Tesla
and the
Lemurian
Gate

by Gary Gentile

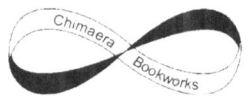

The cover photographs were taken by the author.

Dedicated to the works of Nikola Tesla

International Standard Book Numbers (ISBN)
1-883056-49-7
978-1-883056-49-0

First Edition

Printed in U.S.A.

Prologue

Nikola Tesla contemplated the apparatus in his laboratory.

His experiments with high-voltage high-frequency electrical discharges intrigued his inquisitive mind. The generation of artificial lightning had captured his attention like nothing else since his invention of alternating current. Every day he learned more about electricity and its possible uses than he ever imagined possible.

With static charges he could energize the filament of a lamp that he held in his hand, without harm to himself and without the use of wires. With that same static charge he could stun a rabbit, kill a mouse, or vaporize small insects.

He wrote furiously in his notebook. He annotated the time of each experiment, the precise voltage with which the magnetic coils were charged, the measured potential that was transferred across the space between the windings, and the length of the multiple arcs that zigzagged around the room and were captured on photographic plates.

He had time for one more experiment before his assistants left for the day. In the previous experiment, a fly that had accidentally gotten into the laboratory had been struck by a spark so powerful that the fly appeared to have been consumed before his very eyes. He wanted to test the phenomenon again, so he could spend his solitary evening in noting his observations, and appending speculations about each event.

At his command, the primary coils were wound to full excitation. He signaled for his assistant to place his hand on the giant disconnect. He approached a point that was midway between the discharge coils, where he calculated that the spark – actually a form of artificial ball lightning – would appear.

He had not come unprepared. He pulled a stray one-cent piece out of his pocket. He donned a pair of safety glasses to protect his eyes from globules of molten copper that he expected to fly in all directions when he dropped the coin into the spark ball. He signaled that he was ready.

His assistant threw the switch. The momentary discharge crackled like the firing of a thousand rifles. He dropped the copper cent into the pure white ball that crawled with electricity. The small pop of the penny contacting the spark ball was followed instantly by a thunderous explosion that destroyed the equipment and fused the conducting cables and transformer windings.

He jumped backward instinctively. An intense feeling of heat crawled up his spine. This heat was not generated by electricity, but by fear of the sudden forces that he had unleased in the cause of science.

The laboratory was in ruins. Smoke wafted through the room like an impenetrable fog.

Yet Tesla was exuberant. He had lost his cent but not his senses. The Indian head penny was nowhere to be found. Nor were his glasses splattered with tiny blobs of copper, whose heat of vaporization should have melted pinpoint divits in the glass.

The penny had not simply melted. It had been volatilized, torn into its constituent parts. But what happened to those parts?

Late that night, after Tesla finished writing his notes about the day's experiments, he knew that he needed more power. Moreover, from concurrent experiments, he knew where to get it.

In his youth he had had a flash of insight: a perfectly formed vision of alternating current had appeared in his mind like a detailed photograph, or like a set of construction blueprints. He had seen the mechanism and all its working components in an exploded diagram. Now he had a similar flash of insight: one that showed him the exact specifications for an apparatus that could draw the planet's untapped subsurface energy.

With sufficient high-voltage power at his disposal, he knew intuitively that he could accomplish two goals simultaneously. He could draw electricity from the ground and transmit it without wires to distant appliances, and he could discover the principle behind the disappearance of the penny.

Now was the time to close his shop in Colorado Springs, and commence the greatest experiment in the history of mankind.

Chapter 1

"It wasn't here three months ago, before the earthquake." Woody Carnathan gazed in surprise at the barrier. "It wasn't."

The chainmail fence stood seven feet high. The galvanized finish was burnished and unblemished by the weather, confirming that the steel barricade had only recently been erected.

"I sure didn't expect this." Woody's older brother Darby stuck his fingers through the diamond-shaped openings and tried to shake the sheet of chainmail. There wasn't much give because the silvery poles stood close together and were deeply embedded in the ground, and half a dozen stainless steel hose-clamps secured the crosshatched links to each upright. He panned the clearing on the other side of the fence.

Amber pinched her thin brown eyebrows. "They can't fence off a National Forest." Amber's harsh tone expressed her anger. "It's not legal."

Darby fingered the padded straps of his canvas knapsack in order to shift the weight of the spelunking gear on his shoulders. "Somebody did, and I don't think it was the Forest Service."

"And why would they back up a tractor-trailer to the cave entrance? There's not enough guano inside to fill a grocery sack."

Just then a yellow forklift emerged rear-first from the open end of the trailer. It stopped on the lift gate, rotated backward ninety degrees in a jerking fashion, reached the end of its turning radius with its rear tires precariously close to the edge of the platform, and wobbled as if it were about to tip over. The load on the pallet was top heavy. After the wooden crates steadied, an elbow appeared around the sidewall of the trailer, and a gloved hand pressed down on a black ball-shaped lever. Slowly the lift gate lowered to the rocky ground.

The forklift driver trundled the heavy freight over the

downward angled lip. Once again the crates swayed perilously, separating slightly from each other. After the jostling motion stopped, the forklift driver gently – but still jerkingly – drove forward over a path that had been cleared of trees and loose rock. He steered awkwardly into the cave, barely clearing the low overhang.

Woody pushed up the brim of his rock-climbing helmet. "Look at the size of the opening!"

Darby stared silently.

"The last time we were here the entrance was concealed behind a rhododendron thicket." Amber's pronouncement was a whispered shout. "And you had to scrunch down and crawl into the entry chamber."

"Maybe the Forestry Service decided to use the cave for storage."

Amber pouted. "But they've got that big shed on the highway."

"That's mostly for salt, for melting snow on the high roads. Maybe this is *cold* storage, for storing perishables."

"Like what?"

"I don't know. Maybe lost hunters."

Amber cuffed the back of Woody's head, knocking off his helmet. "You!"

Woody caught the helmet after it bounced off the fence and before it hit the ground. "Watch it, girl. You almost broke my headlamp."

"It can't break. The bulb's an LED."

Woody smoothed his unruly mop of dirty-blond hair in the back and fitted the helmet on his head. "Just the same . . . "

"Okay boys and girls. Or should I say boy and girl? Let's just wait and ask somebody what's going on."

Amber and Woody glared at each other, but neither responded. All three stood silently and watched as the offloading procedure was repeated two more times.

Darby pointed to a stack of neatly trimmed timber and an adjacent pile of debris. "Looks like somebody cut down the trees to make a path from the service road, then bulldozed the stumps out of the way."

Parked next to the logs was a brand new silver pickup truck from which the tailgate had been removed. A pair of thick sturdy planks like doubled joists stretched from the bed to the ground.

Woody gasped. "And ripped out the rhododendrons and blasted open the entrance."

Now Amber's ire was really aroused. "And now you can walk into the cave two abreast without ducking."

"Not with your two breasts." Woody's mischievous grin vanished when Amber cuffed him again. This time he caught his helmet before it hit the fence. "Hey, watch it."

Amber pursed her lips at him. "You."

"I was just trying to keep Darby abreast of the situation."

This time Amber's open palm smacked the back of Woody's bare head so hard that his scalp bounced off the links. "Hey!" He rubbed the sore spot.

Darby shook his head in consternation. "Can you two lovebirds quit the banter?"

"She started it."

"And I'll finish it if you don't mind your manners." Amber faked a cuff.

She and Woody glowered at each other.

The lift gate rose, indicating that the last load was being carted into the cave. The trucker jumped down after the lift gate folded and tucked itself under the rear bed. He yanked down on a thick nylon strap to close the trailer door.

The clang of steel on the bed of the trailer sounded uncommonly loud in the quiet forest. A flock of squawking mourning doves fluttered out of a grove of nearby pines. Crickets stopped chirping for a moment, then gradually recommenced their chatter. A soft hush whispered through ponderosa needles on a gust of wind. A lone butterfly zigzagged drunkenly across the scene.

The trucker opened the cab door. From the driver's seat he pulled a clipboard with a sheath of papers. As he walked toward the rear of the trailer, the forklift driver met him halfway way. He took the proffered pen, signed the top sheet, tore it off, folded it, tucked it into his jacket pocket, and nodded. He walked past the trucker toward the locked gate.

The trucker climbed into the cab, closed the door, and wasted no time in starting the diesel engine.

Although Darby, Woody, and Amber stood only a few steps to the side of the swing-gate, the forklift driver did not bother to glance in their direction. He spun the dial on the combination padlock, yanked the bolt out of the case, and pulled the chain out of the links. He swung open the gate.

In first gear, the tractor-trailer moved forward at the pace of a snail. As the cab passed through the opening, the grizzled trucker grinned down at the threesome and favored them with a wink. The phrase "Ted's Trucking Service" was emblazoned in red on the blue door of cab. "Independent Movers" and "Wemoveanything.com" were painted in white on the dull metal sidewall of the trailer. Second gear enabled the eighteen-wheeler to reach turtle speed.

No sooner did the rig pass out of the opening than the forklift driver swung the gate closed. The man was short and stocky with dark olive skin and pitch black hair that covered his ears. He wore work boots, corduroy pants, and a beige flannel shirt under a worn black leather jacket.

"Excuse me, sir." Darby approached the man with a smile on his tanned face. "I was wondering. We came here to explore the cave – "

"This is private property." He locked with gate with finality.

Undaunted, Darby peered through the fence. "But I thought this was forestry land – "

With a piercing gaze, the man jerked a thumb over his shoulder. "Forest boundary is outside the fence and up the hill."

"Well, we were wondering – "

"You can't come in here." With that he put his back to them and marched away.

After a moment of silence, Amber yelled, "The same

to you with feathers on it."

The man entered the dimness of the cave without a backward glance.

"He needs to work on his people skills."

"You said it." Woody still held his helmet in his hand. "Now what're we gonna do?"

"Climb the fence after he leaves." Amber gritted her teeth with a snort. "After sundown."

"The cave will be dark then."

Amber cuffed the back of Woody's head. "You."

"Okay, teenagers, let's quit the violence." Darby was five years older than his brother, and ten years more mature. "Can you finish your high school project without a last look inside?"

"Uhn-uhn."

"No way."

Darby thought for a moment. "How about another cave?"

Amber didn't hesitate. "Maybe Woody can, but I started my baseline in this one, and it's too late to start another baseline in a different cave, even if there was one in the neighborhood."

"I need to take pictures of the crystals. There won't be any perceptible growth since I was here last fall, but my flash wouldn't fire that time. I need visual proof for my advisor."

Darby studied the fence. It extended in a sweeping curve in both directions, like the perimeter of a hemisphere that was half the length of a football field, with the ends butted against the rock face on both sides of the cave entrance. The cement foundations for the posts were fresh and white and rock solid. The fence was not crowned with barbed or razor wire, just the extended tips of the crosshatch. It would be a simple task to climb over the top.

"We could always rappel down the rock face," Woody suggested.

"Yeah, and no one would see us at night." Amber rolled her narrow shoulders so that the mountaineering gear rattled in her pack. "I've got the Jumar ascenders for that steep pitch to the lower level."

The cliff face above the cave was sheer for twenty feet, then angled back for another twenty feet until the naked rock disappeared under a cloak of topsoil covered with emerald green moss. Small ponderosa pines clung precariously to the slope higher up, seeming to ignore the law of gravity. The thin forest then covered the mountainside for several thousand feet in elevation, to the tree line where green turned to brown on barren ground on which only lichen could survive.

Darby was more cautious. "I think we'd better find out what's going on first. The forest rangers should be able to tell us. Let's drive down to the salt shed and talk to them."

Amber grumbled louder than Woody, but ultimately they both calmed down and followed Darby down the newly cleared dirt roadway to the place where the car was parked on the service road. The old but well-kept four-wheel-drive vehicle was Woody's pride and joy. Woody slid into the driver's seat of what he liked to call his jalopy. Amber rode shotgun. Darby stretched his long muscular body across the rear bench seat. Packs and headgear were stowed in the after compartment.

Woody and Amber maintained a nonstop repartee that fell somewhere between argument and argumentation. Darby quietly put the noise out of his head.

The dirt service road plowed circuitously through the plush woods on a nearly level plane. When the four-by-four reached the intersecting highway, Woody turned downhill on the macadam, away from the summit trailheads. The forestry shed lay a couple of miles beyond the base of the mountain. Woody turned into the driveway. The single-bar gate was closed and locked, meaning that no one was home.

Amber threw up her hands. "*Now* what do we do?" After a sustained male silence, "How about stopping at headquarters in town?"

"Good idea," Woody offered.

Darby shrugged, although neither of those in the front seat could see his body language. Finally he vocalized, "Sounds okay to me."

Woody backed into a tight turn, proceeded forward onto the highway, and continued away from the snow-covered peak. The road descended gradually through ever-thickening game land. A small herd of mule deer was grazing in a grassy meadow; strays browsed on pine needles that lined the edge of the grass. A few raised their heads at the passing of the vehicle, but quickly returned to their habitual pastime.

The front seat banter never ended. Darby ignored the badinage. He peered out the windows at the lush greenery where he had been wont to explore in his formative years: riding his bicycle partway up the mountain road, then stashing it in the weeds while he hiked up streambeds and flipped over rocks to look for salamanders. Life seemed so simple at the time, bereft of responsibility and the conflicts of adulthood. He sighed in fond remembrance.

He almost wished that he could be a teenager again. If only he hadn't had to study so hard to make the grade . . .

He awoke from his reverie at the outskirts of town, where scattered farm houses began to appear and the land had been cleared for crops. Small pastures dotting the landscape were occupied by horses that didn't have to till the land for a living; they had only to bear occasional equestrians along nearby wooded trails. One cattle ranch raised Belted Galloways that had been imported from Scotland for their nicely marbled beef, but the current generation lived a life of endless food and luxury, and had to give only milk in return for their keep – until they became too old to produce. Because of their distinctive pattern – a broad white belt encircling the middle of the body was sandwiched between glossy black hair at shoulders and rump – as a carefree kid he used to call them Oreo cows.

So idyllic . . .

Then urbanized civilization blighted the pastoral landscape: stores, housing developments, strip malls, fast food restaurants –

"Stop the car!"

Darby's order was so loud and emphatic that Woody jammed his foot on the brake pedal at the same time he spun his head from side to side, looking into his mirrors and out the windows for trouble. The dual-lane highway was largely devoid of traffic. The cars in view moved slowly in their proper lanes. The next intersection lay half a mile ahead.

Woody let up on the pedal and let the vehicle coast. "What?"

"Sorry. I didn't mean to scare you."

Amber didn't yell at Darby the way she did at Woody. Her tone was soft, almost mellow. "What's the problem?"

"No problem. But I just saw the moving van behind that diner back there."

"What moving van?"

"The tractor-trailer that we just saw at Lone Bat Grotto."

Amber was quick on the uptake. "Hey! Maybe the trucker knows what's going on."

"That's a great idea." Woody pulled over and paused on the shoulder, looked both ways and checked his mirrors, then did a U-turn and headed back to the diner.

"How come my ideas are good but his are great?"

Woody ducked his head between his shoulders as if he expected to be cuffed. Amber let him off this time – perhaps the only time throughout their relationship. A defensive riposte would only get him into worse trouble.

Darby sighed . . .

Chapter 2

The diner was bright and cheery. Patrons were few because late breakfasters had left and early lunchers had not yet arrived. A solitary waitress fidgeted behind the counter.

Darby spotted the trucker in a booth in the far corner, next to a window that offered a view of his cab. He headed in that direction. Amber and Woody followed in silence.

The trucker was stout enough for his stomach to touch the table. His short gray hair matched his whiskers which, now that Darby could see him close-up, was not as much grizzled as it was trimmed short. His unbuttoned dungaree jacket was spotlessly clean.

"Excuse me, sir."

The trucker looked up, placed his fork on his plate with a half-eaten slice of apple pie, finished chewing, and swallowed. "I remember you from the compound."

"Yes. We were there."

The trucker glanced his Darby's companions. "What can I do for you folks?"

"Well, we were wondering – could we have a few words with you?"

The trucker swept his gaze at the trio again. "Sure thing. Have a seat." He slid close to the window. "The young lady can sit next to me."

"Thank you." Amber swept onto the plastic cushion with grace and aplomb. "Woody never calls me a lady."

Woody opened his mouth to speak, but then thought better of it. He sat on the bench opposite the trucker, and scooted to the window so there was room for his brother.

The trucker took a sip of his coffee. "So, what's on your mind?"

Darby managed a weak grin. "Well, uh . . . "

"We were hoping you could tell us about the man at the cave. He wouldn't talk to us."

The trucker chuckled. "So the young lady gets right to the point. So, I don't usually talk about my customers, but I've been itching to tell somebody about this strange bird. It might as well be you. Mister Pacal Kinich is not a friendly fellow."

Darby fiddles with a place mat. "So I noticed."

"What kind of name is that?" Amber wanted to know.

"Foreign. So, I don't mean he's *un*friendly. He's just – businesslike. I run into all types in this line o' work, and he's the coldest dude I ever met. But as long as he pays the bill he can be a sourpuss if he wants to."

Darby cleared his throat. "Well, uh, did he say anything about the cave? Or what he's putting in there?"

"It's not my job to be nosy, but when I haul freight I've got a responsibility to know what I'm hauling. There's regulations, you know, and I have to abide by them. Some things can't be hauled across State lines without a special permit, like hard liquor and such. Other things need authorization to go through tunnels: inflammables, compressed gas, and such. And they're really strict when you cross the border into Canada or Mexico, because of import duties. Now what this dude tells me I'm hauling is wine."

Woody erupted, "I told you it was for cold storage!"

At that point the waitress arrived. She did not acknowledge the outburst. "Can I get anyone anything?"

Darby raised an index finger. "I'll take a coffee. And a refill for mister, uh – "

With a wink, "Call me Ted."

"I'll take an orange pop with no ice." Woody hated to have nothing more than two sips of soda and a glassful of frozen water cubes. Pop was always kept refrigerated anyway. "And a straw."

Amber smiled. "Apple pie for me, and a glass of water with a twist of lemon."

"Sir?"

Ted shook his head. "One slice is all this belly can handle, but you can warm my cup." After the waitress departed with the orders, "Wine my ass! Oops, pardon me, lady."

"Call me Amber."

"Pardon me, Amber."

Darby and Woody added their names to the mix.

"So, I've been hauling freight for thirty years, and I can tell you for sure and for certain there's no wine in those crates."

Darby: "How do you know?"

"There's a lot you can tell about freight by the way it's packed: whether it's in wooden crates, cardboard boxes, steel cylinders, glass or plastic carboys, and so on. You can also tell by the size and shape of the container. I've hauled wine before. Bulk is transported in barrels. Bottles are packed in cartons, four or nine to the carton, wood in the old days but nowadays mostly cardboard, with the bottles separated by corrugated sleeves to prevent breakage."

Woody was impressed. "Wow, you really know your stuff."

Ted shrugged. "It comes with the territory. So, you can also tell by sound. No matter how snug bottles are packed, there's always movement. I don't mean bottles clanging together, but a soft kind of tinkle that occurs when the corrugations are spread and flattened as the bottles sway sideways on a rough stretch of road. I can tell you this: there's no wine bottles in those crates."

Darby: "Doesn't wine also come in plastic liners and cardboard totes?"

Ted scoffed. He waited for the waitress to distribute the drinks and Amber's pie before he continued. "Cheap wine, yes. But that doesn't need any kind of special storage. You can keep it in a garage or a stockroom. And besides, it sells so fast that long-term storage isn't an issue. This guy claims that this stuff is vintage wine that had been kept on racks in a cellar for years, or decades, until they needed the space and had to move the whole kit and caboodle to that cave.

"Besides that, the crates are heavy and they're the wrong dimensions. They're long and narrow instead of square like liquor crates. They're tall enough to hold bottles, sure, but they must weigh a ton. I know, because I had to reposition some of them after he loaded them in the trailer. He's purely an amateur as a stevedore and forklift operator."

Darby: "I noticed that."

Ted sipped his coffee. "I don't mean the way he drives, but that too. I mean the crates weren't banded or wrapped in plastic sheeting to keep them from shifting and toppling. You must have seen that from the fence."

"I did."

"So, from the looks of things I think he hand-loaded the trailer one crate at a time. He followed my instructions about placement and weight distribution, but the crates weren't secured to the pallets the way a professional would do it." Ted took another sip. "So, I've done my share of long distance hauling from one coast to the other. Even took a couple of loads to Alaska a few years back. That was when I worked for big freight hauling companies, before I bought my own rig and went independent. Now I tow trailers for half a dozen outfits. I usually pick up an empty trailer from a yard, tow it to a warehouse or distribution center where it's loaded, then tow it to the customer's place of business. Instead of a salary I work T and M."

"Time and material?"

"That's in construction. In my line o' work it's time and mileage. I get paid for the distance of the tow, and for the time I spend sitting in traffic. I still do some interstate work, but mostly I stick close to home, in North Cal and lower Oregon. That way I get to spend more time at home with the missus. So, for this job I picked up the trailer from a freelance furniture mover and left it on a ranch north o' town. A big sprawling two-story house that must be a hundred years old, judging by the style, but maintained to perfection like you see in housewife magazines. Had two huge barns and a corral full of llamas.

"Now here's the crazy part. He had me park the trailer in one of the barns, a hundred feet from the house. The crates were already there. That means the wine – if it really was wine – was sitting in a hot barn for who knows how long. Seems to me he should have left it in the cellar till he was ready to transport it.

"So, I went back two days later after Pacal had loaded the trailer. Stowage is a science. You can't have all your weight on one side or the rig will tip over on a sharp turn or a curved exit ramp. You also can't stack your freight to the ceiling because a high center of gravity makes the rig top heavy. He did all right in those regards – paid attention to my instructions – but when I inspected the load I saw the crates were stacked unbound. They would have vibrated off each other in the first five miles. Good thing this was a furniture moving trailer that was equipped with interior framing. I put straps around the pallet loads and snugged them to the sidewall slats. So, no professional mover would have left the crates loose like that. That's why they teeter-tottered when he drove them into the cave. Pacal made himself out to be in the winery business, but my guess is that this is a fly-by-night outfit. His first.

"And another thing. Liquor boxes are small so women and out-of-shape men – " Ted patted his ample tummy. " – can handle them in the stores. Your average stock boy isn't a body builder."

Woody slurped his pop. "Wow, that's really fascinating. So what do you think is in the crates?"

"Don't have a clue. I just know it's not wine. Now I want to tell you something else that's strange. Darn strange. The barn had a workbench that was a tinker's delight. Took up almost one whole side of the building. Forty feet long if it was an inch. Had more tools than a hardware store and machine shop combined. All neatly arranged on pegboard, and power tools in drawers. Two drill presses. Routers. Grinders. Dremel kits. And a lot of other things I didn't recognize.

"The workbench was littered with springs and metal parts and canvas bags and nylon straps and saws and other woodworking tools. I think he knocked those crates together himself, and for some unknown reason he screwed eye bolts to either end and both sides. But one thing caught my attention." Ted paused to take a bite of his apple pie, and swill it down with coffee. "So, I spotted a gleam of light that nearly blinded me, where a sunbeam came in through the barn door and hit a lump of something about half the size of a golf ball, but distorted, like a partially melted blob with protrusions. Like those feet that amoebas have – "

"Pseudopods," Amber furnished.

"That's it. Pseudopods. So, I got curious, so I moseyed over after I unhitched the trailer, and picked it up. It was heavy as lead and smooth to the touch."

Ted leaned forward over the table. He glanced around the diner, looked at each of the trio's eyes in turn, and lowered his voice to a whisper. "It was a gold nugget."

Amber's intake of breath was louder than Woody's hushed "Wow!" Darby blinked.

Ted nodded and winked. "It weighed two or three pounds if it weighed an ounce. I did some calculations. Taking the middle ground, sixteen times two and a half is forty ounces. Bullion is going for more than a grand an ounce. That means that chunk of gold is worth some fifty thousand dollars! More money than I make in a year, after taxes. And he left it laying on a workbench. So what do you make of that?"

After a prolonged silence, there was another prolonged silence. No one knew quite how to respond to such a fact.

"I wiped my prints off the nugget with my handkerchief, dried snot and all. I didn't care. I just didn't want Pacal to know I touched it. Or even saw it. Who leaves something like that in the open? And where did he get it? It was gone this morning when I picked up the trailer."

There was another prolonged, prolonged silence.

Finally, Darby posed a question. "Do you think he got it from the cave?"

"No way!" Woody hunched his shoulders. "Sorry. Didn't mean to shout. But Lone Bat Grotto is the remnant of a lava flow – actually two lava flows, one over top of another with a breakdown between them. Gold nuggets are found in streambeds and alluvial deposits; never in igneous rock."

Ted showed a mouthful of teeth. "Now who knows his stuff?"

"Well, I'm studying to be a geologist. That's why I need to get into that cave. So I can finish my senior project on cave crystals."

"My senior project is on speleobiology." Amber smiled proudly. "What I really want to major in is xeno-biology – "

Ted raised bushy eyebrows.

"The study of alien life forms. But I can't find a college that offers any courses. In the meantime, I'm counting the number and species of insects and other creatures that occupy the cave from one season to the next."

"So, what exactly *is* a senior project?"

"It's like a thesis that's scaled down for high school. We each get to pick a subject – any subject at all as long as our advisor accepts it – then we research it and write a report on it. It counts toward graduation grades. And you can't graduate without it."

Woody took the torch. "And they don't have to be academic subjects. One kid in our class is forging a sword. Another is building a dune buggy on a Volkswagen chassis."

Ted shook his head. "They didn't have that when I went to high school. Only college."

"You went to college?" Amber rolled her eyes as soon as she said it. "I didn't mean – "

"None taken. I've got a liberal arts degree."

"Uhn huhn. Then why are you driving a truck? I mean – "

Woody quoted: "Even a fish would stay out of trouble if it kept its mouth shut."

"Because the money is good. The only job you can get with a liberal arts degree is flipping burgers at a fast-food joint. As a trucker I got paid to travel all over the continent, and visit interesting cities along the way."

Amber showed understanding by nodding and pursing her lips. She kept her mouth shut.

"So, I saw you had hard-hats and headlights at the compound. I take it you already knew about this – what did you call it? – the Bat Cave."

Darby snickered. "Lone Bat Grotto. That's my name for it anyway. It doesn't have an official name because, until today, I didn't think anyone but us knew about it."

"How'd you find it?"

"I used to ride my bike up here as a kid – "

Woody: "As long as Mom didn't find out."

" – and hike through the woods, or climb the mountain. One summer I was out late, wandering around. I wasn't lost; I was exploring. Anyway, around dusk I was hiking along the base of the cliff when I saw a bat fly out of a rhododendron bush. I didn't think anything much of it, and anyway I was in a hurry to get home. I told Woody . . . "

Woody smiled. "I was a baby. Go ahead and tell it. I don't mind."

"Well, I told him I saw a bat, and he thought I meant a baseball bat. When I told him it was a flying bat, he didn't believe me. He said 'bats can't fly.' I couldn't get him to understand that a bat is also an animal."

Amber cooed. "Oh, that's so cute. You never told me."

Woody shrugged.

Darby: "Anyway, a few weeks later I went back to the same spot because there's a pond nearby; one that I had found the day I spotted the bat. This time I took my fishing rod. I caught a couple of sunnies – six inchers. I didn't keep them. I measured them with a ruler and wrote it down in a notebook, then put them back. Caught the first one a second time, too. I filed off the barbs so they would tear up the mouth, but that one had a tiny hole in almost the same spot."

Amber quoted, "Even a fish would stay out of trouble if it kept its mouth shut."

"Anyway, I stayed late because I was catching, until I ran out of bread, which I was using for bait – I pinched it into a ball between my fingers and thumbs – then passed the same bush on my way back to my bike, and another bat – or the same one – flew out of the bush. I didn't think bats lived in bushes, so I crawled into the thicket to see what they were doing there. That's when I found the cave entrance. I didn't go inside. I didn't have a flashlight. But I went back later – I mean, another day – with my grandpaw's kerosene lantern, and kept going farther and farther inside every time I went there. I only ever found one bat living in the cave, and only in summertime – "

"They migrate to Mexico for the winter," Amber interjected.

"When Woody got big enough, I took him there too."

Woody took the torch again. "I think that's what got me started in geology. I was scared at first, but once I got used to walking in the dark – Darby let me hold the lantern – I got to liking it. That's why I chose it for my senior project."

Ted pushed away the uneaten remains of his pie. "So what're you gonna do now?"

All three of them shrugged.

"So, I'm really curious about this guy." Ted the trucker reached into his back pants pocket, pulled out a worn brown leather wallet, extracted a business card, and handed it to Darby. "Let me know if you find out anything about him. And let me know if I can help."

Chapter 3

"I've been thinking."

"I thought I smelled smoke."

Darby ignored Amber. "Woody, do you remember the two summers I worked as a gopher for that landscaping company, before graduating?"

"How could I forget? You were always bringing flowers home for Mom. And you gave me a couple of cactus plants that I had for years."

"Yeah, they used to have leftovers from the jobs. Well, one of the errands they had me go for was getting photocopies of plats from the county recorder of deeds, in the municipal building."

"Okay . . . "

"Well, they have plats of every property in the county: public and private. The landscapers wanted to make sure they weren't planting shrubbery on a neighbors lot, because some people didn't really know where their property ended and the neighbor's began. In fact, some of them were dead wrong about their property lines. So the company surveyed the boundaries to make sure they wouldn't get sued, or have to tear out a garden they accidently put on somebody else's lawn – "

"You want to see if that Kinich character really owns the cave." Amber twisted in her seat and stared wide-eyed at Darby. "That's brilliant."

"Well, he might actually own the land, or some of it, but we can check the plats to make sure. And I'd rather not tip our hand to the Forest Service in case we have to, uh, go in at night."

Amber reached between the bucket seats and grabbed Darby's hand. "I'm in like with Woody but I love you."

Woody frowned.

Darby shrugged. "If we have to sneak it at night, we won't do any damage, and no one will even know we were ever there. We'll just look around and get the stuff you need for your projects. But maybe there's another way . . . "

The original part of the municipal building was a hundred years old: a red brick façade on a native stone edifice that would likely stand for another hundred years. As the county population grew, so did the need for storage and administrative space. Now the core structure was surrounded by stuccoed wings, clapboard annexes, and connecting breezeways whose utilitarian architecture conflicted horribly with the inaugural design.

Darby had no difficulty in navigating the complex arrangement of office add-ons: a convoluted path akin to a puzzle maze. Despite an absence of five years, he went straight to the office where the plats were kept on file. He didn't recognize the clerk who worked there now. "Where are the withdrawal forms?"

The clerk smiled pleasantly. "We don't use them anymore. All the plats have been microfilmed onto a single roll and categorized by a plat numbering system." She escorted the trio to the microfilm reader, switched it on, and issued general instructions on how to use the machine and locate sites on individual frames. "Use this dial to enlarge the picture, and press this button to make a copy. Print-outs are fifty cents each."

The county map was divided into quadrants similar to a geological survey map. Instead of contour intervals, the map showed roads, property lines, utility right-of-ways, and other significant features. The county map was organized in rows and columns, first from west to east, then from north to south, with each quadrant numbered and keyed to the master plat. Darby had to scroll through half the reel before he located the frame on which the cave entrance would have been shown had the county surveyors known of its existence. He twisted the dial to enlarge the image.

A smile spread across his face. "Well, we won't have to rappel, although I was kinda looking forward to it."

Woody peered at the screen. "I don't get it."

"Neither do I."

Darby traced the property lines on the screen. "Okay, the whole mountain is National Forest down to the surrounding ranges and farm fields except for these isolated plats. These landowners either didn't want to sell, or they were holding out for more money and the Forest Service let them go. This – " He enlarged the image again, almost as far as it would go. "This is the highway, and here's the service road bearing south." He zoomed in all the way. "And here's the plat that's owned by the – " He had to squint because the ink on the original paper plat had been blurred. " – the Consolidated Tabernacle Society."

Amber groaned. "Oh, no. A spiritual or religious cult. A bunch of nuts in search of a jar."

Woody: "Maybe they worship bats."

"Or guano."

"Teenagers, please." Darby reduced the image a tad so it showed more of the surrounding National Forest. "The area of the private plat is, uh, one point five nine five acres, and measures four hundred feet by one hundred fifty feet by three hundred twenty-three feet by one hundred seventy-one feet."

"That's not very big."

"Just enough to control the cave entrance." Darby pressed the print button. "I want to show you something but we'll do it outside."

The clerk was nowhere in sight. Darby left two quarters on the counter on his way out the door. They found a bench in the open air. Darby motioned for Woody and Amber to sit on either side of him. He held the print-out so they both could see it, on his kneecaps where his head didn't cast a shadow from the bright sun.

"This isn't a topographic map so it doesn't show contour intervals, but it doesn't matter. This north-south line here is the eastern property line, the uphill side. And really, it doesn't matter where the cave entrance is inside private property, because the plat is so small. Woody, do you remember the Tom Sawyer hole?"

"The Tom – ?" His pale face was a reflection of perplexity.

"You were pretty small but had an easier time than I had."

"The Tom – the Tom – Yes! The back door to Lone Bat Grotto."

Amber pouted. "Is this a private joke or can you let me in on it?"

"You tell it, Darby! You found it!"

"Okay, okay." He turned to Amber. "Did you ever read *Tom Sawyer*?"

"Of course. Everyone has read *Tom Sawyer*."

"Well, in the book, Tom and Becky Thatcher get lost in a cave – "

"McDougal's Cave," Woody inserted.

" – and they run in to Injun Joe, who wants to kill them, or at least kill Tom. Tom and Becky escape through a hole so small that Injun Joe can't fit through it. When the main cave entrance is closed to prevent other people from getting lost, Injun Joe is still inside, and he starves to death."

"And Darby found a hole that leads to the lower tube. We crawled through it once. Darby called it the Tom Sawyer hole."

A grin slowly emerged on Amber's face. "Is this going where I think it is?"

Darby nodded. "The hole is more than a thousand feet from the main entrance. It's not on private property. In fact, almost none of the cave is on private property. Only the entrance. We can go in the back way and not be trespassing."

"Gee, and I was looking forward to rappelling down the cliff in the dark."

Darby folded the print-out and stuffed it into his jacket pocket. "Some other day, when you don't have a project to finish. And I know a cliff that's higher than that one."

Chapter 4

Woody drove past the service road that led to the cave entrance. He went another half mile before Darby told him to pull over and park on the dirt shoulder.

"We can bushwhack from here."

They piled out of the vehicle and retrieved their packs and helmets. Darby pulled out a lensatic compass, sighted a bearing through the crosshairs, pocketed the compass, then led the way. He had no need to refer to the map; he had memorized it. One compass reference was enough for him. Once he got a bearing, he automatically gauged the direction of travel from the angle of the sun (when it was visible through the leaves) or the direction of the shadows (when it was not). He pocketed the compass; he would not need it again unless the sky became overcast.

Woody and Amber chatted and chattered constantly, in an endless contest of bashing, with Woody getting bashed more than once, and not only vocally. After a while they all started nibbling on cheese and crackers, and sipping water from their canteens.

The pine forest was open and largely devoid of thick understory. The few sticker bushes that had managed to take root in the overwhelming shade were easily avoidable. A woodpecker tapped sporadically somewhere in the distance. Sunbeams stabbed through the spaces between trees like Olympian spears, illuminating with effulgence the light brown needles that blanketed the ground, and the huge pine cones that Woody kicked aimlessly every so often.

There were no signs of civilization. There was no hustle or bustle. There was no lurking danger. For Darby, there was only a feeling of freedom . . .

Darby had crawled through the Tom Sawyer hole only twice: when he had discovered it from inside, and when he took his brother through it from the outside. He considered the possibility that the opening might have caved in since then, but he did not mention his concern. They walked across a clearing that lined a boulder field, then stumbled and hopped across the boulders for a hundred yards or more. The boulders were rounded after millennia of advancing and retreating ice fields.

The boulder field ended at a talus slope that climbed hundreds of feet up the mountain. Darby skirted the edge of the slope, then angled into the woods away from the summit. Several minutes later he spotted a familiar outcrop. He pointed an index finger to the top of the cliff.

"Amber, that's where I'll take you for a rappel ride. The height is about twenty feet short of a rope length." He didn't bother to state that a mountaineer's rope length was one hundred sixty-five feet, figuring that with her experience she already knew it.

She tilted her head back so far that her climbing helmet fell off. A full head of thick chestnut hair escaped in the process. "I want to do it."

"That's what she always – "

Amber cuffed Woody so fast that he didn't even see it coming. His helmet flew off his head like a baseball heading for center field. "You!"

Darby shook his head at their antics. After they recovered their headgear, and glowered at each other in silence for a moment, he proceeded past the vertical bluff toward a lower escarpment. "There it is."

Woody poked his head forward. "Where."

"I don't see any hole."

Darby snickered. "That's why we call it the Tom Sawyer hole. Because it's practically invisible. From the outside. The only way I saw it from the inside was because I spotted a glimmer of light. At first I thought it was a reflection from my flashlight, off a glossy piece of rock, like mica or pyrite."

Woody approached the base of the cliff, and crouched. "This is sedimentary rock." He ran a finger over the surface. "Lava is igneous. How can that be?"

"You tell me. You're the geologist."

Woody flung off his pack, then lay down on his belly.

"I can feel a cool air flow so this must be the opening. But it sure doesn't look like I remember it."

"That was a long time ago. You were pretty small, and there may have been some collapse since then."

Woody flicked on his headlamp as he crawled forward to investigate. "I don't see any loose breakdown on the floor." He played his light beam from side to side. "I think it's stable. At least as far as I can tell from here." He backed out, then clambered up to his hands and knees. "It's gonna be a tight fit."

"I like a tight . . ." Amber shut her mouth and glared at Woody, daring him to make a lecherous comment. He didn't.

"We'll have to push our helmets ahead of us, and drag our packs behind."

"I'll go first." Darby doffed his pack and helmet. After running his fingers through his dirty-blond crew-cut, he removed a pair of leather gloves from his pack, and donned them, after which he put the compass into the pack with his other caving paraphernalia. He twisted his head sideways as he squirmed into the low opening. "It's not tall but its wide. Decide whether you want to crawl on your belly or your back, because once you get in here you can't roll over."

Woody followed on his stomach. Amber bunched her long silky hair into a pony tail and bound it with a rubber band. Because the crack was so broad, she lay on her back and wiggled like a sidewinder on a hot stretch of sand.

It was smooth going for the first fifty feet. Then came a distinct demarcation, after which the floor and ceiling changed in texture, and became rough and knobby. Darby got wedged in a restriction. He backed up, turned sideways, then slithered ahead in order to pass his muscular chest through a spot with greater clearance, while passing his flat lower abdomen over the tight spot.

Shortly after that, another chokepoint spread all the way across the crack. The restriction extended only a foot or so in the direction of travel. In order to proceed, Darby took five or six deep breaths, felt sufficiently hyperventilated, expelled all the air from his lungs, collapsed his chest, forged ahead quickly, and inhaled deeply on the other side of the pinch point. The experience made him realize how slender he had been in his teens, before his final growth spurt and weightlifting regimen.

Woody stopped to examine the geological rift. "This is where the sedimentary rock ends and the basalt begins. The Tom Sawyer hole isn't a solution cave; it's a bedding joint between layers. The fracture zone terminates at a thin spot in the crust of the lava tube. It's not part of my project but I can add that as a footnote to my report." With his slender, underdeveloped body, he had no difficulty in passing through the restriction that had been such a breathless obstacle for Darby. He stayed on his brother's tail.

"Hold up. I'm stuck." Amber tried to wriggle sideways through the restriction but got hung up in the middle. Her torso was snugged tightly between the ceiling and the floor.

Woody started laughing. "Hey, Darby. Amber's tits are too big to fit through the narrows."

Amber struck out with her foot and tried to kick Woody in the leg, but he was out of her reach. "You! I'm gonna get you." With great effort she squeezed the soft and squishable parts of her anatomy past the restriction, then sidled toward Woody with a scowl that would scare a rhino. "I'm gonna get you."

"Uh, oh."

By this time Darby was standing upright in the lava tube.

Woody crawled out of the notch, placed his hands on the floor of the tube, and brought his knees down next to them. He reached up and hauled his pack and helmet off the ledge. He ducked behind his older and larger brother. "I'm in trouble now." Then he giggled rapturously.

Darby readjusted his clothing, which was twisted around his body after scrabbling over rock. "Don't get me in the line of fire."

Amber came out of the notch feet first. She sat on the ledge with her feet dangling above the floor of the lava tube. Her denim jacket was rumpled, her flannel shirt was partially unbuttoned, and her double-D sports bra was pointed south by west.

Woody knew what was coming. He made matters worse because the opportunity was too good to pass up. "Looks like you got a little discom*boob*ulated in there."

Amber quietly shifted her bra to the foreground and repositioned her udders inside the cups. She buttoned her shirt meticulously, leaving the tails out over her jeans. She shook out her jacket so it hung straight. She brushed grains of dirt and dust off the sleeves. Then she leaped off the ledge and proceeded to beat the guano out of Woody, pummeling him with both fists, as if he were a punching bag and she was practicing for the championship featherweight. He took his punishment like a man. By the time the beating was over, they were both laughing so hard that they fell down in a heap.

Amber found a bootlace untied. She bent over to retie it. "That was pretty good."

Rubbing his sore shoulder: "I thought so."

She tossed off one last mock punch. "Very clever."

"I was just trying to keep Darby abreast of the situation."

She punched him again, playfully. "You already said that."

Darby shook his head over their juvenile antics. He was getting used to it. "If you two kids are done with your verbal foreplay, can we get on with it?"

A lava tube was formed after a volcanic eruption, when the top layer of lava cooled and solidified but the hot liquid underneath was insulated and continued to flow until it drained, leaving a hollow that was generally tubular in shape. Some lava tubes were miles in length. Some were nearly a hundred feet in diameter. The main channel of Lone Bat Grotto was somewhat flattened, with a height of fifteen feet and a width of eighteen feet: dimensions that were fairly consistent throughout its mile-long length. It led to an upstream junction where

two smaller tubes met and formed the larger downstream tube. One of the upper tubes bifurcated into two
additional branches.

Furthermore, there was a lower tube that was
formed by a previous lava flow. The lower tube measured
some thirty feet in diameter. It's only connection with
the outside world was the Tom Sawyer hole. Midway
along its length the ceiling of the lower tube passed diagonally under the floor of the upper tube. The thin separation between tubes had broken through long ago.
The trio had to hike only a hundred yards or so to reach
the confluence.

"Hmmnn." Darby looked up at the opening in the
ceiling. "I hadn't thought of that."

"Yeah, we brought rope to climb down, not up."

Amber's ponytail bobbed as she played a light beam
on the three-story wall. "Jumars won't do any good without a rope in place."

Woody ran gloved fingers over the rough lava surface. "I should be able to climb it. It's got – it's got a
sandpapery surface and a lot of fingernail ledges."

Amber concurred. "Like the Lower V pitch in the
Basin." To Darby: "We did some climbs on the north face
last summer, with Mr. Patel, our eleventh grade science
teacher. It was three times higher than this one."

"Yeah, but we were top-roped." Woody pulled off his
gloves to get a better feel of the texture. "I've been doing
fingertip pull-ups whenever I walk through a doorway in
the bungalow." He flexed his fingers. "I'll never play the
piano but I can go up a wall like a housefly."

"You should see him, Darby. He climbs like poetry
in motion."

"Iambic pentameter, too. Tie the rope to my waist,
Amber."

"Are you sure – "

"He can do it, Darby. You haven't been around for a
while so you don't know how good he is." She shrugged
out of her knapsack, pulled out the rope, and lashed it
around his slender midriff, leaving the loop loose enough
so it would not constrict his breathing. "He can almost

outclimb Mr. Patel, and he's been doing it for years."

"Well – "

"Give me a boost, you two." Woody grabbed a couple of finger holds and placed one boot on a nearly invisible knob. The knob was rounded so his sole slipped off. Once Darby and Amber hoisted him upward, each with a hand on an adjacent buttock, his foot found another knob, and his fingers located firm grips over his head. "Keep pushing."

Amber groaned with the effort. "This is like raising the flag over Iwo Jima."

"Just keep pushing!"

After Woody climbed higher than Amber could reach, Darby bore all his weight. A moment later Woody was on his own. He didn't rush. He calmly surveyed his choices. Darby aimed his light to Woody's left, while Amber aimed hers to his right. Woody stepped sideways before climbing upward again.

Darby stood directly beneath his brother, with his arms outstretched so he could break Woody's fall should he slip.

"It's not too bad."

"Oh, Woody. Please don't fall and hurt yourself."

"I'll be careful, hon."

Amber looked at Darby and hunched her shoulders. "He calls me hon."

"Only when you're around. When you're not around he calls you Atilla."

Amber stared nonplussed for a moment. Then she guffawed loudly. "Did you hear that, honey. Darby made a funny."

"I'm trying to concentrate here." He was twenty feet high with ten more feet to go. His bare fingertips were dug into sharp lava ledges, and his soles were balanced on tiny protrusions. He leaned back so he could see higher up the rock wall. "Can you aim your lights . . . Yes, that's better."

Woody kept his reaches short enough so his elbows were always bent. This climbing method afforded better leverage than long reaches in which his elbows were locked open.

"Don't rush it, honey."

He let out a yelp and lurched backward, nearly losing his grip in the process.

Darby stiffened for the catch, but Woody didn't fall. "What is it?"

After a few sharp intakes: "Biggest darn centipede I ever saw, in a hole about two inches from my nose."

"Don't *scare* me like that."

"Red beady eyes like a tiny demon."

To Darby, "That's the first body count for my biology report."

By this time Woody had one hand clutching the upper lip. Still he didn't rush it. Most climbers fall because they move too fast without considering all their options. This was particularly important on a free climb. The lip had a slight overhang, which meant that Woody had to lean back away from the wall in order to proceed: a difficult maneuver under good lighting conditions.

Slowly, Woody tested nearby grips that fit the geometry of his lanky body. He was looking not only for the next handhold, but for succeeding handholds that followed from the next one. Climbing was like playing chess: you had to look multiple moves ahead.

After he had his moves plotted, he levered himself up and over the edge into the upper tube. "Made it."

Amber took a deep, deep breath.

"Finding a place to tie off the rope is gonna be the hard part."

Unlike limestone and dolomite caves that were formed – and deformed – by waterborne carbonic acid, which dissolved easily soluble minerals, lava tubes usually lacked flowstone formations such as stalactites and stalagmites. Instead of floors that were littered with rocks that fell from overhead, most lava tubes looked like highways or tunnels that had been swept clean of debris.

Woody lowered the end of the rope through the opening. "There's nothing to tie on to but I think I can hold the rope against a bump in the floor. Amber, you come up first and you can help me hold the rope for Darby."

"Okay." Amber clamped two ascenders to the rope. A cam allowed the ascender to slide upward but not downward. To each ascender she snapped a carabiner from which a short length of rope was suspended; a stirrup was affixed to the bottom of each length. When she was ready to put her weight on the rope, she shouted. "On belay."

"On belay."

She grabbed the handgrips of the ascenders and placed her feet in the stirrups. She took the weight off one stirrup, slid the attached ascender up the rope, released the cam so the ascender bit into the rope, put her weight on the stirrup, stood up, then slid the lower ascender up the rope to the bottom of the upper ascender. In this fashion she "walked" up the rope. The most difficult part was clambering over the lip: her weight on the rope would not permit the ascenders to proceed past the place where the rope was bent over the edge. For the last bit she had to reach over the lip and force her fingers under the rope that led to Woody. It wasn't easy but she accomplished the feat.

She pulled up the rope, secured the ascenders to the bottom, lowered the works, then helped Woody hold the rope down against the bump in the floor. "Let us know when you're ready."

Darby followed the same procedure and soon reached the top. "Good work, Woody. You too, Amber. I guess you know it'll be harder climbing down."

"We'll manage – "

"Oh, no. I forgot to look for the centipede."

"You wouldn't have seen it anyway. You came up a different route."

"I'm counting it anyway."

"I swear I saw it."

"I believe you." Amber coiled the half-length of rope over her elbow, then placed it neatly on the ground next to the wall, along with the ascenders. "The crystals are downstream so let's shake a leg." She did.

They strode slowly side by side with Amber in the

middle.

Darby caught his toe on a ripple. He stumbled and scraped his helmet against the wall. "That's what helmets are for."

Amber bent at the waist and played her light on the floor, then swept the beam from one side of the tube to the other. "Let me know if you see any bugs. Most of them are near the entrance. I hope that guy is gone by the time we get there."

"The heck with bugs. I'm looking for gold nuggets, even if they don't grow in lava."

"They don't." Nonetheless, Woody kept his eyes peeled, and not necessarily for crystals. "He can't chase us away, right, Darby?"

"Well, all he can do is keep us off his part of the cave, which ends a few feet back from the entrance."

"You'll tell him that, won't you?"

"I'll tell him."

"What if he doesn't listen to you?"

"I've got the map in my pocket."

"Quiet!" Amber held up an index finger. "Do you hear something, like a buzzing sound?"

"Turn off your lights."

All three doused their headlamps. The cave went pitch black. As his eyes gradually adjusted to the darkness, Darby could discern a dim yellow glow ahead, emanating from around a sweeping bend in the tube. And now that he was paying close attention, he could hear a faint hum in the distance ahead.

"I think it's a generator."

Chapter 5

Woody's youthful exuberance subsided. "Do you think he'll yell at us if he thinks we're on his property?"

"He might." Darby stared down at his feet. Except for small stones and ripples, the floor of the lava tube was fairly smooth. Scattered chunks of lava that had fallen from the ceiling were faintly visible as silhouettes in the glow from ahead. "Let's try not to antagonize him."

Woody pulled out a miniature camera with close-up capability and a built-in flash. "The best clusters of crystals are close to the entrance, where the overburden is shallow so a lot of water seeps through the rock, then precipitates minerals as it evaporates from the ceiling. Continued seepage induces growth. But there are smaller clusters farther back that I can photograph for my report."

"Well, let's just wait and see what's what. He might turn off the generator and leave."

"Then we can have the cave to ourselves. Hey, there's a cricket on the floor." The cricket and another one hopped away and vanished in the shadows. Amber pulled a small pad and pencil from her jacket pocket, and entered a notation. "That's another entry for my report."

The light was brighter around the curvature of the wall, revealing a large square silhouette.

Woody whispered "Looks like a pallet of crates."

The trio walked softly into the shadow of the stack of wooden boxes. Something fluttered overhead, flitted from side to side, then zoomed past them into the nether reaches of the cave.

"That was Belfry. Something must have disturbed it."

Darby peered at Amber in the darkness. "Belfry?"

"I named the lone bat Belfry." Amber hunched her shoulders around her head. "It must have gotten back from its winter vacation south of the border."

Voices emanated from the light zone. The words were indecipherable, blurred by echoes. It soon became apparent that people were shouting.

"Sounds like he has company. Maybe that's what spooked him."

Figures appeared distorted because the string of bulbs was stretched along one corner of the floor. Long shadows were cast on the ceiling and opposite wall of the tube. Half a dozen garishly costumed people hove into view. They wore black knee-length boots, maroon leotards or pantaloons and matching shirt, a metal breastplate, and a strange looking helmet with a crest and pointed brim. Black, scraggly beards hadn't been trimmed in ages.

"What the heck . . . " Amber crouched on the floor and peered around edge of a crate.

Woody bent over top of her. "You can say that again."

"What the – "

"Quiet!" Darby ducked to eye level so he could look over the stack.

One oddly dressed character was shoving someone from behind. The one who was being pushed was dressed in modern denim. His shock of thick black hair bounced every time he was poked in the back. The group stopped at a stack of crates some fifteen feet away. More shouting erupted. Despite the proximity of the shouters, their words were still garbled by echoes.

One character punched the denim-clad person in the solar plexus with the butt of an antique arquebus. The victim folded over in the middle and fell forward onto his knees. Now Darby could see that his hands were tied behind his back with sisal rope.

"I get it now," Amber whispered. "They're making a movie in here."

Woody agreed. "Yeah. That's why that guy was so secretive. These crates must be full of stage props."

"I don't see any cameras, so this must be a dress rehearsal."

"Those are actors dressed as conquistadors!"

"This is exciting."

"Wow! I'm gonna put this in my report."

Darby watched the scene in silence.

The conquistadors took turns shouting at their victim, and speaking loudly among themselves in what sounded like Spanish, but wasn't exactly. Without closed captions, none of the trio could interpret their dialogue. The victim shook his head but refused to reply to their inquiries.

One conquistador pressed the point of a dagger to the victim's throat. Another drew a long-sword from a scabbard that was belted to his waist. Hunched over, the victim shook his head again. The conquistador raised his sword high in the air. He yelled in what must have been a form of ancient Spanish. The victim continued to shake his head. The sword descended swiftly . . .

. . . and chopped off the victim's head.

The head didn't fall to the ground but hung onto the neck by the muscles and skin of the throat. The victim gradually teetered forward and fell awkwardly to the ground, with the head bent to the side at an unnatural angle. Red liquid spurted from severed arteries.

The scene was so realistic that Amber couldn't help but squeal like a frightened javelina.

All heads turned in her direction.

Woody spoke in a hushed tone. "Amber. It's only a special effect. Now you've given us away."

Amber slapped a gloved hand over her mouth, drew in a deep breath. Her body lurched as if she were going to vomit.

"Well, there's no sense hiding anymore." Darby stood tall and sidestepped past Woody and Amber to the middle of the lava tube. "We didn't mean to interrupt the scene. We're just doing some scientific studies – "

The conquistador who had lopped off the victim's head strode forward. Pinched eyes perched above a thin nose and narrow face that was shaped like a wedge. His grim visage could have been carved from stone. He held the bloody sword in front of him threateningly.

Amber reached out and grabbed the cuff of Darby's pants. "Darby."

"Let me handle this." He didn't glance away from the dark eyes of the strangely clad actor.

The conquistador stopped within sword's reach of Darby, fingering the hilt. He spouted angrily in ancient Spanish. Another conquistador joined him – the one who was armed with the arquebus, which he now pointed at Darby. Darby scrutinized the matchlock. The flash pan was filled with black gunpowder; the match on the end of the serpentine burned dimly, like a pilot light on a gas stove.

Darby stood a head taller than his opponents. "You'll have to speak English if you want to hold a conversation."

The sword wielding conquistador spoke again, but not in English. His arquebus-toting companion responded in kind. They shouted at Amber and Woody, who were still hiding behind the stack of crates. The swordsman directed his attention and his words to Darby. When Darby stood mute, the swordsman stabbed his weapon straight at his midriff.

With lightninglike speed, Darby twisted sideways just as the steel point penetrated his jacket and slid past his ribcage. He slammed his open palm against the back of the wrist that held the hilt, grabbed the sword by the guard with his other hand, and wrenched the blade out of the wielder's hand, breaking the wrist in the process. Instantly he spun around and jabbed his left palm against the conquistador's nose. A perceptible crack and a gush of blood attested to broken cartilage.

The other conquistador triggered the arquebus at the same time that Darby struck up against the iron barrel with the tightly held sword. A flash of light was followed a moment later by the explosion of propellant through the touchhole. A large caliber ball scored the side of Darby's polycarbonate helmet, and flaming gunpowder singed the side of his face.

Darby staggered with the blow. He was knocked against the crates, momentarily stunned, but the crates supported him so he didn't fall to the ground. The arqusbusier was now at a disadvantage, for his ancient weapon was a muzzle loader, and there was no time to grab his powder flask, pour powder down the barrel, top it with a wad, a ball, and another wad – tamping each item in place with a ramrod – and relight the match, before Darby recovered his senses and smote the would-be shooter alongside the crazy-looking helmet with the flat of the blade.

The stricken conquistador no sooner bit the dust with a clatter of rusting armor than his comrades-in-arms leaped into the brawl. A chain-mailed pikeman made a stab which, once again, Darby deftly avoided. He yanked the pike from the surprised conquistador's hands, then drove the blunt end into his belly below the breastplate. The thrust not only knocked the wind out of the pikeman, but threw him back into his companions, who stumbled about in a muddle.

Just as the uninjured conquistadors formed into ranks, Woody flashed his camera in their faces, temporarily blinding them and causing more confusion, even fear.

Darby let go the pike in order to grab the teenagers by the sleeves and pull them upright. "Let's go!"

Woody was wide-eyed and Amber was weak-kneed, but neither one faltered when it came to following Darby's instructions. They switched on their headlamps and raced along the lava tube in the direction from which they had come.

"That – that wasn't in the script," Woody murmured.

Light beams bounced erratically from their headlamps. The trio soon reached the breakdown that connected with the lower gallery. Glancing over his shoulder, Darby glimpsed a conquistador trotting behind them, leading his way with a flaming torch. Despite the uncertain illumination, the other conquistadors were not far behind. "There's no time to climb down. Keep going."

They passed the connecting passageway without slowing down. They soon outdistanced the conquistadors – or at least, they could no longer see the bobbing torchlight because of the twists and bends in the tube.

They maintained a steady pace for half a mile, until they reached the fork where two smaller tubes merged to form the larger one that they now occupied.

"Now which way," Woody wanted to know. "They're both dead-ends."

"The left tube is smaller and has a sharp bend where we can lay an ambush."

"Then what?"

"Yeah, then what?" Amber stared frantically along the tube. She was breathing hard.

Darby looked at Woody. "You have your rock hammer, don't you?"

"Yes, but – "

"Let's keep going." Darby jogged at a pace that he could maintain for hours.

Amber and Woody had no difficulty in keeping up with him, but they were getting more winded with every step. The tube took a long sweeping curve to the left, like a track in subway tunnel, then angled sharply at a restriction and . . .

. . . led to a coruscating brilliance that spanned the height and width of the cave where it pinched together like the waist of a wasp.

"What the heck . . . " Amber stopped so fast that Woody collided into her back.

He peeped around her shoulder at the unnatural light. "What *is* that?"

It reminded Darby of an oil slick except that in addition to blues and purples, vivid hues of every color in the rainbow swirled kaleidoscopically on a seemingly flat surface: merging and parting, blending and separating, turning and churning, streaming and rotating, in a fantastic, chromatic pin-wheeling chiaroscuro whose effect was both dizzying and mesmerizing. Tiny white sparks and long red streamers crackled softly around the perimeter where the pirouetting palette touched the uneven lava walls.

No one moved. They simply stared. Darby was unable to comprehend the weird auroral display that stretched across the tube, seeming to block the way that he knew continued beyond the pale.

The more Darby concentrated on the dazzling spectacle of iridescence, the more translucent it became. Instead of an oil slick, he now perceived that it was more like a thin film of soap before it was blown from a wand to form a bubble. Despite interference from rich mobile color slicks, he was able to peer through the opalescent membrane into the dim cave that stretched to infinity on the other side of the polychromatic barrier.

Slowly, almost imperceptibly, Darby raised his left hand and moved it toward the . . . unknown. His heart beat faster. He stretched his fingers as he cautiously placed his palm flat against the eddying emulsion . . . or almost against it. At a distance of several millimeters he halted. He gulped. The follicles on the back of his hand stood straight up, mildly tickling his skin. It felt like the charge of static electricity that resulted from touching an old-fashioned cathode ray television screen.

When his hand contacted the prismatic field, his entire body tingled as every hair stood on end. The feeling was not painful; it was disturbing and – somehow exhilarating. Every pore on his body was alive with electrical energy. Yet he felt only slight resistance to penetration, like one would encounter from pushing against a thin sheet of rubber, or perhaps a layer of cellophane food wrap. He shoved harder through the nacreous illumination.

His hand "burst" abruptly into the other side. It was visible but somehow distorted, or refracted, the way a fishing line appears to be bent or offset when it is seen through the watery interface. He pulled his hand back out. Once clear of the static field, it looked and felt normal.

Darby inhaled deeply. "I don't know what it is. Some aberration of light, like a reflection, maybe?"

Amber stepped to his side. She repeated Darby's experiment. "It's more like – a force field. A weak force field."

"How come we've never seen it before?" Woody didn't touch it, but he cupped his hand over his headlamp with an air of scientific detachment. "It doesn't reflect light. It absorbs it – or dissipates it. Some local phenomenon is generating the – whatever it is."

"Maybe it's a kind of low frequency electromagnetic field effect that excites our visual cortex."

"You mean, like an illusion that we can perceive but that really doesn't exist? Except inside our head?"

"Something like that. Strong magnets focused on the brain can cause hallucinations."

Woody put his face close to the boundary line and squinted sideways along the apparent surface. "Whatever is causing it must be self-sustaining."

"This is very weird. First it's make-believe conquistadors lopping off heads, now it's a colorized misperception."

"Maybe this whole thing is a dream sequence."

Darby indicated the torn material. "This hole in my jacket isn't a dream, and neither is this – " He pointed with his chin toward the immaterial coloration. " – whatever it is."

Further discussion was curtailed by the clattering sounds of approaching conquistadors, and the flickering glow of hand-held torches, which emanated from around the bend.

Darby took one step back, braced himself, and leaped through the lambent plane of radiance. "Let's go!"

Raw energy flowed through his body like a mild electric shock. There was neither pain nor pleasure, just a weird sensation that he had never experienced before. His equilibrium vanished into a miasma of conflicting impressions. He felt disjointed, displaced, disturbed. His vision blurred with a cacophony of loud colors. His tongue tasted the scent of jasmine. His body was knotted, twisted like dry water being wrung out of a wet towel. He tried to catch himself from falling into nothingness. He braced himself for the inevitable crash . . .

. . . when his foot touched something solid. He stumbled forward, as if he had expected to drop from a great altitude, but fell only the height of a staircase riser.

His headlamp illuminated the limestone floor of a

cave. Instead of thrusting out his arms to stop his fall, he rotated the upper half of his body, hit the ground with his shoulder, and rolled over his knapsack, unhurt but dazed. He fought disorientation.

A moment later Woody landed next to him, followed immediately by Amber. All three lay together in a heap.

"What just happened?" Amber's helmet had been knocked off her head in the – transference. Her ponytail lashed from side to side as she tried to get her bearings.

"Hey! Stop whipping me with your horsetail." Shaking his head, Woody hesitantly pushed himself up to his knees. "Hey, what happened to the lava tube?"

Woody's pronouncement made Darby aware that the cave in which they had "landed" differed dramatically from the one from which they had departed. The glimmering pane of light still spread across the restriction, but the cave beyond had changed from a tube to a house-sized chamber that was adorned with long, spindly flowstone formations: stalactites and stalagmites, plus a single fat column that was fluted for its entire thirty-foot-tall length.

"This – this is impossible."

Amber donned her helmet. She played the beam of her light-emitting diode on the rugged designs of the speleothems. The dull brown lava had been replaced by glistening white walls with gypsum intrusions whose curled "leaves" sparkled like translucent gems.

"I don't think we're in Kansas anymore."

Chapter 6

"You can say that . . . No, don't say it again." Woody crawled on hands and knees to a pool of limpid water that stretched twenty feet across. On the far side, a submerged tunnel angled downward farther than his headlamp reached. He peered into the shallow depths nearby. "Hey, what are those squiggly things on the bottom?"

Amber scampered to his side. "Where?"

Woody pointed. White wormlike critters squirmed sluggishly on a number of spindly legs across inundated rocks. Each one measured less than an inch in length.

Amber inhaled loudly. "They're isopods. Albino isopods. Cave isopods. Do you know how long isopods have to live underground before they lose their pigment? Thousands of years. Thousands of generations. This is – this is unbelievable."

Darby stood to his full height. He looked not at the reflective pool but at the coruscating pattern of colors that constituted a gateway between the world he knew and one that he could not possibly fathom. "Do I have to remind you people that there's a gang of armed cutthroats after us?"

Amber and Woody spun around as if they had been stung by a hive of bees.

"And if we came through that splotch of color, so can they."

Darby leaned forward and put his face against the spectral barrier without actually touching it. Diffuse orange nimbuses appeared to move in three dimensions behind the lambent pigmented plane. When deeply saturated tints eddied away from the point in front of his eyes, to be replaced by translucent pastels, he was able to peer momentarily through the thin remaining dye spots, and catch a glimpse of human figures in the lava tube, which was dimly lit by flaming brands held high in the hands of approaching conquistadors.

"They're there, and they're coming this way."

"Then let's get out of here." Amber looked frantically around the chamber. "Over there! There's a tunnel."

The trio retreated. They entered the passageway on the opposite side of the chamber. Darby let the others precede him. He hung back, flipped off the headlamp switch, and observed the chamber from behind the fat ornate column.

Without artificial light, the decorated chamber was softly but weirdly illuminated by various hues that emanated from the colorized screen, as if a beam of white light were being refracted through a glass prism. The scene was reminiscent of a commercial tourist cave, in which the operators installed colored floodlights to highlight flowstone formations for the public.

Suddenly, a torch poked through the fabric of clashing colors, followed immediately by a sword-wielding conquistador from a point about a foot above the adjacent floor of the chamber. The man lurched forward, staggered, and regained his balance. Two more conquistadors strode through the pigmented barrier; they all stumbled as a result of the difference in floor levels. The conquistadors Darby had smote in hand-to-hand combat did not appear.

Darby melted into the shadow of the tunnel. He didn't dare to switch on his headlamp just yet, so he shuffled forward slowly, feeling his way with his boots until he glimpsed a pair of bobbing beams in the distance. He crouched low to the floor so he could spot rocky obstructions in silhouette. He hastened his pace.

He found Amber and his brother waiting for him anxiously. "They came through the barrier as if they knew about it."

"What is this place?" Amber wanted to know. "And *where* is it?"

"And how did it get connected to the lava tube? We've never seen this part of the cave before. This system isn't even the same geological formation." Woody swung his arms around at the walls and ceiling of the broad tunnel. "This is limestone, and the flowstone back there was formed by calcium carbonate."

Darby shook his head. "I don't have any answers for you."

"Not only that, but this new system is colder than the lava tube." Woody glanced at his pocket thermometer. "Instead of a constant 52° year round, like I noted in my preliminary report, here it's only 48°. It doesn't make sense. None of this makes sense."

"I agree. All I can say as that these conquistadors mean business. That wasn't a special effect we saw back there. That was a real execution."

Amber started to whimper. "I can't believe it. I can't believe it. I mean, I believe it, but I just can't believe it."

"Let's keep going."

Woody: "Where?"

Darby jabbed a thumb over his shoulder and offered sage advice. "Away from them."

Unlike lava tubes, which tended to be fairly straight, level, and uniform, solution caves were convoluted and without particular shape. They were created and continued to grow by seeping groundwater that carried naturally occurring carbonic acid, which dissolved soft stone such as chalk, salt, dolomite, and limestone. The result of erosion was an erratic configuration, as soluble minerals liquefied while minerals that were higher on the Moh's hardness scale were largely unaffected.

Woody: "Looks like we're following a fault or bedding plane."

The fairly smooth floor of the passageway soon yielded to a large chamber that was filled with car-sized boulders: chunks of rock that had fallen long ago from the unsupported ceiling. Breakdown made travel difficult, for the trio now had to clamber over, duck under, or climb around these massive angular blocks. Then they had to ascend a short escarpment whose surface had been smoothed by deposited flowstone. Streaks of orange in the marbleized surface were caused by iron in the groundwater.

"You feel that?"

They all stopped, but neither Darby nor Amber

sought to answer Woody's question.

"It's airflow. Coming from ahead. We must be near an entrance."

Amber tilted her head. "I think I can hear it."

They continued onward. Minutes later a whistling sound became perceptible to all. In a few more minutes the rush of moving air was downright raucous.

"It's getting colder." Amber's observation was all but drowned out by the wind. "And look at that!"

That was a manmade wall built out of stone slabs laid atop each other without mortar. A narrow doorway led to a room that was as large as a meeting hall. Cloth remnants that looked like bedding and blankets lay strewn across the rock floor.

"Forget it." Darby sensed that they were close to the entrance. Yet there was nothing but blackness outside the sharp beams of their headlamps. After passing the doorway, they rounded a right-angled bend and encountered . . . not the warm welcome of the radiant sun, but the unexpected spectacle of a raging blizzard. The outside of the cave was as black as night. A fierce howling wind blew a wall of snowflakes sideways.

"This – this is impossible."

Woody took a more practical approach. "What do we do now, Darby?"

"Well . . . " Darby was nonplussed. He switched off his headlamp, returned to the bend, and peered around the edge. He saw nothing in the dark corridor, but thought he heard the clattering of chain mail. Back at the entrance. "We have to keep going."

Amber was incredulous. "Into that?"

Darby nodded.

"Okay. Let's go." Woody cinched his chin strap. He stepped into the blizzard. His LED beam bounced off snowflakes as if they were tiny mirrors.

Darby grabbed his brother by the shoulder. "Hold on, partner. Let's go slow till we know what we're getting into."

Woody hesitated. "Yes. You're right. You want to go first?"

"If you don't mind."

Woody made a sweeping gesture with his arm. "After you."

"Let Amber follow me. You bring up the rear."

"Okay."

"Okay, Amber?"

Amber was shivering, either with cold or with fear. She nodded.

Darby buttoned his jacket up to the neck, and raised the collar. He stepped off the rock floor into ankle-deep snow. The scree collar kept most of the white stuff out of his boots. Above the noise of the gale: "They'll be able to follow our footprints."

"You think they'll come after us?"

"They looked like pretty tough hombres. Let's see if we can find some solid rock to walk on."

He marched straight away from the cave entrance, treading lightly because he could see no farther ahead than a couple of body lengths. The ground sloped gently downward for a hundred feet or more, then leveled out. What Darby took to be a plateau seemed to end abruptly. Due to darkness and whiteout conditions, he could not see more than a few feet downwind. They could have been standing on a slightly elevated ledge, or on the lip of a thousand-foot cliff.

Darby had to shout in order to be heard above the wailing of the wind. "Stay here for a minute." He retraced his steps to the entrance of the cave. He doffed his pack, then walked backward while sweeping the pack back and forth over their tracks. This action only partially obliterating their trail, but he was hoping that newly fallen wind-blown snow would soon fill in the shallow depressions.

"We must still be on the mountain somewhere, wherever that other cave took us. We have to watch out for crevasses and ice slides."

Amber bared her wristwatch. "Has it occurred to anyone that it shouldn't be dark yet? And that it should-n't be snowing like this in April."

Woody's words were nearly drowned out by ambient

noise. "And that the sky was clear and sunny when we went into the cave less than an hour ago?"

Darby hunched his shoulders. "I don't understand any of this, but we have to deal with what we have."

"Good thing we dressed for the temperature of the cave."

Amber had difficulty in articulating her words. "I'm cold even in my long-johns."

"Let's get moving, then." Darby picked a direction that was perpendicular to their escape route from the cave. He pivoted his headlamp downward; in the horizontal position its beam reflected off falling snowflakes the way a car's high-beams bounced off fog. Now he could at least see where he was putting his boots.

They soon reached a shallow depression in which the snow had accumulated to a depth of several feet. The fluffy dry snow reached above their knees, reducing their forward progress to a crawl. Despite being nearly blinded by flying ice crystals, which hammered into his eyes, Darby managed to observe the approach of a precipice.

He usually found it exhilarating to hang his toes over cliff faces, to stare down thousands of feet into valleys below, or to stand on the lip of a high waterfall. But in this instance he was afraid that a strong gust of wind might knock him off balance. He dropped down to all fours and peered over the edge. A sheer vertical drop extended as far as his light could reach. Cautiously he backed away. He was not concerned about drop-offs that he could see; he was concerned about crevasses that he could *not* see: deep crevices whose tops were bridged by a thin layer of snow that could crumble under his weight.

He changed direction and kept going. Soon the snow reached his crotch. He felt as if he were wading through molasses. He looked back at his companions. They fought silently and without complaint to keep up with him, even though he was breaking trail.

Darby shouted, "Woody, give me your rock hammer. We're gonna bed down for the night."

Woody returned an expression of perplexity, but wasted no time in slinging his pack off his back and digging out the tool.

"Are you crazy? We can't sleep out here in this storm. We'll freeze to death. I'm half frozen already."

"It's okay, Amber. I know what I'm doing. We're gonna dig a snow cave."

"A snow cave!"

"It'll be a new experience for you." Darby removed his pack. He scooped snow with his hands until he reached a layer of ice, where snow from a previous storm had been melted by the sun, then refrozen when the temperature dropped below freezing overnight. He chopped through the ice with the rock hammer. The snow underneath was wet and packed to a consistency that, under different circumstances, he could have used to make snowballs and snowmen. He lay down the rock hammer.

Amid the raging storm, Woody and Amber watched helplessly as Darby tossed out armful after armful of compacted snow. He dug down about a foot and a half below the ice layer, then, on his knees, he started tunneling sideways into the tall drift. As he shoveled snow backward between his legs, Amber and Woody crouched behind him and removed the snow that he excavated.

It took only a few minutes to hollow out a tunnel that was long enough to cover his torso. He backed out. "I've hit more ice. I'll have to chop through it." Taking the rock hammer, he lay down on his side and started chopping away at the thick layer of ice. The frozen barrier curved downward at the angle of a staircase. He spent ten minutes making a hole that was large enough to crawl through. Then he lay aside the rock hammer and started scooping out soft snow by hand.

He shoved handfuls of snow alongside his body as far as his waist. "Pull it out, Woody."

Woody lay down at Darby's feet and squeezed into the narrow tunnel. He reached past his brother's knees in order to grab the snow that Darby was removing from farther inside the tunnel. Woody then shoved the snow past his own body to where Amber, without being told, picked up handfuls and piled it around the hole.

Darby had to chop through two more ice barriers before he reached the bottom of the drift. It took half an hour to hollow out a cave that would accommodate all three of them.

"Back out, Woody. We're done."

First Amber, then Woody, backed out of the narrow entry tunnel so that Darby could squirm out feet first. He was overheated from his exertions. After working so hard, neither Woody nor Amber complained of the cold. When all three were crouched in a circle, and facing each other in the hole by the entrance, only their helmets and mounted headlamps were battered by wind-driven snow.

Darby raised his voice. "I suggest that we squirt before crawling inside."

Amber was apoplectic. "What? Bare my ass in this weather?"

"Unless you think you can make it through the night without peeing in your pants."

After an extended staring contest: "I'm not leaving this hole."

After another extended staring contest, Woody said, "Our plumbing exposes less skin."

Darby nodded. "Okay. We'll go. But Woody – don't go far. You might get lost in this blizzard."

Woody climbed out of the hole and floundered no more than a yard through thigh-deep snow before stopping.

Darby did the same in the other direction. To Amber: "Let us know when you're done."

No more than two minutes passed before Amber called out, "Okay. You can come back now."

When all three were back in the hole: "Woody, go in feet first. I'll hand you the packs."

"Okay."

Woody wiggled backward until only his outstretched arms poked past the tunnel entrance. Darby placed the straps of two packs in his hands. Woody squirmed all the way to the end of the snow cave. "I'm in."

"Amber, I'll go next. You come in right behind me, feet first."

"Okay."

Darby dragged her pack into the cave. When his feet touched the back wall, he used his shoulders to work his back to the side opposite his brother. Amber slid in between them. LED's from the headlamps reflected from the surrounding snow and fully illuminated the close confines of the makeshift igloo. It was barely high enough to enable them to roll over without scraping their shoulders on the ceiling.

"Woody, use the packs to block the opening, but leave breathing holes."

Woody did as his brother instructed. After plugging the opening, the sound of the wind outside was barely audible.

"Switch off the lights to save the batteries. They drain pretty quick in subfreezing conditions. You can use your helmet for a pillow."

"This isn't too bad," Amber observed. "Cozy even."

"I'm hungry. How do we call for room service?" Woody kibitzed.

Despite being packed together like sardines in a can, Amber managed to find Woody's head in the dark, and cuff the hair above his nape. "We still have our lunch."

"Good idea." Woody opened his pack and removed a sandwich. "Ham and cheese."

Although moving around and rolling over was difficult, Darby and Amber did the same.

"Peanut butter and jelly. And it's frozen."

"Put it between your legs."

Amber cuffed Woody again.

"He's right, Amber. Your body heat will warm it up a little. And stick your water bottles inside your jacket, or it'll freeze.

They all warmed their sandwiches by pressing them between their upper thighs. Darby ate and drank in silence, while Woody and Amber jabbered in their usual manner. No one touched on the subject of their fantastic predicament, or the preceding improbable events.

Eventually, at Darby's suggestion, they rolled onto their sides and nestled together like spoons. No one made any off-color jokes. This was a matter of survival.

Chapter 7

Darby carefully withdrew his arm from Amber's waist without rousing her. He rolled back a tad until his shoulder blade contacted the wall of snow behind him. His wristwatch was covered with snowmelt, but the black plastic casing was waterproof to a depth of one hundred meters. He pressed one of the function buttons. According to the illuminated face, six hours had passed since the trio had blocked themselves inside the snow cave.

He waited patiently for the others to awaken.

Amber jolted in the darkness. "Wha – ?"

Darby placed his hand on her upper arm. "Take it easy, Amber."

Woody stirred, tried to roll onto his belly. "Is everyone alive?"

"Affirmative." Darby raised his head above his helmet and switched on the headlamp. Their bodies were jammed so tightly in the cave that most of it was cast in shadow. "Did everybody sleep okay?"

"I kept hearing a clicking sound, like drumsticks on stone."

Amber cuffed Woody. "You. That was my teeth chattering."

"Sorry."

Darby took charge of the situation before a mock argument started. "Let's move the packs so we can get out of here."

Darby and Woody stowed their water bottles and pulled their packs aside. Amber donned her helmet, then tucked her pack under her chin. A solid wall of snow was spread in front of her.

"It should be mostly fluff, from spindrift."

Amber grabbed a handful. The snow was so light that she could blow it off her gloved palm as if the flakes were motes of dust. "You're right." She dug her way out of the tunnel by pushing her pack ahead of her. "The hole is completely filled. No, wait." She pawed some of the snow to her side. "I can see sunlight."

Then she struggled out of the tunnel and beckoned for the others to follow. Woody pushed his pack out next; Darby brought up the rear.

There wasn't a breath of wind.

The morning sun was blocked by the mountain, but its glorious light filled the western sky and shone down on white puffy clouds below. To the inhabitants of the valley floor the sky was overcast, but to the adventurers on the upper slopes the visibility was unlimited. Several distant summits protruded through the cloud layer, adding a three-dimensional quality to the cloudscape. The mountainside was blanketed with snow as far as Darby could see.

Amber stood in awe. "This – this is beautiful."

"I'll say." Woody was less enthusiastic. He turned to his brother. "Darby, do you know where we are?"

Darby shook his head. "Nothing looks familiar. We're on a part of the mountain – " He glanced uphill, calculated compass bearings by the position of the sun. " – that I've never seen before."

"How's that possible? You've climbed all over this mountain."

"I . . . don't know. It looks different with all this snow."

Amber was not dismayed. "I'll bet it does. But as long as we're facing west, all we have to do is go downhill until we reach the service road, then turn north."

"You're right." When Darby looked south, he saw that their tracks from the night before had been completely obliterated. Smooth, untrammeled snow spread all around them. He also saw that what he had feared might be a precipice in the dark, turned out instead to be a mere step – but beyond that step the slope descended precipitously over a series of wide ledges that reached as far as the low-level clouds, and probably beyond. "Well, let's go."

"Wait! Shouldn't we rope up, or something?"

Amber shook her head. "I don't have the rope any

more. Don't you remember? We left it on the floor by the opening to the lower gallery."

"Oh. Yes."

Darby: "It doesn't matter anyway. Roping up only works with experienced climbers, who know what to do when somebody slips. And you need ice axes to arrest a fall. With us, a rope would only be a false sense of security, and would make you less cautious. If one person slipped, he would drag everybody else down with him. We'll do kick-steps. Watch."

He shuffled through deep snow to the ledge, crouched and sat on the lip, then stretched his legs to reach the angled platform of snow-covered rock below. He stepped hard through the top crust.

"See how kicking a hole acts as an anchor? The top layer of snow or ice is slippery, but when you kick through it, it holds you in place. I'll break trail, and take short steps so you can step in my tracks. Or you can kick your own steps."

Woody followed Darby over the ledge, then held his hand out for Amber, whose much shorter legs made the step more difficult for her to descend. They floundered for a bit, but the farther they descended, the less snow covered the ground. They scampered over occasional outcrops where naked rock was exposed. Wherever there was snow, Darby stepped hard through the fluff or crust, and made sure that his footing was secure before taking his weight off the anchored foot and taking another step. The descent was hard work and slow-going, but it was safe.

At one place the surface snow was loose and the slope was gradual. Darby showed them how to glissade. He sat down with his feet in the air in front of him, and coasted downhill on his butt as if he were sitting on a sled or toboggan. He descended several hundred feet in a few seconds, then gradually slowed to a stop as the angle of the slope flattened.

Woody whooped as he followed in his brother's wake. Amber screamed all the way, but immediately started laughing as soon as she ground to a halt. The level plain extended for several hundred yards before tilting downward again, forcing the trio to resume kick-stepping.

After half an hour of slow progress, they entered the cloud zone. The scene of splendor vanished because they were now surrounded by thick mist: a condition that was known to mountain climbers as whiteout. Visibility was reduced to less than fifty feet. Now they had to be extra careful not to slip on the thin layer of ice that covered the rocky substrate.

Shortly afterward, the cloud layer brightened. Sunbeams penetrated the mist and reflected off droplets in suspension. After that it took only a couple of minutes for the clouds to dissipate. The sky cleared around them, and the golden orb peaked over the upper ridgeline. Sunlight bathed the valley in all its brilliance.

There was no sign of the fields and pastures that ringed the base of the mountain. The town that should have been visible in the middle distance was absent. Nowhere was there any indication that mankind had ever cultivated or settled the land below.

Amber sat on a shelf of bedrock that was concealed by only a smattering of snow and particles of ice. "We are definitely not in Kansas."

"This isn't California, either."

Darby studied the scene in silence. Gone were the pine forests and groves of redwoods. Gone were the pastures that fed cattle and horses. Gone were the roads. Gone were the ranch houses on the outskirts of town, and gone was the town. In their stead grew vast open grasslands and huge tracts of jungle: a patchwork wilderness expanse that extended to the horizon. In the far distance stood the mountains whose peaks had been visible above the cloud layer.

Darby slowly shook his head. "It doesn't even look like – North America."

Woody and Darby huddled on either side of Amber. Lost in thought, all three contemplated the impossible landscape. They could have been looking at a museum diorama of prehistoric times. All that was missing were Indian teepees and . . .

"Is – is that a herd of – bison?"

Woody followed Amber's pointing finger. "I – can't tell."

Amber humphed. "I wish I'd brought binoculars. But who takes binoculars on a caving trip?"

"If they *are* bison, it's the biggest herd I've ever seen. There must be thousands."

"More than exist in the world."

"Put that in your biology report."

Amber did not try to cuff him for his impertinence. "Yes. Right below conquistadors. *That* has to be a pretty rare sighting." Amber removed her helmet and rewound her ponytail. "So what now, Darby?"

"Well, uh . . . I guess we better keep going downhill. Do a little exploring. . . . Maybe we'll find an explanation for – whatever happened."

"Do you think we went back in time? To the era of conquistadors, Indians, and herds of bison roaming the plains?"

"Where the deer and antelope play?"

This time Amber cuffed Woody hard, knocking off his helmet. He winced, and managed to catch the helmet in his lap.

Darby slowly shook his head. "I don't know. But this doesn't look like any part of the world I know of. Uh, don't they look like palm trees at the base of the mountain."

His brother squinted and shaded his eyes. "Hey, I think you're right. We're definitely either in a different time zone or some other zip code."

Amber cuffed him again. He ducked so that her hand merely ruffled the hair on the back of his head. "You. North California hasn't been subtropical since the Pleistocene. Before the last Ice Age, ten thousand years ago. Right?"

"Right. So, what – you think that peacock feather thing we went through sent us back in time?"

Amber raised light brown eyebrows and gave a long exaggerated shrug. "I don't have a clue."

Speculation was getting them nowhere but confused. Several more minutes of silent contemplation ensued.

"Well, we don't need these anymore." Darby took his pack off his back, loosened the straps, removed a clear plastic bag of snacks, and stowed his helmet inside.

Woody followed suit. "Good idea. I can use a double handful of gorp."

"I've got landjager and dried fruit."

Amber checked her supplies. "I've got cheddar cheese and bannock."

They spread the food on the rock ledge behind them, and settled down for a welcome repast. They soon drained their already nearly-empty canteens. After stowing the leftovers, they resumed their descent, with Darby leading the way and Amber between him and Woody.

It wasn't long before they crossed a snowmelt runoff. They tanked up on clear cold water, and refilled their canteens.

The lower slopes were devoid of snow. Loose rocks were the only hazard. They proceeded swiftly to the tree line, and even then the vegetation was so sparse that there were no impediments to speak of: only the occasional log or gully. They did not have an altimeter, but Darby was certain that they had passed the elevation of the service road. Considering the circumstances, the fact that they did not cross it came as no surprise.

Ground cover consisted of a wide variety of ferns. The soil was soft and loamy. Clumps of bright green moss grew on isolated hummocks. In some places the land was swampy, forcing the trio to make detours in order to keep their footwear dry. The band of understory constituted a transition zone between exposed bedrock that sported multi-hued patches of lichen, and the flat plain where tall shrubbery sprouted gigantic leaves that created a canopy that blocked the hot rays of the sun.

Amber was the first to doff her jacket. She tied the sleeves in a knot around her waist. "Anyone have a machete?"

"I always take one on caving trips. You never know when you might have to cut off someone's head."

Amber asked for it, so she didn't bother to turn around and cuff the back of the Woody's head. She plucked a leaf that was the size of an elephant ear. "This vegetation is more tropical than subtropical. Or maybe a little of both."

"It's almost like jungle, but it's not." Darby moved through the thickly tangled underbrush by bending limbs down instead of pushing them ahead. That way they didn't spring back and strike Amber in the face. He also suggested that they keep their distance from each other, in case someone tripped.

The ground now consisted of hard dirt and twisted roots. Darby found himself either ducking under limbs that were too thick to push out of the way, or climbing over them. Thick lianas now wound around fat boles that were covered with smooth bark: trees that neither he nor Amber, despite her biological knowledge – her strongpoint was fauna rather than flora – was able to identify.

Nor did they recognize the jungle sounds. Several chirps and whoops overlapped each other, so they must have originated from different sources, but whether they emanated from the throats of birds or the rubbing legs of insects was impossible to ascertain. They caught a glimpse of a small flock of purple macaws. Once they heard a howl from the treetops which might have been the territorial call of a squirrel or monkey, but they couldn't locate the animal.

Eventually the quasi-jungle thinned. They jumped over a couple of rivulets that swarmed with water striders: insects that were familiar to all three explorers. They also found themselves swatting green flies whose nasty bites left large red welts.

Darby entered a small clearing. "Now that's a tree I recognize."

"Coconuts," Amber called. "I hope they're ripe."

"I wish I had an entrenching tool."

Woody lay down his pack. "How about knocking them out of the tree with a rock hammer?"

"That'll work."

It took Woody three throws before he managed to strike a coconut, and then it didn't break free. On the next throw, the hammer almost landed on his head. He stepped farther back from the tree before he made his next toss. It missed. But two throws later he was successful in striking a coconut hard enough to break it off the stem.

Darby took his survival knife out of his pack, unsnapped the retaining strap, and slipped the blade from its brown leather sheath. The knife could be used as a weapon, but it was designed primarily as a tool. The bottom edge of the six-inch blade was as sharp as a filet knife, as was two inches of the top edge; the rest of the top edge was serrated and was intended to saw wood. The stainless steel shank protruded beyond the leather handgrip; the flat end served as a makeshift hammer. An attached pocket contained a whetstone bonded to flint.

With deft tangential strokes, Darby sliced thin layers off the outer husk until he reached the smooth shell. He then used the point to rout a drinking hole. He handed the coconut to Amber. She took one sip of milk, passed the coconut to Woody, who took a sip and passed the coconut back to Darby. They continued the round-robin until the cool liquid was all imbibed.

Darby placed the shell on a log and beat it with the blunt end of the knife.

"My rock hammer can break it open faster."

"I know. I just want to prove a point." After splitting open the shell, Darby handed large slivers to each of the others. Darby used his survival knife to peel off the meat. Amber used the blade of a multi-tool. Woody whittled away with the chisel end of his rock hammer.

"Is this what you call living off the land?"

"Well, it's a start. Let's get three more for the road. Uh, the trail."

With practice, Woody quickly became proficient at knocking coconuts off their perch. Darby sheared off the husks. The shells didn't take up much space in the packs because they fit nicely inside their helmets. They

all stuffed their gloves and jackets into their packs. Then
they stripped off their outer clothing – Amber maintaining etiquette by changing behind a tree – so they could
remove and stow their long-johns.

"Don't roll up your shirtsleeves, Woody. They'll protect your arms from bugs and thorns."

Dungarees and flannel shirts were not the best outerwear for the tepid conditions, but they provided the
protection that Darby warned against. Darby reeved the
knife sheath through his belt, for quick access to the
knife.

They proceeded through a forest of date trees and
palms, with occasional coconut trees. After a while they
encountered sporadic mango trees, but the fruits were
too high to reach. Then came a grove of papaya trees.

Woody picked a fruit off the ground. He brushed the
outside with his hands to wipe off dirt and dust, then
took a healthy bite. "Tastes good. And juicy. It doesn't
look as if we'll starve around here."

"Sure are an awful lot of fruit trees around here."
Amber scooped up a papaya and bit into it. "Doesn't
make sense."

Darby studied the trees around them and made a
startling observation. "That's not all that doesn't make
sense. These trees are growing in a row."

Woody paused in mid bite. "Hey, you're right."

Amber did the same. "Could be a nurse tree."

"A what?"

"A nurse tree. It happens a lot in rain forests. A tree
falls down, rots, and seeds take root in the log. But this
. . . " She sidestepped to a better vantage point. "They
aren't growing just in a row. They're growing in rows and
columns. These – these trees were planted!"

"Not only that, but I think I see a path over there."

"Where?"

Woody ignored her. He started walking between the
trees. Darby and Amber followed. What appeared to be
a well-worn dirt animal trail led out of the grove of papaya trees through a hedgerow to a patch of what at first
glance appeared to be familiar palm trees, but which

proved to bear nuts the size of a baseball. After a minute's walking the path opened onto a broad clearing that was occupied by a gigantic stone structure.

All three stopped, stunned.

Amber breathed, "Omigod! It's an Egyptian pyramid."

Chapter 8

The pyramid-shaped structure stood more than fifty feet tall. It was constructed of massive stone blocks that had been cut to fit the stepped contours. The four corners were mitered. The smooth facings on the steeply sloped tiers were disrupted by inset staircases in the middle of each triangular side. Atop the flat apex rose a wood and adobe edifice with a flat thatched roof.

"Wow," was all Woody could utter. Absently he took another bite of his papaya.

The tall grass that fringed the base had gone to seed. Worn depressions in the limestone steps attested to long-time usage, yet the covering of dust or pollen implied long-ago abandonment. Some of the adobe had been melted away by rain. Chunks of thatch lay scattered around the crowning edifice, while pieces of wood littered the uppermost tiers.

"Let's go check it out." Amber hiked through the knee-high grass and clambered up the steep narrow steps, using all fours for stability because the stair treads were so narrow.

She reached the summit before Woody was halfway up. Darby climbed at a more leisurely pace; he noted that the slabs had been fitted without mortar. When he stooped to slide the sharp edge of his survival knife between two slabs, he discovered that there was not enough space between them for the blade to penetrate.

The facing of the stones that comprised the topmost tier were carved with caricatures of human skulls, and bordered by zigzag vertical and horizontal grooves that were connected to each other like a squared sine wave. Embossed between paired skulls were two symbols that looked like ritualistic daggers: one pointed upward and the other pointed downward.

The wood and adobe edifice was empty. Its outer walls were inset, allowing the trio to walk around the outside promenade and see the land in all directions.

The mountain they had descended towered to the east. To the north and south lay thick junglelike vegetation. The western landscape was comprised largely of shapeless open fields that were connected by dense jungle growth, with fruit trees predominating in between: an irregular or asymmetrical patchwork that hinted at organized cultivation.

Nowhere was there evidence of recent habitation.

"On second thought, this isn't an Egyptian pyramid. It's Aztec, or Mayan, or Incan. What do they call it?"

Woody furnished the answer to Amber's question. "A ziggurat."

"That's it. A stepped pyramid."

Darby scanned the horizon to get the lay of the land. He was more interested in their future than the archaeological past. "There are more buildings westward. Why don't we mosey over that way and take a gander?"

Amber and Woody agreed. They climbed carefully down the stone staircase to the surrounding grassland, then struck out in the direction of the now westering sun. They found that curved and recurved pathways connected the clearings in a bewildering, snakelike manner that was reminiscent of a maze. Most of the clearings were just that: areas that were clear of trees or jungle but overgrown with weeds.

Whenever a path forked they found a wooden post, either standing or lying on the ground and overgrown with moss. The posts were carved on all four sides with calligraphic symbols reminiscent of Chinese characters, but very different and incorporating curlicues.

In one clearing Amber plucked a handful of long stems. "Looks to me as if these meadows used to be tilled. The green stalks aren't all wild grasses. Some of them are edible grains, although I can't identify them. They continued to sprout naturally after the field was left fallow. Judging by the way the wild grasses have encroached on the grain, and are taking over the crop, I'd say this field hasn't been seeded manually for decades."

They crossed two more farm fields before encountering a clearing that contained a number of buildings: a rectangular central structure that looked like a German pillbox because it was made of stone blocks, surrounded by outbuildings or blockhouses that were framed with hardwood poles and plastered two-feet-thick with adobe. Each building they checked was devoid of furnishings, although several had built-in wooden shelves. The pillbox had a stone roof, but the thatched roofs of the blockhouses had long since collapsed into the interior.

"I wonder who lived here?" Woody wanted to know.

"And where did they go?" Amber added, just before she let out a screech and fell over backward.

A pair of armadillos looked up in astonishment, blinked, then skittered into a burrow at the base of an adobe hut.

"Sorry." Amber stood up and dusted herself off. "I know they're harmless, but they startled me."

"I think you startled them, too." Woody backed away, but apparently Amber didn't consider that his comment was worth a cuff.

A tall thick beam stood at the far western edge of the clearing, in front of a jungle whose trees were encumbered with lianas. They ambled in that direction. The beam was actually the bole of a fat tree whose top hamper had been lopped off about fifteen feet above the ground, and whose limbs had been sheared even with the trunk. The bark had been scraped off, and the inner core had then been smoothed to a light brown sheen. Contorted human faces and fabulous creatures were carved in the wood.

Woody stared. "Wow. A totem pole."

"Not *just* a totem pole, but a *living* totem pole." Amber pointed to the base of the tree. "It's still rooted in the ground."

Darby studied each human caricature and stylized animal as they alternated in place on the sculptured column. The humanoid features were finely drawn but distorted or twisted out of perspective. The animals were unrealistic: imaginary constructs that at first appeared to be prehistoric, but upon closer examination looked like nothing that had ever lived on Earth. There was a wingless batlike miscreation with hypothetical Ubangi lips; a piglike monstrosity with six giant legs; a sloth with bulging eyes and a wasp waist forward of its hind legs.

Amber screamed at the top of her lungs.

Woody winced and placed his hands over his ears. "Amber, please! Do you have to keep screaming like that. I think you punctured my eardrums and broke every glass within two city blocks."

The look on Amber's face was one of abject horror. Darby reached out to her; he placed a hand on her shoulder. "Amber . . . "

Five seconds passed before Amber inhaled. Then her ample chest heaved as if she had just completed a marathon.

"Wow, is she okay?"

"That . . . that . . . " She didn't seem to be able to formulate her thoughts. She put both hands on her chest, and tried to control her breathing rate. "That top figure turned its head and – looked at me."

Darby glanced at the totem pole. "Take it easy, Amber. It's only a wooden statue."

Woody did the same. "Maybe it's like a painting where the eyes seem to follow you as you move around the room."

"No! It – turned – its – head."

The crowning miscegenation looked like an overweight chameleon with dark round eyes and a truncated beak, but coated with gaily colored plumage instead of scales, and equipped with a long feathered tail that curled around its legs. Soft down covered the narrow breast. The deformed animal stood on its hind feet with its claws gripping the scalp of a graven Neanderthal skull. The arms, or forelegs, were tucked close to its sides, rendering the fingers hidden or out of sight. It could have been a drunken artist's vision of a cross between a lizard and a parrot. It was the size of a barn owl.

All three of them stared hard at the topmost sculpture, soaking in every detail. It stood as still as a – well, as a statue, or perhaps a cigar store Indian. The carving was meticulously rendered even though the creature it depicted was freakish: not monstrous like the other images, but a conglomerate of limbs and body parts seemingly from disparate animal species.

Then the carved creature blinked.

Amber didn't scream, but she inhaled so sharply that Woody put his hands over his ears in anticipation.

A moment later the creature unfolded a long pair of wings, started flapping, and lifted off the hominid cranium. It hovered for a moment, then spun around and soared into the jungle, its long, dragonlike tail whipping back and forth behind it.

Woody was the first to find his voice. "Wow. It was some kind of bird-lizard perched on the totem pole."

After a frozen moment, Darby cautiously approached the pole and tapped on it with his knuckles. "The rest of this thing is solid wood. At least as high as I can reach."

"Okay. Okay." Amber closed her eyes. "The eyelid came up from the bottom. It was filmy and translucent, like a nictitating membrane found in some birds and reptiles. Which makes sense if this was a composite of the two."

She swung her pack off her back, dropped to one knee, removed her notebook and pencil, and started sketching the flying reptile while the mental image was still fresh in her memory. No one disturbed her until she was done.

"Does anyone remember the color combination?"

Woody reeled off as if from rote: "Brown head, green breast, red and yellow wings, and, uh, dark blue or indigo body."

Amber didn't have crayons, so she improvised by writing the color schemes in the appropriate places. "Dark brown or light brown?"

"Uh, I'd say reddish brown, like burnt sienna."

"Good."

Darby felt left out of the conversation. "Well, is this some kind of tropical – whatever?"

"Not on this Earth. I mean, not on *our* Earth, in *our* time."

Woody shivered. "That's a scary thought."

"I know what you mean."

"Well, it makes about as much sense as everything else, which is no sense at all."

"You got that right." Amber put away her writing materials. "I don't know where or when we are, or how we got here, but even though it scares me, I have to admit that this is a fascinating place."

"If you're going to be stranded someplace, it might as well be someplace interesting. Right, Darby?"

Darby nodded slowly. "I guess."

"Oh, come on. You're the great explorer. You're the one who spent all your spare time as a kid in the woods, exploring. And took me with you when I was old enough."

Darby smiled. "Yeah, and got in trouble for it, too."

"Sometimes. Now you get to explore till you're heart's content, without . . . well, you know, now that Mom and Dad . . . "

Darby kept nodding. "But it's different when you're grown-up."

"Different how?"

"I don't know. Just different."

"You mean you don't like exploring anymore?"

"No, I still like exploring. I just like doing it – I don't know – where I have some idea of where I am. Where – "

"Whatever happened to your favorite saying: 'I'm not lost. I'm exploring.'?"

Darby chuckled. "Well . . . This is all so – so different. Like it's not even the same planet we grew up on."

Amber waited for an appropriate pause. "Okay, I know where you're coming from. But we're here and there's nothing we can do about it – except go back to the cave and go back through the looking glass. The conquistadors are probably gone by now. But hey! This is spring break, and no will miss us for a week, until we – " She indicated Woody and herself. " – don't show up for class on Monday morning. And you have time to make up your mind about what to do next: to look into your career opportunities. So let's spend a few days checking this place out before we go back to the rabbit hole – "

"You're mixing books."

Amber would have cuffed Woody except that she was still on her knees and he was standing several feet away, prepared to take a step backward. "You."

"It's not that. It's . . . I guess – I guess I'm a little concerned, you know, about your safety."

"That's good, Darby. And I appreciate it. I'm concerned, too. But this place – " She spread her arms wide, and sounded wiser than her years. " – is incredible. We've got ancient ruins and strange animals – "

"And colored soap films," Woody interjected.

" – and flying statues and who knows what else. This place – this place is more exciting than a dry senior project about bugs in a lava tube."

"Yeah."

Darby shrugged. "Well, I don't mind it at all. It's just that this isn't – it isn't a game. We're into something really big. Something not understandable. We can't call it quits and go home when we're tired of it. We're stuck here until we figure out where we are."

"Or when," Woody interjected.

"Or when. Or how to get back home. And we don't know what to expect in this – place." Darby looked toward the jungle. "Like that jaguar over there."

Amber and Woody whipped their heads around so fast that their necks cracked.

"It's been watching us for a couple of minutes."

The jaguar switched its tail. It looked curious rather than angry – or hungry.

Amber started to scream, but controlled herself with scientific detachment. "Woody, look at the fangs."

"I see them. It's not a jaguar. It's a – "

"Smilodon."

"Yeah. A saber-toothed tiger."

Darby made a face. "You mean, like the skeletons they dug out of those tar pits."

"Exactly. La Brea."

"But I thought they were extinct."

Amber: "They are in our world. As of ten thousand years ago, thereabouts."

Woody suddenly threw down his knapsack and pulled out his rock hammer. The tableau lasted quietly for half a minute, with Amber and Woody staring wide-eyed at the tiger, Darby seemingly relaxed, and the tiger switching its tail with a look that might have been interpreted as boredom, or disdain. Silently the tiger put its back to the trio, and strolled into the jungle with total lack of concern.

Amber grabbed her notebook. "It didn't have black spots like a jaguar, but more like dark brown splotches on a gray background, faintly connected by light brown lines, almost reticulated like a giraffe."

"Put that in your report."

"Report! I could write a book on this place."

Darby remained calm and collected. "All right. From now on we start carrying weapons."

"What? Penknives and multi-tools? I'm sure that'll scare off the lions and tigers and bears."

"Oh, my." Woody grinned.

"No, but we can make spears." Darby looked up at the sun. "We have a few hours of daylight left. Let's scrounge around and look for wood. I want long straight fresh cut limbs for spears, deadwood for a fire, and more fresh fruit and coconuts for food. We'll go back to that stream, drink as much as we can, and fill our canteens."

Woody threw off a mock salute. "You're the boss."

"We stick together. Nobody gets out of sight – "

Amber frowned, but before she could object, Darby continued.

"If you need to take care of some personal business, go behind a bush. But no farther. We stick together. Always. Is that understood?"

Both Woody and Amber nodded.

"Good. We'll stay in that stone hut for the night, then decide what to do in the morning."

It took until nearly sundown to accomplish all their tasks. Not only did they stock up on coconuts and papayas, but they found a mango tree that Woody was able to climb. They gathered armfuls of twigs, sticks, and dry moss from the ground. Darby and Woody hefted logs onto their shoulders, while Amber dragged some to their temporary fort. Darby used his survival knife to saw off three eight-foot limbs of one-inch thickness.

"Any longer and they'll be too heavy and unwieldy."

The stone hut measured ten feet by twenty. It had a doorway on each side. Darby stacked the kindling in the middle of the room.

Woody compared his rock hammer with Darby's survival knife. "How are we going to cut them into logs?"

"We're not. We're gonna use an old Indian trick."

Darby laid the logs in three of the four doorways. He made a loose pile with the moss, then stood tiny twigs around the moss and leaned them inward. The result was a miniature wigwam. Outside the twigs he stood thicker sticks. He struck his knife against the flint until one of the sparks ignited the moss. He blew gently on the tiny flame until it spread throughout the pile. He leaned back on his shins while first the twigs and then the sticks caught fire. When a good-sized blaze was going, he poked the ends of the logs into the flames.

"As the ends burn off, all we have to do is push the logs farther into the fire."

The temperature dropped as the sun slipped beneath the horizon. After donning their long-johns and jackets, they lay around the crackling fire and ate from their ample food supply. Darby whittled a point on one end of each spear, and singed the points to harden them. The last thing he did before turning in to sleep was to scatter loose sticks outside each doorway.

Darby slept soundly through the normal nighttime sounds, but his subconscious mind was constantly on alert. Any unnatural sound – such as an animal making noise by stepping on the outdoor sticks – would instantly bring him to full awareness and ready to fight.

He wondered idly how roasted armadillo would taste.

Chapter 9

The night was fairly quiet. There was the usual chorus of frogs and insects, and the distant grunts of foraging mammals, but no prowlers came close or made sounds out of the ordinary.

The fire was low but still burning because everyone had pitched in by pushing the pre-positioned logs into the center of the hut whenever he or she awoke to change positions on the stone floor, which was hard despite a matting of leaves and grass. Darby could always feel that pea at the bottom of his makeshift mattress.

As usual he opened his eyes at first light. He stared at the glowing red embers, enjoying the warmth and pre-dawn moments when he had his thoughts to himself, before he was forced to face the mysterious challenges of the day. The dank odor of wicking long-johns was a familiar scent. Perhaps it was the only thing that was familiar about this world into which he and his companions had been thrust against their will. One item in his favor was that he felt more informed about this strange land today than he had felt on his previous awakening.

Familiarity bred confidence and security – to a point.

His brother had been right in his assessment of Darby's personality. He liked exploration of the unknown. Yet he was still nagged by the fact that the kind of unknown territory that he was used to exploring was at least understandable. This antediluvian wilderness, this never-never land, was not subject to orthodox boundaries, and held secrets which at first blush appeared to be unknowable. It played by different rules of engagement: rules of which he was largely ignorant.

As soon as the others stirred, Darby rose and exited the hut, surfeited with more introspection than he felt comfortable in probing. His last such thought concerned walking out of a life that was pat and predictable, into one that was neither. Whatever that meant . . .

Once again the snow-capped mountain blocked the

dawn. The surrounding jungle – or rainforest (it was neither, or it was a combination of both) – was growing
louder with each passing minute. A bee buzzed past his
nose without slowing down, bent on some obscure mission that only another bee could comprehend. A pair of
red and blue macaws cawed loudly as they flitted from
branch to branch on a tree at the perimeter of the clearing. An ordinary green grasshopper leaped through the
tall grass several feet from the doorway, while others
chirruped nearby. The scene appeared almost . . . normal.

He stripped, redressed without his long-johns, and
squirted on the grass before stepping back inside.
Amber was still curled into a ball on the floor, with her
gloved hands clenched tightly between her legs. Woody
was sitting upright; he nodded in greeting. Finally,
Amber stretched, leaned up on one elbow, and scooted
toward Woody so she could lay her head in his lap.
Woody fondled her tangled tresses.

"So what's on the agenda for today?" Amber wanted
to know.

"Go west, young woman. Go west."

"Why west?"

Darby furnished the answer. "Well, northwest actually, because the open plains are in that direction."

"How do you know that?"

"Don't you remember seeing it yesterday, from the
mountain?"

"Sure, I saw what looked like bison on rangeland,
but how do you know it's relationship to where we are?"

"Well, I – I guess I memorized the landscape. You
know, for future reference."

"You don't know my brother. He's got everything to
the horizon mapped in his head."

Amber sat up. "You can do that?"

Darby shrugged.

Amber reached for a nearby fruit. "Drat."

"What's wrong."

"Some critter chewed up my mango."

Woody squinted at the fruit as she held it up for him

to see. "It didn't eat much."

"You." She lightly cuffed the back of his head.

Woody's hair was so messed up that the cuff didn't disarrange it in the least.

Darby grabbed one of the spears and started honing the blackened point on the stone wall of the hut. "Anyway, we'll head in that direction. There's no hurry."

Amber and Woody went to opposite sides of the hut to do their morning ablutions and remove their undergarments. After a hearty breakfast of coconut milk and meat, papaya, and mango, Darby handed out the spears. I cut two feet off yours, Amber, so it won't weigh as much.

"These are for thrusting only. Don't try to throw them because they won't fly true till we lash some weights near the front."

There was no need for Darby to look at the sun for direction. He observed shadows, then compensated mentally for the height of the stellar orb. They walked at an easy gate. Woody and Amber sustained their usual mindless banter, to which Darby paid no attention. Now that he knew for certain that predators roamed the forest, he kept a constant vigil for spoor, sound, and sight of saber-toothed tigers. Behavior patterns could not be inferred from fossil evidence, but he worked on the presumption that they could be every bit as sneaky and fierce as the modern day jaguar or mountain lion.

A tribe of howler monkeys swung through the treetops with long arms flailing. One paused momentarily to look down at the trio. It stood on a thick limb with the tip of its prehensile tail curled around the trunk. It reached between its legs, hurled something that landed at Amber's feet, then tore through the upper canopy and was soon out of sight.

Amber scowled. "Nothing to get upset about. They're known for throwing feces at their enemies."

"Yuck. So much for this being a Garden of Eden."

"Just don't eat the apples."

Around mid-morning they encountered a river. It wasn't a raging torrent but the flow was fast and the depth uncertain.

Darby was unconcerned. "Let's walk upstream and look for a wide spot."

Woody was nonplussed. "Don't you mean a narrow spot?"

"No. Water bunches up at the narrows, and spreads out thin where the river is wide."

"Hmmnn. Makes sense."

They hiked for a mile and a half before they found an acceptable ford.

"Use your spear as a cane. Plant it downstream and lean into it. Rocks might be loose and will be slippery if they're covered with algae."

The river was a hundred yards wide where they crossed it. The water was only shin-deep for Darby and Woody; knee-deep for Amber. The major impediment was not the depth, but the speed of the current which threatened to bowl them over. Woody went down to his knees on one occasion, and almost toppled over completely before he pushed himself upright with the aid of his spear. It took ten minutes of careful treading to reach the opposite bank.

They sat down for a breather.

Next they tried to follow the bank upstream, but rhododendron thickets were so tightly entwined that they were soon worn out from stooping, crawling, and clambering over and under the limbs. The word "impenetrable" came to Darby's mind. He struck out perpendicular to the river until he gained high ground, where the forest was relatively open. They he turned and led the procession parallel to the river on an ever rising course. The woods ended abruptly at a vast open plain.

"Bison!" Amber shouted triumphantly. "I knew it. And talk about amber waves of grain!"

"No pun intended."

Thousands of grazing bison populated the rolling hillsides that stretched seemingly to infinity.

"But so many. Wow."

"Take a picture before they get away."

Woody slung his pack to the ground. "I don't think

they're going anywhere." He rummaged through the pack until he located the digital camera. He snapped several carefully framed shots. "And we're here at the perfect time – high noon – when the overhead lighting is the best."

Darby sidled along the edge of the forest. "Let's try not to disturb them. I don't want to start a stampede."

The sight was so magnificent that they couldn't take their eyes off the herd. Every once in a while, an astute bull spotted them skirting the edge of the forest. After eying them steadily for a minute or so, the bull invariably returned to his chronic pastime.

"I don't think they're afraid of us."

"Put that in your report."

"You know what's really strange? I mean, stranger?" Amber squinted as she cupped her hands over her eyes. "The ones that are on that hill to the left look bigger than the ones that are closer."

"Yeah, and they're coats don't seem as dark. Must be the lighting."

Almost as an afterthought, Darby said, "Woody, doesn't that camera have some kind of zoom?"

"Yes! I can't believe I didn't think of it before. I bought this model because of its close-up capability, for shooting crystals, but it has a twelve x telephoto lens. Optical, not digital."

Woody held the view screen in front of his face and pressed the zoom button all the way. At such extreme enlargement, the displayed image bounced around so much that the animals were little more than a blur. He pressed the shutter release halfway down, locked in the autofocus and image stabilization, and snapped a picture. The resulting digital image was clearly displayed in color. Woody switched modes to the saved images file.

"It looks like – like a – a moose. But with a funny looking hat rack."

"Let me see that." Amber grabbed the camera out of Woody's hands. She studied the image overlong. "I don't believe it."

"What is it?"

"If I didn't know better I'd say it was an Irish Elk. Extinct for ten thousand years."

"Like the saber-toothed tiger?" Darby asked.

"Exactly." Amber let Darby look at the view screen. "See the palmate antlers? They're distinctive. And distinctly different from moose antlers."

"So, we're definitely in the – what did you call it – the Ply . . . "

Woody took the ball: "The Pleistocene. The geological epoch that preceded the Holocene: the epoch we live in. Or used to, anyway."

"Is that when cavemen lived?"

"Kind of, yes, but in an earlier stage. The Pleistocene goes back two and a half million years, and ended with the last Ice Age ten thousand years go."

"Oh, yes. I remember from yesterday."

Amber: "The ice age killed off a lot of mammals that used to be plentiful."

"Like that elephant over there?"

"Omigod!"

"Wow!"

The elephant in question was the size of a stake-body truck. It lumbered along casually without eliciting special attention from nearby bison. Its trunk swung fore and aft between a pair of white, inward curving tusks, while its slender tail twitched in the manner of a startled squirrel, only slower. It's broad flank was patterned with swirls that trended from off-white to various shades of gray.

No sooner did the pachyderm clear the trees than another, smaller one emerged from the forest. The trio had barely gotten over their surprise when a smaller one yet brought up the rear. The last in line stood only one third the height of the second; it was a baby.

Amber shouted, "Take a picture! Take a picture!"

Woody fumbled with the camera, got the elephants in focus, and tripped the shutter. He then activated the zoom, zeroed in, and snapped another picture. The elephants were much closer than the Irish elk – less than half a mile across the veldt – so the resultant images showed more detail, and the enlargements showed less pixilation.

Woody enlarged the saved image before passing the camera to Amber.

Amber needed only a glance. "They're not African elephants because the ears are too small. Must be Indian."

"Could they be woolly mammoths?"

"No, Darby. Woolly mammoths are, er, were, woolly. They had long hair. These have smooth skin. Well, skin that looks smooth at this distance. It might look rumpled if we were closer. Great shots, Woody."

"Thanks. Now if I could only get some crystals for *my* report."

"I think reports for our senior project are the least of our worries."

"Yes, I guess you're right."

"Besides, my advisor wouldn't believe this anyway."

The family of elephants grazed alongside isolated bison without any contention occurring between species. Likewise with the Irish elk in the background. All was peaceful on the prairie.

The trio squatted in the tall grass and munched on various fruits as they watched, enthralled, a scene that predated recorded history.

Woody practiced hacking on a coconut with Darby's survival knife. "I don't get it. If we've gone back in time, to an epoch when prehistoric animals were still alive, how does that account for an elephant from another continent?"

Amber chewed thoughtfully on a papaya. "You're right. It doesn't make sense."

Darby slowly shook his head. "None of this makes sense to me. I mean, conquistadors go back only a few hundred years. Not ten thousand. So what are they doing here – that is, if this is where they came from before we met them in the cave?"

"That's a poser." Woody finally gouged a jagged sipping hole in the coconut shell. It wasn't as good a job as Darby could do. He offered the coconut to Amber. "And we're from an altogether different time zone. It's like we passed through some kind of international date line. Only instead of skipping back twenty-four hours, we've skipped back twenty-four decades, or twenty-four millennia. Or both."

Amber quoted Lewis Carroll: "Curiouser and curiouser."

They dawdled over their food not because they were so hungry, but because they found it difficult to leave such an incredible vista. When they finally resumed their trek, they hiked through the low understory a short distance inside the forest, where they could see the herds of herbivores by peering through the foliage but where their presence was mostly concealed from the eyes of the grazers.

They found the trampled trail that the elephants had trod on their way through the forest to the open plain. It appeared to be well used. Darby decided to backtrack on the trail to see where the pachyderms had come from. The route of flattened vegetation was easy to follow. The trail led uphill to exposed bedrock, which overlooked a valley in which an aged aqueduct channeled water past a ziggurat and a collection of abandoned stone structures that were all connected by a contiguous stone pavement that was sprinkled with shrubs which had taken root in a veneer of windblown soil.

It was then that they heard a scream, and spotted a woman in distress on the plaza below. She was in the clutches a pair of armed conquistadors.

Chapter 10

Darby didn't take time to think. He just reacted instinctively.

He raced down the hill with amazing celerity, leaping from rock to rock like a mountain goat. He reached the stone plaza at a full gallop. Instead of running normally from heel to toe, he rolled his boots on the outside of the soles so they didn't make slapping sounds on the stone. The conquistadors were so absorbed in their wrestling match with the woman that they didn't hear his silent running until it was too late to fend off his attack.

Darby didn't stab the nearest conquistador, but wielded his spear like a pugil stick. His upstroke caught the turning conquistador in the midriff. He bent forward with a whoosh of escaping air. Darby's downstroke slammed against the back of the conquistador's helmet, smashing him to the ground and sending the helmet clattering across the plaza.

The sound of metal on limestone alerted the other conquistador. He let go of the woman, spun around in surprise, and drew his short-sword from its sheath. The steel blade was only partially extracted when Darby slammed the side of the spear against the conquistador's elbow. The sharp crack of breaking bone was followed by a howl of pain and anguish.

The woman charged up from the ground, yanked a dagger out of the conquistador's belt, and stabbed him in the back. Another yelp erupted from his mouth. When he turned to face his female opponent, the dagger was ripped out of her hand; it stuck in his back like a pin on the tail of a donkey until centrifugal force threw it free. She threw a clenched fist at his face. His turning motion threw off her aim. Her knuckles slid past his forehead but managed to catch his ear. He howled. She immediately followed her first punch with another one to the cheek.

Darby swung his spear into the conquistador's kidney. He staggered once, fell to one knee, then toppled to the ground on his side. The woman kicked him in the chest. She yanked the spear out of Darby's hands, slammed the butt into the conquistador's thigh, then swung it around as if it were a baton, and cracked it against the back of his neck. He coughed twice, gurgled, and expired. The woman didn't take her eyes off him until he ceased to twitch and his face turned blue.

Both Darby and the woman were breathing hard. Their chests were heaving.

After a long moment, Darby caught his breath and shifted his gaze from the dead conquistador to the Amazonian combatant. She was short and stocky, with a short crop of pitch-black hair that barely covered her neck. His jawed dropped in astonishment.

"Maia, uh . . . "

The woman looked fiercely into his eyes, equally surprised. "Darby Carnathan! What the hell are you doing here?"

"Well, uh, I don't know. I don't even know where 'here' is. And I guess I could ask you the same question."

A long silence ensued, during which her intense gaze gradually softened. "Did you come through the portal in the cave?"

Darby nodded slowly.

"Of course. You had to." She changed her line of vision to the two people who were cautiously making their way down the hillside. "Are they with you?"

Darby turned his head, kept nodding.

"I figured, from the way they're dressed." She didn't say anything else until the pair arrived. "Is this the whole gang, Darby?"

"Yes, uh, Maia."

Amber screeched, "You know this gal?"

"Well, yes. We went to high school together. Uh, this is my brother – "

Woody stammered, "Derwood, but everyone calls me Woody."

"Call me Maia. And your name?"

Amber took a moment to calm her voice. "My birth

name is Hortense Elspeth Cornthwaite, but if you ever call me Hortense I'll scratch your eyes out. And if you shorten it I'll do worse."

Maia hesitated, but if she was intimidated by Amber's outburst, her face didn't show it. "So what should I call you?"

"I go by the nickname of Amber."

"Amber. That's cute."

"She chose Amber because she likes fossil tree sap."

Amber cuffed Woody so fast that he didn't have time to cringe. "And he goes by Woody because he's always got one."

"You two must be married."

"Not yet. Maybe never, if he keeps it up."

"You wouldn't go with me if I didn't keep it up." Woody ducked, but he was way too slow on the draw to avoid the cuff. Taking a chance on another cuff: "We're in lust with each other."

Amber scowled.

"I see." Maia turned to Darby. "Are they like this all the time?"

"Well, I'm afraid so."

"Cute. Very cute. You swing a mean spear. Next time use the point and stab to kill. Did you bring any guns with you?"

"Well, no, we – "

"What were you doing in the cave?"

"Well – "

Amber interrupted. "If it's any of your business, we were working on our senior project."

"You climbed over the fence – "

"We did not. We went in the back way, through a crawlspace in the lower gallery."

Maia's eyes widened. "There's a rear entrance?"

"Well – "

"My brother discovered it. He took me through it when I was a kid."

"You've known about the cave?" Maia looked up at Darby. "Since we were in school?"

"Well, yes. I first found it in junior high."

"I'll be damned. I thought only our group knew about it."

"You belong to a spelunking club?"

"Not exactly."

"Then what were you doing in the cave?" Amber wanted to know. "And how did you get here?"

Maia pointed with her chin to the bodies on the ground. "I was abducted by these bloodthirsty bastards. They entered your 'verse and dragged me back through the portal."

"What do you mean by verse? You mean a poem?"

Maia pursed her lips. "Do you have any idea what this is all about?"

"No. And if we did, we wouldn't be here."

"Then why did you go through the portal?"

"What portal?"

"The one in the cave. The luminescent partition that separates 'verses."

"I don't know what poetry has to do with anything, but we were chased here by a troupe of actors dressed up as conquistadors. Like these guys. One of them took a stab at Darby with a sword, and another one almost blew his head off with a medieval rifle. They trapped us near the end of the lava tube, and the only way to escape was to go through – that colorized screen."

"So you're not gunrunners? You're here by accident?"

"Gunrunners? No."

Maia inhaled deeply. "Didn't they come after you through the portal?"

"Yes, but Darby led us out of the cave. We holed up in a snow cave for the night."

"Very resourceful. It shows good survival skills."

"When we woke up in the morning, we thought all we had to do was climb down the west flank and head for town. Then file a complaint with the actors guild. But – but – "

"But the world was different. And now you're trapped here because they're guarding the cave – were guarding it as soon as you passed through the portal. You're lucky to be alive. No, not lucky. You're smart. You're brave. You're adaptable."

"Darby gets most of the credit. He's the one who got us out of there, and down the mountain."

Maia turned her attention to Darby. "This isn't the first time he's come to my rescue."

"Well, uh – "

"Eleventh grade." To Amber and Woody: "I was being homeschooled until my parents were killed in a car crash. The State, in its infinite wisdom, forced me and my brother to attend public school, and taught us reams of academic nonsense that we didn't want to learn and had no reason to know. The kids in homeroom started picking on me right away. They called me flat-face because of my nose. They started shoving me around. Until Darby saw what they were doing. He told them to leave me alone. He said it softly. He was bigger than most of them. They glared at him, and one guy stepped up to him, but after a short staring contest he backed away." To Darby: "What would you have done if he hadn't backed down?"

"Well, uh, I guess we'll never know."

To Amber and Woody: "Watch out for the quiet ones."

After a pause, Amber asked, "So, how did you come to be in the cave? And get captured by the conquistadors?"

"That's a long story."

Amber glanced up at the sun. "We've got time."

"Not as much as you think. I'll explain later. Right now I want to question the conquistador who's not dead yet. I see his breastplate moving."

Maia knelt by the fallen conquistador. She relieved him of a leather flask that was tied to his belt, took a long gulp of water, then squirted the remainder onto his face. The conquistador blinked and spluttered. His eyelids opened partway; he was only semiconscious. She slapped his cheeks with the flask until he moved his hand to protect himself.

"You better take his weapons away," Darby cautioned.

"You're right." Maia tossed his poniard out of reach, but kept the short-sword gripped tightly in her hand. She thumped his cheek with the flat of the blade. He tried to push her away when he regained a sense of awareness. "These two thought they were going to have some fun with me. Now it's my turn."

She spoke to the conquistador in a strange guttural language that sounded nothing like ancient Spanish. He spat at her. She slammed the side of the blade against his cheek with such force that the edges left bloody parallel grooves in his skin. She raised her voice almost to a shout. Darby couldn't understand his answer, but there was no mistaking the arrogance in his voice and facial expression.

The twosome parried words for half a minute, after which Maia placed the point of the sword against the conquistador's throat, in the hollow over the trachea. Now she screamed. The conquistador suddenly grabbed her hands above the guard and attempted to push the sword away. Maia resisted. She overreached her strength so that the point pricked his skin and penetrated half an inch into his throat. She halted for a moment, yelled, then shoved hard. The blade emerged from the side of his neck.

She yanked the sword free, and let it drop to the stone floor of the plaza. "He wasn't going to talk anyway." She wasted no time in removing a large leather pouch from the conquistador's belt. "At least his food sack is full." She stood and turned away from the gurgling body, still in its death throes, as if she had done nothing more than swat an annoying insect.

Maia stared blankly at the stunned expressions that faced her. "Those bastards killed my little brother." After a moment: "And they enslaved my entire race. If you people ever want to get back home, you'll have to help me raise an army to defeat them. Otherwise you'll never get past them to the portal."

None of the trio said a word in reply.

Abruptly Maia burst into tears. She covered her face

with her hands as the tears flowed voluminously down her cheeks. She wailed like a banshee.

Amber rushed forward, threw her arms around Maia's shoulders, and hugged her tightly. "Oh, Maia, I am so sorry for you."

Maia didn't resist Amber's comforting gesture. She sobbed for at least five minutes. Finally she wiped the tears off her face with her palms, and wiped the mucus from her nose with the sleeve of the blue cotton shirt under her leather jerkin.

"Sorry for the display of tears. I guess I've been holding that in too long." Tears flowed again, and she sniffled some more, but she did not convulse completely out of control. "My baby brother."

While Amber and Woody were totally captivated by Maia's tearful outburst, Darby kept a sharp, three hundred sixty degree lookout. "Are there more conquistadors around here?"

Maia wiped off the remnants of her latest flood of tears. "No. The main group is ahead of us, heading west to Teomotl. I was with a splinter group that was bringing up the rear. Six conquistadors and a llama. They were keeping me alive because they don't know how to operate the guns, and I wouldn't show them. My legs were hobbled, my hands were tied behind my back, and a rope around my neck was tied to the llama. They didn't notice that I picked up a chunk of quartz crystal and used it to cut the rope off my hands. I kept them together as if they were tied.

"After we stopped for a break, two of them – these two – untied me from the llama and let the rest of the group go ahead so they could take turns raping me. They threw me on the ground on my back. They had to take the rope off my legs to get my pants off. I let them think that I wasn't going to resist, but as soon as my legs were free I kicked one in the face and bashed the other one on the ear with the crystal. Then I ran like crazy. I would have gotten away except for the bola.

"It wrapped around my ankles and tripped me. By the time I got the rope unwound, they were on me." To

Darby. "That's when you showed up. By this time the rest of the group should be at least a league away. They won't expect us to catch up until sundown."

"Let's not make any tactical assumptions. These conquistadors are pretty bad hombres. They might be smarter than you give them credit for."

"You're right. We shouldn't assume anything. That must come from your ROTC training. What – what do you suggest?"

"Well, first we should put some distance between us and the conquistadors. What direction did you come from?"

"South."

"Then we'll head north. Let's take their weapons and anything else of value."

"Good idea."

Amber: "It's not a good idea. It's a great idea. And Darby is full of them."

"Yeah. Big brother has a head for this kind of stuff. And the experience."

Maia crouched by the bodies and removed the armament. "So I've noticed. I'm good with a sword. Who wants the other one?"

"I'll take it. I've never used one before but I can probably figure it out. Give the knives to Woody and Amber."

They all strapped their newly acquired weapons to their belts. Maia found another food pouch and leather flask on the other conquistador, making two of each; she tied all four items to her belt opposite the sword. The conquistadors did not carry packs, and their pantaloons had no pockets. The armor was useless because the conquistadors didn't stand much over five feet in height.

Maia marched northward. "I know the area so I'll lead the way."

"Well, can I make a suggestion?"

Maia stopped and turned around.

"In case a search party comes after them, let's cover our tracks."

"How do we do that?"

Darby broke off a bunch of tall pampas grass. "I'll

bring up the rear and sweep our tracks as long as we're walking on this dusty stone. You take point but don't step on any weeds. Nobody does. We don't want any broken stems to show which way we went."

Maia nodded. "Pretty smart, Darby. Pretty smart."

"I told you so," Amber added.

Darby: "Not to be a poor sport, but do we have any particular destination in mind?"

Maia nodded again. "If I have my bearings right, there should be a path up ahead that leads to another outpost a couple of leagues away. We can hole up there for the night. It's not occupied but it should have some amenities."

Woody: "You mean, like a shower and a salad bar?"

"Not exactly."

"I didn't think so. One more question." After a wordless pause: "What do you call this place?"

"This outpost is called Zaca-Ruba. The one we're headed for is Zaca-Nola."

"No, that isn't what I meant." Woody swept his arms wide. "I mean this – place."

"Oh. We call it Lema-Rea, which translates literally as Open Sky. It's equivalent to your Earth. The conquistadors refer to it as the Great Land to the West, or the Western Reaches, because in relation to North America this landmass lies west of California, which in your 'verse is the Pacific Ocean. They corrupted the pronunciation the way they corrupted everything else in Lema-Rea. In your 'verse, this place, as you call it, it has come to be known as the lost continent of Lemuria."

Chapter 11

The overgrown plaza was ringed by encroaching vegetation. Maia looked down at engravings in the stone, then angled northwest. Soon the stone floor ended and a dirt trail appeared, barely visible through lush, overlapping leaves. She glanced at a wooden post on which symbols were carved.

"This is the way."

"Tell me more about – "

Maia interrupted. "Not now, Amber. Save your breath. If we jog we can reach Zaca-Nola in an hour. Then we can relax and lick our wounds."

She did not wait for a consensus of opinion, but started off at a pace that would eat up the miles while not leaving them too much out of breath. Darby found it difficult to jog with a sword that was only loosely secured to his side. The sheath bounced at every step, oftentimes crossing in front of his lagging right leg to a position behind his leading left leg, nearly tripping him at the next step. To counter this annoying interference, he had to hold the sword tight in order to prevent it from swinging. He held the balance point of the spear in his left hand. The items in his pack didn't clatter because the straps were drawn tight in standard military fashion.

A six-mile jog was well within Darby's ability, despite the fact that he was wearing hiking boots instead of jogging shoes. As high school students with academic ambitions, Amber and Woody had not maintained a strict regimen of physical exercise. They were soon breathing hard, but not in evident distress. They kept switching the spear from one hand to the other. Their youth worked in their favor. Every time Darby caught up with Amber, he slowed his pace so as not to crowd her, and poke her in the gluteus with his spear tip.

After thirty minutes of steady jogging, Maia slowed to a fast walk that she called a resting pace. Darby welcomed the reduction in speed, but not as much as Woody and Amber, who took the opportunity to gasp for air. Five minutes later Maia resumed the fast clip, her short but nimble legs blurring like the limbs of a scurrying mouse.

Eventually Maia stopped and stared at a wooden post.

After Amber nearly caught her breath: "Why do you keep doing that?"

"Doing what?"

"Looking at those posts?"

"I'm not just looking at them. I'm reading them."

"What? You mean you can decipher those hieroglyphics?"

"Of course. They're written in my native language."

"And what language would that be?"

"Lema-Rean. These are signposts. Like your street signs except that they give distance and direction."

"Wow!" Woody expostulated. "And I thought it was just a lot of scribble, like Indian graffiti."

Maia simpered. "A lot about this 'verse you don't perceive."

Amber threw up her arms. "What is it with you and iambic pentameter?"

Maia sighed with a mock smirk. "I'll explain it to you. To all of you. But first let's reach Zaca-Nola. We should be safe there." She turned on the heel of a brand-name jogging shoe.

They soon reached the outskirts of another stone plaza. Huge paving stones extended in all directions, past vertically walled structures and between a pair of small ziggurats to a larger ziggurat in the distance. Darby was beginning to understand that these so-called plazas – which were bigger than shopping malls – were equivalent to paved towns or villages, spaced at irregular intervals throughout the jungle on geological high grounds whose height offered a commanding view of the surrounding territory, especially from ziggurat summits whose extra elevation rose above adjacent tree tops.

Although it looked as though the plazas had been

carved out of the jungle, in fact the jungle had grown up around the plazas after ordinary upkeep had ceased. Darby noticed that the vegetation encircling the perimeter of stone blocks consisted of small trees and young shoots instead of mature plants: second generation growth. Creepers lay everywhere, and trellises of vines hung from dilapidated adobe huts.

Maia didn't head for the central ziggurat, but wended her way unerringly between structures to the eastern edge of the plaza, where the stonework yielded to what must have been a lawn before low weeds and grains supplanted the grass. Lowering sunbeams glinted off the surface of a pond that was thrice the size of a hot tub.

"This is a communal bath, which I'm sure we can all use."

"Woody does. He smells."

Woody corrected her English. "*You* smell. *I* stink."

Amber cuffed him. "You."

Darby laid down his spear and pack. "Well, I do feel pretty scuzzy."

"Then feel free to descuzzify yourself with a brimstone bath." Woody knelt and stuck his hand in the water. "This is a hot spring. The faint odor of rotten eggs comes from sulfur."

Maia threw down her belt along with the sword and the various pouches and flasks that were secured to it. One by one she stripped off items of clothing and folded them in a neat pile. She stepped into the pond totally nude. Her torso and legs were covered with welts, purple bruises, and swollen areas of skin. No one else made a move to disrobe. When she stood knee-deep in water, she turned to her companions and spread her hands. "Come on in. A long soak is guaranteed to be therapeutic."

After a few seconds of stunned silence, Woody reached for his pack. "Wow. You remind me of *September Morn*. Can I take your picture?"

Amber cuffed him so hard that he fell forward onto his face. "You."

"Hey! It's a famous painting by Paul Chabas."

"I know what it is, and you're not taking it."

Darby unzipped his jacket and unbuttoned his shirt. "When in Rome . . . or Lema-Rea." He undressed boldly until he was down to his shorts.

Maia settled in the water at the far end of the pond until her chin rested on the surface. "What's that nasty gash on your chest?"

Darby looked down at the side of his ribcage. A four-inch furrow was carved deep into his skin. Dried blood stretched from below the cut to his waist, where it had been stopped by the elastic band of his long-johns. "Well, it's where that conquistador got me with his sword, back in the cave."

Amber scolded, "You never told us you were hurt!"

"Well, there were other things happening. By the time we got bedded down in the snow cave, it didn't hurt anymore. And it wasn't bleeding . . . "

"Of course it wasn't bleeding. The blood was frozen."

Darby shrugged. After a moment's hesitation, he removed his shorts and strode into the water. It was pleasantly lukewarm.

Amber stripped next. Woody turned away from the pond, removed his outerwear, and backed into the water. After he submerged to his chafed neck, he sidled to Amber's side.

"Can I make a suggestion?" No one responded to Darby's question. "Let's spread out so we're opposite each other. That way you can see past the person you're facing in case anyone – or anything – is coming." He shrugged. "It's standard combat procedure."

Woody and Amber separated so that Woody faced his brother.

"May I make a suggestion?" Maia received the same response. She pulled up a handful of dark green slime and rubbed it over the sore spots that decorated her body. "This algae has special curative enzymes that promote healing. Dig some up from the bottom of the pond, and rub it onto any wounds, injuries, scratches, bug bites, anywhere that hurts. Let it soak in, then reapply it every few minutes. It helps to relieve pain, too."

Amber jerked a thumb in Woody's direction. "Will it cure a headache."

"Hey!"

"Only kidding, honeybunch."

Woody scowled.

Maia dunked her head to wet her thick black hair. Darby did the same. He also grabbed a handful of slime and patted it gently on the deep chest laceration. Irritating the partially healed wound caused a stinging sensation, somewhat like the antiseptic action of aftershave on a face full of razor cuts: exquisite in the comfort of knowing that the alcohol in the lotion was doing good by preventing infection. Soon the sharp tingles faded to near numbness, as if a doctor had applied a local anesthetic before stitching a wound.

Amber held a handful of slime to her nose. "This stuff smells. Or stinks. Whatever."

"You'll get used to it. It also softens and moisturizes the skin."

"You sound like a commercial." Woody spread the paste on thorn pricks that adorned the backs of his hands. "So tell us about the Technicolor screen back there in the cave."

Maia stared up at the cloudless blue sky. "Have you ever heard of piezoelectricity?"

"Sure. It's a primary branch of study in crystallography, with lots of useful applications in everyday life that people don't even know about. That's the reason we were in the lava tube. Well, Amber was there to report on subterranean fauna for her senior project. I was there to determine the presence and growth rate of crystals. According to the textbook, uh, let me see if I can remember it right, 'the piezoelectric effect is the generation of an electric charge in compressible solids by means of an applied mechanical force.'

"In plain language, if you exert pressure on a crystal, or certain other solid materials, it squeezes out electrons and makes them travel between layers in the lattice. The flow of electrons is defined as electricity. You can generate thousands of volts by pressing or deforming a crystal, although the amperage is minimal. When you beaned that conquistador with that quartz rock you picked up, you actually created a small electrical charge, although not enough to feel a shock."

"Very good, Woody. I'm impressed."

"He's pretty smart," Amber allowed.

Woody tilted his head from one side to the other. "Geology is my major. I mean, it's my major interest, but it'll be my major subject when I go to college."

Maia nodded. "Good. That will make it easier for me to explain what caused the chromatic shield, or what we call the chromashield, translated loosely. It's like a gateway or portal between 'verses."

Darby: "Not for me. I was never any good at science."

"I'll simplify it for you. Woody, feel free to butt in if you think you can clarify anything. You obviously know about the Ring of Fire – the border of geological instability that surrounds the Pacific Ocean, where temblors and volcanic activity predominate."

"Temblors?"

"Earthquakes. A generic word that's used to describe large-scale seismic movements, particularly those that don't occur on planet Earth, such as Moonquakes and Marsquakes."

Darby nodded.

"It's well known in your 'verse that electrical discharges precede temblors – "

Amber raised her hand as if she were in class, but before she could speak . . .

"I'll get to that in a moment. Atmospheric turbulence is caused mostly by temperature differentials. High-speed winds cause airborne molecules to collide with such force that electrons are knocked off the outer shells of atoms. Clouds of ions – stripped atoms that need to recapture electrons in order to regain the balance of the positive and negative charge between the nucleus and the outer shell – move above the surface of the Earth, dragging free electrons through the ground until the potential becomes great enough to cause a static discharge known as lightning, like the kind you see during thunderstorms. Contrary to popular belief, lightning arcs from the ground up into the air, not vice versa. The air-to-ground strike is an optical illusion."

Darby rubbed his temples. "You're making my head hurt."

"Stay with me. You can drive a car without understanding the workings of the internal combustion engine, and with proper training you can repair an engine without knowing how to drive a car. You can forget the background information."

"I already have."

"Anyway, seismic movement alternately compresses and decompresses rocks and minerals in the earth. This plastic cycle creates an electric charge in the ground. Tectonic plates extend deep into the Earth's crust, all the way to the mantle: a depth of anywhere from thirty miles to two hundred miles, depending on who you believe and which theory is currently in vogue. Think about how much material is under pressure as those plates grind against each other, like an irresistible force against an immovable object."

"Wow, I never looked at it that way before."

"It's not taught in school, and the concept itself has been suppressed – but I'll get to that some other time. Anyway, what I'm leading up to is that there's an enormous amount of electricity flowing through the earth – googleplexes of gigawatts of raw energy: enough to create electrical disparities in the atmosphere when the potential reaches the breaking point, and enough to induce a magnetic field that can deflect a compass needle and make it point away from the North Pole or go into a spin.

"Rock, as you know, is porous. People think of it as solid, but geologists recognize that it's riddled with voids: minute cracks, crevices, and interstices that water can seep through as if rock were a sponge - which in effect it is. That's why you have artesian wells. Under certain circumstances, usually deep within the mantle but sometimes manifested near the surface, electricity generated by the piezoelectric effect forms a tangential convergence of forces which creates a vortex in the force-matter field, or FM field.

"A vortex is formed whenever a specific combination of conditions is met: sufficient power, a modulated frequency, a confined cavity that can contain the vortex, and the extension of the FM field into similarly shaped cavities in two 'verses that happen to be in alignment, or conjunction. Equilocality is crucial. In this case it means that the same energy level is occurring at the same space in two convergent 'verses. Once the gateway or portal is created, the power requirement that is needed to sustain it is drastically reduced; it will maintain its immanence as long as there are no extraordinary changes in configuration or geographical placement. Then the gate can be opened from either side.

"Your people think of the totality of existence as the universe: the one-all reality that encompasses everything. My people have learned to recognize the variverse: 'verses of endless variety. Your people live in one such 'verse; mine live in another. It's what we call space-share."

Woody squinted. "Is that like a timeshare? Where you own a condo for one week of the year, and other people own it for the other fifty-one weeks?"

"No. Both our 'verses advance in time at the same rate, but our worlds share undifferentiated space. My space is normally separated from your space by the coordinate system of the FM field. The chromashield is an electromagnetic point of convergence between two 'verses. Think of it as a rupture in the field: a gate between 'verses that can exist only underground, where electromagnetic energy can circulate through solid material around two cavities simultaneously. When you stepped through the chromashield, you passed from your 'verse into mine. And, as you've probably noticed, my 'verse is different from yours."

"Wow. Wow. Wow."

Amber raised her hand to cuff him but he was too far out of reach. "Stop it, Woody. You sound like a barking dog."

"I can't help it. What a concept! One that's an awful lot to comprehend."

Darby humphed. "Lucky me. I didn't comprehend any of it."

"I'm not sure I did, either. I mean, I believe you, Maia. I accept it. It's just – " Amber inhaled deeply and exhaled slowly, with a soft whoosh. " – it's hard to bend my mind around it. And I *wouldn't* believe it if I didn't see it. And go through it."

Maia grinned. "There's more."

Darby closed his eyes and rubbed his aching temples. "Oh, no."

"Wait a minute!" Woody rose halfway out of the water. "Before you go on . . . do you mean that the, uh, point of convergence has to be in a cave? I mean, at a place in a cave in one 'verse that coincides with a place in a cave in another 'verse?"

"Not just the same place in a pair of caves, but at a place that has nearly identical strictures or parameters in both 'verses. Think of our 'verses as two sheets of loose-leaf paper, one on top of the other. For the sake of analogy, imagine that instead of each sheet having three holes designed to fit in a three-ring binder, each sheet has only a single hole somewhere on its surface – although, in reality, every 'verse has the potential for multiple holes, and usually does. Anyway, rub the two sheets of paper over each other as if they were being pushed this way and that by variable geological forces, until the two holes – each of the same approximate shape and size, and not necessarily round – come into alignment. Electromagnetism flowing through the rock in both 'verses interact in such a way as to create a vortex that connects the 'verses. When sufficient pressure is exerted by an object on the chromoshield – the fabric that separates one 'verse from another – that object can pass through the aligned openings from one sheet of paper to the other. As I said, the electromagnetic vortex is a gateway or portal between 'verses."

Woody mouthed the word "wow" but didn't vocalize it.

"The paper holes I can understand, but not the vortex and shield." Darby rubbed more slime on his chest, and started applying it to contusions and abrasions elsewhere on his body. "Can anything pass through, or only people?"

"The flow is constant as long as the vortex is stable. Atoms and molecules pass back and forth if they have sufficient kinetic energy to overcome the resistance, which is analogous to surface tension. Likewise dust motes, pollen, pheromones, airborne pathogens; basically, anything and everything in the air. Or in groundwater, because most vortexes are created deep underground. That's why our 'verses are so similar, having the same plants and animals, although most animals pass through the membrane only when the vortex is created at the entrance of a cave; or not far inside; or, rarely, in an arch."

This time Woody found his voice. "You mean an arch like in Arches National Monument?"

"Yes, but only if complimentary arches exist in both 'verses, or if an arch in one 'verse coinncides with a cave in the other. And they have to be small enough to sustain the electromagnetic field. Electromagnetism is poorly understood in your 'verse – mostly the applications that deal with electricity and magnetism, but not many of its other effects, such as organizing and stabilizing astronomical bodies, like the rings of Saturn."

"Wow. How do you know so much?"

"My parents taught me. We're descended from Lema-Reans."

"So, what? You've been crossing between worlds, er, 'verses, living part time in ours and part time in yours?"

"No. I was born and raised in your 'verse. I've never been to this 'verse until two days ago."

Chapter 12

The stunned silence lasted only a moment before Amber expostulated in surprise. "How can that be? You know all about this place: names, locations, distances, the – the portal between worlds, or 'verses. How can you know all that without ever having been here?"

"My parents taught me. I told you I was home-schooled. Except for two years wasted in senior high, I've spent my whole life studying, training, and preparing for the day when a portal would open, so I could help to rescue my people from tyranny and slavery."

"Your people?"

"I am descended from the race that lives in this 'verse. I've been waiting for this day – praying for this day – to avenge the deaths of my ancestors, who were killed off by invading conquistadors from your 'verse."

"From our . . . "

Woody was nonplussed. "Okay, okay. I've accepted the fact that the conquistadors aren't costumed actors making an epic film about the conquest of the Peru, but are you saying that the ones in the cave, and back there at Zaca-Ruba, are real-live conquistadors from our, uh, 'verse?"

"No. They're the evil offspring of the original conquistadors. They invaded our 'verse in the sixteenth century, shortly after they occupied the American continents in your 'verse. I know it must sound confusing – "

"Confusing! You're going from the ridiculous to the absurd."

Maia licked her lips patiently. "Yes, I'm sure it must seem that way. I can explain . . . but not now. The sun is setting, and we need to find a place to bed down for the night where we can prepare some food. We're going to be famished in a little while."

Darby: "Last night we camped in a pillbox and made a fire to keep warm."

"A pillbox?"

"Well, some kind of stone building with four door-ways. With all the buildings in this abandoned city, I'm sure we can find something similar. We can gather wood for a fire . . . "

"Okay, but we'll have to do some scrounging for cookware. The conquistadors fed me quinoa, so that's probably what they've got in their food pouches."

"Quinoa?" asked Amber.

"We call it the Mother Grain. It's a kind of cereal that grows at high altitude. It's a highly nutritious source of protein. What have you been eating since your arrival?"

"After finishing our snack food, we've been living on coconuts, mangoes, and papayas. And they weren't growing wild – "

"My people have been farming them for thousands of years."

"Thousands – "

"Later, Amber. For now, let's get moving so we can get our chores done before sundown." Maia stood up and stepped out of the pond. She used her fingers to wipe most of the droplets off her body. "You two gather wood. Darby and I will search the city for supplies – "

Amber followed Maia's example by not showing concern about her nudity. "Darby gave us strict instructions to stay together. *All* together."

"But not *in* the altogether," Woody quipped, from the safety of the pond where Amber couldn't cuff him."

Amber glared.

Maia stood to her full five-and-a-quarter-foot height. She stared from one to the other. "I'm sorry. I'm used to giving orders to our hired hands." To Darby: "You're instructions are wise – for the three of you, because separation would leave at least one person alone in unfamiliar territory. How about if we split into pairs, like I just suggested?"

"Well, uh, okay as long as we stay within earshot. And, uh, I think one of us – I mean, you and me – should go with one of them." To Amber and Woody: "Don't take this the wrong way, but we've got more experience – "

Woody interrupted his brother. "You won't get an argument from me. One adult fighter with each kid who's not a fighter."

Amber reached for her clothes. "Makes sense to me too. I *want* to be paired with one of you. I couldn't go after a conquistador the way Maia did, even if I do have a knife."

Maia addressed Darby. "I like the way you think. You obviously know more about small group dynamics than I've been able to learn from books. We'll do it your way. Who gets who?"

Darby felt conscious of his nudity as he climbed out of the pond. "You take Woody. I'll take Amber. Do you know bird calls?"

Maia tried not to smirk but could not restrain herself. "I'm afraid that subject wasn't in my curriculum."

"That's okay. Woody knows them."

"Is that what I missed by dropping out of high school?"

"No. We picked it up on our own."

As proof of his prowess, Woody rendered perfect imitations of a crow, a blue jay, and a mourning dove. Each time, Darby replied in kind.

Maia raised black bushy eyebrows. "What? No owls?"

"Owls don't usually hoot in the daytime. It's a dead giveaway that Indians only use in Westerns."

"I'll remember that."

They spent a few minutes wiping down and getting dressed, then went on parallel ways in order to do their assigned chores. Darby collected large deadwood while Amber gathered kindling. Unless a stone structure or ziggurat got in the line of sight, they were almost always in visual contact with Maia and Woody. Whenever the two teams were out of view from each other, they kept in touch by means of comfort calls.

Maia ducked into several huts, emerged with her hands filled with useful objects, and handed them to Woody.

Finally, they all met with loaded arms at the base of a massive ziggurat that rose over a hundred feet in height. Maia led the way to a nearby rectangular building where she and Woody had stashed a horde of items.

"This is a communal bunkhouse so most of what we need is already here."

Amber was amazed at the array of goods that lay scattered around the great-room: painted pottery of various sizes, metal pots and pans, utensils carved from bone, hammocks woven from cotton fabric, and blankets made of textiles.

"All this stuff was left behind when the people evacuated the city before the conquistadors' advance. The conquistadors stole everything of value – that is, of value to them: mostly gold and jewels – and didn't take time to destroy what they didn't want."

Darby nodded slowly. "How long ago?"

"I don't know. Our historical records are scratchy after the original invasion, when interverse travel was brought mostly to a standstill. Since then communication has been sporadic: only when a new portal opened, or an old one regenerated. But first, let's get a fire going and start cooking."

Darby assumed the fire-starting chore. Maia added rocks to the partially demolished ring around the central pit. Once the fire was blazing, she inserted two iron rods into holes that were bored into the stone floor, on opposite sides of the pit, and hung a cooking pot filled with water and quinoa on a spit that stretched from one rod to the other.

While the quinoa was cooking, Maia munched on a slightly overripe mango. "The most important fact that you people need to understand is that you're trapped here. You can't get back to your 'verse unless we oust the conquistadors who are guarding the portal. Now that you've escaped them, and I'm on the loose, the conquistadorian army will be more vigilant than ever. The only way we can overcome them is to get our guns back."

"What guns?" Amber wanted to know.

"The guns that we were transporting for the relief of Teomotl. The last we heard, which was more than a century ago, Teomotl was one of the few Lema-Rean cities that was holding out against the conquistadors. A lot may have changed since the closing of the last working portal, after the San Francisco earthquake in 1906, but that's our most recent intelligence. Even if Teomotl has fallen, our objective would then be to liberate the city and initiate a counteroffensive against conquistadorian rule: first in Teomotl, then in the rest of Lema-Rea.

"I can't force you to help me, but it's in your best interests to do so. By working together, we might be able to rally some troops and make a beachhead against the conquistadors. Especially if we can knock out the enemy caravan and get more gunrunners."

Amber opened her mouth . . .

"I'm a gunrunner. That's why I was in the cave when the conquistadors came through the portal. My family has been collecting and hording guns for decades, buying them legally whenever possible, or on the black market for outdated military rifles, hand guns, and other conventional weapons. We've got enough ammunition stockpiled to support a small army, which is what we hope to do.

"We raise llamas on the farm, ostensibly for their wool, or fiber, but in actuality to use as pack animals in Lema-Rea. We sell llama fiber in order to maintain a façade of legitimate business, but we have all the money we need in the form or gold."

Amber gasped.

"Gold is abundant in Lema-Rea. Far more common than in your 'verse. Despite its attractive luster, for us it has little in the way of monetary value – much like your copper. I don't mean that we don't use gold to make jewelry and ceremonial items, only that's it's not a precious metal or primary commodity. To us, the greatest appeal of gold is its conductivity."

Woody wondered: "You mean electrical conductivity?"

"Yes. Gold is a better conductor than copper: of heat as well as electricity. Not as good as platinum but far superior to copper. We use gold the way you use copper. This pot – " She indicated the vessel in which the quinoa water was now boiling furiously. " – is a gold-alloy. The original inhabitants disguised the precious metal by coating the inner and outer surfaces with pitch, so the conquistadors would recognize it and steal it. There's no word for this alloy in English. By analogy, brass and bronze are common in your 'verse. Brass is an alloy of copper and zinc; bronze of copper and tin. Pure gold is softer and much more malleable than copper, so it has to be alloyed with zinc, tin, and other metals in order to give it strength and durability. The ductility of pure gold makes it ideal for use as an electrical conductor."

"You – you have electricity?"

Maia nodded. "Direct current only. We never had a genius like Tesla to conceive alternating current."

"You mean Nikola Tesla, the inventor of radio?"

Maia scowled and rolled her eyes. "I do mean Nikola Tesla, the discoverer of the principle on which wireless telegraphy is based: the Tesla coil, known generically as the spark-gap transmitter. What I really meant was Nikola Tesla, the inventor of alternating current: the form of electricity that runs the entire world in your 'verse.

"The reason Tesla didn't proceed with the development of radio the way Guglielmo Marconi did, was because he had a grander goal in mind. He concentrated his studies on earth-generated electricity and wireless transmission. I've already explained to you how electricity is generated in the earth by means of the piezoelectric effect. Tesla realized the tremendous potential of this natural law – in both meanings of the word 'potential' – and sought ways to harness it. In large measure, Tesla is the key to the ultimate success of our mission.

"Tesla's breakthrough occurred in 1899, as a result of experiments that he conducted at his laboratory in Colorado Springs. His experiments with high-voltage magnetic induction resulted in phenomena that he didn't fully understand. He induced atmospheric electrical discharges by interacting with the flow of electrons in the ground: a form of artificial lightning. This experiment proved that potential energy existed between the ionosphere and the surface of the planet, and that it could be tapped or siphoned off, then transmitted through conductors to terminals or points of use.

"That led him to the construction of a transmission tower on Long Island. Ostensibly the tower was supposed to transmit powerful communication signals around the globe, like a super powerful radio transmitter. It did that. In addition, the tower was designed to accumulate and store electrical energy that passed through the ground, and to transmit it through the atmosphere without wires, so it could be drawn off by light bulbs, appliances, motors, and so on. That's when Tesla was shut down and ostracized."

Darby thought about rubbing his temples, but decided instead to make no outward show of ignorance. He let Woody fill the temporary hiatus in the conversation.

"Okay, I'll bite. Why was Tesla ostracized?"

"I was going to tell you even if you hadn't asked. Tesla was ostracized because he told his financiers about the true purpose of the tower. To go back a few years, and to simplify the contretemps, Thomas Edison had the monopoly on lighting New York City by means of direct current. He was in constant conflict with Tesla because he invented alternating current, and held the patents on the system. Edison pushed for DC even though AC was a better system. DC can't be transmitted economically for more than a few miles, whereas AC can be transformed to high voltages which *can* be transmitted over great distances with little line loss, then stepped down to usable voltages.

"George Westinghouse wanted to get into the electrical business, so he leased Tesla's patents as a way of opposing Edison. In 1893, Westinghouse funded Tesla's plan to build a dam and utilize the flow of water to turn the armature of a dynamo that would generate alternating current to power the Columbian Exposition in Chicago – an advertising ploy to demonstrate the utility of alternating current. The plan worked, and eventually DC died out except for short-range, special uses: mostly large motors where speed control was a factor, such as in elevators and printing presses.

"In 1900, J.P. Morgan funded Tesla's Long Island project because he wanted to steal a march on Marconi, and provide a global communications service that was better than Marconi's system. By this time, Morgan had bought out Westinghouse's electric company. This meant that he was now in the electricity generating business. After Tesla successfully demonstrated his wireless transmission of communications, he kept working on the wireless transmission of electricity. As Tesla's project neared completion, Morgan realized the adverse implications of the system, so he pulled the plug. He had the tower operation shut down by withholding additional funding and foreclosing on the property."

"I don't get it. What's so wrong with a wireless system that Morgan would want to stop it from happening? You wouldn't need all those thousands of transmission towers and millions of feet of heavy-duty cable that uglify the countryside."

Amber put in her two cents. "Yeah!"

"In addition to owning a power company, one of Morgan's biggest money-making interests was in railroads. And one of the railroad's biggest customers was the coal-mining industry. Coal is burned to generate steam for power plants. Morgan was making money from both ends of the stick: by transporting coal, and by generating electricity. Take away the need for coal, and you take away the need to transport it by rail. Tesla's success would have spelled Morgan's doom. *Wild electricity that is generated by the Earth and extracted from the ground is free.*"

Darby didn't comprehend the science, and economics was not his strong point, but he understood enough to let a whistle escape his lips.

"Yes. Free electricity benefits the public but not the business moguls. Tesla wanted to provide unlimited power for the masses. The planet generates enough electricity to power the world – and that isn't a tautology. The only human investment is in the construction of the plant: the energy accumulators and the transmission

machinery. After the system is emplaced, it operates itself by absorbing electricity from the ground and trans-
mitting it to remote devices."

"Wow!"

"That's the problem with your 'verse. It functions on
greed and selfishness. All other considerations are secondary." After a silence, "Morgan and his associate en-
trepreneurs went all out to vilify Tesla, ruin his
reputation, make him out a crank, when all he wanted
to do was to benefit mankind. He was a modern
Prometheus."

Darby placed a hand over his tummy. "I hate to interrupt this scientific discussion, but my stomach is
grumbling and I feel – faint, or light-headed – for lack of
food."

Maia stirred the quinoa and ladled some into a ceramic bowl. "I told you we'd be famished soon."

"But, how did you know?"

"The bath. I told you the slime had curative powers,
and it does. The enzymes promote healing – somewhat
like the enzymes in chicken broth, but with far greater
speed and more powerful effect. Unfortunately, healing
doesn't come for free. It requires energy. Accelerating the
body's natural healing process increases the consump-
tion of energy. You have to furnish your depleting energy
supply by metabolizing more food.

Darby nodded slowly. "That makes sense." He dug a
bone spoon into the congealed quinoa and shoved it into
his mouth. "Hey, this is pretty good."

"It would taste better if we had some spices to add,
but I didn't find any when I was scrounging for supplies." Maia filled bowls for Amber and Woody. "Eat as
much as you want." To Darby: "You'll need it the most
because you sustained the worst injuries. You'll sleep
well, too, while your body repairs itself."

"I'm already feeling tired."

"Pull up your shirt. Let me see the cut."

Darby did as he was asked.

"Wow." Woody put down his bowl in order to examine his brother's ribcage. "It's – it's almost healed over

and – and there's no sign of a scab."

Maia nodded. "It works wonders."

Amber took another bite, then held out her hand. "Amazing. Those thorn pricks are completely gone."

"The conquistadors heard about the curing ponds, and saw some of their victims who had healed overnight. Even under extreme torture, no one would tell them where the ponds were located or how they worked. The conquistadors thought it was magic. They spent enormous amounts of time and energy searching for a pond, in your 'verse as well as mine. Especially Ponce de Leon. He exaggerated the curative powers, claiming that a curing pond could restore youth and prevent old age. He called it the Fountain of Youth."

Chapter 13

Darby opened his eyes groggily. The sun had long since risen and illuminated the great-room. Amber was kneeling by his side, looking down at him with a smirk on her face.

She cooed softly, "Da-a-a-r-r-r-r-by. Upski-dupski."

He squeezed his eyes tight, then reopened them. His grogginess dissipated, but he felt a pang in his stomach that ached with increasing vigor. When he sat up, Amber shoved a bowl of quinoa in his hands. Without a word, he wolfed it down as if he hadn't eaten in a week.

"Feel better?"

"Lots. . . . I don't even remember falling asleep."

"Maia said that would happen because you were hurt so badly. The rest of us slept pretty soundly, too."

Darby glanced around the room. He saw no one else.

"Don't worry. They haven't gone far. Just outside to see a man about a llama." She handed a holed coconut that was filled with milk, and a plate full of bite-sized chunks of coconut meat. "We've already had some food – enough to tide us over until breakfast. A real breakfast."

"How's that?"

"Maia says there's a rookery nearby, so she's taking us on an Easter egg hunt. That's appropriate, since this is Easter break. We've already packed the kitchen supplies so we can cook on the spot. And I wrapped a bedroll for you."

Darby felt better, but weak. He threw off the blankets and examined his ribcage. A faint line stretched across the skin where yesterday there had been a deep sword cut. "That slime works pretty good."

"All my little scrapes are gone. A soak in the pond and an application of slime certainly rejuvenates the body, even if it doesn't extend your lifespan."

Darby swallowed the last of the coconut milk. He stood up, still chewing the meat. "So what's the plan?"

"We're just waiting for you, sleepyhead."

"I'm ready."

Amber picked up his pack. A bedroll was lashed to the top with short lengths of sisal rope. She waited for him to don his belt and accoutrements before handing the pack to him. She then gave him a spear, kept one for herself. "You can squirt on the way."

"Thanks." He noticed that pale gray fabric was wrapped around the spear about a foot away from the tip, and a loop of the same material was secured in the middle of the shaft. "Who did that?"

"Maia. She said the weight on the end would help to stabilize the spear in flight, in case you have to throw it. Saber-toothed tigers, watch your butt! And the sling is so you can carry the spear on your shoulder like a rifle, or across your back. It's tied with slip knots so you can slide it off the end

"Smart gal."

"I wouldn't want to run into her in a dark alley."

"There are two dead conquistadors who would agree with you."

"Yeah." Amber furrowed her brow, looking wistful. "I'm glad she's on our side. Or we're on her side. Whatever. Come on. They're waiting for us, and I'm hungry for eggs. We've been eating too much fruit for my alimentary tract."

The sun had already appeared above the eastern mountain. Golden beams pierced scattered clouds to illuminate the ancient city complex, which now reminded Darby more of an industrial park than a shopping mall. Groves of trees and fallow fields broke up the monotony of stone buildings and ziggurats. Weeds grew here and there where wind-borne dirt had accumulated deep enough for them to take root. He tried to picture what the city must have looked like when the grounds were kept and the earth-filled patches were effulgent with crops.

Despite the overgrown parks, the layout of Zaca-Nola did not resemble any town square he had ever seen. Cities in his 'verse had trees and flower gardens for the sake of appearance. Zaca-Nola was more utilitarian, with plots of earth that were cultivated to provide edibles in reach of the inhabitants. The hodge-podge manner in which fields separated structures from each other was not accidental; it showed that a great deal of planning had gone into the arrangement and construction of the city.

Darby imitated the distinct call of a bobwhite. An answering call sounded immediately from the southwest. Darby led the way in the prescribed direction. As he and Amber rounded the corner of a three-story edifice, he saw Maia and Woody standing side by side. Woody nodded.

Maia shouldered a bulging burlap bundle that was made portable by means of a tump line and two stout leather straps that wrapped around the bottom. "How do you feel?"

"Well, pretty good."

Maia wore her jerkin but had dispensed with her shirt. Her arms were bare. Her trousers were rolled up above her knees, displaying legs that were shapely despite well-toned muscles. Black and blue marks no longer decorated her smooth olive skin. "Good. From the edge of town we have to go about a league and a half. No jogging today. Our bodies are still healing, so if we push too hard before consuming more food, we might collapse from lack of available energy. Just keep a steady pace."

Woody hefted his pack. He had rolled up the sleeves of his shirt. Darby followed suit. Maia lifted her bundle by the tump line, which she placed across her broad forehead in order to bear the bulk of the weight on her neck muscles, then slipped the side straps over her shoulders. She struck across the stone plaza with her human ducklings in pursuit.

The pace that she called steady was one that Darby considered fast. They passed a grove of fig trees, and another of dates, but none of the fruit was ripe. Maia wove a serpentine route around a suburban neighborhood of adobe huts, leading an unerring course to an obvious trailhead between two tall palm trees, from which a well-worn path carved a meandering footway through the surrounding forest.

The lack of thick understory and the open air that existed to a height of thirty feet, where the stout limbs and broad leaves spread across the trail and provided shade, enabled Darby to hold the spear over his shoulder like a marching soldier on parade. Woody and Amber did the same, keeping up their constant chatter as if they were on a picnic outing instead of stalking conquistadors on an alien planet.

So quickly does fear and wonder become commonplace.

Tropical birdlife became more prevalent as the foursome distanced themselves from Zaca-Nola. Darby spotted numerous multicolored parrots and macaws, dazzling in the variety of color combinations. One pure white cockatoo squawked raucously from a treetop as the party passed beneath its nest. Several species of parakeet watched in silence. Once a purple hummingbird buzzed in front of Darby's face, hovered, stared him in the eye, then darted away like an arrow in flight, to disappear in nearby foliage.

Darby thought idly how Maia's 'verse must have been a wonderful place in which to live before the coming of the conquistadors . . .

Maia called a halt when they reached a glade. The open area was an acre or so in extent. In the middle stood a stone pillar whose four sides were covered with various carvings. Maia studied the glyphs, turned on her heel, and strode toward a path at the opposite end. The path led a hundred yards to the edge of a vast plain that seemed to extend to infinity. Small groves of palm trees dotted the landscape.

"The nests will be located in those woodlets where the copse is dense enough to offer protection for the fledglings. One nest each; they don't like company. Leave the packs and spears here." She tossed off the tump line and let her bundle roll off her shoulders to the ground. She surveyed the plain from left to right. "The coast looks clear. Now we run."

She made a dash for the nearest grove. Darby, Woody, and Amber did their best to stay on her heels. She was fleet of foot when she wanted to be; none of them could catch up with her. She dived headlong into the thick brush, where she waited for her cohorts.

"Now we crawl. Keep your weapons in hand." She drew her sword by way of example. She humphed. "A lot of good this rusty antique will do. Like that knife – " She indicated the one in Woody's sheath. " – it probably hasn't got a sharp enough edge to cut through a conquistador's skin."

"Well, if you – "

"Later. Let's get an egg before mama or papa return from feeding."

Amber did not bother to draw her poniard. "*An* egg? As in singular?"

"We need only one." With that she crept through low-level lianas, holding her sword by the hilt with the blade dragging behind, so the point wouldn't snag in the vines in front of her. "And keep quiet. They have good ears."

About a minute later they encountered a perpendicular animal trail that was broad enough to accommodate an Irish elk.

"Woody and I will go left, Darby and Amber go right. Make a bird call if you find a nest. And don't take any more than one egg. They're not good at math so they'll never know it's gone."

Darby and Amber walked for half a minute when the trail ended in a gigantic pile of loose sticks that could have been the ground nest of a fabulous Arabian roc. It stood four feet tall and had a diameter of twelve feet. In the middle lay what appeared to be four misshapen beach balls, off-white in color and dappled with light blue splotches.

Amber was mesmerized by the sight. "What the heck . . ."

Darby was about to vocalize a blue jay chirp when Maia rushed up behind him. "Nice going. Our way led to the entrance." She climbed onto the pile of sticks and scrabbled to the center. She hefted one of the objects as if it were a medicine ball instead of an egg. Due to the uneven footing on loose and breaking sticks, it was all she could do to roll the egg over the uneven surface, despite its compactness. "Darby, you take the egg."

Darby grabbed the egg as Maia rolled it over the edge of the nest. It felt like a barbell weight; maybe two. He cradled it in his arms, and stepped back so Maia could lever herself out of the nest and onto the ground.

"Let's get out of here." She hurried back to their point of entry, dropped down to all fours, and skedaddled.

Amber followed.

Woody looked at his brother with his hands held out as if in supplication. "Is she crazy?"

Darby raised his eyebrows and rolled his shoulders. Woody shook his head as he ducked into the narrow opening. Darby put the egg on the ground and rolled it through the rabbit trough in front of him. The egg was out of round – not egg-shaped like an ordinary chicken egg, but flattened at the poles like the Earth. It wobbled from side to side as he rolled it along the tight-knit tunnel. He emerged from the thicket in time to hear an explosive squawk – not unlike one of Amber's screams but three times louder.

"Uh, oh." Maia stood up, waved one arm, and, like a marine sergeant yelling to his squad on a beachhead landing, shouted, "Follow me."

The "me" was almost lost in the breeze because she had already turned toward the forest and was running flat out. Darby saw why. What he took to be a parent of the oversized egg was racing across the plain in their direction. It was still a couple of hundred yards away, charging through the grass on a pair of disproportionately short legs that were as fat as utility poles. The neck was equally as thick; it supported a monstrous beaked head that stood ten feet above the ground. It was like a giant ostrich, but bigger, taller, and meaner. It didn't stick its head in a hole, but kept both fiercely squinted eyes on the stolen egg.

Darby stood alone, for Amber and Woody were already halfway to the forest. He ran as fast as he could with a hefty weight in his arms, and a sword banging away at his side and threatening to trip him at every step. Maia was already on an intercepting course with the giant bird, wielding a spear in both hands.

She stood her ground as Darby rushed past her into the forest. He dropped the egg harder than he intended, but the thick shell didn't crack. He grabbed one of the other spears. He turned in time to see Maia take a sideswipe at the bird's long neck. The glossy yellow beak was snapping at her head when the shaft struck its neck in mid-squawk.

Darby slammed the shaft against one massive leg. The bird backed away, peered down at them from its towering height, and issued a half-hearted squeak. It blinked back and forth at Maia and Darby. The eyes glowed with chatoyant emerald green and sapphire blue that was mystifying if unnerving.

"Cover the egg!" Maia shouted over her shoulder.

Woody and Amber reacted simultaneously. They tossed their packs on the egg so as to hide it from the giant bird's line of sight.

"Stare it down, Darby. Stare it down."

After a minute or so, the bird turned away and stalked across the plain on pile-driver legs to the woodlet, where it was joined by another, larger specimen. They entered the thicket one after the other.

"They're as stupid as chickens, but when you're that big and strong you can afford to be stupid.

Woody intoned, "Strong like bull, dumb like tractor."

Amber cuffed him out of reflex. To Maia: "What *was* that bird?"

Maia lay down the spear and inspected the egg. "It doesn't have a binomial nomenclature because it doesn't exist anymore in your 'verse. Your people exterminated them in the seventeenth century. The genus is *Aepyornis* and the species is related to the *maximus* of Madagascar. It's a flightless bird like your ostrich."

"It may be flightless but it can run faster than some

birds can fly."

"I'll grant you that. I've been told about these avian herbivores all my life: studied their habits, learned where to find them, how to steal only a single egg, how to repel an attack – as you saw, they back off a fight if you show them who's boss and where they stand in the pecking order – but I have to admit that I had my doubts there for a moment, when it looked like it was going to run me down. Real life isn't the same as reading a book." As an afterthought. "We have moas and dodos, too, but they live in colder climates." To Darby, "Thanks for backing me up."

Darby nodded slowly.

"I also have to admit that actually meeting one was quite a thrill."

"Those kinds of thrills I can do without. I'll stick to crystals and leave fauna studies to Amber. Crystals won't kill you."

Amber shrugged. "I wasn't thrilled. I was scared witless. I think I'll keep my studies on cave bugs. You can keep your *Aepyornis*."

"Believe it or not, they're supposed to taste like chicken."

"I like mine extra crispy."

Amber cuffed Woody again. "You." To Maia: "Anyway, we don't have a skillet big enough to fry anything that size."

"No, but I brought a pot that's big enough to boil an egg." She pointed to the rounded bottom of her makeshift pack, which Darby now saw was made of a thick blanket to which Maia had tied shoulder straps and the yump line. The top was lashed shut with a length of hemp.

"I was hoping for an omelet."

Amber lifted her hand to cuff Woody for his comment, but let it go.

"Maybe next time, when we have some vegetables and mushrooms to add to the mix. There should be a cookhouse half a league from her. Darby, can you carry the egg that far."

"Sure."

They made good time. The cookhouse was located next to a spring in a clearing that was a five-way intersection of dirt pathways. The cube-shaped edifice was built of odd-sized stones that were fitted together without mortar. The roof consisted of heavy, overhanging timbers whose covering of thatch had rotted into particles that littered the hard dirt floor; it would offer scant protection from rain. The inside was bare except for a fire ring. Conquistadors had long since looted the cookhouse of kitchenware items.

All four adventurers gathered sticks and rotting logs, and soon had a small fire blazing.

Maia located the metal rods that were meant be assembled in the form of a spit. She poked the relevant rods into holes in stones that were intended for the purpose, and placed the cross-piece between them. She rolled down the sides of her burlap bundle as if she were peeling a banana, to reveal a huge gold-alloy pot that constituted the bottom of the bundle. The pot was filled with utensils and other paraphernalia, each of which was wrapped individually in variously colored cotton fabric. She emptied the pot, hung it over the fire, and filled it partway with water that she obtained from the spring.

The gold-alloy transmitted heat to the water so well that it was soon bubbling furiously. When Maia inserted the *Aepyornis* egg, the water rolled up around the sides of the shell and barely covered the top. "It won't take long." She rolled the egg continuously with a pair of thick wooden swizzle sticks. "It'll be hardboiled in no time."

"Unless it has a chick in it," Woody noted.

"It doesn't. Two of the others did. I tapped them all to make sure."

"Kind of like an ultrasound test, huhn?"

"Yes, although if an embryo had started to form, we could still eat the meat and what was left of the albumin."

Amber made a face of disgust but remained silent.

After Maia announced that the egg was sufficiently cooked, she ladled some of the hot water into ceramic mugs that she brought out of her bundle, and sprinkled what looked like pollen into each one, by rubbing two bulbs together. "This is a kind of Lema-Rean tea, made from a sweet spice that I picked while we were hiking." She passed mugs to each of the others. She picked up a rock with a pointed end. "For the main course we break open the egg while it's still in the pot."

"I have a rock hammer," Woody offered.

Maia put down the rock. "Be my guest."

Woody retrieved the hammer from his pack. He used the pick end on the shell, which proved to be an inch thick and difficult to break. He finally succeeded in cracking the eggshell. He chipped away at the cracks until chunks broke off the shell. Amber plucked away the pieces.

When the hole reached an irregular diameter of four to five inches, Maia signaled for him to halt. "That's enough." She handed bone spoons to each of the diners. "Now we eat the egg right out of the shell, like scooping ice cream from the box."

Darby found the albumin as bland as that of a chicken egg. He wished he had some salt. The yolk was reddish rather than yellow, and somewhat pungent: a taste that would bear getting used to. He found that by taking portions of both ingredients together, the combination – while not particularly palatable – was at least edible. He washed down each bite with Maia's spiced tea, which proved to be very tasty if somewhat bitter.

After they ate their fill, Maia left the remaining portion inside the shell, and sealed the top with a moistened cloth. "We'll save the rest for lunch."

She was about to use the remaining hot water to pour more tea when the room darkened. Sunlight entering from the lone doorway was blotted by a massive shape. For a moment, before Darby's eyes adjusted to the reduction of dayshine, it looked as if a shaggy carpet had been thrown across the entrance. Then the shape folded in the middle, stepped under the lintel, and stood to its full height of seven and a half feet.

Long, scraggly, reddish hair lay matted on a lean body like that of an over-tall orangutan. Abnormally elongated arms and legs completed the simile. The head was shaped like a watermelon standing on its end. Ebony eyes peered out from under a protruding brow ridge. The lips of the biped pulled back to reveal a mouthful of yellow, inch-long teeth.

The creature growled.

Chapter 14

Darby reached for his spear so fast that his hand was a blur.

"*Don't hurt it!*" Maia screamed. She leaned past Amber and grabbed Darby's forearm.

Darby's eyes were the size of saucers as he glared at her.

"Let it go. They're harmless."

Darby looked back at the monstrosity, his spear still gripped tightly in his fist. Woody and Amber were wide-eyed statues.

"It smelled food. It only wants to eat. It won't hurt us, even if we don't give it food."

The beast growled again – not like an angry wolf but like a frightened dog.

Maia stood and faced the thing. The anthropoid took a step backward, banging its skull on the lintel. She held out her hand. The creature scrunched into the doorway. Slowly Maia turned and retrieved the leftover *Aepyornis* egg. She proffered it to the hungry cur.

The creature accepted the offering, grunted several times, stepped into the daylight, and lumbered away while looking constantly over its broad rounded shoulder.

Amber sighed so deeply that her exhale deflected the flickering flames. "*That* is going in my report."

"What was – *that*?" Woody wanted to know.

Maia faced them with an uncertain, half-hearted smile. "Loosely translated, it was a Shaggy Person." She wiped sweat off her brow. "I had it drilled into me that they're harmless, that they roam the forests but are seldom seen because of their natural timidity." She snickered. "According to the storytellers, they're so shy and reclusive that they won't even approach each other, which is why you never see their young. The only time they're bold enough to come near a human being is when they're starving, and looking for a handout."

"Wow," was Woody's only comment.

"It obviously has a hominid background," Amber offered.

"Yes. I suppose it shared a common ancestor with *Homo sapiens* – like monkeys and great apes." Maia regained her composure. She poured another round of tea, using a triple-folded blanket to lift and tip the scorching gold-alloy pot. "They shelter in overhangs in the wild, or in abandoned forest buildings when no people are around. Every once in a while one slips through a portal into your 'verse. Sightings are uncommon because they seek solitude and wilderness, and, as I said, they're exceedingly timid. Your people call it Bigfoot, or Sasquatch."

"Wow!"

"So the legends are true. Bigfoot and Sasquatch really exist, but only in your world, uh, 'verse. Humph. On second thought, I'll leave that out of my report. No one will believe it, especially my project advisor. *I* hardly believe it, and I saw it." After a pause: "So, what other animals exist in your, uh, 'verse that don't exist in ours? We saw what I thought was a herd of Irish elk."

"And a family of elephants," Woody added.

Darby volunteered, "I thought they were woolly mammoths that had shed their winter coat."

Maia grinned. "We have woolly mammoths but they live farther north, in the subarctic zone. What you saw was either a mastodon or a Columbian mammoth. They used to live on your American continents, but they were either killed off or they died out during the Ice Age, along with the Irish elk."

"Why didn't they go extinct here?" Amber wanted to know.

"For one thing, our Ice Age lasted longer than yours – thousands of years longer – and it didn't end abruptly the way yours did. It fizzled out gradually, giving animals time to adapt or to migrate to gradually warming climates. For another, my people didn't hunt species to extinction. We have a lot of animals that no longer live in your 'verse."

"Yeah, like conquistadors."

Amber was about to cuff Woody for his comment, but changed her mind. "That's a good point. How come you still have conquistadors?"

"As I told you before, they are not *our* conquistadors. They came from your 'verse, bent on conquest and the search for gold and jewels. After they raped and pillaged your 'verse . . . " After a moment of silence. "Look, I can explain everything, but first we have to get moving if we're going to intercept the conquistadors before they reach Teomotl. Are you still with me?"

The trio traded looks, expressions, and shrugs. It was obvious to Darby that Woody and Amber wanted him to be their spokesperson. "Well, uh, sure. Okay. We're still with you."

"Good. Then let's go. But first, let me show you the lay of the land." She used a stick to draw a diagram in the dust. "Here's Mount Pech-Nim – that's what we call the mountain – where we came through the portal. The best I can figure from your description, you went pretty much straight down the mountain and kept heading west to the Pech-Nima Outpost, and turned northwest to the Cotl River. You followed the river northward for a bit, crossed it, and continued northwest to the Pech-Cotl Prairie. Afterward you swung around southward to where you met me.

"The conquistadors took me and the llama train south along a descending slope almost all the way to the bottom, then switched to north, then south again to the base, where we started heading west. We passed south of the outpost before turning northwest, roughly paralleling your course. The river takes a sharp turn westward, about five leagues downstream of where you crossed it. When we reached the left bank, we turned west and followed it. I escaped here and swam across the river to where you ran into me, here. The llama train kept going west on the other side of the river.

"They'll be plodding along because of the llamas. They're like mules: slow but sure. We can travel light and fast in a southwesterly direction. The river cuts into a deep gorge with sheer walls like your Grand Canyon, but there's a narrows here where there should be a bridge. By taking a diagonal course, we can intersect their trail on the south side, hopefully before they get there."

Darby nodded slowly. "Well, how will we know whether they're in front of us or behind us, when we cross their path?"

"Llama dung."

Darby raised his eyebrows.

"My brother had our llamas grazing not too far from the cave. He drove them there from the farm, right past the ranger station. Twice." She laughed. "They never look out their window, and they never patrol the mountainside. And on the rare occasions when they do go on patrol, like when they have to search for a lost hiker, they see only what they can see from their pickups. They're too fat and lazy to get out and walk around. That's why they don't know about the cave. Anyway, we were going to use the llamas to carry the gun crates to Teomotl. The conquistadors are doing the same thing. So if we see fresh llama dung on the trail, then we missed them."

Darby nodded. "Sounds like a good plan."

Maia wasted no time in repacking the pot and hoisting her pack. She was ready to go before the others got to their feet. She marched through the doorway without a backward glance. "We'll pick food on the way."

Amber twisted her lips. "Great. More fruit."

The entourage did its best to keep apace of Maia, who charged ahead as if she were wearing roller skates, and was carrying only a purse instead of a makeshift backpack whose hard, round, unpadded shape could not have been comfortable. They all crowded together so they could hear her follow-up explanations with regard to extant Lema-Rean fauna.

"We have all the plants and animals that exist in your 'verse, plus all of those that went extinct at the end of your most recent Ice Age. As I said before, the continent of Lema-Rea extends across most of the area that is occupied by your Pacific Ocean. That's why we have bison on our east coast and auroch's on our west coast."

Amber to Woody and Darby: "An auroch is an antediluvian species that was bred into domestic cattle. They lived in Europe and Asia."

"Very good. Lema-Rea spreads as far north as your Aleutian Islands, as far south as Easter Island, as far west as Asia, and it overlaps Polynesia but falls short of Australia."

Woody gasped. "Does that explain the stone statues on Easter Island?"

"You two are very sharp. Yes, it does. There were portals on Easter Island in the olden days. The island was uninhabited until our people crossed over and established a settlement there. They carved the statues and dragged them to their present locations. Our people also immigrated to the Polynesian islands." Maia chuckled. "That was thousands of years ago. Your archaeologists have invented a slew of rationalizations to explain how people reached Easter Island from South America (by sailing reed boats) or from Polynesia (by canoes or catamarans that were blown off course). Your archs are always clutching at straws: making up stupid and illogical theories whenever factual evidence is lacking or doesn't exist. A lot of archs have gotten college degrees by writing theses and dissertations that were based on nonsense, but were written with enough obfuscation and multisyllabic words to impress their advisors or into believing committee members that they knew what they were writing about, when all they were doing was snowballing them with highfalutin lingo and a subject matter based on whole cloth – which was how their advisors and committee members got *their* degrees. A BS based on BS, then a Ph.D piled higher and deeper. Academia. Gotta love it."

Amber laughed out loud. "My biology teacher showed us a published thesis about monotremes and marsupials. In one section, the candidate wrote over and over about animals in captivity displaying what he called a 'stereotypic locomotive pattern' in their cages. It took me quite a while to figure out that the author meant 'pacing'."

"Quite a few archs have made careers by spouting unsupported hypotheses, as long as their gibberish sounded fancy enough to confuse their peers and baffle the public. Some even claim to have translated Mayan writing – with absolutely nothing on which to base their interpretations."

"You mean, like their calendar ending in 2012?" Amber suggested.

Woody humphed. "I missed the end of the world. I meant to watch it happen but I dozed off and slept right through it."

Maia scowled. "First of all, the stupid archs got the dates all wrong. They founded their premise on gross misinterpretations of Mayan symbols. They presumed the wrong starting date, so naturally they got the wrong ending date. And second, the end of the calendar didn't signify the end of the world. It merely showed the point at which we stopped extrapolating – "

"What do you mean, we?" Amber wanted to know.

"Yeah. I thought you were descended from the Lema-Reans." Woody added.

"I am. So is the Mayan civilization. And the Aztecs. And the Incas. And the Olmecs. And the Toltecs. And all the other so-called cultures that your stupid archs named in the mistaken belief that they were all different from each other, instead of the same people living in different locations at different times. Why do you think that American ziggurats are identical with the ziggurats you see in Lema-Rea? It's because Lema-Reans built them in both 'verses.

"That is, Lema-Rean architects designed the ziggurats and observatories and multi-story buildings, and laid out the cityscapes with plazas and parks. We hired local help to quarry the stone and assemble the structures. We've been visiting your 'verse for thousands of years, and during that time we have tried to consolidate your people, create a cohesive civilization, and instill indigenous warring tribes with a sense of community. And in large measure we succeeded. Until the invasion of the conquistadors, who ruined it all in their unholy quest for riches, at the cost of destroying a vast society of peaceful citizens who had quit fighting among themselves so long ago that they didn't know how to protect themselves from foreign aggression, or repel invaders who were bent on conquest and subjugation."

They reached an intersection where Maia called a rest stop. They sat on the grass-covered ground and broke out canteens. Darby subtly maneuvered his cohorts so they formed a square, with pairs facing each other so they could look past their opposite.

After wetting her whistle: "When Lema-Reans discovered the portals that separated 'verses, they found a vast untamed territory that was sparsely inhabited by primitive human beings living in widely separated clans. Some of the clans that lived close to each other exhibited the feral, warlike nature that is established behavior in your 'verse: they fought their neighbors for no reason other than the fact that they liked to kill. Other clans – those that were secluded and not in close communication with distant clans – were friendly and amenable to discourse with visitors.

"My people first transferred to your 'verse without any intention of vanquishing or enslaving your people, but for the purpose of pure exploration of unknown lands; that is, lands that were unknown to them. My people are inherently curious about everything: geography, the sciences, natural law, and most of all, their inner selves. Much like your nineteenth-century mountain climbers and explorers of the Dark Continent, certain individuals felt the need to see for themselves the many wonders of the variverse.

"After the most enterprising adventurers discovered for themselves the challenges of the New 'Verse, as we call your 'verse, others followed in their footsteps. These were people who looked upon the New 'Verse as something akin to a dude ranch: a place to go where living conditions were primitive and less exacting, and that required self-sufficient survival skills. Your 'verse came to be viewed somewhat as an escape, or a vacation from the everyday grind, much like your people view back-packing in wilderness areas as a means to get away from an otherwise humdrum workaday existence.

"Then came the more serious minded folks, those who saw the New 'Verse as an invitation, or an opportunity, to better the plight of an underprivileged segment of mankind: aborigines they viewed as brothers in a disadvantaged realm, and who were living like savages, not because they were inferior either mentally or physically, but because civilization had not yet evolved in their 'verse. These Lema-Reans were like your classical missionaries, except that they didn't try to convert their subjects from their home-grown beliefs to a belief in a fabulous omniscient God, or Allah. Lema-Reans have no gods, no beliefs."

"They sound more like Peace Corps volunteers," Amber offered. "They're goal isn't to intrude in the culture they're assigned to, but to educate the people and provide medicine and health services."

"Yes, I think you're right. Our help-mates – a rough translation of how we referred to them – wanted to introduce civilization into the New 'Verse. They did so not in the way the British created a worldwide empire – by subduing and suppressing indigenous populations, then keeping them impoverished while appropriating their resources – but by improving their lot: something that your Americans do occasionally when they provide aid to beleaguered countries that have nothing they want. Most American aid is a self-indulgent political ploy disguised as altruism."

No one either confirmed or denied her allegation.

Maia announced that the break was over by standing and shouldering her pack. The rest followed suit. She glanced at the crossroad sign.

"Some of our people remained in your 'verse and intermarried with the locals. There was no mass pilgrimage, but there were always enough trained help-mates – either permanent cadre or transients on deployment – to oversee construction of city complexes, like those at

Machu Pichu, or Chichen-Itza, or Teotihuacan, or Palenque, or Tucume, or any one of hundreds of other ancient metropolises that were abandoned after the earth shifted and the nearby portals were closed. Whenever that happened, we closed shop at one location and moved to another. All the major cities were built close to portals, in order to facilitate transferences. If a portal was located vertically underground instead of on the side of a mountain or in a cliff face, a ziggurat was erected on top of it.

"Our greatest achievement was in channeling the contentious energies of the American aborigines from belligerence to constructive activities, like husbandry, quarrying stone, transporting building blocks, erecting ziggurats, carving art, learning our language, and so on, all on a massive scale that involved hundreds of thousands of eager participants.

"Don't take this personally, boys, but do you remember how you used to build forts in the dirt when you were kids? My brother did. We took that inborn aspiration and directed it toward *con*struction instead of *de*struction. When men and women are busy, they tend to be happy. Discord is generally a function of dissipation. Whenever a new portal opened, we built a new city at the site, and kept expanding it until the portal closed. It wasn't just a make-work project, because ongoing construction also increased support services: agricultural, keeping livestock, manufacturing, and so on."

The conversation didn't occur all at once. Maia spoke a sentence or two at a time, followed by many minutes of silence when the trail led uphill and breath had to be conserved for inhaling air instead of exhaling words. They also took time to gather fruit on the fly. The sun stood high overhead when they reached the east-west extension of the Cotl River.

The canyon walls that boxed in the river stood fifteen hundred feet high. The distance across measured more than two hundred feet. The adjacent ledges were spanned by a rickety looking rope bridge that had seen better days – and those days were decades in the past.

One of the support ropes, which also acted as a hand-hold or guardrail, was ragged and frayed. Many of the footboards were either missing or badly splintered.

Maia grinned mischievously. "I told you there was a bridge."

Darby made one of his rare funnies: "You forgot to mention that it was condemned."

Chapter 15

Woody peered over the edge in evident dismay. The rock walls were rough but almost as sheer as a pane of glass, and looked just as slippery. The crashing waves of a cataract were white with foam. "I think it might be safer to dive and swim across."

Amber placed the toe of one boot past the rim. "What a rappel!"

Maia lowered her pack to the ground. She knelt by the end of the bridge to inspect the maguey fibers. She pulled on the two primary suspension ropes, each of which was thicker than Darby's thigh. They were secured to a natural rock abutment that had been drilled or cored to allow the rope to be passed through the holes and tied together. From each massive rope hung thinner ropes that supported a bottom rope that spanned the abyss. Each of the bottom ropes was connected to the other with cat's-cradle supports for the footboards. She yanked and twisted all the ropes within reach. "It's not as bad as it looks."

"No. It's worse." Woody backed away. "What do you think, Darby?"

"Well . . . " He shot an uncertain glance at Maia's sober face, from which he received no encouragement. " . . . It's – it's best to spread out your weight. Never put all your weight on one foot, but lean down on the guide rope with your hands spread apart."

"Great. One lies and the other swears to it."

Amber: "I'll go first. I'm the lightest."

Maia scowled and placed her knuckles on her hips. Her fierce dark eyes were level with Amber's hazel orbs. Maia was chunky compared to Amber's slenderness.

"That's combined weight, with packs."

"Nice out," Woody commented dryly. "Good save."

The two women stared at each other for a moment. Finally, Maia conceded Amber's point with a single nod. Amber stepped onto the first wooden plank, tested it with her full load, heard an ominous crack, but proceeded anyway.

Darby cautioned her. "Don't step on the middle of the boards. Keep your feet close to the edges, where they're resting on the suspended rope."

Amber followed his sage advice. Despite her avowed confidence, she advanced unhurriedly, taking short, experimental steps while sliding her hands along the guide rope.

"Don't lean against the top rope," Maia advised. "If a section snaps you'll fall overboard. Stand straight, and press down on the top rope with your elbows bent."

A gentle breeze made the rope bridge sway. Amber gasped, gripped tightly, and refused to budge until the gust passed and the bridge stabilized. Then she resumed inching her way across the gorge, crawling like a caterpillar on a slender twig.

Woody was clenching and unclenching his fists. His face was sallow and firm, with his teeth gritted and his jaw working unconsciously in a circular pattern. His respiration was so shallow that his chest neither expanded nor contracted. "Be careful," came out like a croak.

One third of the way across, Amber reached the first place where planks were missing or broken in two, and hanging by a thread. Now she had to step directly on the suspension rope. The guide rope and the suspension rope were connected by means of cross-hatched fibers in the design of triangles, or half diamonds, with each bundled strand angled diagonally from top to bottom, then diagonally from bottom to top. Every time she pressed down on the suspension rope, her poundage pulled down the guide rope immediately above her foot.

Standing still did nothing but prolong the agony. She did her best to keep moving at a steady pace. Halfway across the gorge she stopped and glanced down at the rapids nearly a quarter mile below. No one said a word, but Darby knew Amber well enough to imagine that she was enjoying – if not ecstatic over – the experience. She liked heights as much as he did. Perhaps more. If she hadn't had strong academic ambitions, she could have pursued a career in walking high steel on skyscrapers. As long as they let her rappel to the ground when the whistle blew at the end of the workday.

Darby didn't realize that he was holding his breath until Amber stepped on solid rock on the other side of the gorge.

She grinned like the Cheshire cat as she waved them on, hollering, "A walk in the park."

Woody whispered, "That's easy for you to say because you're on the other side." He looked up at his brother. "Who's next?"

Both Darby and Maia stared him down.

Reluctantly, Woody stepped onto the first wooden plank. "You know, maybe the heaviest person should go next. Then we would know that it's safe for everyone else."

Darby: "You'll be okay. Just don't jump up and down like a grasshopper."

"Grasshoppers only jump up. Gravity brings them down." Woody moved across the bridge with somewhat less aplomb than his girlfriend had exhibited. Instead of crossing smoothly and nonstop, he halted and hesitated whenever he trod on loose or broken planks. He wasn't afraid of heights – altitude never bothered him – but he displayed trepidation about the structural integrity of a rope bridge that had not been maintained or repaired for ages. "It's not so bad." He didn't sound as if he meant it.

When Woody reached the other side, he made a motion of wiping imaginary sweat off his forehead. Amber hugged him.

Maia turned to Darby. "Do you want to flip for the privilege?"

"Well, uh, I think maybe you should go next."

"It's nice to know that chivalry isn't dead. Okay. You can be the rearguard."

When she reached for her pack, Darby bent over to pick it up and hold it while she slipped the straps over her shoulder. He was astonished at the weight of the burden. "This thing must weigh eighty pounds."

"It's pretty heavy." Maia gracefully slipped her arms though the straps, pulled the tump line over her head, and positioned the pack for balance. "With your height and bulk, I bet you weigh more than I do with my pack."

"Maybe so."

Maia started across the rope bridge without a backward glance, as if she had spent her entire life crossing deep canyons on hand-woven threads. She scampered across the gorge with full confidence, swinging her arms and legs in a continuous fluid motion the way a monkey swings through trees without being bothered by height.

Darby watched her acrobatics intensely. She never faltered or slackened her pace despite the considerable load on her back, as if she were merely playing hopscotch on a cement sidewalk. She reached the opposite side without a single misstep.

Now it was Darby's turn. Like Amber, he loved height, so he had no fear of the distance that separated his feet from the raging river below. Plus he had plenty of experience in climbing techniques, from childhood monkey bars to military ropes courses. His only concern was rot in the hemp. Also like Amber, he took a moment in the middle of the bridge to stare down at the water, imagining how much fun it would be to paddle a life raft through the enormous rapids. He was not necessarily a thrill seeker, but he did enjoy challenges.

He stifled a grin as he stepped on terra firma.

Maia had not bothered to remove her pack while waiting for Darby the cross the gorge. "The river picks up a lot of snowmelt as it passes along the base of the mountain before it turns westward. That's why the water level was so low where you waded across it, and so high where it cuts through the canyon."

Three paths led into the forest from the left bank abutment. She immediately turned and marched along the one that pointed southwest. "We can't catch up with the conquistadors today, but if we hurry we might be able to intersect their route tomorrow. We'll eat on the way and hike until dark."

Woody threw off a mock salute that Maia didn't see.

Amber rolled her eyes as if to say, "You got that right." Darby simply brought up the rear.

Maia resumed a thread of dialogue as if she had not been interrupted by crossing the gorge. "The archs in your 'verse are constantly speculating about why pre-Columbian civilizations collapsed; why the American cities were abandoned. They are always propounding new and totally unsupported theories about so-called cultures wasting away from decadence, or dying out from disease, or being riven by internal strife, or being invaded by neighboring enemies. They treat the word 'culture' as if it were mold growing in a jar.

"Those civilizations didn't collapse; the people moved away. The people emigrated from a city whenever a portal between 'verses was closed, and transference was no longer possible. Your archs can't accept that a civilization can abide for millennia without noticeable change, despite the fact that they can readily observe such an ancient and established civilization in their own puny 'verse. China has existed for thousands of years without social alteration, and without stagnating. While it's true that until recently there was little if any technological advance in Asian civilization, the fallacy or failure in logic in condemnation is that your archs equate gains in scientific knowledge or engineering improvement with cultural endurance, when in reality one has nothing to do with the other.

"Your archs use progress as a barometer to quantify the continuance of a culture, claiming that a culture that doesn't advance – whatever *that* means – must inevitably die out. Instead they should use peace and personal happiness as their measuring instruments. We have lived for untold millennia in harmony with our environment. We may not have had the wheel, or printing presses, or the internal combustion engine, or time-saving kitchen appliances, or computers, or television, or amusement parks, or video games, or gambling casinos, or snuff films, or guns, or war, or atomic bombs, or total dependency on oil and coal to keep our precarious civilization afloat, but we had long-term stability – until the conquistadors destroyed our peaceful American civilization and pursued us into our 'verse."

After such a harangue, there didn't seem to be any defensible comment that the trio from Earth's 'verse could make. Amber took a stab at it anyway.

"Maia, according to my American history teacher, there was constant fighting among rival Mesoamerican and South American, uh, peoples."

"That what the school system wants you to believe. But let me ask you this: where did that information come from? Where was it documented?"

"Uh, well, I guess it came from our history books."

"How did it get in the history books? What are the primary sources for that information?"

"I guess . . . I guess I never really thought about it."

"That's why my parents didn't want me to attend public or private schools. Because the textbooks they use aren't factual, and when they are, the facts are sanitized so as not to offend anyone. Instead of describing history the way it actually occurred, school system textbooks tell history the way the administrators and teachers wish it could have been, or the way they want their students to believe it was. There is nearly as much propaganda in textbook writing as there is in your government's news leaks and public announcements.

"If you want to sell textbooks to schools in Tennessee, you leave out all the parts of biology that discuss evolution. If you want to sell textbooks to schools in Massachusetts, you gloss over the parts that deal with witchcraft. If you want to sell textbooks to schools in California, you pander to Hispanics by making the conquistadors out to be heroes."

Darby had a sudden flash of memory. "Didn't you get in an argument in class about, uh, the Spaniard who discovered the Pacific Ocean?"

"You're damn right I did. Mr. Ramirez rhapsodized about Balboa's endurance and bravery in forcing his way across the isthmus of Panama and reaching what he called the Southern Sea. He neglected to mention that Balboa slaughtered thousands of native people along the way, and stole their valuables, and burned their villages, and raped their women. Somehow those facts were left out of the textbook and Ramirez's lesson plan. He wanted the Hispanics to believe that their forefather was a famous Spanish explorer instead of a brutal mass murderer. That's one of the reasons why I dropped out of school as soon as I was able to emancipate myself in accordance with your country's nonsense laws."

Darby brushed an annoying insect off his nose. "Seems to me you spent most of the term correcting him."

"Of course I did. He was always wrong. He was teaching carefully worded fiction instead of cold hard fact. He didn't necessarily lie all the time, but when he did tell the truth, he purposely left out contradictory information that would have shed a totally different light on events. Like failing to note Balboa's pillaging and extermination of the indigenous population in pursuit of his primary objective: not exploration but conquest."

"I remember the day you walked out of his class and never came back."

"Ha! I was so upset over his twisting the facts that I almost vomited on my desk. Even when he knew that what I told him was true – I could tell by the way he hesitated and mumbled – he refused to admit it. He would rather spread misinformation than let the students know the truth about their heritage, and the ruthlessness of their ancestors. I had to leave the room before I punched him in the face. He . . . watch out for the bushmaster."

Amber screamed. Woody jumped sideways. Darby reached over his shoulder for his spear.

"It's venomous, but it you leave it alone, it'll leave you alone."

The snake was coiled around a clutch of white eggs. It was impossible to determine the length, but Darby guessed that it measured six to eight feet uncoiled. The scales were patterned with black and orange-brown triangular shapes. The head rose slowly, the tongue extended and retracted, but otherwise the snake made no aggressive movements.

Maia kept walking as if the bushmaster were nothing more than a rubber toy. "He knew that I had traveled extensively in Central and South America. When my parents were alive, they took me and my brother to most of the ancient ruins. At Chichen-Itza, I overheard a tour guide tell his entourage that less than three percent of all the Mayan hieroglyphics had been translated. What an exaggeration! Not a word of it is true!

"Wartime code breakers knew that it was impossible to decode an encrypted message without the key. They needed a starting point. And even then, with the most sophisticated computers in the world in the 1940's, they were able to decode only a fraction of intercepted German and Japanese radio traffic. They didn't break the Nazi naval code until they captured an Enigma machine. Even modern-day translation programs can't translate foreign languages without first inputting every word in the language and all their possible meanings. Many meanings depend on grammar and context for the correct interpretation."

"All too often the translation programs yield gibberish. 'Out of sight, out of mind' was once translated as 'invisible lunatic.' Remember that for two thousand years, no one knew how to translate Egyptian hieroglyphics. Even after the discovery of the Rosetta Stone, it took a host of scholars and a language genius like Champollion twenty years to transliterate hieroglyphics by comparing them with Greek and Demotic script. Now you have archs and language experts who claim to have deciphered whole volumes of Mayan glyphs and pictographs. They have written entire books about their supposedly 'successful' interpretations.

"In high school, I knew more about ancient American languages than anyone in the world except my parents and other members of the CTS: the Consolidated Tabernacle Society, a fictitious name that our group adopted. Imagine being forced to sit in a classroom with a college dropout for a teacher – one who took ten years to get his teaching degree by attending night school, taking online courses, and buying a fake diploma and transcript – and having to listen to his insane ravings about sixteenth-century warmongers who conquered the savages that inhabited the Americas."

Darby almost wished that another bushmaster would interrupt Maia's tirade – even though he sided with her point of view. He had kept a low profile in American history class until the end of the semester only because he needed a passing grade to graduate. He barely made it.

By this time the sun sat low on the horizon. When they reached another crossroad, Maia stopped to read all four sides of the signpost.

"There's a way station not too far ahead. Let's double-time."

Darby was amazed that Maia could jog with that heavy load on her back. Yet she didn't seem to mind, and didn't even break into a sweat. Darby had carried oversize packs on hot and steamy jungle operations, compared to which this was a cake walk. His only concern was for Woody and Amber. After a while they started to lag behind the feisty Amazon. Instead of crowding his brother, Darby fell back in order to give him some leeway.

The rest house was barely standing, and in a sad state of disrepair. Years of rainfall had eroded the adobe until it stood barely six feet high. The roof timbers that had supported the thatch had rotted through; they now littered the earthen floor.

Woody threw down his spear and knapsack in a state of utter exhaustion. "What's the point of sleeping inside?"

Amber was too tired to comment. She and Woody forwent their usual banter.

"Well, the walls will give us protection from wild animals," Darby noted.

"Wild animals are the least of our worries. How many times have you camped in the woods and worried about lions and tigers and bears, oh my?"

Darby saw her point. He didn't bother to mention the

time a wild boar wandered past his position. The low walls would make a good barricade against conquistadors, if any happened to be this far off their beaten track.

It took only half an hour to clean the interior of rotting logs and debris, most of which they stacked neatly against one wall because it could be used as fuel for the fire. They didn't have to gather wood. There was ample water from a nearby spring. Maia cooked the other sack of quinoa that she had taken from the dead conquistadors. They munched on various fruits for both appetizer and dessert.

When night fell, all was quiet except for croaking frogs and a number of stridulating insects. Darby took little satisfaction in the fact that Maia looked as tired as he felt. Or maybe her face reflected something other than fatigue: concern, uncertainty, or even anxiety.

He stretched out on his back and lay with his head pillowed on his clasped fingers. Without light pollution from city streetlights, the firmament was crystal clear: a deep purple backdrop that was sprinkled with white sequins. Atmospheric heat waves caused the stars to twinkle. The Milky Way shone in all its splendor. The four of them moved close to the fire, and gazed skyward. Woody and Amber huddled in each other's arms.

Woody whispered, "Did you ever wonder what the ancients were smoking when they looked at the Big Dipper and saw a bear?"

Amber humphed.

"Or when they named Orion when all they could really see was his belt?"

Amber humphed again, barely audibly.

"Or how they got Cassiopeia out of a W? And what the heck is a Cassiopeia, anyway?"

Darby was drifting off to sleep. He shifted his gaze to each constellation as his brother called out their names. He easily identified Sirius, the Dog Star, because it was the brightest star in the nighttime sky; it was located in Canis Major: a constellation that didn't look anything like a big dog. He followed the Big Dipper's pointer stars to the dim stellar pinpoint that was known as Polaris, the North Star.

After all the odd happenings, strange sights, ancient architecture, and extinct animals, the heavens above lent welcome familiarity to his home 'verse: perhaps the only part of Maia's 'verse that was the same as his.

Suddenly he became disoriented. He squinted, trying to see if a wisp of cloud lay close to the eastern horizon, blocking his view of the lower firmament. He rubbed his eyes with his forefingers. Still he could not find the Evening Star, despite the fact that it should already have risen; and he knew precisely where to look for it.

Then the reason came to him: there must be a slight time differential between the two 'verses. That could explain why the trio left their home 'verse in daylight, but arrived in this 'verse after dark. He posed this supposition to Maia.

She answered sleepily, "You must have been in the cave longer than you thought. The electromagnetic force that bonds the space-share fabric is stronger than the force of gravity, which is the weakest of the four fources. It maintains the planetary alignment in each 'verse. Deviations caused by external forces are short-lived, because any misalignment is soon realigned and locked in place."

"Well, are the seasons the same here as they are on Earth?"

"Yes."

"Then why isn't Venus where it's supposed to be?"

"Because this 'verse doesn't have a planet Venus."

Chapter 16

Darby rolled onto his elbow and stared at Maia in the soft flickering light of dying embers. The red glow faintly illuminated her face. Her eyes were closed.

Woody sat bolt upright. "What do you mean there's no planet Venus?"

"Can we talk about it tomorrow?" Her voice was soft, a barely audible whisper.

"No!"

"While we're hiking?"

"No!"

Maia rolled her head. She pleaded with half-lidded eyes. "Please?"

"No!"

She sighed deeply. To Darby: "See what you started?"

"Well, I'm just as curious as Woody about why you don't have a Venus."

Woody winked at Amber's stirring form. "Present company excepted, of course."

Maia threw aside her bedroll, sat up halfheartedly. "In the variverse, the various 'verses are similar but not identical. Remember: 'verses of endless variety? You don't exist in my 'verse. And people in my 'verse don't exist in yours. The natural law of parallel evolution is responsible for your 'verse and mine producing similar species, and cross-fertilization through portals accounts for why those species, or variations of them, exist in both 'verses. That's because life – that is, the fundamental basis of life – is a fixed and consistent chemical process.

"No matter what 'verse you're in, hydrogen bonds with oxygen to form water. Likewise, organic molecules form the same way in all 'verses due to the natural proclivity – or valences – of carbon atoms to bond in the same fashion. The double helix of DNA will eventually form in every 'verse in which planetary conditions allow organic chemical bonding to exist: even in 'verses that don't communicate with each other. In that sense, life is like gravity. No matter what 'verse you're in, when you let go of a stone it hits the ground at your feet – and it falls at the same rate of acceleration on planets of the same mass.

"Life is an inevitable occurrence in all 'verses on all planets that possess the proper proportions of atmosphere, water, acceptable temperature range, radiation shielding, and so on. Likewise, the laws of physics work the same in all 'verses: the formation of stars, the birth of planets, celestial mechanics that maintain the stability of solar systems, electromagnetism, and so on. In other words, the fundamental forces in all 'verses are determined by natural law. Life is as predictable as the formation of basalt from cooling lava. Stages of life are similar but diverse. The processes are variversal."

Amber also sat up. "My biology teacher is fond of smashing the watchmaker argument. Creationists believe that a complex design implies an intelligent designer; that something as complex as a human being couldn't evolve without purposeful influence – which a logical person perceives as exactly what you're describing: natural law. Creationists keep saying that if you dumped all the parts of a watch – wheels, springs, pins, screws, and escapement – into a bag, and shook them up for all eternity, they would never come together to form a working watch. The fallacy of the argument is that metal parts don't obey natural laws, whereas atoms and molecules do. They're building blocks that assemble themselves in accordance with the laws of chemical affinity."

"Your biology teacher is wise. Subservience to – "

Darby rubbed his temples because he felt a headache coming on. "Excuse me, but what does this have to do with Venus?"

"Sorry. I got off track and lost my train of thought."

Woody snickered. "You didn't just lose your train of thought. You lost the whole railroad."

Amber muttered an indifferent, "You."

"Okay, okay." Maia could not help but grin. To Darby, "Before I get totally derailed, have you ever heard of Immanuel Velikovsky?"

"If it has to do with science, I'm afraid not."

"Understood. Velikovsky was a medical doctor and psychiatrist by occupation, but he was also a learned mathematician, linguist, and pre-Christian historian: basically a polymath, an interdisciplinary scholar who was self-taught in a number of scientific subjects. In this age of specialization and finely tuned university degrees – learning more and more about less and less until you know everything about nothing – he was the kind of person who no longer exists: a scientific eclectic, if you will.

"His abundance of avocational studies led him to noting some remarkable coincidences in the recorded texts of ancient civilizations: the mythologies of all of them – Sumerian, Babylonian, Mesopotamian, and others – contained remarkably similar accounts of a worldwide catastrophe that afflicted mankind in the prehistoric past.

"Among additional anomalies he discovered that none of the earliest writings mentioned the planet Venus. It was as if the ancients had no knowledge of its existence. Only later histories referred to the second brightest object in the nighttime sky, after the Moon. Ancient civilizations were well versed in astronomy: their so-called priests knew about the equinoxes and the length of the day, they recognized the relationship between tides and the phases of the moon, they produced ephemerides of astronomical objects and catalogued their magnitudes, they could predict lunar and solar eclipses – all of which begs the question: why didn't they ever annotate the planet Venus?

"Even more anomalous were the stories of ancient gods, and the fights they had in heaven. Velikovsky came to realize that the classical gods were not gods in the sense of supernatural beings, but analogues for planets. Furthermore, every mythology includes a description of a huge fireball, a comet, that was born or separated from the planet Jupiter, advanced toward

Earth, and caused massive destruction at its nearest approaches: incredibly high tides, volcanic eruptions, ground upheavals, fierce lightning storms – exactly the way the Hebrews described such disturbances in the *Bible*.

"Wow!" Woody shoved a log farther into the fire.

"Velikovsky postulated that the earliest legend of the Noachian flood wasn't fictional, wasn't just a fabulous story, but that it recounted an actual event that occurred in prehistoric times; that later myths were based on fact and were passed down through word of mouth from one generation to the next before writing was invented; that the biblical accounts of catastrophes – the destruction of Sodom and Gomorrah, the collapse of the walls of Jericho, the plagues of Egypt, the seismic wave that wiped out the Pharaoh's army in pursuit of Moses during the Exodus, Joshua's account of the sun standing still in the sky – that all these events resulted from return passages of Venus in its irregular orbit around the sun; and that human civilization was far older than archaeologists were willing to concede; that historic timeframes of these events are disordered and confused.

"After many years, as the comet blundered through the solar system in a long elliptical orbit and made subsequent passages in close proximity to the Earth, it settled into a stable orbit around the sun. Velikovsky started publishing his work in 1950. As you can imagine, such a radical challenge to traditional astronomy met with great resistance. He was vilified, branded a crank, called a crackpot, and his unconventional theories – about the birth of Venus and restructuring the timeline of ancient civilizations – were called preposterous.

"Most scientists refused to review his evidence. Instead, they assassinated his character, claimed that he lacked credentials, called his theories farfetched, and placed him and his so-called pseudoscience on the lunatic fringe of academia. Yet, many of his extrapolations turned out to be true.

"He predicted that, as a newborn planet, the surface

temperature of Venus would be in excess of 800 degrees; that it would have a retrograde rotation; that its atmosphere would contain oxygen; that hydrocarbons would be found in the upper atmosphere. All these predictions have since been confirmed by unmanned probes – both Russian and American – without giving credit to Velikovsky's prior extrapolations.

"He declared that Jupiter was a proto-star with a hot core, and not a cold, ice-covered body that astronomers claimed it was. Subsequent space probes proved him right. He declared that Jupiter possessed a magnetic field that would emit radio noise. Decades later, scientists detected radio emissions and a magnetic field around Jupiter.

"He predicted Earth's magnetosphere decades before it was discovered. As he had professed, Earth's magnetosphere was found to extend far beyond the Moon.

"He declared that the Moon would be found to possess thermal gradients and structural instability due to tidal distortions from Venus's close passage; that the Moon was not completely dead, as was presumed by astronomers. He was proven right. Thermal gradients have been found, and moonquakes have been detected, by instruments that astronauts left on the Moon.

"He also declared that lunar rocks would possess weak magnetism that was leftover from electrical discharges between Venus and the Moon. The rocks that astronauts brought back from the Moon displayed this remanent magnetism. Rather than credit Velikovsky for predicting this phenomenon, scientists today ignore him and remain baffled by it. They're also baffled by pockets of radioactivity that have been found on the Moon, even though Velikovsky predicted that such local anomalies would exist as a result of interplanetary electrical discharges.

"He declared that the comet Venus must also have interacted with Mars as Venus passed it during its fall into orbit around the sun. He predicted that the surface of Mars would be riddled with rifts that resulted from Venus's large gravity field. This turned out to be true.

He also predicted that electrical discharges would create radioactive hotspots as it did on the Moon. This also turned out to be true. And he predicted that the surface of Mars would show recent flow formations, like those that are formed by flash floods. Again, he was right.

"Velikovsky predicted that the Sun was electrically charged – years before that fact was firmly established.

"Yet, as bold as these solar and planetary predictions were, his most important contribution was in the field of celestial mechanics. He audaciously asserted that gravity was not the sole force responsible for the stability of solar systems and galaxies: that electromagnetism played a large and crucial role in determining the motions of celestial bodies, stars as well as planets. Scientists scoffed at such a suggestion at the time he made it, but now they all recognize the universal affect that electromagnetism plays in stabilizing orbits.

"The rings of Saturn are a primary example. *Voyager* and *Cassini* spacecraft found that millions of tiny particles are kept in position by a mechanism that can't be explained by orbital mechanics alone. Scientists now suggest that Saturn's magnetosphere and electrostatic repulsion are responsible for the formation and orbital resonance of the rings. Again, Velikovsky received no credit for being the first to predict the significance of electromagnetic charges that controlled the mechanism.

"What Velikovsky didn't know was precisely *when* Venus was ejected from Jupiter. But *we* know. Or, at least we can approximate its age. We've been making astronomical observations since before the dawn of your 'verse's civilization. We didn't actually witness the birth of Venus in your 'verse, but we are better able to accept its origin – not only because our 'verse doesn't have a planet Venus, but also because in our 'verse Jupiter doesn't have a birth scar: what your astronomers call the Great Red Spot."

"Wow! That's an awesome concept, and brilliantly explained. Not bad for a high school dropout. You should have been a teacher."

"Or a college professor," Amber added.

"Or a special ed tutor," Darby conceded. "Even a dodo like me understood a lot of what you said. Except for the big words, that is."

"You're not a dodo, Darby. You just have skills in areas other than memorizing trivial academic subject matter and regurgitating it on cue. Besides, we have dodos in this 'verse, and you're a lot better looking."

"Ooooooh" Amber sing-songed, "Maia has a crush on Darby."

Maia's olive skin blushed. "You woke me from a sound sleep. I'm allowed to be mushy."

This time it was Woody who went, "Ooooooh."

"Okay, okay. Enough of that. As I was saying, it's not difficult to imagine that Jupiter could conceive and eject a body the size of Venus, when Jupiter is more than thirteen hundred times the volume of Venus, and only one thousandth the volume of the Sun, which means that Jupiter's escape velocity is much less than the escape velocity of the Sun. By comparing geological differences between your 'verse and ours, we've been able to determine that the first near passage of Venus occurred ten thousand years ago, give or take a grand."

"Hey! That's about the same time as the Ice Age."

"Give the man a gold star."

Woody grinned broadly. "I meant the last Ice Age."

"I figured."

"I meant the *end* of the last Ice Age."

"Of course. If it hadn't been for the birth of Venus, its heat and electromagnetic interaction with the Earth wouldn't have ended the Ice Age when it did. That is, it wouldn't have accelerated the gradual rise in temperature that was taking place ten thousand years ago. Lema-Rea took longer to warm up than Earth: a natural process that undoubtedly kept our civilization from advancing at a quicker pace. My people were working too hard at keeping warm and growing food to build pyramids, cityplexes, and starscrapers.

"Because we were closer knit – fighting our environment instead of each other – our advances were more in the fields of introspection and social conscience; living *with* the land rather than off it. As a result, our science and engineering lag considerably behind yours. But then, neither did we possess the territorial imperative that led to war. We were content to live peaceably as *part* of nature instead of above it. And we lived that way until your bloodthirsty conquistadors arrived."

Only the crackling fire and bursting air pockets in logs broke the ensuing silence.

Finally, Amber asked, ""How did that happen?"

"They followed our retreating people and escaping local inhabitants, and discovered some of the portals. Not content with plundering your Americas in their insatiable quest for treasure, they invaded our 'verse as well. Before too many of them got through, though, we cut them off at the pass, so to speak, by doing something that we had never done before: we closed the portals."

Woody kept the fire going by pushing in logs and stirring the embers with a stick. "How – how did you do that?"

"Remember I said that the creation of a portal depends on a pair of corresponding cavities of the same size and configuration, one in each 'verse? It's the junction or intersection of both electromagnetic force fields that connect two 'verses. To close a portal, all you have to do is alter the shape of one of the cavities until the force field goes out of alignment and breaks the connection."

"You mean, chip away some stone."

"Precisely. That doesn't necessarily mean that another portal won't open nearby, when the forces are diverted, especially if the cavities are tubular and parallel – those are the longest lasting portals. But if the cavities cross perpendicular to each other, a broken portal usually stays broken – until some cataclysmic event shifts the cavities into alignment.

"So that's what we did when we found that the conquistadors had discovered the portals. No more of them could come through, but by that time the damage was done. Once the invaders had a foothold in our 'verse, it was like having a fox in a henhouse. We were defense-less against their rapaciousness. They raided and ran-sacked our outposts, stripped them of everything that they considered valuable, tortured and murdered the residents, then moved on to the next village or town or city."

"Why – why didn't you fight?"

"Because my people didn't know how to fight. They were pacifists. They didn't have the inborn disposition for waging war. The only weapons they had were de-signed for killing game, or for slaughtering livestock. I don't mean that my people were a nation of sheep. There were individuals who were more aggressive than the av-erage citizen, and who defended themselves from the conquistadors, but they were few in number. Our soci-ety's moral mindset repudiated war. In fact, it was my people who quelled warfare among your American tribes, with the unfortunate side effect of making them vulnerable to invasion."

"How do you mean?"

"Please, Woody, no more questions. Can we talk about it tomorrow? I need some sleep. We all need our sleep. Tomorrow we have a long trek through the Great Gloomy Swamp, and we have to do it fast enough to reach Paca-Zula, where we can spend the night indoors. That will be our last stop before hopefully catching up with the conquistadors before they cross the Chiruba Mountains."

Acquiescence was silence.

Chapter 17

The Great Gloomy Swamp looked pretty much the way it sounded. Maia explained that it was a literal translation. At first the ground sloped downward so gradually that it seemed almost level. The transition from rainforest to swampland was accompanied by an increasing incline to water level. Sequoias and massive conifers yielded to cypress trees and tupelos. The wetlands understory was a tangle of ferns, vines, and sawgrass. The four musketeers rolled down their pants legs as soon as they started to get slashed by the sharp leaf edges.

The insect population grew dramatically: in numbers as well as in species. The most annoying were mosquitoes; they buzzed constantly above stagnant puddles, and once they detected the scent of human blood, they followed the adventurers in hordes. Swatting did little good. For every mosquito killed there were ten to take its place. Rolled-down sleeves kept the bloodsuckers off arms, but face, neck, and hands were constantly under attack.

The path that led the way through the rainforest was fairly straight. After it descended to the lowlands it twisted and turned, sometimes in semicircles and curlicues, in order to follow the topography and to stay above the worst of the water-filled pockets, ponds, and mud-sucking miasma. The longest and deepest wallows were bridged by hewn logs resting on submerged crossmembers, many of which were rotted beyond repair.

"No sense trying to keep your boots dry. We'll have to wade through areas where long-time lack of maintenance has let crossings return to nature."

"Couldn't we have gone around this swamp?" Amber wanted to know.

"We could have taken wide roads that are like two legs of a right triangle, but the hypotenuse is shorter and ultimately faster for unburdened travelers."

Amber and Woody complained about the stench, but Darby had experienced worse. He rubbed a thin film of moist clay on his exposed skin, as a way to ward off biting bugs. None of the others felt like following his example.

"As I was saying, my people discovered your 'verse thousands of years ago – I'm not sure when because our records that long ago are sparse. At first they paid only short visits to your Americas because the natives there were mostly hostile. Instead of trading with their neighbors for mutual benefit, they engaged in constant battles with them, in order to steal whatever they needed or wanted. My people found such behavior abhorrent. Eventually . . . watch out for the water moccasin."

Amber's piercing scream flushed a flock of resting cormorants.

Woody clapped his hands to his ears. "Amber!"

"Sorry."

The sleeping snake opened its beady eyes and glared at the passing foursome. It's forked tongue darted out of its white cottony mouth. It was so big and fat that it reminded Darby of a coil of anchor hawser. It made no other movements.

"Anyway, to my people your 'verse was just another parcel of land that lay adjacent to their home. If the locals didn't want to trade, we figured on leaving them alone. Eventually, a portal was discovered in the highlands where your natives never ventured. Out of curiosity they started passing through the gateway to explore the mountainous terrain. Some people stayed for a while, camping in the wilderness. It was much like a holiday to them, the way your people go backpacking in national parks and state forests, or spend their vacations on dude ranches, or join environmental groups such as Earth Watch. It was all done as a diversion.

"After a while, the portal in the Andes grew so popular that the influx forced our people to expand their horizons, until they encountered a tribe of your people who were living in virtual isolation. They were friendly. Trade relations were initiated. This led to meeting more distant tribes, some not as friendly. Yet our people exerted an influence over the hostiles because we had something that they needed and couldn't steal: knowledge. We knew about agriculture, animal husbandry, architecture, and most important, herbal medicine.

"Your people were primitive. Some were savages. We refused to deal with those who were inhospitable; avoided them, in fact, because we were unable to defend ourselves against their warlike ways. Slowly – and this took hundreds of years – they began to adopt more peaceful manners: not necessarily because they wanted to, but because it was to their advantage to do so.

"The tribes that accepted our invitation to a lifestyle that was pastoral rather than contentious lived far better and healthier than those that didn't. We became voluntary consultants, helping disadvantaged people who were willing – sometimes eager – to ally themselves with us. This wasn't planned. There was no grand scheme. Our involvement in your 'verse simply grew from our natural inclination to share and share alike. Your philosophers refer to this social grace as altruism, or selflessness, but in nature it's simply a standard behavioral pattern: a danger reduction facet of the herd instinct. In the big picture, the protection of the multitude equates to protection of the individuals within that multitude. Individual safety as well as overall safety is vastly increased.

"Our people were exchange teachers at first, but after the natives became civilized, many of them integrated with the local population. The natives lived in thatched huts and makeshift tents until we taught them how to build permanent residences of adobe. They . . . I'm sorry. I'm repeating myself. I guess – I guess I want to make sure you understand that we did not consolidate the backward inhabitants of your Americas the way Alexander the Great Executioner killed off his competitors, or how the Romans created their empire – by slaying all those who opposed subjugation – or the way Ghengis Khan butchered everyone in his path, or like Hitler's failed attempt at world domination by slaughtering millions of innocent people."

Amber was sympathetic. "I understand. I think we all do."

"Then enough said." Without preamble, Maia picked up the thread of an earlier conversation. "The so-called Mayan calendar that your archs claim to have interpreted was a Lema-Rean calendar. It was written in a language that they had no way to decipher. Remember what I told you before: it's impossible to translate an encoded message without first having a key, or a known starting point – something to work from, at the very least some familiarity with the language to be decrypted, and the repetition of certain letters or words: like the letter 'e' in the English alphabet. It's doubly impossible to translate a foreign language that has no correspondence whatsoever with any other language in the 'verse, and an alphabet that is totally different and that pronounces different sounds.

"The Lema-Rean language is largely glyphic, somewhat analogous to your Chinese logographic languages, but not like them at all. I won't go into syllabary and other language structures and symbolisms because – pardon me for saying this – you haven't studied the subject the way I have, so you probably wouldn't understand it."

"I don't," Darby said.

"Anyway, it's irrelevant. What your archs did was to start from an assumption of what they believed certain glyphs might mean, then proceed from there. You're familiar with the computer acronym gigo – garbage in, garbage out? If your assumptions are wrong, then everything that follows those assumptions is also wrong. That's how your archs 'deciphered' the so-called Mayan language and calendar. They started with garbage, ran it through a garbage disposal, then claimed that they had interpreted the meanings of the glyphs."

"That I can understand."

"Good. Then understand that nothing of what your archs think they know about the Mayan language – or the many dialects that existed throughout Central and

South America – has any basis in fact. It's nothing but academic gibberish to fool themselves, their peers, and the masses. It's true that there was a Mayan calendar – actually, a Lema-Rean calendar – and that it had a termination date, but the translated dates were wrong, and the reason for the termination date was wrong.

"That I don't understand."

"I can explain it so you will understand. In your 'verse, ancient sky watchers created astronomical tables that enabled them to predict eclipses, phases of the moon, equinoxes, and the locations of the planets, all with a remarkable degree of accuracy considering their lack of instrumentation. Modern astronomers have refined those tables. They can now extrapolate not only when the next eclipse will occur, but the one after that, and after that, and after that, ad infinitum. But there's no reason to keep extrapolating a thousand years into the future. They won't be around to make observations. So they leave it to future astronomers to make additional extrapolations.

"The same is true for the so-called Mayan calendars, which were created to assist in observations of Venus. The termination date did not signify the end of the world. It signified only that there was no reason for our astronomers to extend it any farther at that time."

"That makes sense."

"I thought it would. In the same regard, the primary reason for creating the calendar and building observatories in your Americas was to observe the peregrinations of Venus – a planet that doesn't exist in our 'verse. At least, not yet."

Woody was flabbergasted. "What do you mean, not yet?"

"If Jupiter ejected a planetary body in your 'verse, there's reason to believe that it might do the same in ours. And that it might cause the same kind of global cataclysm that it caused in your past. My people started studying Venus before it fell into a stable orbit around the sun. During Venus's erratic near-passages, they suffered the same catastrophes that your European civilizations suffered. Except that we had an escape clause.

"When devastating upheavals and enormous deluges started occurring in your 'verse, my people – that is, the Lema-Reans, and those inhabitants of your 'verse who wished to accompany them – migrated in mass to this 'verse. And they stayed here until the disturbances on your planetary surface subsided."

"Wow."

"I'll second that," Amber said.

"Now do you understand why there are no distinctions between Mayans and Aztecs and Incas and all the other so-called cultures that your archs claim to have recognized? They are all parts of the same civilization, the way North Dakota and Nebraska and Alabama are States of the same Union. The people may speak with different accents, but culturally they are no different. Your archs make a big – "

Maia stopped short at the edge of a large body of still water. Chirping frogs of various species sang choruses in different pitches, from bass through soprano. Tupelos grew in scattered confusion. Although there was no country known as Canada in Maia's 'verse, Canada geese honked melodiously in nests that were sequestered at the base of branching boles. One anhinga stood on a partially-submerged log, drying its wings. Several cormorants imitated the anhinga in treetop safety.

A series of boulders stretched across the pond's narrowest point. Many of the logs that had served as bridges between them had slipped off their perches into the dark tannic water alongside. The onetime causeway was now a series of bridgeboards and gaps.

"Don't worry. If we have to wade, the water shouldn't be too deep. I'll go first."

Maia jumped to the nearest boulder. It was the size of a compact car that had sunk halfway the windshield. Then she danced along a rotted timber to the next boulder. Woody followed. Then came Amber and Darby. The hopscotched across the pond without throwing jacks.

Darby was about to leap onto a boulder behind

Amber when he saw the boulder tilt under her weight. She slid down the sloped side and splashed into the stagnant water on her butt. She gulped but didn't scream. The boulder then rose a foot into the air. A giant head poked out of the end that faced Darby. A pair of saucerlike eyes opened and stared at him. A gaping mouth hissed like steam from a broken valve, warm and fetid.

Darby froze. The disguised boulder rose on four columnar legs. Darby had seen Galapagos tortoises in the zoo; this individual was half again as big.

No one spoke. Amber didn't scream, although her mouth was open.

"It's okay, Amber." Maia's arms hung limply at her side. "It should move away."

Woody spoke to Maia, but never took his eyes off the tortoise. "I wish you would use the word 'will' instead of 'should.' I'd feel a lot better."

As if on cue, the tortoise turned away from Amber. Its fat tail unfolded from between its coal-black carapace and dark-gray plastron, and accidentally thumped across the top of Amber's head. She gasped. Her ponytail remained intact. The tortoise lumbered across the pond to a landing, where it climbed onto dry ground and stalked away.

"Put *that* in your report," Woody said. "Sideswiped by a giant turtle."

Amber was too flustered to reply. Woody stepped knee-deep into the water beside her, held out a helping hand. Amber grasped his fingers. He pulled her upright. She stood there dripping, unmindful of the soaking as long as the tortoise had quite literally turned tail and departed. She made no attempt to cuff him.

"They're vegetarian," Maia offered.

Amber nodded, her eyes still staring at the landing where the tortoise had pulled its disappearing act. "Thanks."

Woody put his hands on his hips. "I don't get it. In the books, Tarzan gets attacked by every wild animal there is, all in his first day in the jungle. So far, every animal we've seen has ignored us . . . uh, except for Big Bird."

"That's because Burroughs never even saw a jungle, much less lived in one. He was clueless about predator behavior and predator-prey interaction. He thought that predators spent every minute of every day attacking everything within reach, as if they had nothing better to do."

Darby's face was bland. "I had a run-in with a wild boar once." He shrugged. "It turned away when I made some noise."

"That's the reaction you're most likely to get unless the predator is hungry or territorial. And boars are not necessarily predators; they're basically scavengers that will prey only on animals that are much smaller than themselves, such as newborns and ground birds." Maia shifted her focus. "Are you hurt, Amber?"

"Only my pride. But I feel icky." She wiped stinky mud off her hands, using the dry upper portion of her shirt, then the back of Woody's pack. "Yuck."

Woody kept his mouth shut.

The foursome trudged across the fetid water without further altercation. Despite their leaping from hummock to hummock, everyone ended up with wet feet and trousers. Teeming insects and swarms of gnats were a constant annoyance. A foot-long centipede shuffled up a tree trunk on some mission known only to itself. Unseen cicadas sang up and down the scale.

They ate lunch on the fly.

Maia picked up a lost thread almost as a non sequitur: "Your school books are rife with errors due to academic manipulation and school board propaganda, but books that deal with pre-Columbian civilizations are worse; far worse. Everything you ever read about the original inhabitants is false, and for one obvious but always ignored reason: the source material of all historical information was created by conquistadors. They were the biggest braggarts and greatest liars that ever roamed your 'verse. They told tall tales that put Paul Bunyan to shame. And when they weren't lying outright, they exaggerated tenfold."

Woody humphed. "They sound like politicians."

"Not only did the conquistadors have incredibly huge egos, but they had to convince their Spanish backers that they were earning their money. So they made up stories about the indigenous population: they were bestial, they were barbarians, they fought constantly among themselves, they committed atrocities against neighboring tribes: all the things that the conquistadors actually did themselves.

"In fact, the locals were peaceful, agrarian people – largely, I might add, due to Lema-Rean influences that went back thousands of years. They welcomed the conquistadors with open arms because they had never encountered a race of such depravity. They – "

"Excuse me, Maia." Amber was solicitous. "Don't take this personally, but what about the story that when Cortes invaded Mexico, the Aztecs thought that men on horseback were, uh, something like centaurs, a single animal, melded together, and that the Aztecs got on their knees in supplication."

"How stupid do you think they were? How . . . Sorry. I didn't mean to shout. But that's a sore point with me. Of course they recognized men on horseback. Don't you think that they had ridden llamas and alpacas before? And what happened when the conquistadors dismounted. Don't you think the Aztecs would have recognized that the conquistadors were human and that horses were a different kind of beast of burden? Don't *you* take this personally, but a person would have to be an idiot to believe a story like that. Montezuma never bowed to anyone. He treated the conquistadors the way he would have treated any group of visitors: with simple respect, because that was the custom.

"The conquistadors made up that story about Montezuma and his people, to convince the folks in Spain how backward the locals were, how unworthy they were of not being subjugated, or obliterated. Let me repeat: everything you ever thought you knew about pre-Columbian America is false. The conquistadors burned every codex they could find, because the codices told the true history of America: a truth that they didn't want anyone to know.

"Later, to bolster their fictitious sagas, they had friars write bogus accounts of local history: accounts that couldn't be repudiated because mass burnings had destroyed most of the evidential documents that were written on bark paper, and because the ancient stone carvings that couldn't be expunged were written in a pictorial language that couldn't be translated by modern-day survivors. The conquistadors vandalized some of the stonework anyway. Then they had friars write boastful accounts of their own courageous actions against purportedly brutish and belligerent people: first the Aztecs, then the Mayas and Incas.

"The *Popol Vuh* – the so-called sacred text – is a fake. It's a mixture of biblical and mythological creation stories that were blended with fictitious names and genealogies in order to impute an impression of authenticity to a work of imagination. It's a *be*trayal of New World history instead of a *por*trayal.

"The conquistadors not only falsified past and current events, but they glamorized their own participation in those events. They claimed to have exterminated huge numbers of the local population as if they were nothing more than infecting vermin, when in fact most of the people escaped through portals to Lema-Rea, then closed the gates behind them. The conquistadors who remained in your 'verse were never able to solve the riddle of how so many natives disappeared, so they pretended to have killed them all – the way those events are portrayed in your history books.

"It's true that the conquistadors killed anyone who got in their way. But it's also true that they inflated the numbers, and that they overstated their hardships, in order to glorify their ill-gotten reputations. Then they added fabrications about virgin sacrifices, and the beheading and disemboweling of captured enemy soldiers."

The swamp ended abruptly at a cliff face. When

Darby looked up, he saw that a set of steps had been carved into the stone. The steps ascended diagonally for two hundred feet, after which cutouts climbed straight up for the final twenty feet to the top.

"Now you can see why this route was used only by message runners. Llama trains took the roundabout road because it's graded and paved, much like the Roman's Appian Way."

The climb was deceptively straightforward until they reached the final pitch. Then they had to scramble up shallow indentations that resembled rungs on a ladder. Finger grips had been carved into the level stone at the top. They would have facilitated clambering over the lip if they hadn't been filled with dirt and grass. The last bit required some bending at the waist and stretching arm's length to grab onto nearby shrubbery.

Maia executed the maneuver with ease, then helped the others over the edge. By this time the sun stood barely above the horizon. "Paca-Zula lies just ahead. It's a major complex where we can spend the night."

"Ahead" turned out to be half a league away. They crossed a fallow farm field before encountering the scattered remains of roofless adobe dwellings: Lema-Rean farmhouses. After passing through a grove of hardwoods, the foursome reached the edge of an expansive plaza. A lone ziggurat stood in the center of a handful of stone outbuildings. A waist-high platform was encircled by flat-topped rocks that were the height of seats.

Maia grinned mischievously, pointing out salient features. "The kiosk at the top of the ziggurat is where virgins were sacrificed. That platform is where human bodies were dismembered."

Chapter 18

Woody sputtered, "But – but – "

And so did Amber, "You – you said – "

"I know what I said, and I meant it." Maia kept the mischievous grin on her oval face. "You're forgetting what I said previously. The conquistadors consistently falsified and dramatized everything that had to do with the local inhabitants, in order to paint them in as bad a light as possible. What I'm saying now is that they took our traditions, customs, and celebrations, and twisted them out of whack to suit their purposes. Take this reclamation platform, for example . . . "

Maia led her companions to the edifice: a single block of limestone that had been chipped laboriously into a bricklike shape about twice the size of the casket that it resembled. The flat top was surrounded by a sloped groove that could channel bodily fluids to the lowest corner, where a drip spout funneled the liquid into a fine ceramic vase whose patterned shards lay spread on the plaza stonework.

"The conquistadors reported that people were tortured alive: skinned, bled, mutilated, butchered like livestock or game animals, and so on. Most of that is true. The major falsehood is the word 'alive.' When a person expired, the body was placed on this dissection block for honorable dismemberment. The decedent's relatives and closest friends occupied the stone seats; distant relatives and acquaintances brought wooden chairs which were placed outside the ring of permanent seats. That's why the reclamation platform is isolated, with plenty of space for all participants in the grievance ceremony.

"We did not have religious rites or rituals. Attendees celebrated the life of the deceased by sharing memories with each other: a retrospection of the decedent's life and accomplishments. This gay celebration is very similar to your secular memorial services. When all the attendees were satisfied that they had grieved long enough to achieve reconciliation, the body was reclaimed.

"The reclamation process started by bleeding the body. The fluid contents were drained and collected in spouted vases that were shaped like your gravy boats. The fingers and toes were separated from the hands and feet. The limbs were sliced into small pieces. The digits, flesh, and organs were collected in ceramic containers for later distribution. The torso was dissected. The bones were crushed in a jade metate with a gold-alloy mano – equivalent to your mortar and pestle – then ground into fine powder. All these remnants – fluids, body parts, chunks of flesh, and bone powder – were then used to fertilize crops."

Amber was aghast. "That's gross!"

Woody was less mortified. "That's a hundred and forty-four."

If Amber heard his irreverent comment, she made no attempt to cuff him for making it.

Maia shook her head. "No, it was practical, and not too dissimilar from the organ donor process in your 'verse. The lives of people who were born and grown by being fed from the earth, were honored by being allowed to nurture the earth for the next generation. Passing their flesh to their children, so to speak. Only wicked individuals, who were deemed unworthy of continuing afterlife, were mummified or interred out of sight intact. This was done out of personal disgust rather than any ill-founded belief in contamination of the soil.

"Compare the callous manner in which an autopsy is performed in your 'verse. A body is plunked on a post mortem table like a slab of meat, and examined from head to foot. Its chest is cracked open and the organs are removed. The top of its skull is cut off so the brain can be extracted. The internal parts are removed, inspected, then discarded as waste. The outer shell of the corpse is stitched back together. The blood is drained and replaced with embalming fluid. The body is then clothed in an expensive suit or dress. So much makeup is applied that the face resembles a horrible cartoon caricature. The body is placed in a casket that costs thousands of dollars. Then the hollow shell that was once a person is buried in a cemetery where it takes up space – forever. Does any of that sound appealing to you?"

Amber pursed her lips. "Well, when you put it that way . . . "

Maia looked up at the sky as she led the procession to the distant ziggurat.

Dark ominous clouds were forming. The gentle breeze was picking up speed. The temperature dropped a few degrees. Maia seemed not to notice the cold, but Darby felt goose bumps growing on the skin of his exposed arms and legs. Maia's quiet delivery made the hackles rise on his nape. Yet everything she said made sense in a way that was . . . different. At first he thought that the Lema-Rean treatment of the dead was no better or worse than the way they were treated in his 'verse. Then he acknowledged that the Lema-Rean treatment was more sensible than the ritualistic disposal that was commonly accepted in his 'verse.

"Where do you think the Amerindians got the idea of planting a fish head in the ground with corn seeds?"

"Did your people range that far north?"

"Not really. We established an outpost in New Mexico when a portal opened in a cliff crevice, and we built an observatory complex that your people call Chaco. We tried to consolidate the North American tribes but they were far too brutal and warlike. Peace was anathema to them. They're still warlike, only now their weapons are lawyers instead of tomahawks, doing everything they can to disrupt harmony in America." Maia shrugged. "We left them for more quiescent pastures, and let them fight their senseless tribal conflicts among themselves."

As they passed a freestanding stone wall, Maia stopped to read the glyphs and carvings that covered every inch of the surface. Distorted faces and truncated torsos were carved between lines or ornate symbols. Maia smiled.

"What's funny?" Woody wanted to know.

"We left walls like this in your 'verse. Some of the graven images were purely allegorical, corresponding to your Halloween masks. Others, including statues, were visible reminders or material representations of venerated individuals. Your breast-beating archaeologists interpreted them as depictions of our gods, and that this was how we worshipped them. Now I ask you: do your people pray to billboards on the highways or to statues in city parks?" She laughed out loud. "If they only knew the truth they would shrink with embarrassment, and hate me for ruining a fanciful theory with ugly facts. This is a storyboard, something like your first grade reader for children."

Woody pointed to a pair of faces that were nose to nose. "Is that Dick and Jane."

"The equivalent. This wall is also like your coloring books. The script instructs children how to read by rewarding them with finger painting. The paint is pretty much worn off, but you can see flecks of color here and there."

The three visitors from another 'verse leaned forward to inspect the carvings closer.

Darby spotted dabs of pigment: not on the outer facings but on the bottom protrusions of the reliefs, where they had been applied partially out of the weather. "I don't think this city has been abandoned for very long."

"That's what I was thinking. It must have been reoccupied after the conquistadors stripped it of its valuables." She glanced around the stone plaza, squinting. "Which they appear to have done in haste. We may be in luck . . . "

"So what are Dick and Jane saying to each other?" Woody wanted to know.

Maia scanned the wall in its entirety. "It's a tale about actors who are donning costumes before going on stage. In preparation for their performance, they have to apply makeup to their faces and choose what color clothes to wear in the play. The directions are explicit, and read something like 'Color my cheeks red,' and 'give me green pants,' and 'I want a blue dress,' and so on. The teachers would have handed out paint pots. In order for the children to finger paint, they first had to learn how to read the script."

"Great incentive. It beats a ruler over the knuckles if you didn't get it right."

"I suppose you could call it progressive education. Now over here . . . " Maia meandered to the adjacent wall. "This is a commemorative wall, crediting Naxal for his victory over Senotl, and describing how he out-flanked the attacking warriors."

"But, I thought your people didn't have wars."

"This wasn't a war. It was a contest. The description is for re-enactment purposes." Seeing that she was sur-rounded by raised eyebrows, Maia rolled her eyes and chortled. "Okay, I guess I need to disabuse you of con-quistadorian concoctions again." She took a deep breath. "When we first entered your 'verse, the natives we found consisted of tribes that were constantly war-ring with each other, for no other reason than that's the way it had always been. Fighting was so ingrained in their lifestyle that we met great resistance in trying to quell it. So, instead of . . . "

Maia looked around at the scattered buildings. "I saw a sign for an armory a ways back – "

Darby was startled. "Why didn't you tell us? We could use some better weapons."

"They won't do us any good. They're just . . . Okay. I'll show you. Let's grab some coconuts from that grove, and any other food that we can scrounge. We should get under cover before this storm breaks."

Gathering darkness was made darker by black clouds overhead. An occasional sprinkle forecast wors-ening weather.

Maia led the way between buildings and freestand-ing walls. Stone pavements wended around farm plots and past outbuildings that dotted the cityscape, toward the distant ziggurat of virgin sacrifices. All four plucked ripe fruit whenever they found it. The way passed over a stream whose water was hemmed in by stone walls, and was directed through various groves and fields where the ground was irrigated. A stone bridge crossed a cor-beled arch that stood five feet above the surface of the water.

Maia kept up her monologue. "We figured that if we could channel their peaceful energy into building stone structures to replace their hovels, we could also channel their warlike energy into ways that didn't lead to injury and death. It took years – centuries – as we expanded our influence throughout the Americas. Eventually we convinced the locals to stage mock battles in which no one got hurt. The advantage was obvious: everyone got to go home after the fight. In your 'verse, contact sports accomplish much the same goal. Those who didn't want to fight became spectators. Or umpires."

"Umpires?"

"Sure. Someone had to determine who won the game. Umpires accompanied the contestants so they could watch the competitors in action." In aside, "And to make certain there wasn't any cheating."

She stopped in front of a building with a rectangular floor plan. A red and green blanket covered the only doorway. Maia fingered the soft cotton. "These fibers have been woven recently. Someone is maintaining – or attempting to maintain – this city."

Woody humphed. "Too bad no one maintained the suspension bridge. Or the swamp trail."

"That was always done by local volunteers who aren't around anymore because of the conquistadors. It was like your people – employees of nearby businesses – who adopt a stretch of highway to keep clean of litter."

She unhooked one side of the blanket and hooked that side onto a peg, in which position light was admitted to augment the light that entered through paneless windows. The interior was dark and dismal as a result of the cloud cover and approaching twilight. Maia lay her pack on the ground and stepped inside. The others left only their spears outside, so they wouldn't have to duck under the low lintel. All four stood within the entranceway until their eyes adjusted to the dimness. The walls were lined with wooden shelves that were cluttered with assorted weapons that appeared to have been tossed in disarray, but which on closer inspection were found to be somewhat in order – for whatever that was worth.

Maia picked up what looked to be a short-sword and handed it to Darby by the hilt.

Darby looked it over carefully, fingering the blade. "It's made of wood. The edges are blunt. There's no tip." He glanced at Maia. "The end is carved flat, like a dueling foil in a fencing match."

"That's my point. Or rather, that's not my point."

Woody humphed. "This isn't an armory. It's a toy store."

"Where do they keep the dolls?" Amber wondered.

Maia nodded. She knelt to the floor and pulled a worn ceramic jug from beneath the lower shelf. It was filled with a purplish substance that had long since dried and cracked. "The tip and edges of the sword were painted. When opponents engaged in a contest, the one who got touched with paint was considered to be wounded or dead. Umpires made the call as to whether he or she could stay in the game."

Woody humphed. "Like calling a strike or a ball, or a foul."

Now it was Amber who humphed. "Great. A primitive form of paintball."

"Yeah!"

Maia nodded again. "The winner and loser touched foreheads after the contest was called. Our way of shaking hands between rivals. Contests started small. Sometimes between individuals, but usually between neighboring tribes. After a while, tribes joined ranks and played against other cooperating tribes. Before long, they were waging full-scale competitions in which thousands of contenders participated. What started small became a national pastime. The contests were always followed by huge celebrations, and singing, and dancing, and rejoicing, and a lot of drinking intoxicating or mind-altering beverages." Maia laughed. "That kind of behavior is pretty much standard in both our 'verses.

"Then, when some engagement turned out to be memorable or otherwise spectacular, it was recorded for future generations, who then might re-enact it as another form of entertainment." She paused. "Don't look so stunned. Last year's re-enactment of the Battle of Gettysburg included fifteen *thousand* re-enactors – all dressed in period costume and carrying vintage rifles (loaded with blanks, of course) which each individual furnished for himself, and *eighty thousand* spectators. It was the biggest turnout ever."

"How do you *know* all this stuff?" Amber asked.

"It's my business to know. Someday, when the conquistadors are ousted from our 'verse, we hope to reunite with our people in your 'verse. Then I'll become that teacher that you credited me with being. But that day is a long way off." She sighed. "Now you can understand how the conquistadors oppressed and occupied the Americas so easily. The practice of hurting or killing opponents had long since been driven out of the local cultural heritage by the time they arrived. Of course, there were some people who were willing and able to fight – with real weapons – but they numbered in the minority. Plus they didn't have any fighting weapons, only those that were designed for slaughtering livestock, or hunting. Our people welcomed the conquistadors with open arms, and were beaten, killed, and robbed for their generosity."

A somber silence ensued.

Darby wandered around the roomful of stage props. "I don't see any bows and arrows."

"They were outlawed by the rules of the game. Too much chance of poking out an eyeball, or otherwise hurting someone. The same with atlatls and blowguns. Contestants were allowed to use spears, but only for stabbing and parrying. They weren't allowed to throw them at people; only at targets. There were competitions for distance and accuracy, which was useful for hunting game."

Darby ran his fingers over a shield that was shaped like a clover leaf. The perimeter was bent from a length of vine; one vertical and one horizontal cross member in the form of a Christian cross kept the outer rim in place. Several layers of stretched hide had been bonded and dried on the frame to create a material that was as impenetrable as armor. He picked up a bludgeon or mace. The business end of the lignum vitae shaft was coated with a heavy black substance that was somewhat resilient.

Maia explained, "The head is coated with rubber – "

"Rubber!" Woody exclaimed.

Maia snickered. "In your day and age of synthetics, have you forgotten that rubber latex originated as an organic material, extracted from South American gum trees the way syrup is tapped from maple trees?"

"I knew that," Amber gloated.

"Nowadays, in your 'verse, it's mostly synthesized from petroleum. We don't keep gum trees inside the city because the produce isn't edible, but plantations are maintained outside city limits. Weapons were coated with rubber to prevent injury." Maia squeezed the rounded end of the mace. "This rubber has mostly solidified. It's softer when it's freshly collected, in coconut half shells. We also use rubber to make basketballs."

"Basketballs!"

Amber cuffed him. "Woody, don't be a dunderpate. Do you have to repeat everything she says?"

"But – basketballs?"

"It's our national sport. Actually, 'hoop ball' is a more accurate description, but the way it's played is closer to your basketball." Maia squinted at the ceiling as rain pattered hard on the thatch. No water leaked into the room. "This roof has been repaired, and recently."

"So where is everyone?" Amber questioned.

"I don't know. But we had better get going." Maia walked out of the armory, then rehung the blanket over the doorway in order to keep out the drizzle. "This way."

After five minutes of dodging raindrops, the foursome found themselves standing at the base of a ziggurat whose four slanted sides each sported a steep staircase with tall risers and narrow treads.

"Are you ready for this?"

Amber shrugged. "I've got nothing to lose."

Woody fluttered his eyebrows and got soundly cuffed

for his impertinence. "I only meant that there's not much incentive for keeping your virginity. If you're on the sacrificial list, you can get off it by getting laid before the ceremony."

Amber raised her hand, but Woody ducked and stepped aside.

Maia started climbing. "It's okay to lean forward and use all fours."

Amber did. Woody counted out loud. Darby noted that the wet steps were slippery. He couldn't understand how Maia could carry her heavy pack to the top without getting out of breath, but she did.

"One hundred fifty steps," Woody announced, when he stepped on the ultimate platform.

The view from the summit was grandiose. Darby could see the city in its entirety. The paved square measured several miles in either direction. In some places the surrounding forest had encroached on the perimeter. In other places the plaza looked as if it had been swept clean. Several smaller ziggurats dotted the cityscape. Outbuildings were visible in the countryside, where nature was in the process of reclaiming the land. Groves of fruit trees had been pruned. Plowed fields were filled with crops.

No people were in sight.

"The last we heard – at the time of the San Francisco earthquake – there were itinerant clans, or nomads: people who moved around in order to avoid confrontations with the conquistadors. They might have occupied Paca-Zula until the new portal brought conquistadors this way . . . although we're off the direct route between Teomotl and the portal."

"Are there food depots along the way?" Darby wondered.

"No. Only an outpost southwest of here. We should reach it tomorrow. That's where we pick up the main road over the mountains. Are you thinking that they came here to reprovision?"

"That's what an army does when it has to live off the land."

The lull passed. Rain fell heavier. Maia motioned for the others to follow her into the stone edifice that occupied the center of the ziggurat's top platform.

"In good weather the virgin sacrifices were conducted in the sun. In bad weather they were moved inside." Maia looked around the open-air room, whose four spacious doorways were unblocked. The floor looked like a cement sidewalk with grooved expansion joints. But the floor was constructed of stone slabs that were fitted together like the squares on a checker board, except that a small wedge or triangle was cut out of each corner. Glyphs and symbols were carved into every stone. "We *are* in luck. The sacrificial components are undisturbed."

She indicated the stone in the middle of the room. It measured two and a half feet square. "We don't have the official tools but we can make due. Amber, Woody, insert your spear butts in these indentations, and pry."

They did as Maia instructed. The stone levered upward an inch or so. Maia dropped to her knees and shoved her knife into the slit between that stone and the adjacent one. She didn't pry, but held the knife in place and instructed Amber and Woody to reposition their spear butts, and to pry again. This time the end of the stone lifted free.

"Darby, help me lift it."

Darby crouched next to her and slid his fingers into the crack. Together, he and Maia lifted the thin stone slab to a vertical position.

Maia pointed with her chin. "Now lay down your spears over there."

After the spears were in position, Maia and Darby rested the stone upside down on the wooden shafts. The stone could now be easily replaced by slipping fingers under the edge and levering it over and into its previous position. The stone was in fact a lid that covered a pit in the middle of the platform. Maia reached down into the darkness, felt around the sides, located a ledge, and pulled out a knife whose blade was made of black obsidian, one end of which was glued inside a wooden handle.

Maia held up the knife for inspection. "This is the sacrificial knife."

The point and both edges were razor sharp. Maia demonstrated the sharpness by placing the edge on her forearm and slicing off a few short hairs.

Darby fingered his light brown beard. "Would it be sacrilegious for me to shave with that knife."

"We didn't have religion so nothing could be sacrilegious. But you probably couldn't shave very well because the edges are scalloped and uneven. You'd cut yourself to ribbons. Shaving with an obsidian knife – and our men did it – requires patience and practice that you don't need with a safety razor. Besides, you look good with a beard."

Amber and Woody did a singsong duet. "Ooooooooohhh."

Darby grimaced and shook his head.

Maia grinned broadly. "That's enough of that." She held up the blade for inspection. Its sleek black surface was as shiny as shoe polish. "The part that performs the sacrifice is the tip. Either the bride or the groom takes the knife by the handle, pricks the left palm of the other, then hands over the knife so the other can do the same. They place their hands together and mix their blood. This represents their marriage vow. Then they climb down into the inner chamber and sacrifice their virginity – to each other – in the old-fashioned way."

Chapter 19

Woody's jaw was agape. "That's it? No torture? No death? No blood and guts? Just having, uh, making love?"

"Is there something wrong with that? You do the same thing in your 'verse. It's called consummation."

Woody spluttered so much that he couldn't formulate any recognizable words.

Amber took up the slack. "What he means is, that isn't what we were taught in Latin American history class."

"Of course it wasn't. I told you that already. Everything you thought you knew about pre-Columbian civilization was pure propaganda that the conquistadors wanted the rest of the world to believe. They had to make the Pope and the European nations believe that my people were barbarians, that we were degenerate, that we conducted unspeakably horrible and atavistic rites, that we were nothing more than bloodthirsty animals that didn't deserve to be called human. So they invented the most abominable falsehoods they could imagine. Or they blamed the indigens for the despicable acts that the conquistadors themselves committed.

"Years later, when explorers from other countries found that the local inhabitants were peaceful, the conquistadors feared that their atrocities against the local population would be made public. So they hired a group of monks to write a fictitious history of the conquest of the Americas: a history in which the roles were reversed so that the carnage of the conquistadors was attributed to the local heathens. You'll never read about the true reign of terror in your textbooks."

Darby nodded. "No wonder you walked out of class and never came back."

"I never felt bound by your rules and regulations. I was an alien in your 'verse, forced to live there because the only way my ancestors could escape the pogrom of the conquistadors was to close all the portals between 'verses. I considered myself to be an involuntary exile, caught in a nightmare 'verse while waiting for repatriation."

Woody broke a long and uncomfortable silence. "So, if none of what we were taught is true – and I believe you – how do you explain the skeletons of sacrificial virgins that were exhumed from Mayan cenotes?"

"By now it should be obvious that . . . No, I guess it isn't obvious to you because of your educational background. I – I suppose – it must be difficult for you, for all of you, to have your world of knowledge suddenly turned upside down. First, look at the absurdity of your statement. Virginity can be ascertained only by examining soft tissue, not skeletal remains. Therefore your archaeologists have no basis for the allegation that female skeletons that were found in cenotes were virgins.

"Second, some of those women may actually have been virgins. But the reason they were found in cenotes had nothing to do with ritual sacrifice. The conquistadors threw those women into the cenotes alive, and pulled up the ropes, because they refused to let themselves be raped. . . .

"Ropes?" Amber queried.

"The Yucatan peninsula has thousands of cenotes, ranging in size from a balled fist to a football field. Underground rivers were the primary source of drinking water, and cenotes or sinkholes provided the means to reach that water. But they had other uses as well: swimming, bathing, laundering, trash disposal, and so on. Some of the sinkholes didn't have ready access from ground level: the walls may have been undercut or unclimbable, or the surface of the water may have been far below the rim. Inaccessible cenotes had rope ladders secured to the sides, the same as your docks and finger-piers in marinas. Popular cenotes had lifeguards.

"Conquistadors also threw women into cenotes when they were finished using them. Maybe they struggled too hard against rape and weren't worth the effort to reuse. Or they were too badly damaged in the process. To conquistadors, women were nothing more than orifices to satisfy their sexual urges; men were slaves to do their work and bidding.

"As for trinkets found in cenotes – or artifacts, as your archs like to call them – most of them were discarded because they were broken or worn out. Some intact items were dropped by accident. Other objects were deliberately cast into the water the way your people toss coins into a fountain, and make silent wishes that they know won't come true: it's nothing more than a quaint and fanciful tradition. Nothing was thrown into cenotes to propitiate nonexistent gods.

"Your archs ardently espouse that everything that pre-Columbians did must have had religious connotations. Yet they don't have a shred of evidence to support that contention. They just made it up in their heads and wrote it down as if it were substantiated fact. They're just as bad as the conquistadors when it comes to fabricating history from whole cloth. They make us out to be subhumans who practiced dark satanic rites, and who worshiped depraved gods who demanded virgin sacrifices.

"Look around you. Could savages build a city like this? Or like the ruined metropolises in your 'verse. To build a city like Teotihuacan, which housed more than one hundred thousand people, takes the cooperation of thousands – tens of thousands – of workers to construct. If those people were not treated kindly, there was nothing to prevent them from escaping into the jungle and living the way they used to live before the Lema-Reans unified them. If they worshiped anything at all, it was the safe and healthy lifestyle that was offered to them."

After another prolonged silence, Amber spoke quietly. "Okay, that makes sense. So why do we hear so much about praying to Quetzelcoatl? Where did *that* come from?"

Maia curbed her anger by taking several deep breaths. "It's another invention of the conquistadors. That is, there *is* a quetzalcoatl, a feathered serpent, in this 'verse, but we never worshiped it, any more than

Americans worship the bald eagle. The eagle appears on your coins, on paper currency, on flags, on letterheads, and on the endangered species list – except in Alaska, where the flocks are so large that they're considered a nuisance, scavenging in trash dumps like seagulls fighting over fish guts at dockside cleaning stations. The quetzalcoatl is symbolic, like your national bird."

"That makes sense," Woody allowed.

"Look at it another way. Suppose your country suddenly collapsed near the end of December, because of some global or continental natural disaster, and thousands of years later some future archaeologists dug into the ruins of a city and found pictures and paintings and drawings and billboards and statues of a fat, white-bearded gentleman wearing a red suit and black boots. Would they conclude that your culture worshiped Santa Claus?"

Both Amber and Woody snickered.

Maia humphed with a grin. "They would if they were as prejudiced as today's archs in your 'verse. In our 'verse, quetzalcoatls are flying theropods with richly and variously colored plumage – "

"We saw one!" Amber burst with enthusiasm. "We saw one. It was perched on top of a totem pole."

"Yeah," Woody chorused.

"We keep them as pets, like you keep parrots and parakeets, and took some with us through the portals. The people in your 'verse adored them for their colorful feathers – although you have to be careful. They have sharp teeth, and they can be nasty if you don't feed them regularly. You used to have quetzalcoatls in your 'verse, too, but they died out millions of years ago. It's a species of archaeopteryx."

Amber gasped. "How – how is that possible? They've been extinct for a hundred million years. Or more."

Maia shrugged. "So? In your 'verse, the coelacanth was thought to have been extinct for sixty million years, until some were caught in deep water in the 1930's."

"That's incredible."

Woody rubbed his bare arms. The rain was now a

downpour, and a brisk breeze was blowing cold droplets into the room. "Do you also have a Kukulcan?"

"No. That is, yes. Your archs believe in different American cultures, instead of one culture that lived at different times in different places. They claim that the Aztecs worshiped Quetzalcoatl while the Mayans worshiped Kukulcan, and the Incans worshiped Viracocha. But kukulcan and viracocha are only synonyms for quetzalcoatl. They're all the same animal. Think about the different names that Santa Claus goes by: Father Christmas, Kris Kringle, Saint Nicholas. They all refer to the same person. Or symbol. Or personification."

Woody nodded slowly.

"Your archs insist that every minor difference in architecture, or ceramics, or artwork, pertains to a different culture, instead of to the same culture that catered to individual styles and artistic expressions. Take architecture, for example.

"At Chaco, your archs believe that construction was conducted by different cultures: after one culture died out, the outpost was later occupied by another culture; or one culture invaded the area and ousted the previous inhabitants. These suppositions are based on dissimilar architectural designs: the designs of various buildings, the size and shape of construction materials, and so on. It seems never to have occurred to them that designs were based on need or purpose, or that size and shape of construction materials was based on available stone.

"They point to a wall that was built first by large stones laid sideways, followed by a layer of small stones laid lengthwise, followed by a layer that was pieced together from small pebbles, then claim that different cultures were responsible for building each course. Yet they can see the same kind of inconsistencies in any major North American city. Some buildings are made out of wood, some out of brick, some out of stone, some out of iron beams. The façade might be wood clapboard, or aluminum siding, or stucco, or polished marble, or reflective glass panes.

"All these variations have nothing to do with culture.

An ultramodern office building might stand across the street from a gothic church, or a strip mall, or a tenement housing project. Each building was designed by a different architect, was erected in accordance with the intended function of the building, and in accordance with the current cost effectiveness of materials and labor. Culture doesn't enter into the equation at all."

"If you go to an ordinary craft show, you'll see pottery of all descriptions: short and squat, tall and slender, wide-mouthed, small-mouthed, curved mouth, spouted, and so on. The composition of the clay will vary from earthenware to fine china. Ceramic pieces may have been fired with multicolored glazes or pure black and white in any number of designs, from faces to scenery to pure artistry. Each item is the result of the individual potter's taste, inclination, and artistic disposition. It's absurd to claim that each item was produced by a different culture.

"It's the same way with fine art and statuary. Local artists might paint or carve in scores of different styles that have nothing to do with the culture in which they were raised. Your archs don't realize – or they refuse to accept – that diverse pre-Columbian artwork reflects personal and idiosyncratic styles of artistic expression, not cultural bias."

Amber held up her hands, palms forward, like a traffic cop signaling an approaching vehicle to stop. "Calm down, Maia, or the conquistadors will hear you from Cuzco."

Woody stifled a laugh. Darby nodded slowly.

"Sorry. I got started on a rant and couldn't stop. I've had this stuff bottled inside me for so long that I guess I needed to let off some steam, even if I was preaching to the choir."

Darby followed Woody's example of rubbing the goose bumps on his exposed skin. "Well, now that you're steamless, can we bed down some place warm?"

Maia peered through the doorway. Darkness was no longer gathering; it had gathered. "You're right. Let's go down below, eat some food, and get to sleep so we can get an early start."

Amber: "Down below?"

Maia pointed an index finger at the opening in the floor. "To the bridal chamber." She slipped the obsidian knife into her makeshift pack, lowered it through the hole by the tump line, then climbed down onto a narrow landing from which a spiral staircase led down into the pitch black interior of the ziggurat.

Darby placed his spear on the floor. "Don't we need, well, torches?"

Maia fiddled with a circular stone that was embedded in the wall. "I hope not." The stone was graduated with lines like a dial. She grasped it with both hands, and rotated it. There followed a grating sound like stone on stone. "I think the linkage is broken. Stay put until I find the primary engager."

None of the trio made any attempt to move. Darby could hear Maia feeling her way down the steps, her pack thumping from tread to tread. After a couple of minutes of unnerving silence, a faint glow of golden light suffused the interior, like a candle that didn't flicker.

"Come on down!"

Darby went first. The steps consisted of narrow, wedge-shaped limestone blocks that served as both treads and risers. "Keep your feet on the outside edge where it's wider." He spiraled around the center post like a stripe on a barbershop pole. After ten steps the outer casing corbeled outward like an upside-down staircase that mimicked the exterior of the ziggurat. The hollow interior was a single great-room with no partitions except for a curtained cubical on one side of the chamber. Four glowing purple crystals were positioned at the corners of a wooden platform bed that occupied the side opposite the curtained cubical. All this was revealed by perimeter floor lighting.

Woody was enraptured. "Wow!"

Amber indicated the red blankets that covered the bed. "This gives me ideas."

"Where's the light coming from?" Darby wondered.

"A gold filament that runs along the edge where the

floor meets the walls. Another wire is buried in the grooves between floor stones to illuminate the crystals around the bed."

"But, what makes the filament glow?"

"I told you that we had electricity in this 'verse."

Woody inspected one of the glowing crystals. "How – how do you generate the electricity?"

"We don't generate it. We accumulate it." Maia's face glowed almost as brightly as the gold filament and crystals. "Remember I told you how electrons flow through the earth like a chronic static charge? Just as Tesla did, we learned how to harness that continuous flow of electrons by burying accumulators in the ground." She pointed to a circular well in one corner. "These accumulators capture the earth's electrical potential, store the charge, and distribute the energy as we direct it."

Woody's eyes glazed as he stared unseeing into the distance. "Like – like – a Leyden jar?"

"It's a similar but less primitive concept. The difference is that instead of inducing an electric charge by rubbing amber or using a friction machine – "

"Don't you dare say a word if you want to see another birthday," Amber warned Woody.

" – the accumulator siphons off naturally occurring electricity to charge storage cells."

"So – so, you're using the earth as a kind of giant battery charger."

"In essence, yes."

"Wow."

Darby rubbed his temples. "My head hurts."

"Okay. So you're running a current – direct current – through a gold wire, gold being more conductive than copper or aluminum, and the current heats the gold to incandescence, like the filament in a light bulb."

"Does anybody have an aspirin?"

Woody knelt by the perimeter wire and inspected it closely. "What's the clear coating on the wire?"

"Plant sap with some additives to make it pliable after it solidifies. You can touch the insulation without getting shocked or shorting the circuit."

He did. "So, instead of having a light bulb that's been evacuated or filled with inert gas, you have a continuous fine filament that is sealed from the air, like fiber optic lighting through an acrylic cable. And the open air installation dissipates the heat. Awesome! And the crystals? I suppose the gold wire terminates at the base, and the incandescence is refracted through the facets."

"Very good, Woody."

Darby rubbed harder. "How about acetaminophen?"

Woody said to himself: "Very sophisticated." To all: "Did you know that a DC bulb will never burn out if you leave it burning? What burns out the filament in an AC bulb is expansion and contraction of the filament as the alternating current reverses direction one hundred and twenty times a second. Like bending a piece of metal back and forth; it eventually breaks."

"I suppose morphine is out of the question?"

"And this dial is a rheostat?"

"Yes."

To Darby: "Like a dimmer switch."

Darby groaned. "Can we just eat and go to sleep?"

Maia took charge of the dining and bedding arrangements. The kitchenette was equipped with a gold-alloy hotplate that operated on resistance heat, like the element in an electric heater. She boiled water for tea. Additional warmth was radiated from the glowing gold filament.

She took some of the blankets off the platform bed and spread them on the floor side by side. The blankets were made of vicuna wool. The vicuna was a camelid that was closely related to the llama. It lived at altitudes above ten thousand feet. Its fleece was the finest and warmest wool in the world: softer than mink and warmer than down.

She told the others to take turns in the curtained cubical, which contained a wash station and chamber pots (but no running water).

To Woody and Amber: "You two can have the 'loyal bed.' Try to be quiet."

They were. Almost.

Chapter 20

Maia had a built-in clock. She roused everyone from a sound sleep in the dimness of the bridal chamber. By the time they completed their morning ablutions, drank some hot tea and ate a light snack, then emerged from the ziggurat, the sun was barely peeking over the horizon. She replaced the stone lid so as to conceal the hidden stairwell.

She descended the narrow steps to the stone-paved plaza, and headed southwest at her usual fast pace. "We should reach the highway by noon."

Woody managed to stay a step behind her. "So, about these accumulators. You can build a tremendously high voltage and either discharge it all at once or trickle it piecemeal to operate a lighting system. Do you also have motors?"

"Yes, but not on the scale that you have in your 'verse. Our motors are small and quite elementary. Even though gold is common here, and we have an unlimited supply of energy, we don't rely on electricity. It's a power source that we use only sparingly."

"But, can you concentrate or focus accumulated piezoelectricity to, uh, lift heavy blocks of stone? I mean, if it has enough power to open a portal . . . "

"You mean like a force beam?" Maia laughed. "Sorry to disappoint you, but it doesn't work that way. We transported multi-ton stone blocks the old-fashioned way: with wedges, levers, rollers, and rope, plus lots of sweat and muscle – the same way the Egyptians built their pyramids. And their predecessors. And the Asians. We employed ramps to raise the blocks as the ziggurats grew higher, then tore them down when construction was completed."

Darby ran his fingers through his flattened crew-cut. "In ROTC, they had the whole class pick up a one-room cabin and carry it to the other end of the field. Just to show us what a bunch of guys could do by working together."

Woody humphed. "I thought I was onto something. You can build an awful lot of potential with static electricity. Like lightning, for instance. Nature generates a high-voltage bolt that'll travel thousands of feet from the ground to a cloud . . . just like you said a couple of days ago."

"Lightning is a stream of free electrons, not a force beam. Sorry." Maia didn't pause when she reached the first of a series of terraces. She climbed, followed a path between fallow fields, then climbed up to the next terrace . . . and the next . . . and the next. The terraced paddies were dry and overgrown with weeds. "Like fire, electricity is a destructive force until you learn how to control it."

There were twelve terraces in all. From the top terrace they they had a bird's-eye view of Paca-Zula. The greenery sparkled after the previous night's rain. They could also see the dense vegetation that grew in the swamp on the other side of the city. Then they entered a glade in which the trail forked: one tine leading southeast, the other southwest. Maia made certain of her route by reading the signpost at the split, then proceeded southwest.

Hiking through pristine forest would have been enjoyable if the objective weren't so serious. Always on the alert, Darby's sharp and intense gaze swept the forest for signs of danger. All was quiet on the western front – at least for the next couple of hours.

Amber was cheerfully munching on her third pomegranate – spitting seeds indiscriminately – when her nose twitched in the middle of a chew. "Does anyone smell smoke?"

No one did.

But five minutes later Maia held up her fist as a signal to halt. "Now I smell it."

Woody whispered, "Could it be a campfire?"

"Not in the middle of the day. That is, when conquistadors are on the march they don't build fires in midday. Nomads might keep a campfire going. Let's be careful. And be quiet. Real quiet – not like last night."

Woody and Amber looked appropriately guilty.

The trail erupted from the forest onto a broad dirt roadway that extended east and west in a perfectly straight line as far as the eye could see. Darby scoured the ground for signs of llama dung. He saw none. But he saw what he thought were hoof prints in the hard-pack. He touched it with the tip of his spear.

Maia nodded. "Llamas roam wild so it might not be the caravan." She led the procession westward, toward the faint odor of smoke. "There should be a way station ahead."

The road was as wide as a three-lane highway. The forest now grew thin on both sides. Lateral line of sight exceeded a quarter mile. Three whitetail deer scampered away at the approach of the foursome. The only other movement was the twisting of leaves in itinerant breezes. A thin layer of fog or smoke lay across the road ahead.

Fruit trees growing in straight rows and columns had obviously been planted to furnish the help-mates at the way station with food. The clearings that appeared on both sides of the road were acres in extent. They reminded Darby of interstate highway service plazas, complete with refreshment stands, adobe huts, and outhouses – all in an advanced state of disrepair, or recently burned to cinders.

Darby buried his knuckles into a pile of ash that was all that remained of a small outbuilding. "Almost cold. Probably torched yesterday."

"I smelled singed hair." Amber's sense of smell led her to a stone fire ring. She started screaming as soon as she saw what was smoldering.

Remaining flesh on the human body was blackened nearly beyond recognition. The torso was little more than a collapsed rib cage of white powder. The arms and legs – or rather, the hands and feet – still maintained their form. The victim had been tied to wooden stakes at four quarters of a square.

Amber backed away and kept on screaming. Woody went to console her but was unable to do so: his hands lay tightly across his nose and mouth, and he was fighting convulsions that wracked his body.

After catching a glimpse of the carnage, Darby spun in a circle in order to reconnoiter his surroundings. Nothing moved – not even the other bodies that lay scattered across the sward in grotesque positions.

"Conquistadors!" Maia spouted the word as a curse. She stooped by the body of an elderly woman and flipped over the medallion that hung from her neck by a string. "That's the Paca-Zula glyph. They must have been living or squatting there before the conquistadors routed them, then caught up with them here and massacred them. They didn't take the medallion because it's made of base metal."

Amber stopped screaming and started whimpering. She clung to Woody like a limpet, sobbing uncontrollably. Tears streaked her cheeks and dropped off the turn of her jaw onto the bulge of her shirt. Woody's face was a frozen picture of horror.

Maia and Darby trod side by side as they investigated the bloodbath. The next victim they examined was an elderly man whose gnarled hands had been chopped off at the wrists. The hands lay on a bloody log some twenty feet away, implying that he had crawled to his present location after his hands had been severed.

Woody and Amber stumbled along, stifling cries.

A woman lay on her back in silent repose. Her torso was bare and scarred. Her amputated breasts were nowhere to be found.

Another victim was missing one ear and his nose. His blood-stained skull had been battered and crushed with a rock that lay nearby.

Nearly every victim was missing fingers. Those that still had all their fingers showed marks where their rings had been removed.

A number of female bodies had their privates exposed. All but one had been stabbed in the heart. That one was ripped from breastbone to crotch, and her unborn fetus lay by her side in the dirt, still attached to its mother by the umbilical.

The amount of coagulated blood that surrounded the victims stood as mute proof that they had been mutilated alive. Bleeding ceased after the heart stopped pumping. Had the victims been dead at the time of dismemberment, the wounds where body parts had been severed would not have bled.

Amber wailed. "Wh – wh – why did they do this?"

"Because they can." Maia grabbed Darby by the arm and dragged him out of hearing range of Amber and his brother. "We have to talk."

Darby nodded.

Maia looked Darby square in the eyes with an intensity that he could feel: like sharpened icicles. "This has to be the parting of the ways."

Darby was too awestruck to speak.

"Don't misunderstand me. I'm grateful for what you've done, for your company, for your – your friendship. But you have to understand that I was coming here even if the conquistadors hadn't brought me. Even though I've never been here before, I think of this as my 'verse, my home. I've grown up pining to be with my people, to help free them from subjugation and tyranny.

"This isn't your 'verse and this isn't your war. You came here by accident. You have no reason to be here, and I doubt that once the wonder is over, you will *want* to be here. Or, at least, you won't want to stay here. Your home is on the other side of the cave, in a 'verse that is familiar to you. I brought you this far not because I needed your support – I can survive on my own because I've trained for this my whole life – but because you needed my knowhow in order to stay alive in a 'verse that is completely foreign to you. A 'verse in which you don't speak the language, can't read the signs, don't understand the hazards, and couldn't comprehend how vicious and bloodthirsty the conquistadors are toward people they consider to be nothing more than worms to be trod underfoot.

"I don't want to drag you into a war that isn't yours to fight. I think you and your brother and Amber should turn back now. Take this road due west, to the mountain, to the cave, through the portal, and forget that you ever saw this place. Forget it even exists – "

"I thought you said the conquistadors would be guarding the cave."

Maia looked askance. "They will be. I was hoping to recapture some of our guns, so I could send you back with some firepower. But now . . . I don't know. You'll just have to take your chances. But your chances of fighting your way through the portal are better than your chances of fighting off an entire army."

"But you're willing to fight that army alone. With primitive weapons against an army with guns."

"They *have* guns, but they don't know how to use them. That's why they kept me alive. They wanted me to show them how to load, aim, and fire. Not that they won't eventually figure it out for themselves. They will. Just because they're brutal doesn't mean they're stupid. But they can learn a lot faster from an instructor. Raping me was supposed to be a softening up exercise. Now they have to learn it for themselves."

Darby nodded slowly. "It won't take them long to figure out how to load a gun. And they already know how to pull a trigger. But that won't make them sharpshooters. There's a lot more to hitting a target than they could possibly suspect."

Maia frowned. "What do you mean by that?"

"You know what I mean. You just don't know you know."

"Huhn?"

"You've trained with guns. You told me that. So you know all about ballistics and Kentucky windage. But they don't know that. Those old blunderbusses of theirs were only good for close-up shooting. If they fired a modern gun at you from two hundred meters, they'd drop the bullet at your feet, and probably off the line of flight, to one side of the other."

"I get it. They would aim directly at the target, instead of above it to allow for the trajectory of the bullet."

Darby nodded fast. "They're used to aiming the barrel. They don't know how modern guns are sighted. If they used the crosshairs to shoot at you from close range, the bullet would pass over your head. Most guns are pre-sighted for one hundred meters. To shoot a target at twenty-five meters, you have to aim at the ground in front of the target."

"Did you learn this in ROTC?"

"No. In basic training. Now, I'm not saying they won't figure all this out, but it's going to take them a while to become marksmen. In the mean time we have the advantage. And two soldiers are better than one."

Maia was quiet for a minute. "Darby, I – I appreciate your offer. I really do. And I agree with you. But I was thinking more of Amber and Woody. Look at them . . . "

Darby looked. They weren't wailing out loud any more, but their distress was evident. Woody's legs were shaking, and Amber was still crying quietly. They clutched each other for mutual support.

"Darby, they're not like us. They're just kids. They're intelligent – brilliant even. And they're fearless when it comes to facing the challenges of nature. I've seen that. But they're not mentally or emotionally prepared to deal with – whatever we have to deal with when it comes to fighting conquistadors. They may not know how to use modern guns but they have something that Woody and Amber don't have, and never will have – cruelty."

Darby pinched his eyes.

"We don't have it, either. You and I. But we have the wherewithal to fight it."

Darby nodded slowly. "My platoon sergeant used to say, 'War is bad, but to yield to slavery is worse.' "

"Your platoon sergeant was wise." Maia humphed. "I like to think of myself as a pacifist: that is, a realistic or rational pacifist. Whenever I have doubts about fighting the conquistadors, I think back to World War Two, to two outspoken pacifists who had diametrically opposed attitudes toward pacifism. Bertrand Russell stood against violence under any circumstances. He believed that it was better to surrender his freedom to Hitler than to fight. He was an irrational pacifist. On the other hand, Albert Einstein was a rational pacifist. He stood against initiating violence, but not against defending oneself from violence that others initiated. That was why he signed the letter to the President, in which he advocated the construction of the atomic bomb."

"I didn't know that."

"My point is, there's nothing wrong with fighting if the cause is just. I've always believed – "

Suddenly, Woody and Amber were running toward them, waving their arms.

Woody was breathing hard when they arrived. "Someone's coming!"

Maia gasped. "From east or west?"

"East."

Maia looked hard at Darby. "Maybe we didn't miss the caravan after all. Maybe we're in the middle of it."

Darby took immediate control of the situation. "Quick! Let's get inside that ruined hut."

He led the way and the others followed without questioning. The thatched roof had fallen outboard when the rear wall of adobe had collapsed. The remains consisted of one front wall and partial side walls. The stench arising from a round hole in the center indicated that the hut had been not an outbuilding, but an outhouse. No one complained.

"Any port in a storm," Darby grumbled. To Woody: "How far away were they?"

He shrugged, and tried hard to control his stammer. "Hard to say. Half a mile?"

"Then we don't have much time."

"How many?"

"Too – too far away to tell."

"What are you thinking?" Maia wanted to know.

"An ambush." Darby looked for places to hide that stood closer to the road. The woods provided scant cover. They were far too open. "Woody. Amber. You two stay put."

He got no argument over that.

"And give me your knives." The teenagers handed over their blades. "Keep your spears in hand. Maia, you and I will hide behind that log." Darby pointed to a fallen tree on the edge of the forest. "Now!"

He stood up and ran. Maia was right on his heels. They ducked behind the root ball, then low-crawled to the middle of the log. From there they could see partway along the road to the east. The conquistadors were not yet in view from their angle.

"Okay, let's go over a few things first. You take the poniard because you don't know how to use a knife."

Maia grumbled when Darby placed the hilt in her hand. "What do you mean by that? I used it to stab that conquistador in the back."

"Yeah, and the blade didn't penetrate because you didn't hold the knife right." She gave him a dirty look but before she could protest, "Do you remember how the knife stuck out of his back but didn't slow him down, then fell out? That's because you held the blade vertical."

"So?"

"So picture the human ribcage." He drew a crude diagram in the dirt. "When a man is standing the ribs are parallel to the ground. A vertical blade can't fit between the ribs. It jams. If you're going to stab someone, hold the blade is horizontal. Then it will slide between the ribs."

Maia humphed and pursed her lips. "You didn't learn that in ROTC. Or in basic."

"No. And another thing. You can't get emotional in a fight."

Even though she was lying down, Maia managed to put one hand on her hip.

"You have to stay detached. Stay focused. As soon as you let emotion take control of your actions, you give the advantage to your opponent. You start flailing and swinging wild, to hurt instead of kill. Combat isn't a sport. There aren't any rules. You don't fight to win; you fight to kill – by any means possible. And another thing."

Maia added pinched eyebrows to her expression of discontent.

"Forget taekwondo or kung fu or whatever Asian boxing system you tried on that conquistador back there. That stuff is only for tournaments. Real fighting isn't about competitive self-defense. It's about killing the enemy. You can kill someone with a single punch if you do it right. Even if you miss with the kill punch, you'll incapacitate your opponent so you can kill him with the second one." Darby demonstrated with his hands. "Don't use your fist. If he's facing you, curl your fingers and punch him in the throat with the middle joint of your knuckles, preferably on the Adam's apple; that will crush the larynx. If you come up behind him, punch him in the back of the neck with the top joint of your knuckles; if you don't break his neck you'll at least paralyze him. From either side, extend the knuckle of the middle finger and hit him in the temple; that will burst the blood vessel and kill him instantly.

"If you don't kill your opponent right away, don't pick him up so you can punch him and knock him down again, like cowboys do in the movies. Kick him in the head or throat. If it comes to hand-to-hand, don't try to throw him. I know it looks dramatic on television when people crash into glass cases or shelving units, but it doesn't do much damage except to the furniture. Punch to kill, not to hurt."

Maia breathed deeply but didn't speak until she had control of her emotions. "Okay. Okay. So all those years I spent learning martial arts was wasted. I get it."

"Not wasted. It's good exercise, and it hardens your muscles, and improves your balance and coordination. But it only works when your opponent uses the same rulebook. In field combat we only have one rule: no quarter."

Chapter 21

"So what's the plan?" Maia wanted to know.

"Let's wait until we see how many there are. And how they're armed."

"I take you've done this before."

Darby nodded.

"In the Army?"

"No. The Navy."

"But you were in ROTC. Isn't that Army training? You know: Reserve Officers' Training Corps."

"You can choose any military service you want. And you have to commit to it in college. But not in high school. That's more like pre-ROTC. A weeding out process." Darby kept his eyes on the road. "I got weeded out. I wasn't college material. I wanted to go in the Navy, to be a ship's officer. I studied navigation, but the math was too hard for me. So after high school I joined the Navy as an enlisted man. Figured I might work my way up to an officer." He fell silent.

"And?"

"I never did."

"So? What did you do?"

"I managed to qualify for SEAL training, so that's what I did."

Maia was impressed. "Did you just do the training, or did you go on actual combat missions?"

"I went on missions."

"Where? What kind of missions?"

"They're classified."

"Maybe in your 'verse, but not in this one."

"They're classified."

"Okay. I get it. They're classified."

They lay in silence for the next couple of minutes. They heard clopping hooves and the clattering of loose metal. An armor-clad conquistador hove into view. Behind him came two more conquistadors wearing brown cloth jerkins and bloused trousers: one had an arquebus slung over his right shoulder. Then came another unarmored conquistador leading a llama with two bulging saddlebags and a pair of wooden crates. All the men had swords.

Darby whispered: "Why aren't they all wearing armor?"

"Only officers wear armor. The others are common foot soldiers. These are the stragglers who held me captive."

The conquistadors stopped by the side of the first body, then slowly moved on to the others. They engaged in a lively conversation, complete with windmill gesticulations. The llama chewed its cud.

"Do you know what they're saying?"

"They're angry because they missed out on all the fun. They're hoping to find one alive so they can torture him some more, or rape her again."

Darby surveyed his options. "Okay, here's what we're gonna do. They have only one gun and it isn't loaded – "

"How do you know that?"

"Well, it may be loaded but there's no flame to ignite the flash pan. Unless they have matches, they'll have to strike a spark with a flint and steel."

"Okay."

"I want you to create a diversion by walking out in the open. Slide your belt around so your sword is behind you, but be ready to draw it. Call out in their language if they don't see you right away. I want you to attract their attention. But keep your distance. I'm gonna flank them by crawling through those ferns over there to the road. I'll come up from behind and take out the officer."

"How?"

"With the spear. We never trained in spear throwing, so I'm not going to try it, but it has a longer reach than his sword. Then I'll take out the others."

"And what am I supposed to do?"

"Keep them distracted."

"How? Look pretty, talk dirty, or raise my shirt?"

"Whatever."

Maia's anger was growing. "I happen to be a pretty good swordsman – swordswoman."

Darby nodded. "I'll bet you are. I just – I don't want you to engage when you're outnumbered. When I take out the officer, one or two of the others should come after me. Then you can engage."

After a moment's reflection: "Okay. That sounds fair."

"I'm gonna try to keep the officer alive. See if we can get some intel. But no quarter for the others."

"Agreed. Although under different circumstances, Woody would probably say two dimes and a nickel."

Darby didn't grin. "I'll bet he would. And Amber would whack him upside the head."

As if she had heard her name pronounced in vain, Amber let out a screech that resounded across the clearing like a police car siren. Everyone looked toward the adobe hut: Darby, Maia, conquistadors, even the llama.

"That's our cue. The plan has just been changed." Darby kept a low profile as he peered over the log. The conquistadors were already heading toward the hut. "Wait till they pass. Then we'll both dash out and attack from behind. But me first. Understand?"

Maia didn't hesitate. "I do. I'll give you the lead."

It took only a few seconds for the conquistadors to pass the point at which the log lay behind their peripheral vision. Darby stood, stepped over the log, and walked silently through the brush toward the backs of the conquistadors. Maia followed close behind. She stepped on a twig that snapped under her weight. The crack sounded loud in the relative silence. Two conquistadors turned and faced them. Darby charged.

The officer was on the far side of the group, so again he had to change his plan. The foot soldiers drew their swords. Darby did not slow his pace. He held the spear at its balance point. Just before he reached the closest conquistador, he swung the spear across his midriff, gripped it with both hands, and continued to swing it in an arc so that the butt slammed into the side of a swordsman's head. He fell as if he had been pole-axed, which in fact he had.

Darby swung the spear the rest of the way around, skidded to a stop with the butt aimed at the other foot soldier, then rammed him in the solar plexus with the blunt end. He couldn't afford to get the tip stuck in the soldier's guts. He pulled back the spear just as Maia raced past him.

Screaming like a maniac, she whipped the sword in a vicious circle around her head. The third foot soldier, confused, held up his sword to parry her descending blade. But her sword had so much strength and impetus behind it that it battered down his defense as if he were wielding a feather. Her sword sliced the side of his head, lopped off the ear, and buried itself into the muscles of his shoulder. He yelled as he was knocked to his knees. His sword arm hung limp. She took a step beyond him, spun on her heel, and delivered the coup de grace – remembering to rotate the blade so that it paralleled the ribcage. The point encountered so little resistance that it went straight through his body, stopping only when it met the inside of the breastbone, and stuck there. The hilt was yanked out of her hands when the soldier fell forward the rest of the way to the ground.

The officer was after Darby in a flash, thrusting with his sword like a fencing champion with a saber. The maneuver was his undoing. Instead of adopting the appropriate dueling posture, with one foot forward to stop his momentum, he followed through for maximum penetration. In one swift but coordinated movement, Darby let the spear drop to the ground, stepped aside, and ducked. The sword passed dangerously close to his face.

Darby seized the conquistador's arm, spun, and threw his opponent over his shoulder in such a way that he slammed against the ground on his back, knocking the air out of his lungs. Immediately, and without relinquishing his hold, he executed a pullback that wrenched the shoulder out of its socket.

Maia punched one of the wounded foot soldiers in the side of the head. In the heat of the moment she not only forgot to extend her middle knuckle, but she swung wildly and missed his temple. He staggered with the blow nonetheless. She took a deep breath, and used more precision with her second punch, which effected the result that Darby had predicted.

Like an automaton, she moved on to the last foot soldier. He lay on the ground immobile, either unconscious or dead. She didn't bother to feel his pulse. She yanked out her poniard, pictured his anatomy, and plunge the point under his sternum with a slightly upward angle into his heart. He didn't even groan.

The entire fight had not taken more than half a minute.

The officer howled with pain. Darby kicked his sword out of reach, in case he made a grab for it with his left hand.

Maia fought to control her adrenaline breathing. "I thought you didn't go in for any of those Asian martial arts."

Darby shrugged. "I improvised. Hand-to-hand combat usually doesn't use judo, but the opportunity presented itself so I took advantage of it. That was an osoto gari, uh, with an American twist. We wanted him alive but incapacitated."

"You are one hell of a fighter." Maia held out her hand to shake, like a pair of vanquishing warriors, but changed her mind and threw both arms around his shoulders and clutched him so tightly that he could hardly breathe. She was incredibly strong.

"Well, uh, thanks." He wasn't used to hugging his teammates after a firefight – or whatever you call the kind of fight they just had. He placed his hands lightly on her back. He could smell the sweat on her skin; it was a tantalizing odor. "You're a good fighter too."

Maia broke the clench. She looked down at the groaning conquistador, then askance at the approach of Woody and Amber. Darby looked at the llama – which had gone back to chewing its cud – then at the road. The coast was clear. For now.

Amber appeared inconsolable. "Oh, Darby, Maia, I'm so sorry. I didn't mean to scream, but a scorpion crawled up my leg . . . "

"Did it sting you?" Main touched her arm.

"No. Woody brushed it off. But I was . . . startled. I didn't mean – "

"It's okay. Just take it easy. It's all over."

The conquistador groaned louder now that he was getting back his breath. Maia kicked his dislocated arm. He shrieked louder than Amber but not as high in pitch. She spoke to him in ancient Spanish. He made no attempt to rise, yet he maintained an attitude of arrogance despite his vulnerable position.

After a short shouting match, Maia said to Darby, "He threatened to kill all of us slowly for our impertinence against conquistadorian rule. I couldn't get any useful information out of him. Let's go check the saddlebags." To Woody and Amber: "Keep an eye on him. If he moves, kick him like I did."

On her way to the standing llama, Maia stepped around the still-warm bodies of conquistadors and the dismembered corpses of Lema-Reans. Darby gave Amber and his brother a telling look, then turned and followed Maia. As they approached the pack animal, Darby saw a lump in its throat: a lump that moved up and down, and heard a strange gurgling noise that was like the cough of a person with a sinus problem or post nasal drip.

Maia stopped. Darby stopped alongside her.

She yelled, "Duck!" She pulled down on Darby's arm.

The llama opened its mouth and expelled a wad of mucus the size of a golf ball. It flew over their heads and landed six feet away. Maia immediately jumped up and gave a resounding slap across the llama's muzzle, hard enough to turn its head ninety degrees.

As if the animal understood English: "Don't ever do that again!" To Darby, in a quieter voice: "Llama's like to spit at people."

"I see that."

Darby recognized the wooden crates. They were identical to the ones that he had seen in Lone Bat Grotto, stacked up against the wall, only now they had nylon straps secured to the metal ringbolts by means of brass snap hooks, giving each crate the function of a duffel bag. For balance, one crate hung from each side of the pack animal. Padded straps crossed over the llama's back to soften the load. Darby noticed that shorter straps were secured in the same manner to the ringbolts on the ends of each crate: a tump line so that each crate could be hauled by a porter, or carried in the hands by two of them.

"You can unlatch the top half of the outboard panel."

Darby did as instructed. The half panel folded down to reveal an interior filled with guns of all descriptions. They were partially wrapped in white cloth. The first one he pulled out and unwrapped was a vintage hunting rifle that he didn't recognize: a bolt action model with the name Remington stamped on the side. The rifles underneath it were just as old.

"Where did you get these rifles? At a garage sale or an antique market?"

"We've been collecting for years. You can't go into a gun shop and buy a truckload of M-16's, or the ATF will be knocking on your door. We had to buy them piecemeal, here and there, on the gray market, in different States, under assumed names. It's the only way to stock an army with enough guns and ammunition to start a war."

"Did you get minie balls and grapeshot too?"

"Don't start mouthing off like Woody."

Darby found cardboard cartons filled with cartridges of varying calibers, to fit the rifles that were packed in the same crate. Farther down he found a repeating rifle and some shotguns. He wound not have been surprised to find a Sharps or some Civil War relics.

"Here's one that's more your style." Maia tossed a rifle over the llama's back.

Darby caught it on the fly. It was a Springfield M-1 Garand, the World War Two standard issue for American G.I.'s. It was pre-loaded with a full eight-round magazine.

"Somewhere we have some AR-15's – the civilian

model, of course. We could never get any military weapons – fully automatics, machine guns, grenade launchers, and so on – without fear of blowing our cover. We tried to keep a low profile. The semi-automatics must be in another part of the caravan."

"This will work for me. Do you have – "

Maia tossed him a bayonet. "That was difficult to come by. We bought it at a gun show from a souvenir vendor."

Darby fixed the bayonet to the barrel. "Even though the M-16 is the military rifle of choice – because of its lighter weight and smaller round – I always had a hankering for wooden stock rifles. A plastic stock isn't much good in hand-to-hand." He hefted the weight. "If you hit someone on the chin with this stock, the fight is over."

"Okay. So now that we're armed and dangerous, what do we do about Woody and Amber?"

Darby studied them. Woody was holding a stick against the conquistador's breastplate. The expression on his face was grim but not determined. He looked as if he would jump back out of the way if the conquistador made any kind of aggressive gesture. Amber was whining, and rocking back and forth with a two-fisted grip on Woody's free arm. She stood bent over like a gnome.

"We can't go back. Not now. With these weapons we can steal a march on the conquistadors before they take over Teomotl. Even if they get there first, they won't beat down the city gates right away. Uh, does the city have gates?"

"Better than that. It has drawbridges."

Darby's head jerked back.

"Teomotl is on an island. That's why the conquistadors were never able to conquer it. Unless they have conquered it in the hundred years that we've been out of communication. The lower Cotl River curves back and forth like your Mississippi. At a number of places the river is shaped like an oxbow, with the ends of the bow nearly touching. Like your Mississippi, every once in a while the river breaks through the pinch point and creates an island. Also like your Mississippi, once the course is changed so that water flows through the new channel, the oxbow often dries up.

"Originally, Teomotl was built on an oxbow for irrigation purposes. After the conquistadors invaded Lema-Rea, the inhabitants of Teomotl dug a trench across the oxbow. They regulated the depth of the artificial channel so that flow was maintained completely around the city. Our cities aren't built like yours: a confined urban development in which food has to be imported. Our cities are self-contained: a patchwork quilt of irregular plots that are designated as living quarters, administrative buildings, corrals, hen houses, farm land, and so on.

"After the invasion, all the bridges were converted to drawbridges. The conquistadors laid siege to Teomotl because of the amount of gold that is stored there – it used to be a mining and distribution center – but with nothing other than contact weapons, they could never gain an advantage over the inhabitants. They tried crossing the river by boat but were always repelled. They built fire rafts to try to burn down the city. That didn't work because the bulkheads and adjacent structures were made of stone."

"Well, I guess that answers my question. As for Woody and Amber, I think I can vouch for their safety. I think they'll go along with the mission as long as we keep them in the background, out of the fighting. Uh, what's your plan after we reach Teomotl?"

"The original plan was to bring an army through the portal, not just weapons. For hundreds of years we've had a group – a cabal, I guess you'd call us, or a resistance – of Lema-Rean descendants and in-laws whose sole purpose in life is to free Lema-Rea from conquistadorian rule, and to return to our homeland to live in peace. We have clans and families all along the western seaboard, from British Columbia to Chile, keeping watch on caves that might someday open a portal. We didn't know that the conquistadors were doing the same thing.

"We sent word to everyone as soon as our portal opened. Right now, members are coming from all over the Americas to assemble on our farm, and to transfer our fighting units to Lema-Rea. Then my brother and I got captured, my brother was killed, and the portal was heavily guarded. I hadn't formulated any plans until I escaped from the conquistadors, and you rescued me. I guess I had a hazy notion of rousing the population of Teomotl with the promise that reinforcements were on the way, hoping that there were enough warmongers among them to mount a counterattack on the portal."

"That's a good plan."

"So what's the plan now? How would you go about fighting this war?"

Darby thought for a moment. "Attacking the portal with only two soldiers against an enemy force of unknown size is risky. The cave is too easily defensible. Like the Spartans at Thermopylae, only we don't have a back door to outflank them. That pretty much means that Woody and Amber are stuck here with us. I think we should keep going to Teomotl, but keep them safely in the background if we have to engage the enemy."

"I wish we could leave them out of it – find a safe place to hide them until the fighting is over – but you never know where the conquistadors might turn up. The safest place for them is with us. But like you said, we'll keep them in the background when the fighting begins."

Darby collected the conquistadors' weapons and stowed them in the crates. In short order the resistance caravan was underway. Darby led the llama by the leash while Woody and Amber kept their distance from the spitting camelid.

Maia stayed behind with the injured conquistador. She caught up with them fifteen minutes later. She was alone.

Darby acknowledged her presence with a nod. "Did you get any intel?"

"He wouldn't talk, so I gave him a taste of Montezuma's revenge."

Chapter 22

The spirit seemed to have gone out of the mission after witnessing the depredations of the conquistadors. Until now, the Earth-'verse trio had only Maia's word that the conquistadors were as brutal as she made them out to be. After seeing the mutilated bodies – and knowing (or suspecting with conviction) that the dismemberments had been perpetrated while the people were still alive – there was no doubt in their minds that nothing that Maia had said about the conquistadors was exaggerated.

Woody made a couple of half-hearted quips about the four-legged addition to their party. "I didn't understand the conquistador's language but I know some modern Spanish. 'Como se llama' means 'here comes the llama.' " His lackluster delivery didn't accentuate the punchline.

Amber was so downtrodden that she didn't even try to cuff him.

When Maia complained about the llama's plodding pace, Woody cracked drearily, "He can't go any faster. He's a dally llama."

That time Amber didn't even bother to glare at him. She was in a funk that Woody's weak attempts at wit didn't affect.

Maia commented dryly, "He is a she."

The llama was now carrying three spears and assorted swords in addition to the original load. She didn't seem to mind the extra burden, as the extra weight was more than offset by the removal of two rifles, which Darby and Maia slung over their shoulders by their straps, and magazines of ready ammunition.

The road topped a rise from which a mountain range came into view. The road dipped down toward the base of a cliff face that stood in shadow due to the lateness of the day. The ridge line rose a couple of thousand feet above the plain below.

"We're too late," Maia said dejectedly.

"Too late for what?" Darby wondered.

"The conquistadors are already at the pass."

Darby waited for an explanation.

"Teomotl is on the other side of the Ubah Mountains. The range stretches north and south for hundreds of leagues. The exposed rock at the bottom is basalt: sheer and unclimbable. There are only a few places where breakdown and erosion have enabled us to cut roads through the basalt to reach the sedimentary rock above. The Ubah-Cotl pass is like your Thermopylae: a narrow defile that can be easily defended by a small rearguard."

"I see."

"There's a gap in the range a league or so north of Ubah-Cotl – the outpost, that is, which was named for the pass – where the Cotl River flows through the mountains, but it is impassable. It's worse than your Colorado River. Not only because of rapids but because of waterfalls, the largest of which is a hundred and fifty feet high: like your Niagara only with less water."

"How far is it to the next closest pass?"

Maia shrugged. "Around twenty leagues."

Darby nodded thoughtfully. "Is it possible to shoot our way through the Ubah-Cotl pass?"

"Just the two of us? I doubt it. The pass has bends that the conquistadors can hide behind. Remember that even if they haven't armed themselves with our modern-day guns, they still have arquebuses and crossbows. For that matter . . . The conquistadors use runners to send messages the same as we did. That means that they must know that I escaped when their two officers failed to return. So we have to assume that they left some foot soldiers at Ubah-Cotl – the pass, not the outpost."

Darby nodded again. "Was Ubah-Cotl abandoned?"

"As far as I know, yes. The conquistadors conquered it hundreds of years ago. But they never lived in it. They exterminated the inhabitants then stripped it of its valuables. That's all they ever do."

"Can we see the pass from the outpost?"

"You can see the diagonal scar that cuts across the

mountain higher up, but trees block a view of the entrance. Messengers used to . . . well, never mind."

"How far to the outpost?"

Maia pointed down the road. "Turn north at the base of the mountain and go another league." She shrugged. "Less than an hour."

"Okay, the rest stop is over. Let's – "

Both Amber and Woody protested: "What rest stop?" "We didn't even sit down."

Darby held up his hands, palms outward. "I know you're tired. I am too. But I want to reach the outpost while the sun's still out, so we can see if there are any conquistadors hanging around." To Maia: "If runners warned the main group, they also know that the three of us are on the loose. But they don't know who we are or what we're capable of. That gives us an edge. They might be expecting you to try to force your way through the pass, but they don't know how dedicated you are, or that now you're armed. And they don't know about me."

"So what's your plan?"

"I don't have one yet. I'd like to reconnoiter the outpost to make sure it's deserted before we sneak up on the entrance to the pass, preferably before dark."

"Okay. Let's go." Maia headed the march.

Amber and Woody rolled their eyes. Darby brought up the rear because the llama was slow getting started.

Five minutes later Maia called a halt at a signpost. "The pack trains stay on the road, but we can take the messenger's path. It looks wide enough for the llama."

The shortcut enabled them to reach city limits in half the predicted time. They emerged from the forest at a stone causeway over a tributary to the Cotl River. They passed a couple of overgrown farm fields, and walked through an orange grove that led to a ziggurat and a circular stone building without a roof.

"Let's check this out." Again Maia led the way. She passed through a doorway without a lintel into the roofless building that was the size of a football field, only the floor plan was rounded instead of rectangular. The stone floor was littered with loose lumber, cord made of pita hemp, and what looked like blankets in a dazzling array of colors. "Drat."

Darby hitched the llama to a convenient boulder, and joined the others inside.

"A serape factory?" Woody opined idly.

"No. It's a blimp hangar."

"You've got to be kidding."

"No. Runners with important messages used to fly over the mountain to Teomotl. We also used blimps for recreational crossings, visiting friends and relatives, and so on.

Amber stooped to touch the fabric. "It feels like cotton that's been coated with – something."

"Plant sap. That's what made the material airtight. The sections were stitched together, then the needle holes were coated with the same sap. Look over there. It's a gondola. Or what's left of one."

The gondola was an open crate like the kind that were pictured in nineteenth-century woodcuts. The sides and bottom were woven from thin but rigid vines that gave the gondola the appearance of a chain-link fence.

"It's like a gigantic reed basket."

"What provided the lift?" Woody wanted to know.

"Hot air."

Amber perked up for the first time in hours. "Oh, I've always want to go for a ride in a hot air balloon."

"Not today. I was hoping . . . but it was too much to expect that we could assemble and repair the air bag. Besides, the conquistadors have taken all the gold conductors." Seeing questioning expressions: "The heat was generated by electricity stored in accumulators." Then: "Prevailing winds made mountain hops as dependable as train schedules: easterly in the morning, westerly in the afternoon. Almost like clockwork, except when storm fronts interfered."

Darby nodded. "So we're back to cutting them off at the pass?"

"Pretty much. Unless you can think of a better idea."

"Not yet. Let's go reconnoiter the pass before it gets

too dark to see."

They left the llama behind in case its braying or clopping hooves might give them away. She demonstrated indifference at having the crates taken off her harness.

Maia led the procession on a roundabout route that avoided commonly used roads and pathways. They were all on the alert for conquistadors. When they passed through a ballcourt, Maia pointed to the vertical stone hoops atop opposing sloped walls. "The balls had to be bounced through one of the hoops to make a score."

Ubah-Cotl appeared to be unoccupied. They didn't see a soul until they reached the trailhead.

"They're not trying to hide, that's for sure." Maia didn't have to point to the fire at the entrance to the pass.

No officers were in view, but a foot soldier was warming his hands by the flames, and a couple of others were cooking over another fire farther up the pass. It was difficult for plants to take root in basalt. The escarpment was clear of vegetation for hundreds of yards in either direction.

Maia assessed the situation. "We could take out the guards, but the gunshots would alert the others farther back. And there's bound to be an officer somewhere up the pass, to send a runner to rally the troops. With us here, they can't get down the pass and we can't get up it. Talk about a Mexican standoff."

She and Darby spent several minutes discussing tricks to draw the conquistadors into the open. Nothing either one of them proposed seemed to have any opportunity for success without personal endangerment. After a while Darby heard Woody and Amber whispering behind them.

"What are you two mumbling about?"

They both looked up as if they had been caught with their hands in a cookie jar.

"Uh, we were wondering . . . " Woody started.

"Yes, we were wondering . . . " Amber continued.

"Wondering what?"

"Uh, we were wondering if it wouldn't be possible to free-climb that cliff."

"Over there, below the second switchback."

"On that bulge."

The trail led up the mountain in a series of switchbacks: a short leg to the right that led to the top of the basalt, followed by a longer leg to the left through sedimentary rock, followed by three more legs through dirt that was thinly covered with bushes and small trees. The bulge lay under the turning point at the end of the second switchback.

Amber: "The soldiers are probably over there, to the right, on the lower leg. If we – "

Darby interrupted. "Yes, I see. We'd be above them, and could sneak down the second switchback and attack them from the rear. But – "

"I can't climb that bulge," Maia stated firmly.

"But I can," Woody grinned.

"Woody can."

Darby had his doubts. "And then what? You think I'm going to let you charge the conquistadors from the rear?"

"No, uh, I don't want to do that. But I can lead-climb and you and Maia can climb up after me."

"We left our climbing gear back at Lone Bat Grotto. Did you forget?"

Amber clicked her teeth. "We can also use the stuff at the blimp hangar. That cord was in good condition and it looked thick enough for climbing. We can use some of it to make prussic knots."

A prussic knot was a knot that slid freely up a rope but which gripped the rope when downward pressure was exerted on it. It was a method that mountain climbers utilized before mechanical ascenders were invented.

Darby's stomach was twisted in a knot – and not a prussic knot. He thought nothing of putting himself in harm's way, but the thought of putting his little brother in danger made him cringe. He took a couple of deep breaths. He looked at the bulge. He looked at his brother. He looked at Amber, whose broad grin scared him even more. "Let's work our way over there and get a closer look."

They ducked back into the trees where they couldn't be seen from the entrance to the pass. A few minutes later found them opposite the bulge. From close up they could see that the bulge was sloped rather than sheer: perhaps eighty degrees instead of ninety. Plus it was pockmarked where bubbles of trapped air had burst when the molten basalt had cooled. Dirt had accumulated in the holes, and tiny shrubs had taken root.

Woody was enthusiastic. "You see. There's a slight incline and plenty of handholds and footholds. I wouldn't grab plants because the roots can't go very deep."

"You can do it, Woody. I know you can." Amber patted him on the shoulder.

"And then what?" Darby wanted to know. "You drop a rope so me and Maia can climb up?"

"Sure. Once you're above the basalt you can work your way up through the trees to reach the second switchback."

"I think he's got something," Maia agreed.

Darby nodded slowly. "I do too."

Woody and Amber whispered a cheer.

Darby looked eastward. The sky was already light purple. Half of Ubah-Cotl was in shadow from the mountain range. The crescent moon stood some twenty degrees above the horizon. "Can you climb in the dark, by moonlight?"

Woody squinted at the white hemisphere. "By the light of the silvery moon? Sure. I won't need much light because my face will be only a few inches from the rock."

"Besides," Amber added, "He's so good that he can climb by feel."

Darby thought it was dangerous. Yet he had confidence in his brother's climbing ability. He and Amber did a lot of bouldering and rock climbing together. Darby figured that if Amber thought that Woody could do it, he could do it. She would never condone sending him up a pitch that she didn't think he could climb.

"There was lots of wood in the hangar." Amber noted.

To Maia: "Was it hardwood?"

"The hardest. Lignum vitae. It's used to make gondola frames. It's heavy, but it's strong, so the frames don't fold up in a crosswind. Also sapote wood, which is nearly as strong.

"Good. Then we can cut some up to make pitons."

A complete plan had been formulated in just a few minutes. They hurried back to the hangar and started on their self-appointed tasks.

Maia took a length of cord and made a tether for the llama so she could graze. When she removed the saddlebags, she found that they were filled with food. She appointed herself cook. She gathered kindling and wood for a fire, used Darby's survival knife and flint to strike a spark, and used her gigantic gold-alloy pot to boil water in which to prepare quinoa.

"Anyone for jerked meat?"

If Maia had asked if anyone wanted a pot of gold, the response could hardly have been more ecstatic. The meat wasn't beef; it was probably llama. No one complained.

Amber was largely vegetarian, but exclaimed nonetheless, "I haven't had a bite of meat since we entered this 'verse. I'm about ready to eat my shoe leather."

All of them munched on chunks that Maia sliced with Darby's knife – the conquistador's knife being so dull that it required too much sawing and elbow grease to meet her fancy.

Meanwhile, after Maia was finished with his knife, Darby whittled pitons from lengths of lignum vitae. Due to its density, it was one of the few woods in both 'verses that wouldn't float in water. The wood was so hard that Darby had to work extra hard to cut it into appropriate lengths, despite the sharpness of the blade.

Woody gathered lengths of cord and braided them together, in order to make a smooth continuous rope without lumps that would prevent the prussic knots from sliding easily. He estimated the length that was needed to climb the pitch – about a hundred feet – then added another twenty-five. He was back to his normal self, singing the dwarves' song from "Snow White," with satirical lyrics from grade school: "Hi ho! Hi ho! It's off to school we go. With a shovel and a pick and a dynamite stick . . ."

Amber hummed along with him. She made a pair of prussic knots and foot loops. She cut some cord into short and medium lengths, then tied them into loops that could be used in place of carabiners; the result was so crude and makeshift that any mountain climber worth his or her salt would cringe at the prospect of relying on such means as protection against a fall. But the system would work as long as the loop was twisted tightly around the wooden piton.

Maia returned to the grove of orange trees for a sackfull of fresh oranges. She passed them out to the fabricators, along with bowls of quinoa and cups of herbal tea so that everyone could keep working on station. After daylight failed completely, she stoked the fire to provide light as well as heat. In a couple of hours all the rope was made, the knots were tied, the pitons were whittled, and everyone was full of delicious meat and tea.

Darby summed up the plan. Then: "Let's get some shut-eye. We'll get up at high moon, when all the conquistadors except the sentinels will be tucked into their ponchos. Then we'll show them what Darby's Rangers can do."

Chapter 23

With the moon standing almost at zenith, the stark white glow illuminated the black basalt bulge like an Ansel Adams photograph on a negative plate.

Woody rummaging through his pack for his helmet when he made a startling discovery. "I feel so silly." Attached to the helmet was a headlamp.

So much had happened in the few days after their transference to Lema-Rea that all three visitors from the Earth-'verse forgot that they were outfitted for cave exploration.

Amber shook her head. "You and me both."

"That makes three of us."

Maia humphed. "After all these nights we spent in the dark, you didn't remember that you had flashlights?"

Woody looked for an out. "We were saving the batteries for an emergency?"

"And what do you call this?"

The Earth folks looked sheepish.

There was nothing to do but to proceed as planned – with more than lunar reflection to shed light on the subject. Woody donned his rock-climbing helmet and secured the chin strap. He determined that the battery in the headlamp was still charged, then switched it off to save battery life. He left his pack on the ground. He tied the rope in seat-harness fashion: around his upper thighs instead of around his waist, so it wouldn't squeeze him the breath out of his if he slipped and hung by his weight. The rock hammer he stuck into a belt loop that Amber had jury-rigged. He filled his pockets with homemade pitons. For his final preparation he donned his gloves.

Amber pecked him on the cheek. "You be careful, you hear?"

"It will be easy." He started scaling the cliff face without further ado. "The rock is religious because it's so holy."

Amber didn't cuff him. Instead, she tied herself to a stout tree, then ran the safety rope around her waist so that in case Woody fell, she could belay him by pinching the rope in front of her.

Woody whispered the rock climber's standard call: "On belay."

Amber breathed the standard response: "On belay."

The surface of the basalt was rough and pock-marked like a sponge. The protruding points gripped his boot soles like Velcro. He stuck his fingers into the bubble holes in order to pull himself up. Woody had strong fingers for this kind of climbing. Once again, his strict regimen of fingertip pull-ups was about to pay off.

He scampered up the first twenty feet where the slope was the most pronounced. He found a crack in which to install his first piece of protection. He used the rock hammer to pound a piton into the crack. The piton was shaped like a wedge or doorstop. If the piton had been made of metal, the hammer would have made a sharp ping every time it struck. But the wood helped to deaden the sound. The improvised piton had no eye ring, so Woody had to untie one of the loops that Amber had made, and tie it to the piton in such a way that it left two long tails. Then he tied the ends around the trailing rope. If he fell, he would fall twice the length of rope that stretched between him and his previous piece of protection. Theoretically. Pitons – even metal ones – had been known to pull out of a crack if they were installed incorrectly.

Thereafter, he drove a piton into a convenient crack every ten feet or so; never more than fifteen feet.

The climbing was straightforward and proceeded apace. When he reached the top of the basalt, he scrambled over loose dirt to a bush, thence to a small tree whose trunk was thick enough to support his weight. He did it all without switching on the headlamp.

"Off belay," he called, as loud as he dared.

"Off belay." On the ground, Amber secured the prussic knots in position. Instead of dropping another rope, the revised plan called for using the safety rope for climbing. She gave Darby a peck on the cheek. "You be careful, too."

Darby nodded. He was already wearing his helmet. He swung the rifle over his shoulder. He put his feet into the stirrups, pushed the knot up the rope, pulled down on it to ensure its grip, stepped up, and did the same with the other stirrup. When he reached the first loop, he cut the cord to the piton and kept climbing upward. He reached the top in short order. Woody lent a hand in pulling him over the basalt lip and onto the dirt.

Amber gave Maia a hug. Maia donned Amber's helmet. She took twice as long to make the ascent. She wasn't used to mountain climbing techniques – especially those that had been out of vogue for half a century. She didn't rush. She took her time, and made certain that the prussic knot was firm before she trusted her weight to the stirrup. Darby pulled her over the edge onto the dirt.

Woody followed the plan by descending the rope to rejoin Amber. After Woody reached the ground, Darby untied the rope and threw it down after his brother.

Darby and Maia clawed the rest of the way up to the switchback, using shrubs and tree limbs as handholds. It was no accident that the moon had already passed the zenith. Darby wanted to descend the switchback under the cloak of darkness. Trees on the west side of the roadway blocked most of the light. The gloom was precisely as Darby predicted it would be.

Maia adopted a ready position. She jammed the rifle butt against her shoulder and peered over the sights down the switchback, looking for movement.

Darby whispered, "Maia, do you mind if I make a couple of suggestions?"

Maia turned her head but did not lower her rifle. "This is your show."

"Well, I meant about your fighting stance."

"My stance?"

"Yes, well, uh, where did you learn to shoot?"

"In the backyard of the ranch. I've been shooting targets since I was big enough to hold a gun."

"Did your parents teach you?"

"Yes."

"Did they have any combat experience?"

"No."

"Okay, well, this isn't a movie production. They get it all wrong because they don't have military advisors. Or when they do have advisors, they ignore their advice because authenticity gets in the way of theatricality."

"Those are big words for you."

Darby nodded. "Yes, well, this is a real combat situation where things are different from the way they are on a movie set. There's no choreographer to arrange the martial arts dances, and no director to make the fighting scenes look dramatic. Real combat is never storyboarded."

Maia lowered the barrel of her rifle. "Do we need to have this conversation now?"

"Better than afterward, when it might be too late."

Maia's sigh seemed loud in the relative silence, in which the only sounds were those of croaking frogs and chirping insects and the faint rustling of loose leaves that were wafted by occasional breezes. Darby moved her to a spot where a gap in the trees let the moonlight illuminate the roadway.

"Take your shooting stance."

Maia lifted her rifle to her right shoulder and peered along the gun sight.

"Okay, first of all, your elbow is sticking out like a wing."

Maia turned her head. Her upper arm and forearm stretched parallel to the ground so that her elbow pointed directly away from her torso. "So?"

"And secondly, the whole front of your body is facing downrange."

She tilted her head with a look of defiance.

In a softly modulated voice: "Look, you're not shooting at a stationary target or wild game on the run. You're shooting at someone who will be shooting back at you. That means that you need to make your body the smallest target possible. The first thing you do is turn side-ways, with your side facing the enemy."

Darby demonstrated by placing one foot in front of the other and rotating his body ninety degrees. He turned his head so as to look at Maia over his left shoulder.

"In this position my profile is only half a wide as yours, because the side view is thinner than the front view. That means I present a smaller target to the enemy, and makes me harder to hit."

"Okay – "

"And when you stick your elbow out like a wing, it's more likely to get shot off. Tuck your arm under the rifle and hold it tight against your chest. Now do you see how small I look? I mean, how narrow a target?"

"Yes, I – "

"And don't hold your eye close to the rear sight. I know they show SWAT cops doing that in the movies as they charge through rooms in a house, but it restricts your peripheral vision. In field operations, you can't afford to focus all your attention on a pinpoint in front of your rifle. You need to look around you and see your flanks."

"That makes – "

"The same thing goes for shooting a pistol . . . You did say that some of the crates have handguns, didn't you? . . . Never hold a gun in both hands and display the entire front of your body to the enemy. If the gun is too heavy for you to hold steady in one hand, get a lighter gun. Shoot one-handed, with your body turned sideways and your gun arm extended in line with your body."

Maia pouted. She lowered her rifle entirely so the barrel was pointing toward the ground, while she placed her free hand on her hip. She glowered for a moment, then inhaled deeply. She was flustered. "Okay, I can see the sense in everything you say. It's just – It's just . . . You're right. I've never shot at anything but a bull's-eye. And I'm damn good at it. I'm a marksman – markswoman. I guess – I guess I never thought about shooting at a real person. That is, I imagined it. I pictured the target as a conquistador. But I guess I never thought it through - thought that the target would shoot back at me. I just never thought of it that way."

"Maia, I'm sorry. I didn't mean to ruffle your feathers – "

"Oh, no. Don't apologize. I needed a good ruffle. Here I am going into combat, and I don't know the first thing about combat procedure. How did you say it before? I was flailing? Fighting with my emotions?"

"Something like that."

Maia took several deep breaths. "Okay, I'm settling down. I'm tense, but I'm going to keep my feelings under control. Instead of thinking about getting even with the conquistadors, for everything they've done – mutilating, wholesale slaughtering, ripping fetuses out of their womb – I'm going to picture them dispassionately, as nothing more than hostile targets."

"That's it. Stay calm. But be prepared for the unexpected. The enemy doesn't have a script to follow. And my own personal pet peeve: don't put your hands on your helmet."

"What?"

"Well, I don't expect them to have explosives, but you never know. You haven't had any contact with them for a hundred years. What I mean is, movie soldiers always put their hands on their steel pot when a grenade goes off. It looks so stupid. The steel pot is supposed to protect your head. Why would you put your hands on your steel pot? To protect the steel pot and get your hands shredded with shrapnel?"

"I get it. The actors act as if they're not wearing a protective helmet."

"Right. These rock climbing helmets won't stop a bullet, but they're pretty tough."

"Okay, is there anything else I should know?"

"Well, if I think of anything I'll let you know."

"I'm sure you will. Now let's get started before Woody and Amber think we got lost."

They traveled in silence for a while.

"Oh, yes, I forgot . . . "

"Go ahead."

"When we get close, roll your foot on the outside of the sole. That way it won't slap on the ground."

Maia tossed off a mock salute with her left hand; her right hand gripped her rifle. "Yes, sir."

"And let's fix bayonets."

She pulled her bayonet from the sheath on her belt, and fixed it to the front of the barrel. "Are you always this talkative before going into battle?"

"No. Everyone I work with knows exactly what to do."

"Point taken."

"If we only had night vision goggles . . . "

They reached the top of the first switchback. The blackness was not Stygian. Enough light passed through the forest to show shrubbery and individual trees. Darby's eyes played tricks on him – bushes resembled crouched figures, and hollow logs looked like sentries lying prone – but he knew all about the mind's pernicious knack of creating familiar objects out of amorphous shadows and suggestive silhouettes. What was more important than what he could see – or what he thought he saw – was what he could hear . . .

Snoring . . . from right around the bend.

Darby dropped to a crouch. Maia crouched beside him. He listened intently for a minute or so, then leaned close and whispered into Maia's ear, "Follow my lead."

He stood up slowly. Maia did the same. He took one step forward, then halted and stooped so he could whisper again into her ear, "Try not to step on any sticks."

He paused after every step, and listened intently. They went ten or twelve paces when the snorer gasped and choked. Darby crouched and pulled Maia down with him. Faintly he could see some movement ahead: it appeared to be someone rolling over and punching his poncho.

Darby listened . . . and listened . . . and listened. He crouched unmoving for so long that Maia reached over and squeezed his knee. He squeezed her hand in return. Five minutes passed. Ten. Maia squeezed his knee again. Darby squeezed her hand. After fifteen agonizing minutes, the sounds of breathing and snoring resumed a regular rhythm.

He leaned close and whispered: "No quarter."

Darby's night vision had peaked. The eyes continually produced low-light receptor molecules called visual purple, but they were destroyed by light. In darkness, the retina accumulated these photoreceptors as a way to increase night vision. This scientific fact was only one of hundreds of subjects that SEALS were taught in training for night operations.

They stood up together. They approached the sleepers like wraiths. Two shapes lay on the ground about five feet apart, their heads pointing toward the slinking pair. The shapes were not getting any more distinct. Without armor, it was impossible to determine if one of them was an officer. He squeezed Maia's arm gently, pointed to the sleeper who lay closest to her. She nodded.

Darby stepped past the other figure, swiftly turned around on his heels, and thrust his bayonet into the middle of the elongated shape under the poncho. The bayonet made a squishy noise as it penetrated the flesh and underlying organs. The figure groaned. As fast as lightning, Darby pulled out the bayonet and thrust it forward again . . . and again . . . and again, until the conquistador stopped moving and making noise.

Next to him he heard the other sleeper let out a ragged cough, then a half-hearted yell. Maia had failed to hit a vital spot. She stabbed him once and then held the bayonet in place, twisting it back and forth as if she were digging a hole in hard ground: an action that was painful to the victim but not immediately deadly.

The choked yell aroused the two conquistadors who were supposed to be tending the fire, which had reduced itself to embers; the cooking fire had been extinguished. Darby started to charge, realized that the distance was too great, then in one swift movement he dropped to one knee, brought his rifle up to his shoulder, aimed, and squeezed the trigger.

One fleeing conquistador screamed in anguish. The momentum of the bullet knocked him off his feet and spun him partway around. He took a flying leap through the air and slammed to the ground. He didn't cry or move afterward.

The other conquistador scooped up a crossbow and fired wildly in Darby's direction. He heard a whoosh and felt a puff of air as the bolt passed his left ear. Instead of running down the open roadway, the conquistador charged into the forest and was immediately swallowed in darkness. Darby charged after him.

He could barely spot the conquistador thrashing loudly through the forest, leaping over logs like a frightened gazelle. When he vanished from sight, Darby followed the sound. Fear seemed to have lent wings to the conquistador's feet. He ran, dodged, and jumped like an Olympian champion. Darby was not far behind him at first, but he was forced to admit that he was no match for the fleeing conquistador.

He caught a glimpse of the conquistador as he crossed a small clearing that was bathed in moonlight. There was no time to get off a shot. Then something with the force of a flying two-by-four cracked against the bridge of his nose. He was stunned by the blow. He didn't fall, but he was momentarily disoriented. By the time he regained his senses, the crashing sounds of the conquistador were fading in the distance.

Darby spotted his nemesis. The six-foot-tall Navy SEAL had slammed into a low tree limb that the five-foot conquistador had deftly raced under. Blood trickled down both sides of his nose to his upper lip. He tasted salt. He wiped off the blood with his shirttail.

Maia stopped by his side, breathing hard. "Are you hit? Are you hit?"

"No. I'm okay. I ran into a tree limb."

Maia turned and ran without another word.

"Maia . . . " He watched as she crossed the small clearing. There was no reason to follow her. The conquistador was unarmed and nearly naked. Darby retreated to the roadway to inspect the conquistador's campsite. He switched on his headlamp so he could examine the bodies and take inventory of their belongings.

The two bayoneted conquistadors were dead and covered in blood: one from a punctured heart and one from badly mangled organs. Next to the one that Maia had stabbed and gutted lay armor dress and a helmet. Weapons were displayed neatly between the bodies: two swords, two knives, and one arquebus. A powder flask and a pouch of lead balls were stuffed into a canvas sack, along with a handful of raw potatoes, some beets, and a small bag of grain, probably maize.

He walked past the doused cook fire. A hundred feet away lay the conquistador he had shot in the bare back. He was twitching but unconscious. It was obvious to Darby that the wound was fatal: the bullet had missed the heart but had passed through the right lung. The entry wound was the size of a dime; the exit wound was the size of a silver dollar. The bullet had been deflected by a rib in the rear, then burst through a rib in the front, which now protruded through the gaping hole in the chest.

Even as he examined the wounds – rolling over the body in the process – the last gasp of expelled air from the collapsed lung faded to nothingness. Darby took a moment to control his elation and get back to the business at hand. Feeling sorrow and respect for a vanquished foe was the stuff of second-rate literature and hare-brained movies, penned by authors and screenwriters who had never been in combat. In real life, a victorious soldier felt glad to be alive: glad that the body on the ground wasn't his.

In this moment of solitude and introspection, Darby felt relief rather than triumph.

He did not see bedding or belongings for more than four conquistadors, so they were all accounted for. He imitated the call of a hoot owl. Woody responded in kind.

Darby hollered, "All clear."

Chapter 24

Three of the foursome slept until midmorning.

After the nighttime activities, Darby thought that they should all get a few hours' sleep before starting up the pass, in order to be refreshed for the major offensive that lay ahead. Fatigue tended to reduce alertness, to abet mistakes.

He stoked the conquistadors' signal fire and added more wood. There was no need to have two fires going, so he did not rekindle the cook fire.

In his mind, he replayed the sequence of events that followed the ambush. Darby dragged the bodies into the forest to the north, and left them there to replenish the soil. He bent and damaged the armor pieces to make them unwearable, then scattered them in the opposite direction. He gathered all the weapons: not because they needed them, but to deny them to the enemy.

Woody and Amber left their packs at the entrance to the pass. Darby made them carry swords on their way to the hangar in order to retrieve the crates of rifles. They soon returned with the burdened llama in tow: literally, because she didn't like being disturbed in the middle of the night. They removed the crates from her back, then let her wander on the end of her tether; she eventually settled down.

Darby stowed the captured weapons in the crates.

Maia returned without catching the surviving conquistador. He fled downhill and managed to circle back to the road, after which he dashed into the outpost where she lost him among the buildings, darkened pathways, and overgrown farm patches. She was angry with herself for letting him get away. Darby tried unsuccessfully to mollify her. She wanted to sweep the outpost and track him down. She reminded Darby that he was the one who told her that you never leave an enemy at your rear. Darby acknowledged the military maxim, but vetoed her wisdom nonetheless.

He surmised that the worst the survivor could do was to warn approaching conquistadors that their four-man garrison had been attacked and overrun – something that they would soon learn anyway when they reached the entrance to the pass and found the fires untended and the sentinels dead or missing. Darby allowed that the survivor was a loose cannon, but noted that he was without cannonballs and primer.

Darby didn't want to fall into the trap of complacency the way the conquistadors had done. He ordered guard duty: hour-and-a-half shifts. No one objected. He let the others choose the order, and accepted the one that remained: the last, as it turned out. They wanted him to be in charge of how long they were allowed to sleep. He let them snooze an extra hour, figuring that they were engaged in a long-term campaign and not a time-sensitive mission, so that sixty minutes plus or minus were irrelevant in the long run.

He spent his time in cooking food from the conquistadors' stores – and chowing down more than his share. He didn't have anything against a diet of fruit, but it was good to have meat and potatoes on the bill of fare. He boiled all the quinoa that he found in the newly confiscated rations: ate his fill, left sizeable portions for the others, and packaged the leftovers for the trail. Quinoa wasn't very tasty at room temperature, but it was filling and filled with energy.

Amber rustled, stretched, and yawned. She slid out from under Woody's arm without waking him. She joined Darby by the fire. She crouched on her knees by his side, and wasted no time in examining his injury by daylight. "You were lucky. I mean, not lucky, but lucki*er*, because it could have been worse."

"How's that?"

"The branch didn't break your nose."

"It feels like it did."

"I'm sure it does." She placed delicate fingers on either side of the bridge and gently – oh so gently – exerted minimal pressure.

Darby made a face but did not yell "ouch."

"The bone is intact. You must have had your head tilted back a bit when you ran into the branch. It hit your nose but slid upward so you took the brunt of the blow on the skull between the eyes."

"It that why it hurts there, too?"

Amber wet a cloth with water from her canteen, and wiped off specks of dried blood that she had missed earlier under the beam of her flashlight. "Yes. There's a gash between your eyebrows, and the inside of both eye sockets are purple. You'll be black and blue for a few days from bruising, and you might have a permanent mark. Call it a dueling scar."

"That tree's bark was worse than its bite."

Amber finished her ministrations. "Ooooh. You made a funny." She sat back and stretched her legs in front of her, picked up a bowl of meat mixed with quinoa, and started nibbling. "Seriously, though, it wasn't funny what you did last night. You and Maia. I mean, I know you did what had to be done. It's just . . . "

"I understand."

"Thanks. I mean, thanks for doing what you did."

Darby nodded silently.

"I couldn't have done it."

Woody joined them. Despite his exhilaration of the night before, after successfully scaling the cliff face, he was morose. The gratification of rock climbing was tempered by the reality of death and danger. He picked lackadaisically at a bowl of food.

Maia, the quintessential early riser, slept the longest. Considering her emotional involvement and output, she likely needed rest and recuperation the most. She ate voraciously, all the while grumbling about how she lost her quarry.

After brunch they packed their bedrolls and belongings, loaded the gun crates on the llama, and started marching uphill. Darby kept vigilant. Amber dogged his footsteps and followed suit. Woody made no attempt at banter. Moping Maia brought up the rear – except for the llama, which dawdled obstinately at the end of the leash in Maia's hand.

The switchback trail was easy-going due to the gradual incline. It measured two dozen feet in width, like the east-west roadway, and was paved with compacted dirt. No one got out of breath during the two thousand foot ascent. The most trying part of the trek was watching for (and avoiding) fresh llama dung.

A large clearing extended from the end of the topmost switchback. The centerpiece of the clearing was a huge block of black basalt that must have weighed at least ten tons. The four-sided monolith stood some twenty feet in height, and was intricately carved with lifelike sculptures, fine glyphs, and rows and columns of cabalistic symbols. What looked like a circular swimming pool stood alongside the monolith, adjacent to the road.

"It's a watering trough for llama trains," Maia explained. "It's dry now because the conquistadors don't ever do any maintenance. They just strip and burn. Originally the inhabitants of the outpost kept it filled with water from the river."

Amber stepped onto the stone slabs that surrounded the monolith, and walked all the way around the block of basalt. "Are these more storyboards like the ones you showed us before?"

"Yes." Maia read the inscriptions one by one. "This side is a creation story."

"You mean, like in Genesis?"

"Thematically, yes, but it's a fairytale intended for children – more in the vein of Mother Goose or Aesop's Fables. Although your archaeologists would undoubtedly claim that we believed in spontaneous generation – that is, if they could translate it correctly.

"The next side is a paean to a leader known as Katun, who won a war game with only a handful of followers who crept through a thorn thicket at night and counted coup on the opponent's leader as she slept in her tent – a masterstroke corresponding to a chess match in which a player checkmated the other player's queen in the first five moves without taking any pieces.

"The winner and his followers became, let's see, I

guess 'managers' is the closest word to describe their function, although bureaucrat or politician without the negative connotations would be better suited. They assumed administrative duties until the next war game. They also got to live in the royal suites, dress in fancy costumes, and wear the crown jewelry while they performed their executive responsibilities. They take their jobs quite seriously, although every winner was not necessarily a skilled or efficient manager.

"This one is a song. The symbols are music notes and tempo to keep the time. The lyrics . . . " After she scanned the hieroglyphics all the way to the end, her olive skin adopted a curious shade of red. "It's a bawdy song, for adults only."

Woody finally showed some spirit. "We're all adults here."

"I don't care. I'm not repeating what's written. It's too . . . that is, it describes normal behavior between sexually active partners, but . . . it's nothing that you haven't already done, I'm sure."

Amber was aghast. "Do they let kids read that kind of stuff? I mean, it's on the same signboard as the children's story."

"Children wouldn't understand all the words, or the concepts. But yes, our children are raised in an open-minded fashion, without keeping secrets about sex and procreation. I guess my problem is my puritanical Earth-'verse upbringing."

"Humph. Hanging out with too many prudes, you mean."

"Something like that. Now this one is a set of instructions for runners or messengers . . . Hmmnn. Now that's something I didn't know."

"What?"

"The roadway extends seven leagues south along the ridgeline before turning down the west side of the mountain and zigzagging to a sizeable breakdown that can accommodate a llama train. That means that they have to go another seven leagues north from the bottom of the range, because Teomotl lies directly across the mountain from Ubah-Cotl, on the river bank. But according to this, there's a shortcut that skirts the precipice along the edge of the river."

Darby realized the significance right away. "That means that we can steal a march on them. It'll take them two days to drag llamas along the ridgeline and back along the base to Teomotl, so maybe we can reach Teomotl ahead of them."

"What about the llama?" Woody interjected.

"What about it?" Amber wondered.

"Uh, can it make the descent? If this messenger trail is anything like the one across the swamp, or the part at the end where we had to climb an embedded ladder, the llama won't be able to make it."

Maia pondered his statement before replying. "Let's cross that bridge when we come to it. We can always lower the gun crates and leave her behind. You did pack the rope, didn't you?"

Woody jabbed a thumb over his shoulder. "I stuffed it into my pack, just in case."

"And I've got the prussic knots and the unused pitons," Amber added. "Just in case."

"Then let's go for it," Maia insisted. "If we have to, we can let Spitball go free. She'll be content to graze in the wild."

Woody raised his eyebrows. "Spitball?"

"I changed her name from Fluffball after she grew up and got into the habit of spitting." Maia was surrounded by questioning looks. "Didn't you know that my brother and I raised all the llamas in the conquistadors' llama train? They took them from us when they took the gun crates in the cave."

The light of comprehension flared up around her.

"So that's how you knew she was female."

"Did you think I looked between her legs? No, don't answer that. I knew because I raised her from a kid. Now let's get started. The trailhead is behind that stele." She pointed to a stone signpost on the edge of the clearing. She grabbed Spitball's leash and led the way to the shortcut.

The ridgeline dipped gradually for the next half a league, losing some five hundred feet in elevation on its way to the river. The forest thinned near the end, then opened abruptly onto a broad rock outcrop that presented a grand view of both the river and the opposite cliff face.

Amber strode straight to the lip and hung the toes of her boots over the edge. She raised her arms horizontally to her side as if she were going to fly away like an eagle. She took a deep breath as she stared down at the water some fifteen hundred feet below.

The Cotl River was not anything like it was when the trio had waded across it on their first day in Lema-Rea, so many leagues upstream. An untold number of tributaries had swelled its volume until now it was a roaring cascade of whitewater that measured half a league across. Upriver, the high waterfall that Maia had mentioned stood as tall as a fifteen-story building. If the energy produced by the plummeting water could have been harnessed by a turbine, it could have generated enough electricity to power a small town.

Nor was that the only waterfall in the river's passage through the gap between mountain ranges. Smaller drops would have been a rafter's nightmare. The waterfalls differed from Niagara Falls in that the water flowed in thin streamers instead of in massive quantities.

Woody stood next to but one step behind Amber, with one leg stretched forward. Ordinarily he would have placed his hands on her hips and given her a fake shove, just to hear her scream and make her cuff the back of his head, but he was not in the mood for high-jinx.

Darby made one of his rare comments: "This view is worth the price of admission."

It was Maia's turn to nod silently. Yet her dark but glinting eyes gave away her enthrallment with the vista.

The llama hung back and chewed her cud, oblivious to the grandeur.

Despite the vertical distance, Darby could faintly hear the crashing waves in the ravine below. It was glorious moments like this that made him forget the strife and state of war that plagued the 'verse of Lema-Rea. As if he had been stung in the butt by a bee, he spun around in sudden fear that the enemy might be sneaking up on him while his attention had been diverted.

No conquistadors were in sight.

He allowed himself to take only fleeting glimpses of the remarkable cataract. He kept a tight grip on his rifle, and he kept glancing over his shoulder in case the enemy should appear at his back. He didn't need to remind himself that this was an active war zone; it was not a safeguarded tourist attraction.

If finally occurred to him that he was used to working as part of a unit in which each member was responsible for a particular quadrant; in which each member was assigned a specific task, and paid strict attention to carrying it out. He was not used to being on his own, in charge of a group of civvies.

Maia finally broke the spell. "Let's go, folks. We'll still have the river in view partway down the mountain."

She led the llama along the rock shelves, each one a foot or two lower than the preceding one. It was like walking down a grand staircase on the north rim of the Grand Canyon. The trio tagged along with Darby bringing up the rear. They lost another few hundred feet in elevation – with the river in sight all the while – before Maia turned away from the gap at a stone cairn.

No trail was visible on the exposed rock. The correct way ahead was open to interpretation. The sun stood directly overhead. Quartz intrusions in flat slabs of conglomerate reflected pinpoints of light from a bright blue sky that was dotted with white puffy clouds. An opening between shrubs made itself evident as they approached the nearby tree line. A dirt path under a canopy of intertwined branches curved away from the river. A secondary escarpment stretched westward, perpendicular to the river.

They plodded out of the forest onto more bare rock that extended to the edge of a west-facing precipice. An expansive plain of rolling countryside stretched dozens of leagues to the horizon. To the north, the Cotl River burst from the gap in a raging torrent that flowed and splashed its way to an incredible cityplex that measured many leagues in diameter.

The checkerboard layout included dozens of ziggurats that were spaced evenly among squares that contained living quarters, orchards, corrals, and farm fields. Had it not been for the distinctive style of the stepped pyramids, the scene could have been representative of scores of such rural communities found in the Earth-'verse along the Appalachian Mountains.

The ziggurats were different from any that Darby had seen so far. The two staircases that were in view from this angle shimmered like quicksilver, both treads and risers. The rest of the structure – the stone façade, the uppermost platform, and the topmost edifice – shone like polished brass. Darby was spellbound, and nearly blinded by the reflection.

Maia's voice was filled with admiration. "The steps of the ziggurats are coated with silver-alloy. The rest is plated with pure gold. The city that we call Teomotl, the conquistadors call El Dorado."

Chapter　25

"The fabled City of Gold," Amber breathed.

"Not fabled, just misplaced." Even Maia was in awe of the grandeur of the city, despite the fact that she had learned all about it from her homeschool studies, and knew what to expect. Seeing was better than being told. "The conquistadors who chased my people through portals sent word to their compatriots in your 'verse about the existence of Lema-Rean cities that were made of gold. The message got garbled, and the portals were closed, so the conquistadors in your 'verse were led to believe that riches and great treasure were to be found in the highlands to the west. That's how the search for El Dorado got started. Other fabled cities, such a Cibola and Vilcabamba, are also real and exist in Lema-Rea, although they lie much farther west, and we have different names for them. Cibola lies on a northern latitude. Vilcabamba on a southern latitude.

"Wow!" Woody threw his arms around Amber as he gazed at the spectacular scenery. "A city of gold. Real gold. This is unbelievable."

Maia explained the city's defenses. "From here you can see how Teomotl was built on an oxbow of the Cotl River." She pointed with her finger. "The river turns sharply northward after passing through the gap, then makes a huge semicircle and swings southward. The city was built in that three-sided enclosure. After the conquistadors invaded our 'verse, the inhabitants dug a channel across the place where the horns of the oxbow were nearly pinched together. That diverted some of the water and created an island. The amount of water was regulated by the depth of the channel. Over there you can see where a drawbridge would span the canal. You can see the abutments. Like all Lema-Rean cities, Teomotl is self-contained and self-sufficient. The inhabitants raise ducks for eggs, bison for beef, llamas for their soft woolly fiber, and so on. They grow enough crops to feed everyone, enough cotton to clothe everyone, and there's an endless supply of water for drinking and irrigation."

"Sounds more like Shangri-La."

"Although self-government with a touch of socialism can achieve a near Utopian society, no social order can ever attain the ideal paradise because of vagaries in the human element. We have crime, greed, gluttony, indolence, and other base human vices, but not as much as you have in your 'verse, due largely to our upbringing. All except the worst offenders are punished by banishment or shunning, much like certain religious factions practice in your 'verse. It's usually effective. Most people don't want to live all alone in the wilderness, outside the protection of civilization, and without the creature comforts that society provides. Lema-Rea is very much an extended family community."

Woody humphed. "Like a global neighborhood watch?"

"Pretty much."

One part of Darby wanted to stop the senseless gawking and push on to the bottom of the mountain, to complete what he now perceived to be his mission. The other part wanted to gawk. So he gawked with the rest of them at the architectural conceit that was Teomotl: not an overgrown ruin or an archaeological site from past millennia, but a modern, maintained, living, breathing, thriving city. The word splendiferous came to mind, even though he wasn't quite sure what it meant, or even if it was a real word. It just seemed to fit.

He observed people walking about the broad plazas of polished stone, on peaceful and personal errands. He saw people carrying baskets, leading livestock, minding children, standing in small groups: going about everyday life as if war weren't a moat away. On the other side of the canal, he saw a squad of conquistadors loitering around a campfire as if it were an office water cooler. The dichotomy surprised him.

As fascinated as he was by the spotlessly clean, gold enameled Lema-Rean city, he found himself drawn away from it and studying the military situation that the bird's-eye view afforded: the weakest lines of defense, the best places for concealment, the choice directions for attack, the optimal retreats. In five minutes he laid out an entire plan of campaign.

There were two major flaws that Darby could see in the conquistadors' siege tactics. The first was that Teomotl, while not impregnable as a fortress, could not be forced to surrender for lack of food, water, or supplies. The other was that the present balance of power was maintained by dint of the conquistadors' inadequate armament against the inhabitants' superior manpower. The conquistadors were bound to lose any battle that was fought hand-to-hand, because their long-range weapons such as arquebuses and crossbows could not be loaded fast enough to prevent hordes of defenders from overrunning the attackers.

The conquistadors were more likely to starve than the Teomotlans.

As far as he could determine, the conquistadors' entire fighting force was concentrated at the landing of the drawbridge, with no sentinels patrolling elsewhere along the canal. Whether this was an act of arrogance or bravado, Darby couldn't know. He suspected that they were waiting for reinforcements to arrive with the stolen weaponry. If his self-appointed mission were to have any opportunity of success, it was paramount to take out the besiegers before their backup arrived, and to organize a retaliatory offensive with the Teomotlans using the rifles in the crates.

"It's time to go."

All three turned to look at him, but only Maia spoke. "You have a plan?"

"Yes."

"Then let's do it." She pulled on the leash and got the llama on the move.

Darby let Woody and Amber go next.

The narrow footpath descended diagonally across the mountain. Rhododendron grew so thick and close to the edges that the entangled foliage overhead created a tunnel. The crates on the llama's flanks kept snagging in the branches. Spitball finally got jammed between limbs that couldn't be sprung apart. Maia and Woody worked hard to back her up and detach the crates, then stand them upright behind the llama so that she could proceed along the pathway unhindered by her load.

Maia indicated the tump line that was secured to the upper end of each crate. "Looks like we'll have to carry them the rest of the way." She let her pack slip to the ground. "Woody, you're going to have to carry my pack."

Woody passed his lightweight pack to Amber. She slung it onto her shoulders on top of her own pack. Woody struggled with the tump line and shoulder straps of Maia's heavy makeshift pack, got them in place, but was unable to stand up under the weight. Maia helped to pull him upright until his knees locked in place, then sent him on his way. Woody used both hands to grapple with rhododendron limbs for additional support. He gulped air and stumbled under the weight, but he didn't complain.

Amber encouraged him. "You can do it, Woody. You can do it."

Maia ducked under the tump line of one of the crates, positioned it comfortably on her broad forehead, leaned forward so as to lift the crate off the ground, and started walking.

Darby reversed the position of his pack straps in order to carry his knapsack on his chest instead of on his back. Then he followed Maia's procedure for lifting the heavy gun crate. He could walk with the crate but not comfortably, and probably not for very long. He wondered how a person like Maia, who lacked his bulk and musculature, could carry the weight as easily as she appeared to be doing. Worse, her short stature forced her to hunch forward so the bottom of the crate didn't drag on the ground. Darby was tall enough so that the length of the crate did not present a problem.

The foursome trudged along under bulky loads. Led by Amber, the llama outpaced them.

The trek was made worse by errant rhododendron

branches that snagged the corners of the crates. More than once Darby was jerked to a halt, whereupon he had to step back and free the crate from entanglement before proceeding. Several times he was knocked completely off balance. The only reason he didn't fall to the ground was the confinement: he ricocheted off the thicket on the opposite side of the path.

Eventually they emerged from the tunnel into open forest, thence to bare rock with an overview of Teomotl. They stopped at the edge of a precipice that stood a hundred feet or so above the plain.

Woody was ready to collapse. He started to lower Maia's pack, but as soon as he stood upright and bent his knees, the lack of a cantilever yanked him backward. The pack thumped to the ground, and Woody slid gracelessly after it.

Amber shrugged off the packs she was carrying, and knelt by his side. "Good job, Woody. Good job."

Maia shrugged off her crate. She seemed not to notice the loss of weight. "Now what?"

Darby was grateful for the relief of lowering the crate to the ground. After he caught his breath, he looked over the edge and saw that hollows had been gouged out of the rock wall to form rungs, or footholds and handgrips. "Now we lower the crates with the rope."

Maia pulled the cord out of Woody's pack, tied one end to a convenient tree, and tossed the other end over the cliff to check that it was long enough to reach the bottom. "I'll climb down and untie them." She stepped over the edge and scampered like a monkey down the vertical face. "All clear!"

Darby pulled up the rope. He ran it around another tree to make a binding loop. He tied the nether end to the tump line of one crate, pushed it to the edge of the cliff. Seeing that Woody was still winded and too pooped to move: "Amber, give the crate a shove."

She complied, although she grunted with the effort.

The rope snapped taut but the crate didn't fall because Darby belayed the rope where it was wound around the tree. He released some tension. The friction of the rope on the bole enabled him to control of the rate of descent. If he needed to rest his arm muscles, he bent the rope over the loop so that it bound on itself.

In this manner Darby lowered the crate until he heard Maia yelled, "I've got it!"

He lowered the second crate just as easily.

"What about Spitball?" Amber wanted to know.

"She's next."

"What?"

Darby proceeded to tie the rope around the llama's breast and hindquarters, improvising a sling that would keep her body on an even keel. She protested by gargling deep in her throat. Darby raised his hand to the slapping position. Spitball eyed him darkly, but didn't spit.

"The tricky part is getting her over the edge."

Amber dug a red checkered handkerchief out of her pack. "How about if we put blinders on her?"

"Good idea. That should work."

Amber slipped the handkerchief over the animal's eyes and tied a knot under her jaw. "Unseeing is disbelieving."

It took both Woody and Amber to lift and carry and shove the llama's body over the edge. She weighed twice as much as a crate full of rifles and ammunition. She brayed and kicked her legs wildly in the air.

Darby bound the rope as tightly as he could, but still it slipped through his fingers. "I need help."

Amber and Woody gripped the cord behind him. Gradually they lowered the loudly braying llama. Her long neck twisted and turned as her woolly side scraped along the rock face. Finally the tension eased.

Maia called out, "Got her!"

Darby's fingers were too weak to untie the cord right away. He leaned against the tree for support and took a minute to catch his breath. As an excuse for not fiddling with the knots, Darby grasped the tree with one hand and peered over the edge to watch Maia petting and ruffling the woolly fiber on the llama's head and back, and baby-talking to her with a soothing voice. Spitball was not a happy llama.

Darby eyed Wood and Amber, who were crouched on their hands and knees, breathing hard. He untied the improvised tackle and let it drop to the ground next to Maia. "Thanks for the help. I couldn't have done it alone."

They glanced up at him glassy-eyed, but neither one responded.

After they were all rested, Amber and Woody donned their knapsacks, and Darby donned Maia's jury-rigged blanket pack. In that order they climbed down the cut-out ladder. By the time they reached the bottom, Maia had the crates loaded on the llama and was raring to go. It was half a league through open forest to the draw-bridge. They marched silently, on full alert for roaming conquistadors.

They all stopped instinctively when they heard a thrashing sound in the forest ahead. Everyone dropped to a crouch. Maia and Darby unslung their rifles and prepared to open fire as the crunching of vegetation moved tangentially to their direction of travel. Darby looked all around first, then aimed toward the approaching sound.

A horde of squealing cavies erupted into the open and scattered in all directions. Each wild guinea pig was the size of a small house cat. The reason for the stampede appeared a moment later.

"It's okay. It's harmless." Maia indicated the cause of the commotion. "But stay down until it passes." She touched Spitball behind the knees: the signal to sit. She sat.

"It's – it's a giant ground sloth," Amber whispered. "A Megatherium."

"Yeah!" said Woody, a bit louder. In a barely audible voice: "Are they dangerous?"

"Only to trees."

The sloth measured twenty feet from tip to tail. It lumbered on all fours until it reached an oak tree. Then it stood upright, grabbed a thick branch with its clawed forepaws, pulled the branch toward it cavernous mouth, and proceeded to denude the branch of leaves and twigs.

Bulging muscles rippled under dark brown fur.

Maia added, "Keep a low profile. They're not territorial but they don't like company."

The multi-ton carcass could squash them all by simply rolling over them. Darby kept his rifle trained, praying that he didn't have to use it on so magnificent a beast. Conquistadors he could kill without a qualm, but it would break his heart to hurt a prehistoric plant eater of such awesome stature.

Amber punched Woody lightly on the shoulder, and hissed, "Take a picture before it gets away."

"You've got a camera?" Maia gasped in wonderment. "I forgot."

"Yes, but it's buried in the bottom of my pack." Woody shrugged off the straps, fumbled with the tie-downs, dug through the accumulation of food and equipment, and triumphantly yanked out the miniature format camera. "Here it is!"

He fussed with it so long that Amber punched him on the shoulder again, harder this time. "What are you doing? Take the picture."

"I'm switching off the automatic flash." He glanced around at the surrounding forest. "It's dark in here, and I don't want the flash to startle it."

Amber pursed her lips in a pout. "Okay. You're right."

Woody took a snapshot while the sloth was still standing. The flash did not fire. "Got it." Then: "Another wild animal that didn't attack."

"I know it's boring for you, honey, but I like boring."

They perched quietly but anxiously for another five minutes before the sloth ambled on to another tree that needed pruning. After it strode out of sight, the foursome and the llama continued on their way toward the Teomotl drawbridge landing.

Maia snickered. "We have lots of animals that are extinct in your 'verse, but ironically we don't have lemurs."

Darby steered an unerring course through the forest. Half an hour later found them emerging from the tree line on a sloped plateau that overlooked the conquistador's campsite. He motioned for everyone to stand still. "Maia, tie off the llama. Let's grab extra rifles, magazines, and ammunition. Then I want everyone to lie down flat and low-crawl to that big log up ahead." He pointed with his finger.

In less than three minutes they were all in position, peering over the top of a fallen tree whose trunk measured a foot and a half in diameter. The conquistadors' encampment lay three hundred yards away. The drawbridge landing was in view another hundred yards beyond.

"What's that stench?" Amber turned up her nose and pinched his nostrils.

Darby noticed that the weed-covered ground was sprinkled with black, cigar-shaped objects. "I think they use this log as a sitting post. This is their latrine."

"Yuck!" Amber made a face that would have stopped a truck.

Woody moved away from a recent soft pile, and used a handful of leaves to shove dried-out turds under the log. "Don't they know how to dig a hole and bury it?"

"Sanitation isn't their strongpoint." Maia turned to Darby. "Now what's the plan?"

Darby rubbed his bearded chin between thumb and forefinger. "Well, the first thing is to get a headcount. I'm guessing around ten but I want to know exactly how many we're up against."

Woody grumbled, "That's like trying to count a flock of turkeys in a feeding frenzy."

Only one conquistador was wearing armor. Four foot soldiers sat on the ground in a circle (or a square), facing each other, and playing a kind of game that required tossing sticks in the middle of the group. The others perambulated on various errands: collecting wood, bailing water, stoking the fire, or simply moving about through brush or behind trees. One was working on the gate of an empty corral, perhaps in anticipation of the forthcoming llama train.

Because of their constant movement, and appearance or disappearance, it took ten minutes to obtain an accurate count: eleven. At least two or three were always out of sight.

"Now what?" Maia wanted to know. "We start shooting?"

"Now we wait."

"Wait? Wait for what?"

"For the most advantageous opportunity."

"I don't like it when you use big words. Why can't we just charge and open fire? We've got them outgunned."

Darby took a deep breath. "I can see three crossbows leaning against a log. I can't tell from here but I have to assume their loaded. At close range, a bolt from a crossbow is nearly as accurate as a bullet, and just as deadly. If we attack in the open, the first thing the bowmen will do is shoot their bolts. Then the arquebusiers will light their matches from the campfire. Now, at this distance, the low-velocity ball will probably fall short – they're not used for long-range combat – but it could ricochet off the ground and wound someone. If they charge, we'd have to shoot them all before the swordsmen reach us. Why take the risk?"

"Okay. So what does waiting do for us?"

"Well, now, don't take this the wrong way, but soldiers don't go blazing into a firefight like they do in the movies. In real life they don't engage the enemy unless they have numerical superiority or a tactical advantage – or at least think they do. They either make an advantage or they wait for one. Two against eleven is not to our advantage. So we wait."

"For what?" Maia practically shouted.

"Well – " Darby glanced up at the sun. "Right now they're moving around too much. Some of them are always under cover, even if only accidentally. What we've got here is not a full-scale battle with lots of support, but a skirmish that requires small unit tactics and subterfuge because we're outnumbered. So, we either wait till dark like we did last night, or we wait until they gather around the fire for a meal." He glanced at two men near the campfire: one adding wood, the other setting a kettle on a spit over the flames. "Sundown's in a couple of hours. My guess is they'll eat before bedtime."

Maia frowned. Waiting was not in her makeup.

Woody and Amber listened without comment.

So they waited . . . and waited . . . and waited.

Darby and Maia maintained a vigil. Amber and Woody fell asleep in each other's arms.

And still they waited.

As the sun dipped lower, one foot soldier added items to the kettle while another one stirred the concoction. The wanderers returned from their wandering. The squatters rose and moved about their bedrolls, gathering dinnerware and utensils. One foot soldier separated from the group, and dragged his feet up the hill toward the foursome.

Darby pulled Maia down by the shoulder. He placed a vertical finger in front of his lips. Soon they heard the rustling of boots through tall grass. The conquistador was untying the rope that held up his pantaloons when he stepped over the log – and gasped out loud when he saw Darby looking up at him.

Darby grabbed a fold of cloth at the conquistador's waist, yanked him forward, and pulled him to the ground on his belly. He threw a rabbit punch at the back of the soldier's neck, then slithered on top of him, grabbed both ears, and pressed the swarthy face into the dirt . . . and held it there until he stopped squirming . . . and breathing.

By the time Woody and Amber awoke to the commotion, the scuffle was over. They were aghast at the body in their midst.

"We're done waiting," Darby announced, in a soft voice that was devoid of any emotional overtone. "Woody, crawl over to my other side with your rifle and extra ammo. Amber, you stay by Maia's side. When our magazines are empty, we'll switch rifles and you'll load the spare magazines. Understood?"

They nodded silently. They were not eager to participate in the forthcoming shootout, but they were pragmatic enough to know that it was a necessary evil that had to be consummated.

When everyone lay in position, Darby raised himself
to his elbows so he could peer over the crusty log. He
rested the barrel on the crumbling bark, and studied the
situation. "The officer's armor won't stop a high-speed
bullet, so I'll take him out with the first shot. That'll
leave the foot soldiers without a leader."

"Suppose you miss?" Maia wanted to know.

"I won't miss at this range."

"How can you be so certain with an unsighted gun?"

"I sighted this rifle last night."

"How could you? You fired only one shot."

"Well, that's when I sighted it." After a questioning
glare from Maia, "I aimed for the heart. The bullet struck
high and to the right. I adjusted the sight accordingly."

"That was a moving target."

"So?"

Maia shook her head. "Okay. I guess you know what
you're doing."

Darby nodded. "Now, as soon as I open fire, you do
the same. I'll take the targets left of the officer, you take
the ones to the right. That way we won't both be shooting at the same target."

"Got it." Maia rested the barrel of her rifle next to
Darby's.

"If they start scattering like cockroaches after the
light is turned on, shoot the ones that are farthest from
the core."

"Got it."

"Move a little farther to the right, out of the way of
my expelled cartridges. They'll be hot and will burn if
they hit you."

Maia did as instructed. "You think of everything,
don't you?"

Darby shrugged. "I've done this before."

"I'll bet you have."

"And one more thing. Don't shoot at random into the
crowd. Choose a target and follow it until it goes down."
After a pause: "And another thing, that I know I already
said, but my instructor used to say that feelings are irrational. Emotion in a fight leads to unpredictable be-

havior. Maintain strict scientific detachment. Pretend you're at a firing range shooting clay pigeons, or at an arcade shooting gallery shooting a pellet gun at metal silhouettes."

Maia looked exasperated at first, then inhaled deeply. "You're right. I'm too keyed up. All I want to do is spray them with lead and mow them down like weeds." She inhaled deeply again. "I'll try to remember to track my target and squeeze the trigger slowly."

"Just stay calm. Stay calm."

"I will. I am. I'm calm." Once again she inhaled deeply.

Darby sighted his rifle but did not pull the trigger. Most of the conquistadors had settled around the campfire on upturned log stools. Three of them meandered on the outskirts of the bunch. The cook removed a stirring spoon from the kettle and placed it on the log bench behind him. He used a white ceramic bowl as a ladle. He served the officer first.

Darby held his pose for so long that Maia started squirming. "What are you waiting for?"

"I'm waiting for a frontal view." Darby glanced at her. "Patience, Maia. There's no hurry."

"Okay, okay. I get it. I'm being anxious again, afraid that the clay pigeons will fly the coop."

Darby sighted. And waited. And waited.

The officer started gulping down food. He gesticulated with his spoon. He turned to speak to a foot soldier . . .

. . . and Darby squeezed the trigger.

The report sounded like a crack of lightning. A split second later the officer was flung backwards off his stool. His arms flew up into the air, along with his bowl of stew. His body slammed against the ground, executed a backward somersault, and lay still in an obscene heap. The foot soldiers were startled out of their wits. Three of them looked toward the origin of the report; the others glanced around in bewilderment.

Maia's shot struck a conquistador in the shoulder, spun him around, and dashed him into the fire where he upset the kettle.

Darby's next shot caused a conquistador to fold over in the middle.

Maia wounded another one and kept on firing until the magazine was empty. She threw the rifle to Amber and grabbed the one that was proffered. Darby heard the ping that signified that Amber had ejected the magazine.

The remaining conquistadors scattered in random directions. Two of them ran toward the crossbows. Darby picked them off one by one: not always hitting the moving targets and not always killing with a single shot. After the ping he exchanged rifles with Woody. He took his time, aimed with precision, led moving targets, and took his toll on the enemy.

Maia emptied another magazine before Amber finished reloading the first one. Maia grabbed the rifle and the partially loaded magazine, slammed it into the well, cocked the bolt, and blasted away faster than she should.

Resistance ended abruptly. Two conquistadors fled into the forest. The rest were dead or dying. The entire action had taken less than a minute. Of the two that managed to get away, one was limping badly and the other was gripping his shoulder.

Maia beamed. "That was a turkey shoot!"

Darby was less enthusiastic. He slipped a full magazine into his rifle, and chambered a round. "Woody, Amber, would you saddle up the llama with the extra guns and magazines?" After receiving mechanical nods: "Meet us down there." He looked at Maia and cocked his head. "Let's go, but keep your eyes peeled."

Together they walked down the hillside toward the encampment. Darby strode silently and purposefully. Maia bounced like a rubber ball. She kept repeating, "That was a turkey shoot! That was a turkey shoot!"

Two conquistadors were twitching but unconscious. Darby ignored them. One leaned up onto an elbow and slithered on his side toward the crossbows; he was bleeding badly. Darby slammed the rifle butt against the side of his head. He didn't move after that. Darby peered into the forest where the escapees had vanished.

"They're wounded and they don't have weapons. If they don't die soon from blood loss, they'll die later from infection." To his companion in arms: "Good work, Maia. You did good."

She beamed even brighter. "Thanks. Thanks a lot." She threw an arm around his shoulders – awkwardly, as both of them were holding their rifles in their hands – and kissed him resoundingly on the cheek. "I – I – I couldn't have done that without you."

Amber and Woody joined them shortly. All four, plus the cud-chewing llama, proceeded to the drawbridge landing. Two hundred feet away, on the other side of the canal that served as a moat, a large crowd was gathering.

Woody intertwined his fingers with Amber's. "Now what?"

Chapter 26

"What now?" was a good question. Two hundred feet of racing whitewater separated the foursome from the city limits of Teomotl, some of whose citizens were gaping at them from the other side of the canal. Maia cupped her mouth and shouted. Several citizens also shouted. The noise of the rapids overpowered the loudest voice. Vocal communication was impossible under current conditions.

Standing waves that measured some two feet in height did not look inviting for anyone wishing to take a refreshing dip. Nonetheless, Darby made a suggestion: "If you write a note in Lema-Rean, I can swim it across the river and give it to a delegate, or someone in charge."

Maia looked at him in astonishment. "Are you crazy? You can't swim across this. Look at that current."

"Current has nothing to do with the ability to swim. People swim in the surf all the time."

"But you'll be swept away. You'll drown."

"It's true that I'll be swept away, but the speed of moving water doesn't cause drowning. All it means is that I'll reach the other bank somewhere downstream."

Woody: "He's right. His course over the water would describe a vector: one component being the speed and direction of the current, the other being the speed and direction of the swimmer. The resultant line of travel – the vector sum – would be the hypotenuse of a right triangle. Just like an airplane flying in a crosswind."

Amber agreed. "He's right. Woody got an A in high school physics."

Darby rubbed his temples. "Well, I don't know about physics but I can swim across rivers."

"Okay, okay. I'll take your word for it. But I still don't like it. It's dangerous. It's – I don't want anything to happen . . . " After a moment of strained silence: "Is there any way we could *shoot* a message over the canal, to let them know who we are? That we're not conquistadors?"

"Well – "

"What has gotten into those people?" Amber wondered.

"Yeah. They're pointing . . . " Woody looked upstream.

Darby saw a number of gaily-dressed people gesticulating wildly. He cursed himself for focusing his attention on a single objective and not maintaining peripheral vigilance, the way he had been trained to do. Under different circumstances, this kind of lapse could have been the cause of his death, or the death of his companions. Now he spotted a ragtag group of people approaching along his side of the canal. He instinctively unslung his rifle and assumed a firing position toward the perceived enemy.

They were too far distant to discern details. There might have been as many as a dozen people. It was difficult to count because they were walking in a line that he was seeing straight on. The leader was wearing armor.

"They sure are walking funny," Amber noted.

"I'll say." Woody squinted, and shaded his eyes with his hand. "Looks like a caterpillar the way they're shuffling.

"Okay, you two. Get behind the landing dock." Darby pushed Woody and Amber toward the downstream side of the stone abutment. "And watch our backs. Every once in a while I want you to look into the woods where those two wounded soldiers went. Maia, get behind the llama. We can use her for protection."

"What? I don't want her to get hurt!"

Darby was stunned into silence.

"Just because I slapped her for spitting doesn't mean that I don't love her. I told you that I raised her from a kid. She's – she's – "

He thought fast. "Okay. I didn't mean to use her as a shield. I just want to stand behind her so they don't, uh, recognize us . . . so they won't know right away that we aren't part of the llama train."

Now Maia was stunned for a moment. "Okay, okay.

That's a good idea." She patted Spitball on the back. "But if they start shooting . . . "

"We'll get her out of the way." Darby fell back on his training. He glanced across the canal to make sure that the Lema-Reans weren't taking offensive action against them. "Amber, Woody, keep an eye on the townsfolk, too."

There were too many unknowns and uncertain variables to suit him. They were effectively surrounded on all four sides: escapees to the south, locals to the west, conquistadors to the north, and a trail to the east that could erupt at any time with the llama train. "And watch the trail, too."

"Will do," Woody called out.

Darby trusted his brother. Now he could concentrate on the approaching war party. Some of the people were stumbling out of line, and they appeared to be taking unusually short steps. Darby suddenly remembered how his height had gotten him into trouble before – the bridge of his nose still throbbed – so he stooped behind the llama to the average height of a conquistador. It wouldn't be long before the improvised camouflage failed, and he and Maia were recognized as strangers. He kept his rifle trained over the llama's back. "I don't think they're all . . . "

The officer in front was armed only with a sword, and possibly with a knife that was too small to distinguish from a distance of two hundred yards. The foot soldier in the rear stepped slightly out of line. He was casually dangling a crossbow by his side. But the men in the middle . . .

"They're not soldiers, Darby. They're prisoners. They're slaves."

Darby nodded slowly. He could not disagree with her assessment. He could now see that the men in the middle of the line were shackled together: their legs were hobbled, and each man had a thick rope wound around his neck. Except for the first and last man in line, the neck rope was tied both to the man behind and the man ahead. They were barefoot and hatless, and nearly naked in tattered rags that hardly covered their privates. Their olive skin was covered with sores.

"Okay. Only the ones in front and the rear are conquistadors. The rest aren't armed."

Maia sighted along the barrel of her rifle.

"Don't fire yet," Darby warned in a modulated voice.

"You're not waiting to see the whites of their eyes, I hope?"

"No. I just want them to get closer – until they see through our disguise. We'll both aim for the crossbowman. The officer isn't a threat."

"Got it."

A hundred yards away, the lead conquistador called a halt by raising his hand and shouting something unintelligible. The prisoners bumped into each other like boxcars on a track when the locomotive makes an emergency stop. A staring contest ensued.

"I think he's made us. But don't worry – we have fire superiority."

"Darby, I'm concerned about Spitball. She might buck and throw off our aim when one of us fires."

"Good idea. Let's stand in front of her now that the jig is up. Keep your eye on the bowman. As soon as we have a clear shot . . . "

"You give the word."

The standoff continued. They could now perceive the expression on the officer's face: a frown of stupefaction, uncertainty, and caution, all blended together with stern indignity. He had no idea that he was outgunned. He turned sideways and called over his shoulder. The bowman stepped into the clear and lifted his crossbow . . .

"Get ready."

The crossbow barely reached his shoulder.

"Fire!"

Two shots rang out a split second apart. The muzzle flashes were followed an instant later by the bowman's body jerking abruptly backward. He hit the ground on his back, rolled partway over in a reverse summersault with his legs in the air, held the pose for a moment, then collapsed into a bundle.

"Follow me." Darby sidled sideways along the edge of the canal. "Do not – I repeat, do not – shoot the officer. We're too much in alignment with the prisoners. A near miss or a bullet that passes through the soft tissues of his body might hit the prisoners behind him."

"Got it."

They stopped fifty feet from the conquistador, perpendicular to the work party. Now they had a clear shot that would not endanger the prisoners.

"Talk to him, Maia. Tell him to drop his weapons."

Maia spoke in ancient Spanish. The officer responded in kind. His words were incomprehensible to Darby, but he could tell that they were harsh. The subsequent shouting match was much like the previous one, at the mutilation site. Conquistadors seemed never to back down or listen to reason. Maia matched him in decibels.

In aside, in English: "He's telling us to stand down or suffer the consequences."

There followed another heated exchange in Spanish. The conquistador drew his sword. He waved it threateningly. He shouted arrogantly. He stepped forward with his arm outstretched and the sword leading the way. He charged.

Two more shots rang out. Two bullets penetrated the breastplate and punched the conquistador backward. He crumpled to the ground like a ragdoll, and lay still.

"Stupid bastard," Maia cursed. "He said we didn't reload after we shot the bowman."

Darby humphed. "Yeah, he must have been thinking of arquebuses. He never heard of an old-style repeating rifle much less a semi-automatic." Darby turned his attention to the prisoners. "These guys are in pretty bad shape."

The sloe-eyed gaze that returned Darby's horrified stare spoke volumes. Tousled hair, wrinkled skin, sagging jowls, exposed ribs, emaciated abdomen, and spindly legs added a few more chapters. The man in front was hardly alive. He looked like a refugee from a Nazi concentration camp. He rocked on his feet like an inflatable shmoo toy that had lost most of its ballast sand.

Darby drew his survival knife, dropped to his knees, and slashed the hobble rope in two. The skin above the man's ankles was rubbed raw and bleeding. Carefully Darby sliced through the knots that tied the loops around the legs. He stood quickly and did the same with the coarse hemp that secured the prisoner to the one behind him. As soon as he did, the starving man collapsed like an unstrung marionette. Darby caught him in his arms, and lay him gently on the ground.

Maia was frozen by the sight. As soon as Darby took affirmative action, she shook her head to clear her numbed senses, detached the bayonet from her rifle, and went to work on freeing the other prisoners. There were nine of them. Their eyes were glazed like fired ceramic. The strong ones managed to bend their knees and sit; the weak ones buckled into a heap.

Woody and Amber joined the detail. Woody was stoic. Amber was in tears over the pathetic sight, yet she held her canteen to cracked and swollen lips as tears rolled down her cheeks. Her ponytail flew from side to side as she shook her head in disbelief that the conquistadors could treat people with such inhumanity.

"They need food," Darby announced. "Something they can eat without too much chewing."

Amber jumped to her feet. "We've got coconuts and oranges. They can drink the milk and suck on orange slices."

"Get them."

Woody helped Amber open packs and extract easily assimilated comestibles. Amber peeled oranges and distributed slices to the ex-prisoners. Woody hacked away with Darby's bayonet until he created a drinking hole in one of the coconuts. One by one, he held the coconut to infirm lips and let each man choke down a couple of mouthfuls of milk. When he reached the end of the straggling line, he started again from the beginning. When the coconut was empty, he cut open another one.

Darby and Maia severed the last of the binding

ropes. The men sat or lay listlessly. There wasn't much that could be done for raw tissue, where the rope fibers had abraded through the skin, or for the whiplike lacerations that adorned the backs of the mistreated slaves: they were lacking in medical supplies. They had to make due by brushing off the hordes of biting flies, dabbing the wounds with wet cloths, and washing away the blood.

Despite these constant ministrations, Darby glanced at his surroundings every once in a while, to make sure that no conquistadors were sneaking up on them. During one of these spot checks, he noticed that a multitude of townsfolk were shoving a huge wooden structure along the broad thoroughfare that led to the drawbridge landing on the other side of the canal. At first glance it reminded him of an ancient siege engine or catapult, except that he couldn't see anything that looked like a throwing arm.

The machine was being rolled on fat trimmed logs. After it passed over the last log in the row, men and women hefted the log onto their shoulders, rushed it past the machine, and placed it in front of the foremost log. In this manner the machine was hauled over the stone slabs that comprised the roadway to the west abutment, where a pair of stout wooden chocks prevented it from rolling into the canal.

After its forward motion was stopped, a wide gridiron platform was dragged off the top of the machine, stood on end at the edge of the landing, then tipped over and lowered by means of hemp ropes into the water. Legs of timber that also protruded upward prevented the platform from sinking.

Another, narrower platform was dragged off the stack of platforms, stood on end, then pushed and pulled along the first platform to the nether end. The legs that extended fore and aft prevented the platform from tipping in either direction as it was being propelled. Finally, a number of townsfolk wielding thick shaved tree limbs pushed the top of the upright platform until it overbalanced. The platform didn't topple or crash into the water because other townsfolk held it back by pulling on ropes that were secured to the top.

This process was repeated with ever-narrower platforms until eight of them stretched all the way across the canal to the eastern abutment. After the final section of bridgework was emplaced, townsfolk placed flat slabs of wood across the framework sections to create a smooth roadway.

Darby was astonished at how quickly the drawbridge was assembled and erected across the waterway. "The Seabees couldn't have done it better . . . or faster."

Townsfolk nimbly raced across the drawbridge, carrying colorful serapes that they lay on the ground next to the ex-prisoners. The serapes were used as litters. After a patient was helped onto a serape, stretcher bearers positioned themselves at each of the four corners. They stooped and grabbed a fistful of cloth, lifted the serape in unison, and hustled across the bridge into Teomotl.

Maia struck up a conversation with a handful of locals. They spoke in Lema-Rean. Amber and Woody held hands as the procession of invalids was hustled across the drawbridge. Darby kept his eyes peeled on the forest that bordered the cleared swath that stretched along the canal.

One of the wounded conquistadors straggled into the open, muttering in ancient Spanish and holding out one hand in evident supplication.

Maia broke away from her diplomatic duties. She spoke with the conquistador in his own language. She showed him mercy that he didn't deserve. She shot him in the head without torturing him first.

Chapter 27

What Darby mistook at first for chaos turned out to be coordinated activity. Lema-Reans dashed to and fro and back and forth like a colony of ants, yet on close inspection he was able to determine that they all seemed to know exactly where they were going and what they were doing, and went and did it. Turmoil and commotion were eventually resolved into a regulated pattern. He was amazed.

Spitball was led across the bridge by an experienced handler. A pair of elderly women urged Woody and Amber to follow them. They looked to Darby for guidance.

He shrugged and held out his hands, with palms turned upward and fingers spread wide. "Go ahead. You'll be safe in the city."

Somewhat in a daze, they acquiesced.

Darby turned his attention to Maia and to the men and women who surrounded her. They were all fairly short – about Maia's height – and dressed in brightly colored robes that reached down to their sandals. Each one took turns at speaking in what sounded to Darby like blather. He felt like an outsider except that whenever Maia mentioned his name – the only word that he recognized among the foreign jabber – the people glanced in his direction. He felt like a household pet whose head spun around whenever it heard its name, or the words "food" or "walk."

There were no wild gesticulations, shouting, or overlapping dialogue. Each person spoke softly, then calmly yielded the floor to another who wagged a hand or wiggled fingers overhead. Serious discussion continued for more than fifteen minutes.

Maia waved for Darby to join the palaver. Without preamble: "They have agreed to elect you to lead the defense of Teomotl. You can give orders to me, and I will translate them for the council. I am second in command."

"Wha – what?" Darby was dumbfounded. "You want me . . . ?"

"You're the most experienced warrior among us, and you're the expert in small unit action. The council members have won their management positions by winning competitions of stealth, but never against an armed and deadly enemy. They can win tournaments; you can win battles."

Darby nodded slowly. "Well, uh, okay. I guess I can do that." Exactly what "that" was he had no idea at the moment. He looked down at each council member in turn. Their faces expressed something between bewilderment and hope, perhaps with a touch of futility. "Uh, did you explain to them about the conquistadors capturing your weapons?"

"I did."

He thought hard. "Uh, did you find out how they've been holding off the conquistadors? I mean, how they've managed to keep them from, uh, crossing the canal?"

"Apparently it's been touch and go. The conquistadors have tried any number of times over the past hundred years to raft across the canal. They use arquebuses and crossbows to cover the landing party. The resistance fighters, few in number, have managed to beat them back every time by throwing rocks and spears, but there are usually a great number of casualties. About fifty years ago they starting using bows and arrows, practicing on targets and then shooting arrows at conquistadors from behind cover. That's why their camp is so far away from the canal."

Darby studied the low ramparts that the Lema-Reans had constructed along the inside bank of the canal. The wooden walls had been built piecemeal and pushed forward from the outskirts of the city: a simple but effective means of providing cover for the defenders. But against accurate semi-automatic weapons with plenty of ammunition . . .

Instantly a picture erupted in his mind. He thought he knew how the besiegers planned to overcome opposition. "Did you get any intel from the slaves?"

Maia spoke with the council members. "They said they were building longboats with high gunwales."

Darby nodded slowly. "That makes sense. They were building them upstream so they could row or paddle them across the canal and let the current bring them to the bridge landing. An onboard marine contingent would be armed with your weapons, and so would the conquistadors on the outside of the canal, to lay down a suppressing fire."

"So our guns are going to give them the advantage."

"Only if we let them." Darby kept thinking hard. "We've got to set up another ambush, and hold them off until the rest of your people – the ones who are gathering at your ranch – can get through the portal with more arms, ammo, and trained marksmen. Right now we can't beat all the conquistadors in Lema-Rea – we have to assume that they sent messengers to the other cities to organize a mass attack – but we can hold off the ones that are on the way from the portal. Then, by the time more conquistadors arrive from other cities in Lema-Rea, we may have our own reinforcements and additional armament."

"Okay, okay. So how do we start?"

Darby rubbed the whiskers on his chin. "Well, first we need to destroy their boats. No, first we need to send some scouts up the trail to warn us when the llama train is coming. Then we need to establish a perimeter to protect the landing – and to cover a retreat if that becomes necessary. Get that started!"

Maia issued instructions to the council members. They in turn darted across the bridge to gather personnel and to assign specific tasks. Darby kept thinking while Lema-Rean citizens rushed out of the city to do his bidding.

"I want the boats completely demolished and the timbers either thrown in the river or taken into the city. Station your most aggressive fighters at the conquistadors' campsite. Oh, and remove the bodies, and keep all the weapons, and their other belongings. Arm your resistance fighters with whatever weapons are in the crates, and give them a crash course in loading and firing. And send an armed party to look for the one that escaped."

After a long pause: "Oh, and another thing. It'll look suspicious when the llama train arrives and there's no sign of the soldiers who are supposed to be guarding the camp. So keep the fire stoked and the corral gate open. That may confuse them." After another long pause: "And let's have a group of people a hundred yards upstream, making noise and threatening gestures from behind the rampart. That may trick the conquistadors into thinking that all the bridge guards are up there."

The Lema-Reans hurried to carry out the orders that Darby issued and that Maia translated. Whenever Darby thought of another contingency, there was always a number of citizens hanging around to carry out his orders – without questioning his authority or the reason behind the orders. Word was rapidly disseminated that he was a first-class soldier whose every word was to be obeyed.

This was a new experience for Darby. He was used to taking orders, not giving them. As squad leader, then as platoon chief, he had often given orders; but they were usually orders that had been handed down from officers through the long chain of command.

SEAL teams did not operate autonomously. Their missions and special operations were prescribed by upper echelon personnel who were in charge of overall strategy: admirals, the Joint Chiefs of Staff, sometimes the President of the United States. Tactical control and deployment devolved upon field commanders. Strict rules of engagement had to be obeyed.

In action, collective discipline superseded individual conduct. Now on his own, Darby was finding it difficult to break free of the mold. There were no reliable, highly skilled team members he could trust for mutual support. Maia was dependable but she was also a wildcard – not that Darby would ever tell her the latter. She might take offense. All these thoughts and others continually flooded his mind as he struggled to take command of the situation, and think through backups and contingency plans.

"You know what's really ironic?" Maia inquired during a lull in the issuance of orders.

"What's that?"

"We have a traditional story that we tell our children, about a tall bearded warrior who appeared in Lema-Rea and led the people to freedom from the animals that controlled the world before the appearance of mankind. I don't think there's an equivalent legend in your 'verse. It's a fable that is intended to instill confidence in children, to demonstrate that they possess the ability to triumph over adversity as long as they are willing to work hard enough and suffer long enough to achieve a goal. Your being here makes you that living legend."

Darby was speechless.

"I realize now that I never could have done what you have done. I thought that with my martial arts training, target practice, gun familiarization, and so on, I could successfully lead an army of amateur mercenaries against an entrenched enemy, and free Lema-Rea from conquistadorian rule. I recognize now that hatred and aggression are not only useless attributes to take to the battlefield, but are actually counterproductive. You – you've made a great difference to me . . . and my people.

Darby nodded slowly. "Well, uh, we're a long way from winning. But I guess we're a little closer than we were a few days ago."

"Yes. We've managed to kill some conquistadors, steal back some guns, disrupt the llama train, free some slaves, and galvanize the resistance force to taking action. I'd call that more than a little."

She glanced around at the frenetic activity. Lema-Rean pacifists – those conscientious objectors who disapproved of wielding weapons because they were psychologically incapable of taking the life of a human being – were nonetheless energetically engaged in work details that supported the fighters among them: clearing lines of fire, building barricades, digging foxholes, and so on.

"Can you get me a whistle, or a trumpet, or some kind of noise-maker to use as a signaling device? To sound the alarm when the scouts give the word that the llama train is on the way, or, uh, to open fire."

Maia thought for a moment. "I know just the thing." She issued instructions in Lema-Rean to one of the runners who was standing by her side. To Darby: "I don't understand why you're having those holes dug right at the edge of the forest. Wouldn't it be simpler to place them in the clearing along the canal? One upstream and one downstream, to catch the conquistadors in a crossfire? Why all the extra work to clear lines of fire when you already have plenty of cleared space?"

"A number of reasons. For one thing, you never arrange a crossfire from opposite sides of an ambush site unless you're shooting from an elevated position. Otherwise, your soldiers might shoot each other. And in ground level firing, bullets can skip off the ground because of the flat trajectory, and travel twice as far.

"Sometimes a crossfire is arranged like a triangle, with ambushers positioned at both points of the base and the target at the apex. I've arranged your shooters only on one side because I'm afraid they'll swing their rifles around if the enemy spreads out. Even if I told them not to – uh, no slight against your people – they might do it anyway in the heat of battle." In aside, "That's why I had a breastwork erected on the landing – for us to hide behind – in case your shooters get overzealous and accidentally aim at conquistadors fleeing in our direction.

"For another thing, your shooters have never fired a rifle before. They're bound to be bad shots, so I want them close to the enemy where they're less likely to miss. That's why I gave instructions to make lids for the holes. They're not really foxholes; they're spider holes. When I give the word to sound the alarm, I want them to flip off the lids and enfilade the ranks."

Now it was Maia's turn to nod slowly. "Clever. Very clever."

"A broadside ambush is just SOP in some kinds of terrain, where you can't designate triangular fire. We did this once when we were dug into a sand dune and waiting for a convoy. Of course, we had machine guns and trained marksmen."

"So now what?"

"Now we wait."

"You're good at that, aren't you?"

"As my drill sergeant used to say, 'It never pays to jump the gun.'"

"How appropriate."

"Waiting for the right time to open fire is critically important."

"How long did you wait in the sand dune?"

"Three days."

"In the hot sun?"

Darby shrugged. "It was worth it. The ambush went off without a hitch. Nobody got hurt – I mean, none of our guys – and we completed our objective. Sometimes speed is important, but mostly timing is more important than speed. Take Osama bin Laden. That operation was in the planning stages for six months. Two SEAL teams were trained for the mission. They even built two full-scale replicas of bin Laden's compound to practice on. The entire operation was rehearsed, right down to how many minutes would be required for every element of the insertion, inspection, and extraction."

"Were you part of that operation?"

"SEAL team missions are classified."

"But you know if you were part of the operation or not."

Darby shrugged. "Names are never revealed." Then: "For security reasons."

Maia didn't pursue the point any farther. "So, how do you see this operation proceeding."

Darby studied the layout in front of him. "Well, there's not a lot more we can do. Everybody is in place. The area is cleared of nonessential personnel. Scouts have been deployed. Pretty much, all we can do now is wait for intel from the scouts, then warn the ambushers to duck into their spider holes and put on their lids, then let the enemy walk into the trap. The next phase of the operation is up to the enemy."

So they waited. For hours. And hours.

Food was brought and eaten. Naps were taken. Drinking water was distributed. Snacks were delivered.

And still Darby was alert. Fully alert. While Maia dozed.

The sun was a dull orange ball only one diameter above the horizon when a pair of agitated scouts came running down the trail. With long black braids bouncing over their shoulders, they reminded Darby of Amerindians on the warpath, except that they didn't whoop, didn't wear feathers, and didn't carry tomahawks. They gave new meaning to the submarine phrase "silent running."

They started chattering long before Maia was awake enough to comprehend their words. When she finally understood what they were saying, she issued instructions in Lema-Rean. They both ran across the bridge into the city. To Darby: "They just turned the last switchback. They'll be here in fifteen or twenty minutes. The sound alarm will be here in five."

"Good. The sun is at our back. The conquistadors will be looking right into it. Their eyes will be dilated so they won't be able to see too good. Your people shouting upstream will distract them. They'll be confused. And they won't be expecting an ambush – I hope. From what I've seen so far, they've held the upper hand for so long that they've gotten lazy. Complacent. Unsuspecting.

"My platoon leader had us experiment with TSA guards at airport security checkpoints. We travel in civvies so as not to attract attention. The guards are paid minimum wage, and their boring job has become routine. When they asked for ID, we showed them a library card instead of a driver's license. Their eyes passed over the card automatically without actually seeing it: a mechanical response that came from doing the same thing over and over – thousands of times a day, every day – and never seeing anything different. One third of us got through okay."

Darby laughed out loud. "After that we started call-ing the TSA the Transportation False Sense of Security Administration." Then he got serious. "But that doesn't mean I'm gonna relax my guard. There's always the un-expected."

"So I've noticed." Maia turned to a pair of messen-gers and issued instructions. To Darby: "The hullabaloo will commence when you wave your arm. The snipers will pop out of their holes and start shooting as soon as they hear the signal alarm, but not before."

"Good. I don't want them to go off half-cocked, as my drill sergeant used to say."

Darby heard the rustle of cloth on the bridge behind him. He turned to find two people approaching. The male wore a bright blue caftan that was tightened at the waist by a red belt with a glimmering gold buckle. The female wore an emerald green dress with twin cone-shaped bulges on her chest; a gold ornament in the shape of a skull caricature hung from her neck on a thick gold chain, and rested above her breastbone; a basketful of teased chestnut hair cascaded over her shoulders. He took them for a priest and priestess until he recognized their clean, tanned faces.

"Woody? Amber? What are you doing here?"

Woody opened his mouth but Amber spoke first. "Maia said that you needed an alarm."

"Well, yes. I do. But I didn't want *you* to bring it."

"I didn't bring it. I'm *it*."

Darby was at a loss.

Woody grinned. "Her famous scream. That's the alarm."

Now Darby understood, but he didn't like "it." "But, it isn't safe here. You should be – "

Amber interrupted. "We should be in our own 'verse writing reports for our high school projects, but we're not. We're here, in the middle of a war. And if we don't win this war, we'll never get back to our own 'verse to write those reports. We stood behind you on the last am-bush; we'll stand behind you on this one. And that's final!"

Woody added weakly, "You can say that again."

Darby knew when he was outmanned – outwomaned – outgunned. He still didn't like it. "Okay, you can stay. But you stay behind this barricade, and you don't raise your head under any circumstances."

"That's fair," Amber allowed.

"Yeah, that's fair."

Darby turned to the conniver, but Maia was staring intently up the trail. That made him realize that he should be doing the same. He peered around the left side of the breastwork; Maia was peering around the right.

A strained silence lasted for ten minutes before he spotted an armored conquistador rounding a slight curve in the trail. A few seconds later a foot soldier appeared with a laden llama in tow. Darby waited a full minute before waving to the Lema-Reans who were standing patiently upstream to start a commotion. They started.

The lead conquistador stopped in his tracks. The foot soldier bumped into him because he had been staring at the ground; sagging shoulders and a plodding gait suggested that he was exhausted after a long day on the trail. The officer swung at the soldier: a backhanded roundhouse that caught him below the ear. The soldier staggered but didn't fall. The llama reared when the leash jerked its head. The rope slipped from the herder's grip. The llama did a pirouette, then pranced into the woods where the snipers were hidden in their holes. The herder ran after it.

The officer shouted in ancient Spanish. He pointed to the wooden enclosure.

Maia whispered, "He's calling for the armed guard, and ordering the gauchos to put the llamas in the corral."

"Good. That will keep your pets out of the line of fire. And the herdsmen aren't armed so they won't be a threat." He glanced at Woody and Amber, who were hunkered down on the ground at his feet, next to the spare rifles that were already loaded. "Get ready, Amber."

She nodded.

The conquistador strode forward. Three crossbow-man rushed up from the rear, as did a pair of arque-busiers. The arquebusiers stuck their long matchsticks into the campfire, and used them to ignite the match next to the flash pan. All five men were, in modern parlance, "locked and loaded." The officer drew his sword as he called over his shoulder. They advanced as a body.

Eight herders led their charges into the wooden fence enclosure. As soon as the corral was out of the line of fire of the snipers in the spider holes, Darby turned to Maia: "Leave the guy with the sword till last." So they would not both start shooting at the same target: "I'll take out the crossbowmen. You go for the arquebusiers. And keep your elbow tucked to your side." Down at Amber: "Now."

Unlike a Hollywood soldier, who had to expose his entire body to the enemy before firing, Darby poked only his rifle and his eyeball around the side of the portable breastwork. He was trained to shoot left-handed when necessary.

Woody clamped his hands over his ears. Amber let out a scream that would have startled a wendigo. Darby fired. A split second later, Maia fired. Immediately afterward, like trap-door spiders, the Lema-Rean snipers flipped open their lids and discharged a barrage of various caliber bullets that tore through the bunched conquistadors like large gauge lead shot.

It was all over in five seconds. All six armed conquistadors lay dead on the ground, their bodies riddled with bullets. All chambers and magazines were empty. Gunpowder smoke wafted through the air like thin fog with the odor of victory. The noisy commotion ceased. Silence hung heavily like a calm after a squall . . .

. . . until the llamas in the corral started bleating.

Darby turned his attention to the corral. The unarmed herders were busily opening crates and yanking out weapons. Darby reached for a loaded rifle. Now he peered over the top of the breastwork, with his rifle resting on the uppermost plank. He held his fire but Maia did not. She took long and careful aim before pulling the trigger for a headshot. The skull of a herder exploded, spreading blood and brain matter like stewed tomatoes from a shattered tin can.

The Lema-Rean snipers fumbled with their weapons nearly as badly as the conquistadorian herders, all of them demonstrating panic and their unfamiliarity with loading mechanisms.

Darby looked sternly at Amber and Woody. "Don't move." His voice and expression carried a harshness that was uncommon in his personality. He slung one rifle over his shoulder and carried another one in his hand. He calmly stepped around the breastwork and, despite Maia's continuing fire and ongoing killing spree, walked toward the corral. The only herder that Darby shot was the one who pointed a rifle at him. Darby doubted that it was loaded, but he could not afford to take a chance that it was.

By this time the llamas, frightened by the reverberating clamor of gunshots and crying herders, had battered down the split rails between two posts of the log fence, and were escaping into the woods. Three herders sprinted after them, or rather, behind them: their random scatter made it seem to Darby that they were more intent on escaping the massacre in the stockade than catching their erstwhile charges. He let them go.

The remaining herders – those Maia had so far failed to slay – stood unmoving with their arms dangling by their sides. In their life's experience, and lack of a television upbringing, raising hands to denote surrender was not an automatic response. They cowered in a clot as if their lives were already forfeit . . .

. . . which would have been the case had Darby not intersected Maia's line of fire, and waved his rifle over his head as a signal for her to cease firing. Now the only thing remaining to do was to round up the stampeding llamas and the unarmed conquistadors.

There were no more surprises.

Chapter 28

Darby was more at ease on the battlefield than he was on parade.

He and Maia led a colorful entourage that would have put the Mummers to shame. Although he didn't care for showing off, Maia kept grabbing his hand and raising it overhead like a pair of defeating politicians. Woody and Amber – having bathed and dressed in clean local attire – marched proudly behind the triumphant pair (who were still wearing week-long dirty duds, and whose faces were splotched with grit and grime).

Then came the members of the resistance force: those few individuals who had participated in the ambuscade and who had created the diversion.

The surviving conquistadors straggled along in ragtag fashion: dejected prisoners of war whose fate was yet uncertain in a land that practiced shunning instead of imprisonment or execution. Bringing up the rear were two female wardens who were equipped with obsidian-tipped ornamental spears that they kept perilously close to the butts of the rearmost conquistadors, lest they attempt to escape or by misbehavior disrespect the august procession.

Rounding up the missing conquistadors was still in progress.

Every time Darby tried to lower his arm, Maia forced it upright. "Lighten up, Darby. We've just broken a hundred-year siege. You have to expect the people to show their gratitude."

"Yeah, but the way the women keep throwing themselves at me, I feel like a contestant in a beauty pageant, or a dancer in a strip club."

"Don't worry. I'll protect you. And your virtue."

Darby raised his eyebrows.

"The mores in Lema-Rea are different from the mores that are promoted in America. There's nothing wrong with a little praise for the conquering hero."

"I didn't win a war. All I did was win a couple of skirmishes."

"I'll bet that's what Eisenhower told Roosevelt after D-Day."

Darby wondered if Maia was recalling history or hinting at a portent.

Amber patted Darby on the back. She had already hugged and kissed him any number of times. "You'll always be my champion, Darby. Along with Woody, of course." She pecked Woody on the cheek. "You're both my heroes."

The expression on Woody's face was inexplicable. "Home the conquering hero comes . . . I guess."

Darby stuttered. "Yeah, well, uh, I feel more like one of Dorothy's friends being driven through Oz."

"In Lema-Rea, you're a horse of a different color," Woody quipped.

Amber: "Maia, what did you say the councilors called Darby? The Bearded Paleface?"

"That's a close translation."

Teomotl was laid out much like Teotihuacan, outside Mexico City. By comparison, Teotihuacan was a builder's model or miniature. The outlying districts of Teomotl consisted of multistory adobe dwellings interspersed with haciendas, farmsteads, poultry pens, vineyards, plots of grain, groves of fruit trees, and so on: all thriving, immaculate, and well-manicured. There was plenty of grazing land for penned turkeys, llamas, alpacas, guanacos, deer, and bison; there were no useless lawns of grass.

Capybaras, the largest rodent in two 'verses, were raised as organic garbage disposals. Their sole source of food consisted of unwanted table scraps; their feces fertilized organic gardens.

Tens of thousands of inhabitants turned out to cheer the vanquishing of the besieging conquistadors, who had been harrowing Teomotl for hundreds of years in their endless quest for gold and riches at everyone else's expense. The roadway consisted of dirt that had been compacted to the consistency of kiln-dried mud by scores of generations of sandaled feet. The roadsides were thronged with gaily dressed men, women, and children who cheered the valiant victors like fans at a football game. Dogs of breeds that Darby didn't recognize barked or howled in consort.

When the warriors reached the urban perimeter, where adobe construction yielded to stone, the main thoroughfare that was equivalent to the Avenue of the Dead stretched onward for half a league to the town square, then onward for another half a league. The broad surface was paved with flat, oddly-shaped limestone blocks that were fitted together like pieces of a jigsaw puzzle, without mortar. The top of each cut stone was polished to a smooth finish that gave it the appearance of marble but without the slippery surface.

On either side, parallel lines of ziggurats seemed endless, touching each other in the distance like railroad tracks viewed in perspective. Pure gold façades graced the vertical walls of each ziggurat. The facings might have been blinding in sunlight, but in waning dusk the mirrorlike finish displayed the vivid brassy color without the warm glow and arresting reflection of gold.

The base of the shortest ziggurat stretched over most of an acre; it was stepped with seven plateaus, each one of which was utilitarian in that the outer facings consisted of windows that provided light for rooms that were reached from the interior: like a modern office building in the Earth-'verse. Three steep staircases consisted of hundreds of treads and risers. A square stone edifice with three doorways was inset on the flat-topped summit.

Each succeeding ziggurat towered one plateau higher than the previous one. Thus the ziggurats that bordered the main thoroughfare rose higher and higher, on bases that were greater and greater, until they reached two corners of the town square: a spacious open-air meeting place from which the thoroughfare continued on the opposite side with successively shorter ziggurats. The identical architectural scheme proceeded perpendicular to the east-west thoroughfare, with matching ziggurats extending from the square along an intersecting north-south thoroughfare, the whole layout forming a gigantic plus sign.

The town square was ringed by four ziggurats that measured more than three hundred feet in height. The immense town square was large enough to hold several stadiums or shopping malls. In fact, the vast open space in the middle of the four opposing ziggurats served as a bazaar or trading post. Tents and covered stalls offered meat, groceries, and manufactured goods of every imaginable kind, as well as items that were unrecognizable to Darby. The aisles between stalls were thronged with people who had closed shop or quit bartering in order to join the festivities.

Maia squeezed Darby's hand extra hard. "Just grin and bear it. At least you won't have to make a speech. No one would understand you."

Darby wasn't grinning, and it took all his fortitude to bear it. After most of his previous missions, he returned by landing on an aircraft carrier, where he and his teammates were debriefed in private by a few high-ranking officers on a need-to-know basis. Returning to base from a training mission was no different from going home from a nine-to-five job. Darby tried hard to take his own advice and not let emotion get in the way of upcoming events.

The crowd parted with smiles and cheers to let the procession approach the central stone platform, the outer facing of which was covered with multicolored murals that were carved in high relief. Half a dozen steps led to the top of the platform, thence up another half a dozen steps to a raised stone dais or podium in the middle of the platform. Council members motioned to them with sideways finger flaps that were meaningless to Darby, but not to Maia. She dragged Darby up to the dais, and waved for Woody and Amber to follow.

The scene reminded Darby of a televised media event in which designated speakers were surrounded by microphones and overzealous reporters. In place of high-fidelity electronic transmitters, the dais was outfitted with enormous megaphones or speaking trumpets. Lower down, between the corners of the platform, women wagging semaphores signaled to people who stood too far away to hear the amplified voices: to those who stood at the fringes of the town square, or who assembled on the tiers of ziggurats the way sports fans sat on bleachers.

Woody was again in the quipping mood. "This looks like an Olympics medal ceremony."

"All that's missing is the music," Amber added.

"And the pair of overlapping Ballantine beer signs."

"Since gold is so common in Lema-Rea, what kind of medals to they give out?"

"No medals," Maia whispered. "Usually the winners of a contest are given what you might call the key to the city. They become the next administrators."

Darby was aghast. "The last thing I want is to be a politician. Can't they just let us go with a commendation of some kind? Or an honorable discharge?"

Woody humphed. "Or an escort home."

Amber snickered. "Click your heels together three times. See if that works."

Maia was more serious. "Don't worry. This situation is unique. You three are foreigners from a different 'verse, and you're responsible for saving the city from enemy invasion. They'll give you anything you want. Personally, I would promote you to the status of military advisors in the coming war."

Darby nodded slowly, thoughtfully, silently.

The lead council member waved his hands overhead for quiet. The throng settled down with uncommon dispatch. The only sounds that Darby heard were the wail of hungry babies and the occasional bark of dogs. The council member gave a short oration, then let the other members take turns at speaking to the enthralled citizens. Speeches of council members and cheers from the crowd lasted for more than an hour. The only words that Darby understood were the names of the foursome.

Maia was asked to add her input at the end of the speech-making. Her tale of adventure resulted in multiple conversations with wonderstruck council members, all of which was broadcast to an eager audience that hung on every Lema-Rean word. She promised to tell the Earth-'verse trio what was said, but not until the revelries concluded.

When the final word was spoken on the dais, it seemed as if the thundering roar and clapping of the crowd would never end. When it did, it took half an hour for the multitude to disperse. Then the victorious heroes were ushered to one of the four corner ziggurats. Darby lost sight of the prisoners in the confusion and near darkness. Torches led the procession.

On the ground floor of the hollow ziggurat, Darby and Maia were led to a curing pond where they were invited to take a bath . . . together. They did. Amber and Woody had already taken a curing bath in a pool on the outskirts of town, so they sat on the sidelines and dangled their feet in the healing waters. A woman brought fresh outfits for the newly cleaned and healed. They dressed in the dim glow of electrified gold filaments that surrounded the room along the base of the walls.

The subsequent feast was held in an inner chamber that was the size of a ballroom. This large cavity was also illuminated by glowing gold filaments. Thick stone columns supported the corbeled floor above, aided in strategic places by stout stone columns. Flickering candles added a touch of romance to the dinner. The cutlery was made of pure gold.

An appetizer of llama cheese was followed by a spread of meats and vegetables that were spicy enough to burn down the building, even though it was constructed of granite blocks. Blander food consisted of maize tortillas, breads made from mandioca flour and tapioca flour, peanuts, cassava, and a variety of tubers such as potatoes and yams.

Dessert consisted of a number of confections, plus cakes that were made from fly eggs.

Most of the drinks were alcoholic. One was similar to mead; another was flavored with cacao bean extract. A particular intoxicating beverage went straight to

Darby's head. Maia explained that it was made from the leaves of a local plant. Official chewers first masticated the leaves, then expectorated the saliva-saturated concoction into a ceramic urn, where additives fermented the brew.

Some people inhaled tobacco smoke from a white ceramic jar that was passed around the room.

Maia spent much of the time in close communication with the council members. Afterward, when the lead member announced that they were going to repair to another chamber where the partying could begin, she begged off the gala event for the four of them, claiming with justification that they were exhausted after a week on the road, and after fighting for their lives in death-dealing tournaments against armed conquistadors. Without protest, they were escorted to the top of the ziggurat, to the summit edifice that was known in translation as a royal chamber for visiting dignitaries.

The four of them collapsed onto a room-sized pile of soft bedding: a kind of one-piece mattress that was stuffed with guanaco wool and that did double duty as a carpet. They removed their sandals and left them at the entryway. Cotton ticks or quilts that were filled with turkey down took the place of blankets.

"Five-star accommodations," Woody announced. "At last."

Amber bussed him on the cheek. "We can have some privacy after the candles are snuffed."

"Okay, you two. But please be quiet. Some of us want to sleep." Maia turned to Darby, who was already stretched out on the carpet/mattress with his head cradled on his arms. "You might all want to hear this."

Darby mumbled into the cloth, "Can't it wait till morning?"

"It can, but I think you'll want to hear what I've arranged."

Darby grunted. Amber and Woody postponed their mutual desire.

"Against my – my, uh – my feelings – for the three of you, I pleaded your case to the council – about your being here by accident and wanting to return to your own 'verse. They understood completely. I also explained how my group in the Earth-'verse is congregating at my ranch with more guns and ammunition, but that they might have to fight their way through the portal because the conquistadors are guarding it."

"With inferior weapons," Darby interjected. "But also in a defensible position."

"Acknowledged. Now here's the interesting part. You know that my group makes periodic checks on portal sites, waiting for a vortex to form. Checks are made from this side, too – not only by my people but also by the conquistadors. That's how they learned about the open portal so soon after my brother discovered it on your side. But Cotl Mountain has – or had – more than one portal. There's another cave higher up, near the summit – actually not a cave but a crevice with an overhang – which used to have a portal. Usually, when a cave comes into alignment to form a portal, it's because a shift in the tectonic plate has moved the earth under the mountain that encloses the cave – "

"And opens all the nearby portals," Woody finished.

"Precisely. So the chances are good that the back door is open. The problem is that my brother couldn't reach it. There's still too much snow and ice high on the mountain, from the unduly harsh winter, especially in shaded areas. The crevice is located in a difficult place to reach."

Darby forced himself to sit up, fascinated by the prospect of getting his brother and Amber back home. "So, what? You're thinking of waiting till summer when the snow melts in the heat?"

"No. I'm thinking of locating the portal from this side, then descending the mountain on your side, and attacking the conquistadors from the rear, so to speak."

"That's a good plan except that there's more snow on your side of the mountain than there is on ours."

"We've got cold weather garb, snowshoes, ice axes made from meteoric iron, and so on."

"But – but – " Woody screwed up his face. "But now

that the fighting's over with, I was hoping to see more of Teomotl. A lot more. I mean, we're safe now. We don't need to go back."

Amber agreed. "He's right. It would be a shame to come all this way, through all those ordeals, then turn back before we – I don't know – got to enjoy the fruits of our labor, if that doesn't sound to corny."

Maia could not withhold a gleaming smile, but it quickly dissolved into a visage of harshness. "I couldn't agree with you more. I've waited my whole life for this. I don't want to leave either, after striving so hard to get here. But there's more to consider than our personal wants. Than *my* personal wants. My people have waited for five hundred years for this moment. Teomotl isn't safe as long as conquistadors occupy Lema-Rea. They have to be eradicated like the vermin they are, before anyone is truly safe. And that means preparing a defense and counterattacking in force before their reinforcements arrive from distant parts of the continent. This war isn't over. It's just beginning."

She paused to let the information sink in. "Besides, once we rid the land of conquistadors, you – all of you – are welcome to visit here any time you please. The people of Lema-Rea don't necessarily want to remain isolated from your 'verse. Now that they know what it's like, what benefits you have, they might want to negotiate trade agreements. On a limited basis. The roles are now reversed. This time, your 'verse has more to offer ours than ours has to offer yours."

Amber humphed. "Oh, sure. We have a lot of things you don't have: dictatorships, oppression, slavery, Third World famine, religious fanatics, vice, corruption, fraud, murder, police brutality, income tax – just to name a few."

"I was thinking more in terms of your technology and medical science."

"You can't have one without the other. Others."

"We would have to have restrictions."

Darby: "The biggest restriction – or smallest restriction, depending on how you look at it – is a portal that's only big enough to let in one person at a time. Or one llama."

A sardonic grin spread across Maia's face. "I have a solution for that dilemma."

Woody waxed pragmatic. "You can't increase the size of the bottleneck because it would disrupt the balance of electromagnetic forces that created and sustain the portal. You told us that yourself."

"Very good, Woody. You remember well."

"Then how?"

"By creating an artificial portal."

The stunned silence that followed her pronouncement lasted fully ten seconds before Woody managed to squeak, "And how would you do that? Where would you get enough power?" After a pause: "It can't be done."

With a Cheshire cat grin: "It has already been done."

"When? Where? How?"

"Nikola Tesla did it at his Colorado Springs facility in 1899."

Woody's jaw dropped. "How – how is that possible? How . . . "

"Remember when I told you about Tesla's experiments with atmospheric electricity, artificial lightning, and phenomena related to extremely high-voltage magnetic induction?"

"Well, I remember some of it . . . "

"He made a lot of discoveries that he either didn't understand or didn't have time to pursue: high-frequency discharges, stationary waves, resonant frequencies, and so on. There is only so much that a person can do in one lifetime, especially with limited funds. Had Tesla worked a little harder on projects that were bound to produce money, instead of studying scientific curiosities that interested him but that couldn't ever show a profit, he would have been able to accomplish a lot more than he did. He was too much of a dreamer to think about practical applications.

"He recorded everything he did at Colorado Springs. He kept separate notebooks: some on interesting observations, some on avenues to pursue, some on unexplained phenomena. My people – that is, those who were trapped in your 'verse – learned of his electrical experiments and established a base in Colorado Springs so they could keep in touch with his work. Tesla was not a secretive person. He believed in sharing his discoveries with humanity. That made it easy for them to learn about his discovery of the underlying principle that created portals between 'verses."

A collective gasp resounded in the room.

Maia continued without missing a beat. "He accidentally created a tiny portal and kept it open long enough to send a small object through it. Unfortunately, the transient portal shunted so much high-voltage, high-frequency electricity through the ground that it burned out the dynamos in a nearby generating station, where he drew electricity for his experiments, causing a city-wide power outage. The political fallout and the cost to repair the damage forced him to discontinue follow-up experimentation."

Woody was quick to grasp the obvious. "Why didn't your people pay for the damage and fund his operation? A couple of gold nuggets would have kept him going and solved everything."

"Not everything. You have to understand that the energy required to open and sustain a portal is enormous. The energy field that he generated was only an inch or so in diameter, and it remained open for only part of a second. By chance, a fly got into the laboratory while a high-voltage discharge experiment was underway. Just as Tesla threw the switch to create a super-sized spark, the fly chanced to be in the spot where converging arcs created a transient portal. When the fly disappeared, Tesla thought that it had been 'volatilized,' as he phrased it.

"He repeated the experiment. This time he purposely dropped an object into the temporary spark ball. It was an Indian head penny that he happened to have in his pocket. The one-cent transference created such a large difference in potential between 'verses that it overloaded the system, melted the insulation in the windings of the dynamos, and fused the copper coils to a solid mass. His facility was destroyed. The energy field collapsed as soon as the power went out. At that time, there wasn't enough manmade electricity in the world to create a portal the size of the one in Lone Bat Grotto.

"Tesla didn't even know what he had done. To him the energy field looked like a short circuit: a minute globe of interfering electrons, like artificially induced ball lightning, which endured for a span of time that was slightly longer than instantaneous. When the copper coin vanished, he presumed that it too had been volatilized, or vaporized: melted into globules that exploded into particles that were too small to be seen, or felt. It never occurred to him – it *couldn't* have occurred to him – that it had been transferred to another 'verse.

"My people realized what must have happened when he spent that penny. They got hold of his notebooks and photographed them. It's a good thing they did, because some of those notebooks disappeared, or were lost. Yet they couldn't do anything with the information that Tesla hadn't already done. Not without a lot more power – power that didn't exist except when nature drew it through the earth. At that time there was no way to generate the amount of electrical energy that was needed to create a large-size portal and keep it open."

Woody jumped to the obvious conclusion. "And now there is. At least in our 'verse. Nuclear power."

"Precisely. And what's more, I now have the photographs of Tesla's notebooks. My people managed to smuggle them through a short-lived portal as it flickered on and off at the time of the San Francisco earthquake. The council wants me to take them back to your 'verse, along with enough gold to build our own nuclear generating station.

Amber was doubtful. "That's a pretty grand scheme."

"Yeah. And pretty impractical, too. Do you know how much licensing is required to get approval to build a nuclear reactor? The stack of paper would level a forest and reach from here to the moon."

"Woody's right. Not that I know that much about the

process, but if you read the papers, every time a utility company writes a proposal to build a nuclear power plant, it takes them years, maybe decades, to get approval. Sometimes never. You've got to deal with all kinds of extremists: obstinate politicians, rabid environmentalists, local homeowners who want to use electricity but don't want it generated in their neighborhood. I mean, if all the people who oppose nuclear energy quit using electricity, we wouldn't need more power plants – of any kind. But, like the consumer who wants to eat his cake and have it too, these lunatics want to use electricity but not have it generated."

"Amber's right. And those are just the fanatics. Then you have to contend with quasi-reasonable people: half a hundred regulatory agencies that are so concerned with safety that they go bonkers every time a construction worker or a power plant employee gets a hangnail or an ingrown toenail. I don't know why utility company executives don't die of frustration from having to deal with total irrationality. It's like grabbing smoke and – "

"Okay, okay. I get the point. You're preaching to the choir. Besides, I never said that the plant had to be built in the U.S. Regulations are more lenient in countries south of the border. Especially countries that would welcome low-cost electricity. My people own land in Central and South America, where industry standards are different and where democratic governments are more likely to serve the needs of the people instead of a blue-dotted toad or an inch-long ganoid fish or an uncommon species of orchid."

Woody grinned. "Now *that's* a horse of a different color."

After a while it seemed to Darby that the silence wasn't going to end. He ended it. "Well, you didn't spend all that time talking to the council without finding a way to execute this, uh, far-out plan. So what's the next step? Lead a llama train back to the mountain with saddlebags filled with gold dust, and a guerilla party to climb to the upper portal?"

"Yes and no." After an expectant pause: "Yes, a llama

train will depart first thing in the morning, and it will be guarded by resistance fighters armed with modern weapons. But it will take a week to reach Cotl Mountain. In the meantime we – the four of us – will precede them to the mountain and knock out the conquistadorian sentries before their reinforcements arrive and enable them to strengthen their defenses."

"So what're we gonna do? Jog all the way with a handful of runners?"

"Better than that. We are going to ride on the wind."

Chapter 29

Maia swept her arm with a flourish. "Ta-*da*."

The inflation process had been working all morning. A trained ground crew operated rheostats that controlled the voltage of stored electricity.

"We'll have two accumulators in flight, but we're using four of them plus auxiliary radiators to inflate the gas bag in a hurry." She indicated a group of gold-alloy straws that stood vertically on a baseplate whose legs extended from the floor of the gondola into the throat of the gas bag. "The accumulators provide the electromotive force that is needed to excite the heat emitters to the point of incandescence. If the voltage is too low, the emitters don't reach full efficiency; too high, and the emitters soften and melt. The pilot has to adjust the output continuously as the ambient temperature changes. The proper balance of electrical potential is crucial to achieving the most economical heat exchange, and to maintaining the optimum operational altitude with regard to wind speed and direction.

"The envelope is coated with a thin veneer of pitch, or resin: a naturally occurring polymer that is produced by plants. Because black absorbs heat, the material captures energy from the sun and transfers it through the fabric to the air inside. This helps to maintain the internal temperature while conserving electricity."

Woody shook his head. "Solar panels, no less."

"How do you know all this stuff?" Amber wanted to know. "You've only been here a day."

"Yeah. You sound as if you're reading out of a textbook."

Maia shrugged. "As I mentioned, my parents taught me everything I know. They had strict lesson plans for my brother and me. We spent our youth in preparing for emigration."

After thoughtful consideration: "Can you fly this thing, too?"

Maia inhaled deeply. "In theory, yes." She pursed her lips as she made eye contact with Darby. "But if there's one thing I've learned in the past few days, it's that you can acquire only so much knowledge from books and lesson plans. Sometimes formal training and practical experience are necessary instructors. That's why we'll have a skilled pilot do the flying."

Darby corrugated the skin on his forehead but remained silent.

Woody nodded in his brother's stead. "The same goes for riding a bike without training wheels. No matter how many instructional manuals you read, you'll never ride a two-wheeler the first time out."

Amber humphed. "Don't let the balloon get away from us. We don't have a good witch for backup."

"Don't you worry about that. My people have waited five hundred years for this moment." Maia indicated the four heavy-duty tie-down ropes that secured the throat ring of the hot-air balloon to thick metal eyebolts that were drilled into massive stone slabs that were positioned inside the walls of the roofless aerodrome. "It will take more than a bumbling wizard to let this opportunity get away from us."

Because the gondola was going to be crowded with five people – pilot, Maia acting as copilot, and three passengers – support personnel were stripping down the gondola to the bare minimum. Every other vine in the weave was removed.

"Other than homing pigeons, which can carry only short written messages, balloons were the primary means of communication among cities. They enabled messengers to carry scrolls and codices from one city to another. After invasion by the conquistadors, balloons became practically the only means of such communication. Running was oftentimes too dangerous. Isolated ground stations are spread throughout the land, and are relocated whenever their placements are compromised. City officials can be landed on the outskirts of besieged cities on the other side of the continent in order to discuss current events."

Her tutorial was interrupted by the arrival of a scarecrow of a woman whose head barely reached Maia's shoulder. She introduced the pilot. "This is Chan. Like jockeys, pilots are selected by their weight and size."

Chan smiled all around, then plucked a scroll from under her left arm. She unrolled the parchment and went into conference with Maia, while the others looked on in fascination. After much nodding and foreign language exchange, Chan bounded like a monkey over the top railing of the gondola. She fumbled with the onboard accumulators, checked the connections, and prepared to switch the cables after the external accumulators were disconnected and the supplementary heat producers were removed.

"She's doing preflight checks."

Woody was back in character. "Is she going to tell us to make sure our seatbelts are fastened and to put our seatbacks and tray tables in the upright and locked position?"

"Not likely. Her job is to handle the flight controls. The copilot is in charge of navigation. That's why she showed me the map. Runners don't need to be told what to do. They are actually part of the crew rather than untrained passengers."

"I've been trained," Woody quipped. "I know how to use the restroom."

Amber cuffed the back of his head. "Don't be a smart aleck."

Additional antics and repartee were forestalled by the arrival of the council members. Bloodshot eyes, uncombed hair, and wrinkled clothing attested to the previous night's revelries. They immediately engaged Maia in a spoken exchange that none of the threesome understood. It was obvious to Darby that erstwhile merriment had yielded to the sober duties of office.

By now the balloon was almost fully inflated. The gas bag was straining the mooring lines. The ground crew hefted wooden casks over the top railings of the gondola. The casks were filled with ballast water. If additional lift were needed to cross a mountain or to ascend into a favorable wind stream, small doses of water could be poured through the grated flooring. The casks were stowed in the corners so as to distribute their weight evenly.

Through the wickerwork sides Darby saw that Chan seemed satisfied with her systems checks. She fiddled with her stringy black hair, twisting strands around her index finger the way a little girl might do. She acknowledged Darby by staring at him with a smile, and by holding her hand over her head and wiggling her fingers in his direction. Darby returned the expression and the wave, though he felt silly in doing so.

Time passed. Discussions continued. Darby idled. Waiting patiently was part of his stock in trade. More time passed.

He didn't know that his brother and Amber had gone exploring until Woody ran into his line of sight, breathing hard and excited by the gleaming treasure that was cradled in his arms.

"Look at this crystal! Just look at it!"

The bright blue crystal was the size of a bazooka. From the way Woody held it, it must have been equally as heavy. Amber arrived a moment later with a handful of green crystals that were considerably smaller – about ruler length and thickness – plus a blob of yellowish substance that looked like melted plastic. All the crystals glimmered in the sun like refracting mirrors, shooting beams of colored light in the manner of a prism.

"I know we've got a weight limit but I just have to take this back with us. I *have* to. My science teacher will go wild over it."

"And I have *got* to take this back with me!" Amber lay the green crystals on the ground and, pushing Woody out of the way, proffered her prize in front of Darby's face. "Look at it. Look at it closely."

Wordless despite their enthusiasm, Darby focused his eyes on the yellow-orange blob that Amber held only inches from his nose. Inside the globule of amorphous material floated a small patterned object from which two flat iridescent discs and six hairy filaments extended.

"Is that a – is that a bug?"

Woody didn't seem to mind Amber's encroachment. "Give the man a cigar."

"It's an insect. This is my namesake. It's amber. With a complete prehistoric butterfly inside. In perfect condition."

When Darby scrutinized the insect, he saw that the purple discs were miniature wings.

"Well, it's not really a butterfly. It's an insect whose descendants evolved into butterflies. Isn't it awesome?"

Woody: "They have tons of these crystals. Some were so big that I couldn't even lift them. They grow them in the building next door. They have a whole roomful of maturation troughs that provide a homogenous environment to prevent discontinuities. They're in all stages of growth. They put seed crystals in an aqueous solution to start the nucleation process, then – after the crystal nuclei are soluted – they add solvents and mineralized nutrients to promote the size and direction of growth. They've got a regular factory going. This blue crystal is made from copper sulfate – "

"And you should see their amber collection. It's massive! They have a whole room made from yellow copal with insect inclusions, and a display cabinet made from perfectly clear blue amber that didn't bubble in the polymerization process – "

"Okay, okay, okay," Darby protested. "You're giving me a headache on top of the one I already have."

Amber's enthusiasm continued unabated. "And they have more gold than Fort Knox, but you knew that already. These people are phenomenal. And I don't mean because of what they possess, but because of what they *do* with what they possess. They *gave* us these samples without even asking – "

"And the symmetry of the parallel planes in the crystal lattice is perfect – "

"And there are hardly any occlusions – "

"And they have shops where they electroplate gold, and smelt copper, gold, silver, and platinum – "

"Okay! Okay. I get it." Darby rubbed his temples.

"Now let's just concentrate on what we have to do to get home. And, uh, you'll have to ask Maia whether we can handle the extra weight. We need to take guns and ammunition and stuff. So . . . "

Maia was suddenly standing by Darby's side. "You called?"

"Well, uh, Woody and Amber picked up a few trinkets and wanted to know what our weight restrictions are."

She raised her eyebrows at the size of Woody's crystal. "I think we can handle it. But in an emergency we might have to jettison some baggage – " She was interrupted by a profusion of thanks.

After they settled down, Woody got serious. "You know, Maia, I was wondering. Your people have a whole laboratory for manufacturing crystals. Do they – I mean crystals – do they have some kind of, uh, I don't know, special powers? Like healing, or transmuting negative energy, or maybe as power cells . . . "

Maia couldn't help but giggle. "I'm sorry, Woody. I don't mean to make fun of you, but crystal power is a pseudoscience that doesn't exist in our 'verse. Don't get me wrong. There are scientific uses for crystals: early radio, for instance, and our light refracting lamps, and piezoelectric effects. But crystals don't have magical or metaphysical properties. They don't attune themselves to your vibratory state. Especially so-called Lemurian crystals. The only spiritual effect that crystals have on your consciousness is the one that is inspired by your imagination."

"So, why do your people, uh, have so many of them?"

Maia opened her mouth to speak but before she could answer, Amber interrupted. "Your crystal growers act as if they venerate them, or worship them."

Maia nodded with a smile. "Yes, I can understand how you might get that impression. But really, what I've seen – and this comes as a surprise even to me – is that my people – that is, the people in this 'verse – attack every task with such intense dedication that it gives the appearance of veneration or worship. That's the way they are. Their devotion to duty is a standard work ethic."

Woody looked crestfallen. "Drat! I thought I was on to something. Like maybe your specially grown crystals were some kind of channeling devices that tapped into the energy grid that exists in the earth and charges your accumulators, and creates portals."

"Are you still thinking about the New Age movement, and ways to augment mental powers and lift heavy stones to build ziggurats?"

"Well, maybe so. I guess . . . ever since you told us about static electricity flowing through the ground . . . "

"Don't confuse new concepts of reality with fantasy fiction, like the cosmic forces and collapsing gas belts of James Churchward's Mu."

"Well, I – "

"I'm sorry to disappoint you, Woody, but Lema-Rean crystals are used primarily for decoration. Chemical additives produce a diversity of colors that beautify living quarters and work stations. In that respect, I suppose you could say that they have a calming effect that helps to soothe emotional stress – but no more than dyed curtains or patterned carpets or fancy wallpaper do in your 'verse.

"Crystals are also enjoyed for their tonal quality. Crystals of different lengths, thicknesses, and densities resonate at different frequencies. When struck lightly with a gold mallet, each crystal sounds a distinct tone: kind of like Chinese wind chimes. A cluster of nonuniform crystals can produce harmonic rings and melodies that people find pleasing – but again, no more soothing than Muzak in your 'verse."

"Great. Crystals as artwork and musical tuning forks. That sure puts them in perspective."

Maia shrugged. "Sorry."

A few minutes later, Maia received word from Chan that take-off was imminent. She pointed to the weather balloons that the ground crew had released; they were drifting eastward. Chan disconnected the extra heating elements. The ground crew wrapped thick padded cloths around the supplementary, still-hot tubes, and offloaded them the way a chef would use pot holders to remove baked goods from a convection oven. Chan then connected the onboard accumulators to the remaining pair of radiators.

"Darby, I wasn't paying attention. Did the guns get loaded?"

He nodded. "Four repeating rifles and extra clips and ammo. I picked the rifles by weight and reliability. Like you pick pilots. I saw the ground crew stow them in the gondola, along with our packs. I didn't even have to supervise."

"Good. The air is beginning to shift in direction. We should climb aboard."

Amber muttered, "Good advice, so we don't get left behind in case of a premature take-off."

Without ceremony they clambered over the top railing and into the basket. Woody and Amber brought their souvenirs. Like two pairs of boxers, they sat on the casks in opposing corners. Chan occupied the space inside the legs that held the baseplate for the gold-alloy straws that extended through the throat of the gas bag and into envelope. Thus a semblance of balance was achieved. The casks doubled as kneeling stools as Woody and Amber changed position so they could wave to the workers and council members who were standing by to see them start their journey. Darby twisted on his seat so he could peer over the railing as if it were the top rope in a boxing ring.

The ground crew hooked grapples to the eyelets at the ends of the mooring lines. A loud gong signaled for the simultaneous release of the ropes. With heavy-duty gold-alloy sledge hammers, four tenders each knocked the pin from a clevis with a drift pin punch. The strain on the ropes ceased instantly. The ropes contracted like rubber bands, bounced several times, then hung straight down from a socket that was secured to the throat ring.

The balloon lurched upward and yanked the gondola off the ground. The gondola swung for a moment until it settled straight down below the gas bag. The balloon then ascended slowly and smoothly, like an elevator car. Chan wasted no time in catching each grapple with a gaff, pulling it close, and hooking it over the adjacent railing.

When the gondola cleared the stone wall of the revetment, Darby was astonished to see that thousands of Lema-Reans thronged the streets and center square. Thousands more perched on the horizontal surfaces of the stepped pyramids as if they were benches on gigantic bleachers. The cheering multitude wiggled their fingers and waved their hands above their heads. Maia explained that the send-off drew a greater crowd than yesterday's arrival of the foursome because word had time to spread to the suburbs of Teocotl. People from the far reaches of the city were eager to catch a glimpse of the warriors they hoped would turn out to be their saviors.

As the balloon gained altitude, the gondola rose above the flat apexes of the four dominating ziggurats. The pure gold veneered surfaces shone like, well, like the polished gold that they were. The spectacle would have been blinding if the rays of the sun had not been striking the glistening exteriors at an angle of incidence that made the angle of reflection miss the eyes of the sightseers in the gondola by a narrow margin. Even so, the glare was phenomenally bright.

The westerly wind wafted the balloon eastward, toward distant Cotl Mountain, which housed the open portal that enabled transference between 'verses. From a height of a thousand feet, the intersecting highways and byways of Teomotl looked like the strands of a geometrically perfect spider web, displayed in three dimensions. In and around the town square, the varicolored clothing of the still-cheering inhabitants created brightly hued swatches amid golden dapples.

As the distance from Teomotl grew, the dynamic city center diminished in size in comparison to the patchwork design of the suburbs, where terra firma was interlaced with homesteads, ranches, farm fields, and groves of fruit trees that appeared lush with subtle shades of green and brown. Now the great golden city assumed the aspect of a diadem that stretched across a landscape that lay between flowing blue-green rivers.

Woody gasped a single word: "Oz!"

Amber nodded but was too awestruck to speak.

Tears rolled slowly down Maia's cheeks.

Darby felt a pang in his chest and a twinge course along his spine. He didn't know why.

The hot-air balloon described a vector as it rose and drifted eastward with a buffeting breeze. As the gondola swayed gently, one of Amber's green crystals slipped between the floorboards. She caught the others before they went the way of the first. She carefully placed the amber and the remaining crystals in her knapsack – which the Lema-Reans had laundered along with all her and all the others' clothing and equipment.

As the balloon drifted across the Chiruba Mountains, there was nothing more to do but sit back and enjoy the flight. All but Chan were mesmerized by the forested landscape that passed beneath them. The petite pilot stood by the controls but had little to occupy her attention. She reduced the output voltage a tad: enough to stop the balloon's ascent and to remain in a favorable wind stream. Occasionally she purged air by tugging on the vent cord.

Chan spoke a few words to Maia, who gave a single nod in reply. Darby fancied that she had just declared the Lema-Rean equivalent of "steady as she goes."

After a while, Maia unrolled the map and compared annotated features with the geography beneath them. The wind picked up speed, yet the land appeared to move in extreme slow motion. Darby watched the terrain as it passed under his eyes. The balloon was trending south of their intended eastward heading; he soon lost sight of the great Cotl River as it flowed north of a range of hills.

"Hey! Look at that," Amber shouted.

Woody jumped to her side of the gondola in order to see where her finger was pointing. The sudden shift in weight made the basket tilt. "Sorry."

Maia was unruffled. "It's okay to move around as long as you do it slowly."

"Sorry." Woody turned his attention back to the indicated ground features. He humphed. "It looks like a giant lizard. Or a salamander."

"But it's hundreds of feet long," Amber noted. "And look over there. That looks like a turtle, or a terrapin."

Darby didn't know a terrapin from a hatpin. He peered cautiously over the railing. He didn't need directions to spot the enormous geological figures that resembled familiar animals. A third one came into view: a clearly delineated and elongated fish, complete with a spiny dorsal fin and a pair of pelvic fins.

"Those aren't natural," Woody announced emphatically.

Maia joined the others at the railing. The basket angled more as a result of the additional weight, but the shrouds prevented it from tipping too far. "We call it aerial art, because it can be appreciated best from the air. Usually the designs are dug where the topography is flat and featureless, as an aid to navigation. But here, in clearings surrounded by forest, they're made for artistic expression."

"You mean, like those giant designs they have on the ground in South America?"

"The Nazca lines in Peru, yes. These are more distinctive because the ochre subsoil contrasts with the surrounding topsoil. Even without maintenance they last a long time."

"Quick, Woody, take a picture before we get away."

"I keep forgetting that you have a camera."

Woody rummaged through his pack. "Yes, but the battery is almost dead. I took a lot of pictures of crystals and amber and jade – "

"As I was saying back there before I was so *rudely* interrupted – " Amber spoke in mock anger. " – they have the most exquisite carvings in jade, all very detailed. Mostly mammals. From both 'verses. Mammoths and mastodons and saber-tooth tigers from here. Plus some others that don't exist in either 'verse, like dragons."

"We have dragons," Maia remarked matter-of-factly.

Amber's expression of shock was worth a thousand words, but Woody saved his battery power for more important images.

"They inhabit the western part of the continent; the part that overlaps Asia. They're about the size of your Komodo monitors – which we don't have, by the way – but they are longer and more slender, and they have top fins or sails – like the prehistoric Dimetrodon only smaller – which are used to dissipate heat: they live along the equatorial plane and range as far north and south as the Tropic of Cancer and the Tropic of Capricorn.

"Thousands of years ago, before what we call the Great Shift – which occurred along the western edge of the Ring of Fire – portals connected Lema-Rea with your ancient Oriental civilizations, which were far more cultured and advanced than those of your Tigris-Euphrates Valley. Although communication between our 'verses was sporadic, dragons often passed through portals because they liked to sleep in caves, where it was cool.

"Your Chinese idolized them. They kept them as royal pets. Our word for the species translates loosely as 'warm breath.' They're vegetarian, with peculiar stomach attributes. Some of the vegetation they consume is stored in a compartment in the stomach – much the way cattle store undigested food – where the contents are allowed to ferment. Gases that are generated during the metabolic process exceed body temperature – they're warm-blooded, like the dinosaurs from which they're descended – and are belched in order to relieve internal pressure.

"The transference of dragons ceased after closure of the western portals that resulted from the Great Shift. Members of the Chinese nobility were so possessive of their dragons that they kept them closely guarded. They were never shared, so they never bred. Soon the Chinese dragon population died out.

"By that time, the dragon had become so emblematic

in China that they were something of a national icon,
like your bald eagle. The Chinese embalmed the dragons' dead bodies, but as no more living dragons could
be found, the Chinese turned to reproducing the like-
ness by painting their images on canvas or ceramic, and
by the manufacture of symbolic representations such as
stone-cut reliefs, jade ornaments, woven fabrics, bronze
statues, and in modern parades, paper dragons on
floats. Thus was started a dragon cult in which the natural traits and disposition were enlarged and embel-
lished to create the friendly, slinky, fire-breathing
dragon that symbolizes China today.

"And that, my friends, is a little sketch of history that
took two 'verses to choreograph."

The resulting "Wows" sounded like an off-key duet.
Darby nodded silently. So enthralled were they by Maia's
account of pre-Saint-George dragons that Woody almost
failed to get his snapshots. A thought occurred to him
afterward.

He pressed the preview button, located the picture
he wanted, and handed the camera to Maia. "Can you
tell me what kind of mammoths they are? Or are they
mastodons?"

"Species. Not kind," Amber scoffed.

"Columbian. A whole family." After a moment of
study, "How do you – "

"Press this button," Woody indicated.

Maia scrolled. "These are great pictures, Woody.
You're a natural born photographer."

He put on his best "Ah, shucks" face.

Amber was more practical. "Do you think my biology
teacher will believe they're real?"

Maia kept scrolling. "I don't know. With the computer graphics that movie makers use nowadays, he
might think it's an outtake from an animated motion
picture."

She scowled. "I think so, too. Living mammoths are
too unbelievable to be believable."

"More unbelievable than that is trying to get your
teacher to accept a portal between 'verses: one that leads

to a place where mammals . . . " Maia's voice stopped abruptly. She sat frozen, with an expression of horror molded onto her face. Tears welled in her eyes and flowed down her cheeks in solid streams.

Darby snatched the camera out of her hands. He saw a tilted, poorly framed image of a conquistador standing over the crouched body of a man whose head was dangling by a thread of skin on the floor of a cave. He rolled his eyes at Woody.

Woody scrunched his face. He reached for the camera as if he were about to pet a viper. Amber stared over his shoulder.

"Maia, I . . . I'm sorry. I didn't mean . . . I mean, I didn't mean to take this picture. I was just trying to startle the conquistadors with the flash. To blind them . . . To give us time to get away . . . I didn't know what . . . "

Maia was anything but stoic. Tears dripped off her jawbone like water from a broken faucet. Then she started sobbing out loud. She tried to talk, to explain, but the only words that were intelligible, after a fashion, were, " . . . my . . . brother . . . "

Amber cried in sympathy.

Woody stashed the camera but the damage was done.

Chan spoke softly in Lema-Rean. Maia responded with a few syllables and wiggling fingers. Chan fell silent. She concentrated on piloting the balloon. Eventually, Maia unrolled the map, studied the terrain, exchanged a string of sentences with Chan, then sat morosely on her cask.

Hours passed. The voluntary hush was broken only by the sound of the wind as it twanged the shrouds.

Chapter 30

By the time Cotl Mountain hove into view, the sun had already sunk low in the sky. The blue firmament was still aglow, and light reflected brightly off scattered puffy clouds, but the rainforest that extended from the base of the mountain appeared dull and drab.

In one afternoon they had flown the distance that required a week of hiking.

By ascending and descending over and over, Chan had managed to find a wind stream that added a northerly component to the balloon's easterly heading, so that the balloon was pushed in a wide arc that brought it close to the cave that contained the open portal. Now she switched off the accumulators and allowed the gold-alloy rods to cool down, while at the same time she let hot air escape through the vent in the crown of the gas bag. There was no need to drop ballast.

The water casks were mostly full. The balloon had been made heavier by the accumulation of rain when it had passed through a squall. The additional water was evaporating slowly and adding lift. More than that, the updraft of the wind as it hit the mountain was carrying the balloon up the western face toward the summit.

Darby identified features on the mountain. This enabled him to pinpoint the entrance to the cave. Confirmation came in the form of a recognizable path in the melting snow. "Uh, oh."

Mountain landings were tricky because of the slope. Chan maintained her vigil on locating a suitable platform, but three other pairs of eyes followed his line of sight. Two conquistadors were staring up at the balloon. The distance between the gondola and the ledge outside the cave was only a couple of hundred feet. Both conquistadors raised weapons to shoulders.

"Get on top of the casks," Darby shouted. He yanked Chan out of the pilot's position beneath the baseplate of the radiators, lifted her bodily, and perched her on his lap as he fell back on top of his cask. He heard a report from below. A moment later a lead ball crashed through the wooden floor, ricocheted off the bottom of the baseplate, and came to rest on Amber's pack.

A second later, the bolt of a crossbow whooshed past the gondola and penetrated the gas bag below the waistband. A gush of air followed.

Chan disentangled herself from Darby's grasp. She fumbled with a canvas sack that was tied to one of the baseplate posts. She pulled out a yellow glob that measured a little larger than a softball. As she held it in one palm, she beat it with her other palm until it was flattened like a pancake. She ignored the expended bolt that fell through the throat of the gas bag. She let water from a ballast cask soak into the substance. Like a three-dimensional Frisbee player, she hurled the disc-shaped object up into the interior of the gas bag.

Maia explained anxiously, "It's an aerated resin that expands when wet and acts as a coagulant: a temporary patch until the fabric can be mended."

The whooshing sound of escaping air gradually reduced to a hiss. The balloon quickly drifted out of shooting range, and was scooting along the mountainside at a slow but even pace at a fairly constant elevation. Chan ignored the controls. She pulled one of the grapples off the railing in preparation for tossing it overboard. She watched, and she waited.

The distance between the gondola and the ground shortened: not because the balloon was descending but because it was drifting closer to the sloped mountainside.

Maia studied a map of the mountain: one that depicted the location of the caves. She spoke to Chan, who wiggled her fingers in reply. "The upper cave should be a little farther north. We'll try to land as close as possible. . . . Here it comes . . . "

Much of the rock on the upper slopes was bare of snow. In Darby's experience, this seeming incongruity in the amount of cover resulted from a number of disparate but contributing factors: tall summits stood higher than many storms that deposited precipitation on lower elevations; the upper atmosphere was thin so that the rays of the sun were more intense, causing fallen snow to either melt or sublime; the upper atmosphere was also comparatively dry, so the snow that fell on the upper slopes was powdery; the wind at high elevations was usually strong, so that much of the dry snow was blown away.

Darby saw nothing that looked like a cave entrance. When he thought about the small hole that led into Lone Bat Grotto, he could understand the reason.

Maia shouted a single syllable in Lema-Rean. Darby figured that it must have been the equivalent of "Now!"

Chan dropped the grapple. It hit the ground with a thud, scraped along naked rock, snagged, and pulled loose. A moment later it snagged again; and again it pulled loose. Chan dropped another grapple. Although neither grapple would stay snagged in the rock, the cumulative effect of dragging and snagging reduced the speed of the balloon to a crawl.

Darby yanked his leather caving gloves out of his pack. He pulled then on his hands, donned the pack, grabbed one of the grapple ropes, rolled over the railing, and slid down the rope the same way as he would descend from a helicopter. As soon as he reached the ground he snatched up a grapple, ran with it to an outcrop, and jammed one of the tines into a groove.

He yelled, "Come on down!"

The balloon stopped drifting. The gondola swung under the shrouds but quickly stabilized. Woody and Amber followed Darby's example. Maia used one of the other grapple ropes to lower the guns, ammunition, and supplies. Because she not experienced at rope work, she climbed down hand-under-hand. Chan lowered the last remaining grapple. Darby secured all grapples, not just by hooking their tines, but by tying two of them to a projecting rock.

The foursome donned jackets. Snowshoes and ice axes were unnecessary. In short order they were packed, armed, and ready to go. Woody's knapsack was unwieldy as a result of the long blue crystal that protruded from the top.

Maia shoved the mountain map into a pocket. "This way." She led the group along a ledge that angled downward about a thousand feet below the pointed summit. "You know that if the portal isn't open, we'll have to attack the conquistadors in the lower cave with a frontal assault."

Darby shrugged. "I'd rather sneak up on them from behind, but – we'll do what we have to do."

Drifts of snow lay beneath overhanging ledges, where it was shaded during daylight hours. There the footing was slippery but not treacherous. They stayed on bare rock as much as possible. Twice they had to climb down to a lower ledge, and once they had to climb up to a higher ledge. Then they shinnied down a chimney that ended at a dark hole.

"This is it."

Darby, Woody, and Amber donned helmets and headlamps. Maia shone one of their backup flashlights into the opening. She showed no trepidation at what they might, or might not, find. She boldly entered a tall but narrow tunnel that was shaped like a steeple. She didn't have to crouch or walk sideways. The others followed in her wake of darkness. Darby brought up the rear.

The air in the cave was cool and crisp. Condensation dripped from black dolomite.

"This is a solution cave," Woody whispered.

"I wonder if it's got critters."

"Stay focused, people. I don't mean to minimize the value of your senior projects, but we have larger concerns right now."

Woody agreed. "Yeah, like staying alive."

The cave penetrated some fifty feet into the mountain before it turned a sharp corner and changed dimensions: it grew as wide as a kitchen and shrank to the height of a cupboard. They waddled like ducks until the ceiling sloped high enough to permit Maia to stand. Darby had to crouch.

There was no doubt about which way to go when they encountered a Y-shaped fork. The left passage was big enough to drive a truck through. The right passage was the size of a phone booth; it emitted an eerie luminescent glow that was unmistakably the sign of an active portal.

A moment later the four of them crowded in front of a coruscating multi-colored film that blocked the passageway in one 'verse, but led to a passageway in another 'verse.

"Load a round and switch off your safeties." Darby didn't bother to mention his pet peeve: that on television and in movies the hero always waited until after he stepped through a doorway into unknown danger before arming his weapon. How stupid was that? He heard the satisfying clicks to signify that his suggestion had been taken, even by the two who didn't wish to shoot anyone.

Maia hesitated. "Did you see that?"

After several seconds: "What?"

"A flicker."

Darby was not immune to the mesmerizing effect of the portal's swirling chatoyance. He felt as if he were being drawn into a sheet of pietersite, or tiger's eye – semiprecious gemstones of which his mother had held an inordinate fondness – and swallowed whole. He closed his eyes and shook his head to break the grip on his mind.

"I saw it," Amber said in a low voice.

"What does it mean?" Woody wanted to know.

Maia reached toward the portal but did not touch the many-hued plane that separated 'verses. "It means that the portal hasn't stabilized yet."

The portal vanished even as she spoke. A split second later it reappeared. For the next five minutes she ticked off seconds subvocally. "The minimum period of persistence is half a minute. I suggest that we go through one at a time, immediately after a flicker. To be safe, the next person shouldn't go through until after the following flicker."

"I'll go first," Amber announced.

"*I'll* go first," Darby corrected. He didn't say why, but he held up his rifle as his reason. Because they didn't know what they might find on the other side, Darby didn't want someone who might hesitate to shoot.

Maia never took her eyes of the portal. "You take rearguard." She leaped . . . and was gone. Like Alice stepping through the mirror, her body vanished piecemeal as she vaulted through the plane of swirling colors.

A moment later she returned. "All clear." Then she was gone again.

After a stunned silence, Amber said, "I'll go next."

Woody placed a hand on her shoulder. "Wait for the flicker."

"I will."

Came the flicker. Amber stepped boldly through the portal.

Now Darby placed a hand on Woody's shoulder. "Wait for the flicker."

"You can say that again. But don't." The wait seemed interminably long. When the portal finally flickered, Woody stretched one foot behind the other, as if to get a jumping start. He held the position so long that Darby finally gripped his shoulder and held him back.

"Wait for the next flicker."

Woody took a deep breath. "Okay." After the next flicker, Woody stepped back, hesitated . . . hesitated . . . hesitated . . . and leaped.

Darby glanced over his shoulder. He was greeted by darkness. He turned his head and studied the convulsing colors of the portal. Tenuous streamers moved and merged and mingled. Bold but evanescent patterns suffused through diminishing gradients into adjacent patterns that both thickened and attenuated. Shades of green and blue and red and black and purple and . . .

The portal flickered. Darby inhaled, held his breath, and jumped . . . passed through an infinity of juxtaposed images and discordant modal tones and awkward tastes and creepy feather touches and munificent odors . . . and fell into Maia's arms. With a definite lack of romance, his rifle banged against hers.

"Better than the first time?"

Darby took another deep breath – a breath from his home 'verse. He nodded.

"It usually is."

Woody was jumping with excitement. "We don't know where we are yet."

"Maia wouldn't let us go on our own," Amber said.

Maia pursed her lips. "I think we should stick together. Just in case . . . "

Darby could not disagree. "Well, then, let's get going."

There were no dripstone formations in evidence, yet water dripped from the ceiling and plunked into puddles on the floor. Darby guessed that it was a function of warm outer air causing the cool inner moisture to condense. His LED beam led the way around a sharp bend and along a widening passage whose walls were thickly coated with ice that reflected the coruscating colors of the portal. Three LED's bobbed behind him. He didn't go more than fifty feet when the cabin-sized tunnel came to an abrupt end. The ceiling now consisted of ice instead of rock, and a solid bank of snow sealed the overhang's entrance from the outside world.

Maia strode past him and placed her ungloved hand on the white crystalline surface. It didn't yield or leave an impression. "This isn't entirely unexpected, but I was hoping . . . "

"We've got ice axes." Woody wasted no time in doffing his pack – carefully, so as not to break his giant crystal – and pulling out the Lema-Rean tool. Neither did he waste any time in chipping away at the compacted snow. After a few chops: "This will take a while."

The others lay their packs on the floor and leaned their rifles against the wall.

The pounding of the axe as it chipped against the icy facing echoed throughout the chamber. Woody chopped and chopped and chopped, and when he arm got tired, he switched the axe to his other hand and chopped some more. Amber chopped with her ice axe alongside the hole that Woody was making. The packed snow wasn't as hard as ice, but it was close. In some spots its consistency was almost glacial. By dint of hard work they made a sizeable hole over the course of fifteen minutes: as big around as a whiskey barrel but only half its length. Tunneling through the snow-filled barrier was, as Woody had said, going to take a while.

After two whiles, Woody and Amber had excavated a tunnel that was large enough to contain their bodies. Amber rested frequently.

"Did you hear that?" When no one acknowledged Amber's question, she squeezed Woody's ankle. "Honey, be quiet for a minute."

The sound of dripping water was constant, but Darby also heard something that sounded like rubbing corduroy. "I'll check it out." He didn't have to tell Woody and Amber to keep digging.

"I'll go with you," Maia added.

Solid sheets of ice reflected the eerie light of the portal around the bend in the overhang. Ripples in the ice distorted the image in the manner of curved mirrors in a funhouse.

Amber was only an arm's length behind him when he rounded the corner and smacked into a tiptoeing conquistador who was feeling his way through the darkness along the wall. Darby's light stabbed into dark brown eyes. The crossbow twanged, but the pull on the trigger was merely reflex, and the weapon wasn't aimed for attack. The accidental discharge shot the bolt sideways into volcanic rock. The bolt rebounded like a rubber ball. The distraction gave Darby a split second to shove the startled conquistador into the arquebusier behind him.

Darby followed the shove with a charge: not for the crossbowman who had already shot his bolt, but for the arquebusier who held a loaded weapon whose tiny flame wavered close to the flash pan. He knocked the barrel upward at the same instant that the arquebusier swung the stock like a pugil stick. The butt caught Darby on the shoulder, and the follow-through nipped him on the chin.

He fell sidelong against the wall. He banged his head against the rock but the helmet absorbed the blow. He pushed off the wall with one hand while reaching out for the conquistador with the other. He missed the conquistador completely because the latter stepped aside in order to make another swing with the barrel. This one struck Darby's outthrust arm.

As Darby pitched forward, he turned his falling motion into a twist and swung his other arm in a roundhouse that glanced off the conquistador's armor. He tucked in his shoulder and dived into a roll that carried him a body's length across the floor. Ordinarily he would have used the momentum to come up onto his knees, but he was off balance and his coordination faltered.

He hit the floor hard. The conquistador raised the arquebue and was about to slam the butt into Darby's head when he was suddenly propelled forward by Maia's karate kick to the lower back. The conquistador tripped over Darby. He managed to lift one foot and put it down on the floor before tumbling partway through the film of dazzling colors.

The portal flickered.

That portion of the conquistador that remained in the Earth-'verse collapsed awkwardly onto one knee, stayed in position for a moment, then toppled over backward. The body had been carved diagonally from the left collar bone to the right hip. Blood and internal organs spread over the floor. The same must have happened to the fragment that had transferred to the Lema-Rean-'verse: the head, right arm, and upper right torso. The cleavage was fatal to both parts.

Darby was momentarily shocked by the sight. It took a few seconds for him to gather his wits and realize that he was still engaged in hand-to-hand combat. When he turned his head, the beam of his headlamp illuminated the other conquistador. His chest was convulsing, his face was purpling, and his eyes were slowly closing.

"I hope he was the one who killed my brother." Maia's expression was anything but triumphant.

Blandly, she held up her knuckles. "I did what you said and went for the throat."

A clattering sound diverted his attention. Woody and Amber raced around the bend, rifles tucked to their sides and pointing forward. Amber gasped at the silent tableau. Woody's eyes expanded.

Darby climbed to his feet. To Maia: "Nice work."

"No emotion. Just action."

Darby nodded. He stared at her with an intensity that he always felt after a firefight: a feeling of exhilaration that came not from vanquishing an enemy, but from being alive; the recognition of personal mortality was followed by the glad realization that he had just avoided death. Yet . . . now his emotions were confused and complicated beyond the matter of mere survival. He felt . . . differently.

Maia's jaw was working in such a way that her cheek muscles bulged in and out. Darby sensed an inner turmoil. He spread his hands invitingly. Maia fell into his arms. Her body went limp but she clenched him like an exhausted prize fighter. Darby felt her tremble. She quickly brought the tremble under control, but did not push herself away.

Darby patted her back. He looked askance at Woody and Amber, who stood motionless. Amber tilted her head and raised her eyebrows, but did not say anything. Woody was straight-faced.

Finally the moment passed. Darby and Maia separated without the aid of a referee.

Maia inhaled deeply. "Well, if there were six of them guarding the portal, like there were in the picture, that's two down and four to go. So let's go get them."

Before Darby could say anything, Woody took center stage. "I think we're almost through."

"There's light coming through the glaze," Amber added.

Back at the hole, Woody stooped inside the excavation. He barely had enough room to swing the axe. Amber scuttled in behind him. She scooped out the ice chips as Woody knocked them free, and shoved them behind her. Darby and Maia got down on their knees and used their cupped hands to clear away the white debris that accumulated behind Amber.

A minute later Woody's axe punched through the last layer. "I'm through!" He crawled out of the narrow opening. "Back up, Amber, so I can widen the hole."

Woody took a hard swing that shattered the ice a foot away from the tunnel. With the loss of so much support, the entire wall of ice collapsed and nearly buried Amber as she scuttled backward into the overhang. Darby grabbed her by the armpits and dragged her out from under the chunky burden.

"I'm okay, Woody." Climbing to her feet: "Thanks, Darby."

"Pass out the packs and guns."

It was almost easier done than said. The hole in the ice curtain was nearly as large as the natural rock opening. A couple of minutes later they were all huddled together on a snow-free ledge that stood high on the mountain. Their backs were bathed in the reflected light of the portal.

"Humph," was Woody's comment.

"Yeah, like déjà vu," Amber added.

They were high on the western slope of the mountain. The rising sun had not yet peeped over the summit. A dense cloud cover hid the land below. The only visible features were those on the mountainside above the clouds. The ground around them was nearly devoid of snow cover.

Woody looked at his brother. "Well?"

Darby studied the terrain. He wasn't absolutely certain until he spotted the barest tip of a rocky peak a mile or two away. "This is definitely Mount Shasta. That dark speck poking through the clouds over there is Shastina."

Woody shouted "Hurray!" Amber breathed a sigh of relief.

"But I'm confused." Three faces registered surprise. "Oh, not about where we are on the mountain. About the time. The sun was setting when we left Lema-Rea, but here it's rising. Are you sure there isn't some kind of time difference between 'verses?"

Maia thought for a moment. "I can't give you an answer. My parents never mentioned it, and it's not cited in any of our records. But a lot can change in half a millennia. Our 'verses aren't identical, just similar. Temporal displacement might be one of the dissimilarities."

"Like different species surviving and evolving," Amber suggested.

"Precisely. And don't forget about dislocated continents. And the prevalence or scarcity of certain elements and minerals. And the birth of planetary bodies. Our 'verses resemble each other in many ways. But they are not much more different than Africa is from America. Taken as a whole, there are more congruities between 'verses than incongruities."

Darby nodded.

"So now what?"

"It's an easy descent. All downhill and hardly any snow to speak of. I know the way."

"Then what are we waiting for?" Amber asked exuberantly. "A yellow brick road?"

In less than an hour they stood beneath the clouds in front of the entrance to Lone Bat Grotto. Hesitation gripped the foursome. They had spent so much time in planning on how to reach this point that they hadn't planned on what to do after they got there. And in the few days that they had been together, they had shared experiences of such great intensity that they were all loathe to part.

For several minutes they milled like cattle.

Maia was the first to stop chewing her cud. "I guess – I guess this is the parting of the ways."

None of the others wanted to agree with her – or disagree. To Darby, her pronouncement sounded like another instance of déjà vu. There was more hesitation, more shuffling of feet.

Finally, Darby assumed the leadership role. "Look, we're not really separating. I mean, not for good. We're just going our own separate ways for a while. Taking different paths. We all have different things to do."

No one protested, or offered to comment.

"Woody, Amber, you have to finish your senior projects and graduate high school."

Both nodded glumly.

"And Maia, I know you can handle the other four conquistadors by yourself, but I'd feel better if you let me tag along."

"I – I would like that."

To Woody and Amber: "I mean, we're not really going away. We're just, uh, going through a gate on a short journey to another cave. Or to the other end of this cave. I mean, I know we're going to a totally different 'verse, but it's only on the other side of a gate. We can come back any time we want. And after we clear the way, you can go through any time *you* want."

The sky was gradually clearing. Most of the cloud layer dissipated. Yellow beams of sunlight stabbed the side of the mountain. High up the slope, the crevice with the flickering portal flared with coruscating brilliance as its light bounced off sheets of clear ice and erupted from the overhang like a multihued kaleidoscope. Visual evidence would vanish with the melting of the ice.

"And you can still help. You can help by – " He rummaged through his jacket pocket and brought out a crumpled business card. It was coated with dirt and grime but the printing was still legible. " – by getting in touch with Ted." He handed the card to his brother. "Hire his rig – "

"I can help with that." Maia doffed her new Lema-Rean knapsack. She removed a nugget the size of a golf ball. "I believe you said he was attracted to gold."

Amber brightened as she took the shiny globule. Her hand dropped and her eyes widened. "I didn't know it would be so heavy."

"There's more at the ranch if you need it. Some of my people should be there by now, waiting for me to give them instructions. You can bring them up to speed. Tell them what has happened so far. Tell them what needs to be done."

Woody showed enthusiasm. "Yeah, we can do that.

We can help after school and on weekends. And during the summer, before we start college."

"We can be intermediaries. Your people will want to go to Lema-Rea to get into the fight. So we can take over activities at the ranch, feed the llamas, organize shipments, and – I don't know – just take care of business."

"And we can look for other portals after your people leave. If these portals opened because of shifting tectonic plates, others might open up too. We'll scour the country for other caves – "

Maia interrupted. "Don't scour farther than Nevada or you'll reach Lema-Rea under water. You might drown if you get swept away before you can transfer back. And stay away from the eastern seaboard. Those portals lead to the 'verse of Atlantis."

"Atlantis!" Woody and Amber screamed at the same time.

"Remember the variverse: 'verses of endless variety? There are an infinite number of 'verses. The continent of Atlantis occupies your Atlantic Ocean and overlaps your east coast and the western fringes of Europe. That's how the ancients in your 'verse learned of its existence."

"Wow!"

Maia looked up at Darby. "Darby, like I said, I – I'd like for you to come with me, but you don't have to. It's not your fight. You didn't kill anyone in your 'verse, so you haven't committed any crimes that you can be held accountable for. If you want to guard this side of the portal until my people arrive – "

"I said I wanted to go with you, and I meant it."

Maia's eyes slowly wetted. "Okay. . . . Okay. Then let's do it."

They hugged all around, taking turns. Amber and Maia cried openly. Then Woody and Amber skipped along the dirt road to the place where the jalopy was parked. They left their rifles behind.

Darby waited until they were out of sight before he turned his attention to Maia. He got right down to business. "We have a tactical advantage. They don't know we're coming from this side, they won't be expecting an attack from the rear. They'll think we'll be climbing down their side of the mountain. And even though they'll be on alert because of the two that spotted us, they won't know that they're dead and aren't coming back.

"It'll be dark soon on their side, so at least two of them will probably bed down. I think we should wait a few hours so they'll either be asleep or let down their guard. Then we can sneak up on them."

He was thinking too fast to get his grammar straight.

Maia nodded slowly. "And what about afterward. What are you going to do then?"

"Well, uh, I don't know. I came home to decide whether to re-up for another hitch. But now, I don't know – there's a lot more to do. There's a whole continent to retake. A whole nation to free. That'll take months, maybe years. Conquistadors are spread all over your 'verse. My job in this 'verse is fighting terrorism. I guess I can fight for the same cause in your 'verse. And meanwhile, maybe the two of us, uh, I thought we could spend some time together, uh, between battles . . . "

"I thought so, too. That is, I was hoping . . . " She reached into her knapsack again. This time she brought out an obsidian knife – a ritual knife.

Darby was speechless for a full minute. He was trying to find a way to say what he thought he had to say. After several false starts: "Uh, Maia, I don't know, uh, if this is proper. I mean, uh, I mean, I'm not – not exactly a virgin."

A broad grin split her oval face. "Neither am I. And neither, I suspect, are a lot of Lema-Reans who take the vow. The ceremony is pretty much for show."

Darby nodded. He took a deep breath. He never took his eyes off her expectant gaze. After a moment he held out his hand, and waited for her to prick his palm.

Epilogue

From the *Mount Shasta Intelligencer:*

There has been a lot of talk lately about commercial activity taking place on Mount Shasta. This activity includes the grazing of livestock and the storage of alcoholic beverages, both prohibited by the U.S. Forest Service, which manages Mount Shasta and the surrounding land, and which enforces the rules and regulations of the U.S. Forest Service.

According to ranger Richard Molanda, 51, of Dunsmuir, "There are pockets of private property within many Forest Service land holdings. It's not uncommon. The people who own property that is surrounded by Forest Service land have access rights that the general public doesn't have. And they have the right to do what they want with their land, as long as it doesn't pose a hazard for adjacent Forest Service land. Fire hazards, for example, are prohibited."

Molanda, who has been with the Forest Service for 28 years, said, "Most private parcels are posted. Some people live on their land. Others use it for farming or grazing. The Consolidated Tabernacle Society is one of several religious groups that own property on or around Mount Shasta. Up till recently they haven't worked their land, but now they are, and they have every right to."

We obtained more information from two high school students who were granted permission from the Consolidated Tabernacle Society to examine the cave on their property. Both live in McCloud and attend James Hutchings Senior High. They are collecting information for their senior projects.

Derwood Carnathan, 17, said, "The cave is really a lava tube, created thousands of years ago during one of Mount Shasta's eruptions."

The last known eruption of Mount Shasta was in 1786.

Carnathan, whose senior project is on crystals, said,

"Crystals can grow anywhere that water and chemicals are available, even inside railroad tunnels. The crystals in the society's cave are pretty small, and take a long time to grow. They are fairly insignificant. I wouldn't recommend the cave for further study in crystal formation."

Amber Cornthwaite, 17, is studying cave life for her senior project. She said, "I found several species of fauna which I observed for my report, but they were few and far between, and most live in the light zone. I noted one bat, a few crickets, and a centipede. The lava tube itself is pretty boring. It doesn't have formations like solution caves."

Ted Grozniac, 53, an independent trucker from Weed, has been contracted by the Consolidated Tabernacle Society to transport freight from the society's ranch outside Mount Shasta City to the cave for the past several weeks. He said, "So, I trucked some llamas but mostly I've been hauling wine. The society has been using a cellar on their ranch for cold storage. With their business growing, they needed another location for storage until the wine is sold. The cave is perfect for their needs because the temperature is constant, summer and winter."

Grozniac, who has driven eighteen-wheelers all over the country, said, "As far as I'm concerned, the best thing about the Society is that they pay on time. And the work is local. So it allows me to spend nights at home with the missus."

"Their property is at the base of the mountain and off the beaten track," said Molanda, who inspected the premises. "The number of llamas on the property is small – half a dozen or less. They are kept in a fence-in area so they can't roam on National Forest land. The Society assured me that they have no intention of building on the property. They only want to use the cave for temporary storage, until they sell the wine that's kept there."

Molanda said, "Trucking traffic is light, usually no more than one load per day. It doesn't interfere with hikers and climbers who want to access the trailheads higher up, and the ski park uses a different road."

Maia Kinich, spokesperson for the Consolidated Tabernacle Society, was unavailable for comment. She is currently away on business.

Science Fiction
A Different Universe
A Different Dimension
A Different Continuum
Entropy (a novel of conceptual breakthrough)
A Journey to the Center of the Earth
The Mold
Return to Mars
Second Coming
Silent Autumn
Subaqueous
Tesla and the Lemurian Gate
The Time Dragons Trilogy
    A Time for Dragons
    Dragons Past
    No Future for Dragons

Sci-Fi Action/Adventure Novels
Memory Lane
Mind Set
The Peking Papers

Supernatural Horror Novel
The Lurking: Curse of the Jersey Devil

Vietnam Novel
Lonely Conflict

Nonfiction
The Absurdity Principle
Lehigh Gorge Trail Guide
Wilderness Canoeing

Dive Training
Primary Wreck Diving Guide
Advanced Wreck Diving Guide
The Advanced Wreck Diving Handbook
Ultimate Wreck Diving Guide
The Technical Diving Handbook

Videotape or DVD
The Battle for the USS Monitor

Books by the Author

The Popular Dive Guide Series

Shipwrecks of Massachusetts: North
Shipwrecks of Massachusetts: South
Shipwrecks of Rhode Island and Connecticut
Shipwrecks of New York
Shipwrecks of New Jersey (1988)
Shipwrecks of New Jersey: North
Shipwrecks of New Jersey: Central
Shipwrecks of New Jersey: South
Shipwrecks of Delaware and Maryland (1990 Edition)
Shipwrecks of Delaware and Maryland (2002 Edition)
Shipwrecks of the Chesapeake Bay in Maryland Waters
Shipwrecks of the Chesapeake Bay in Virginia Waters
Shipwrecks of Virginia
Shipwrecks of North Carolina: from the Diamond Shoals North
Shipwrecks of North Carolina: from Hatteras Inlet South
Shipwrecks of South Carolina and Georgia

Shipwreck and Nautical History

Andrea Doria: Dive to an Era
Deep, Dark, and Dangerous: Adventures and Reflections on the Andrea Doria
Great Lakes Shipwrecks: a Photographic Odyssey
The Fuhrer's U-boats in American Waters
Ironclad Legacy: Battles of the USS Monitor
The Kaiser's U-boats in American Waters
The Lusitania Controversies: Atrocity of War and a Wreck-Diving History (Book One)
The Lusitania Controversies: Dangerous Descents into Shipwrecks and Law (Book Two)
The Nautical Cyclopedia
NOAA's Ark: the Rise of the Fourth Reich
Shadow Divers Exposed: the Real Saga of the U-869
Shipwreck Heresies
The Shipwreck Research Handbook
Shipwreck Sagas
Stolen Heritage: the Grand Theft of the Hamilton and Scourge
Track of the Gray Wolf
Underwater Reflections
USS San Diego: the Last Armored Cruiser
Wreck Diving Adventures

Visit the GGP website for availability of titles:
http://www.ggentile.com